THE
NIGHT
GUEST

THE NIGHT GUEST

FIONA McFARLANE

ff

FABER AND FABER, INC.

AN AFFILIATE OF FARRAR, STRAUS AND GIROUX

NEW YORK

Faber and Faber, Inc.
An affiliate of Farrar, Straus and Giroux
18 West 18th Street, New York 10011

Copyright © 2013 by Fiona McFarlane
All rights reserved
Printed in the United States of America
First edition, 2013

Library of Congress Cataloging-in-Publication Data
McFarlane, Fiona, 1978–
      The night guest / Fiona McFarlane. — First edition.
         pages   cm
      ISBN 978-0-86547-773-5 (hardback)
         1. Widows—Fiction.   2. Caregivers—Fiction.   3. Australia—
Fiction.   I. Title.

PR9619.4.M38355 N54 2013
823'.92—dc23

                                                    2013022511

Designed by Jonathan D. Lippincott

Faber and Faber, Inc., books may be purchased for educational, business, or
promotional use. For information on bulk purchases, please contact the Macmillan
Corporate and Premium Sales Department at 1-800-221-7945, extension 5442, or
write to specialmarkets@macmillan.com.

www.fsgbooks.com
www.twitter.com/fsgbooks • www.facebook.com/fsgbooks

1   3   5   7   9   10   8   6   4   2

FOR MY PARENTS

1

Ruth woke at four in the morning and her blurry brain said "Tiger." That was natural; she was dreaming. But there were noises in the house, and as she woke she heard them. They came across the hallway from the lounge room. Something large was rubbing against Ruth's couch and television and, she suspected, the wheat-coloured recliner disguised as a wingback chair. Other sounds followed: the panting and breathing of a large animal; a vibrancy of breath that suggested enormity and intent; definite mammalian noises, definitely feline, as if her cats had grown in size and were sniffing for food with enormous noses. But the sleeping cats were weighing down the sheets at the end of Ruth's bed, and this was something else.

She lay and listened. Sometimes the house was quiet, and then she only heard the silly clamour of her beating blood. At other times she heard a distant low whine followed by exploratory breaths. The cats woke and stretched and stared and finally, when whatever was in the lounge room gave out a sharp huff, flew from the bed and ran, ecstatic with fear, into the hallway, through the kitchen, and out the partially open back door. This sudden activity prompted an odd strangled yowl from the lounge room, and it was this noise, followed by louder sniffing, that confirmed the intruder as a tiger. Ruth had seen one eating at a German zoo, and it sounded just like this: loud and wet, with a low, guttural breathing hum punctuated by little cautionary yelps, as if it might roar at any moment except that it was occupied by food. Yes, it sounded just like that, like a tiger eating some large bloody thing, and yet the noise of it was empty and meatless. A tiger! Ruth, thrilled by this possibility, forgot to be frightened and had to counsel herself back into fear. The tiger sniffed again, a rough sniff, thick with saliva. It turned on its great feet, as if preparing to settle down.

Ruth sent one courageous hand out into the dark to find the phone on her bedside table. She pressed the button that was programmed to summon her son Jeffrey, who would, in his sensible way, be sleeping right now in his house in New Zealand. The telephone rang; Ruth, hearing the creak of Jeffrey's throat as he answered the phone, was unrepentant.

"I hear noises," she said, her voice low and urgent—the kind of voice she'd rarely used with him before.

"What? Ma?" He was bumping up out of sleep. His wife would be waking, too; she would be rolling worried in bed and turning on a lamp.

"I can hear a tiger, not roaring, just panting and snorting. It's like he's eating, and also concentrating very hard." So she knew he was a male tiger, and that was a comfort; a female tiger seemed more threatening.

Now Jeffrey's voice stiffened. "What time is it?"

"Listen," said Ruth. She held the phone away from her, into the night, but her arm felt vulnerable, so she brought it back. "Did you hear that?"

"No," said Jeffrey. "Was it the cats?"

"It's much larger than a cat. Than a *cat* cat."

"You're telling me there's a what, there's a tiger in your house?"

Ruth said nothing. She wasn't telling him there was a tiger in her house; she was telling him she could hear one. That distinction seemed important, now that she was awake and Jeffrey was awake, and his wife, too, and probably at this point the children.

"Oh, Ma. There's no tiger. It's either a cat or a dream."

"I know that," said Ruth. She knew there couldn't be a tiger; but she wasn't sure it was a dream. She was awake, after all. And her back hurt, which it never did in dreams. But now she noticed the noises had stopped. There was only the ordinary outside sound of the breaking sea.

"Would you like to go and investigate?" asked Jeffrey. "I'll stay on the phone with you." His voice conveyed a serene weariness; Ruth suspected he was reassuring his wife with an eyes-closed shake of the head that everything was all right, that his mother was just having one of her moments. When he'd visited a few weeks ago, at Easter, Ruth had noticed a new watchful patience in him, and a tendency to purse his lips whenever she said something he considered unusual. So she knew, from the funny mirror of Jeffrey's face, that she had reached the stage where her sons worried about her.

"No, darling, it's all right," she said. "So silly! I'm sorry. Go back to sleep."

"Are you sure?" said Jeffrey, but he sounded foggy; he had already abandoned her.

Jeffrey's dismissal made her brave. Ruth rose from her bed and crossed the room without turning on any lights. She watched the white step of her feet on the carpeted floor until she reached the bedroom door; then she stopped and called, "Hello?" Nothing answered, but there was, Ruth was sure, a vegetable smell in the long hallway, and an inland feel to the air that didn't suit this seaside house. The clammy night was far too hot for May. Ruth ventured another "Hello?" and pictured, as she did so, the headlines: "Australian Woman Eaten by Tiger in Own House." Or, more likely, "Tiger Puts Pensioner on the Menu." This delighted her; and there was another sensation, a new one, to which she attended with greater care: a sense of extravagant consequence. Something important, Ruth felt, was happening to her, and she couldn't be sure what it was: the tiger, or the feeling of importance. They seemed to be related, but the sense of consequence was disproportionate to the actual events of the night, which were, after all, a bad dream, a pointless phone call, and a brief walk to the bedroom door. She felt something coming to meet her—something large, and not a real thing, of course, she wasn't that far gone—but a shape, or anyway a temperature. It produced a funny bubble in her chest. The house was quiet. Ruth pressed at the tenderness of her chest; she closed the bedroom door and followed her own feet back to bed. Her head filled and shifted and blurred again. The tiger must be sleeping now, she thought, so Ruth slept, too, and didn't wake again until the late morning.

The lounge room, when Ruth entered it in daylight, was benign. The furniture was all where it should be, civil, neat, and almost anxious for her approval, as if it had crossed her in some way and was now waiting for her forgiveness, dressed in its very best clothes. Ruth was oppressed by this wheedling familiarity. She crossed to the window and opened the lace curtains with a dramatic gesture. The front garden looked exactly as it usually did—the grevillea needed trimming—but Ruth saw a yellow taxi idling at the end of the drive, half hidden by the casuarinas. It looked so solitary, so needlessly bright. The driver must be lost and need directions; that happened from time to time along this apparently empty stretch of coast.

Ruth surveyed the room again. "Ha!" she said, as if daring it to frighten her. When it failed to, she left it in something like disgust. She went to the kitchen, opened the shutters, and looked out at the sea. It lay waiting below the garden, and although she was unable to walk down to it—the dune was too steep, and her back too unpredictable—she felt soothed by its presence in an indefinable way, just as she imagined a plant might be by Mozart. The tide was full and flat across the beach. The cats came out from the dune grasses; they stopped in the doorway, nuzzling the inside air with their suspicious noses until, in a sudden surfeit of calm, they passed into the house. Ruth poured some dry food into their bowls and watched as they ate without ceasing until the food was gone. Something about the way they ate was biblical, she had decided; it had the character of a plague.

Now Ruth made tea. She sat in her chair—the one chair her back could endure for any length of time—and ate pumpkin seeds for breakfast. This chair was an enormous wooden object, inherited from her husband's family; it looked like the kind a Victorian vicar might teeter on while writing sermons. But it braced Ruth's back, so she kept it near the dining-room table, by the window that looked over the garden and dune and beach. She sat in her chair and drank tea and examined the new sensation—the extravagance, the consequence—she had experienced in the night, and which remained with her now. Certainly it was dreamlike; it had a dream's diminishing character. She knew that by lunchtime she might have forgotten it entirely. The feeling reminded her of something vital—not of youth, exactly, but of the urgency of youth—and she was reluctant to give it up. For some time now she had hoped that her end might be as extraordinary as her beginning. She also appreciated how unlikely that was. She was a widow and she lived alone.

The pumpkin seeds Ruth ate for breakfast were one of the few items in the pantry. She spread them out on her left hand and lifted them to her mouth, two at a time, with her right. One must go in the left side, at the back of her teeth; the other must go in the right. She was like this about her daily pills, too; they would be more effective if she was careful about how she took them. Through this symmetry—always begin a flight of stairs on her left foot, always end it on her right—she maintained the order of her days. If she had dinner ready in time for the six o'clock news, both of her sons would come home for Christmas. If that taxi driver didn't ring the front doorbell, she would be allowed to stay in her chair for two hours. She looked out at the sea and counted the pattern of the waves: if there were fewer than eight small ones before another big curler, she would sweep the garden path of sand. To sweep the sand from the path was a holy punishment, a limitless task, so Ruth set traps for herself in order to decide the matter. She hated to sweep, hated anything so senseless; she hated to make her bed only to unmake it again in the evening. Long ago she had impressed the importance of these chores upon her sons and believed in them as she did so. Now she thought, If one person walks on the beach in the next ten minutes, there's a tiger in my house at night; if there are two, the tiger won't hurt me; if there are three, the tiger will finish me off. And the possibility of this produced one of those brief, uncontrollable shivers, which Ruth thought of as beginning in the brain and letting themselves out through the soles of the feet.

"It's nearly winter," she said aloud, looking out at the flattening sea; the tide was going out. "It's nearly bloody winter."

Ruth would have liked to know another language in order to revert to it at times of disproportionate frustration. She'd forgotten the Hindi she knew when, as a child, she lived in Fiji. Lately, swearing—in which she indulged in a mild, girlish way—was her other language. She counted seven small waves, which meant she had to sweep the path, and so she said "Shit," but didn't stir from her chair. She was capable of watching the sea all day. This morning, an oil tanker waited on the rim of the world, as if long-sufferingly lost, and farther around the bay, near the town, Ruth could make out surfers. They rode waves that from here looked bath-sized, just toy swells. And in every way this was ordinary, except that a large woman was approaching, looking as if she had been blown in from the sea. She toiled up the dune directly in front of the house, dragging a suitcase that, after some struggle, she abandoned among the grasses. It slid a little way down the hill. Once she had made her determined way to the top of the dune, the woman moved with steadfast purpose through the garden. She filled up a little more of the sky with every step. Her breadth and the warmth of her skin and the dark sheen of her obviously straightened hair looked

Fijian to Ruth, who rose from her chair to meet her guest at the kitchen door. Her back didn't complain when she stood; that, and the woman's nationality, made her optimistic about the encounter. Ruth stepped into the garden and surprised the woman, who seemed stranded without her suitcase, exhausted from her uphill climb, encased in a thin grey coat, with the thin grey sea behind her. Perhaps she had been shipwrecked, or marooned.

"Mrs. Field! You're home!" the woman cried, and she advanced on Ruth with a reckless energy that dispelled the impression of shipwreck.

"Here I am," said Ruth.

"Large as life," said the woman, and she held out both hands cupped together as if they had just caught a bothersome fly. Ruth must offer her hands in return; she offered; the woman took them into her sure, steady grip, and together they stood in the garden as if this were what the woman had come for. The top of Ruth's head didn't quite reach her visitor's shoulders.

"You'll have to excuse me," said the woman. "I'm done in. I was worried about you! I knocked at the front, and when you didn't answer I thought I'd come round the back way. Didn't know what a hill there'd be! Woof," she said, as if imitating an expressionless dog.

"I didn't hear you knocking."

"You didn't?" The woman frowned and looked down at her hands as if they had failed her.

"Do I know you?" Ruth asked. She meant this sincerely; possibly she did know her. Possibly this woman had once been a young girl sitting on Ruth's mother's knee. Perhaps this woman's mother had been ill in just the right small way that would bring her to Ruth's father's clinic. There were always children at the clinic; they dallied and clowned, they loved anyone who came their way, and they all left punctually with their families. Maybe this woman came out of those old days with a message or a greeting. But she was probably too young to have been one of those children—Ruth guessed early forties, smooth-faced and careful of her appearance. She wasn't wearing makeup, but she had the heavy kind of eyelids that always look powdered in a soft brown.

"Sorry, sorry." The woman released Ruth's hands, propped one arm against the house, and said, "You don't know me from Adam." Then she adopted a professional tone. "My name is Frida Young, and I'm here to look after you."

"Oh, I didn't realize!" cried Ruth, as if she'd invited someone to a social event and then forgotten all about it. She stepped away from the bulky shadow of Frida Young's leaning. In a fluttering, puzzled, almost flirtatious voice, she said, "Do I need looking after?"

"Couldn't you use a hand round the place? If someone rocked up to my front door—my back door—and offered to look after me, I'd kiss their feet."

"I don't understand," said Ruth. "Did my sons send you?"

"The government sent me," said Frida, who seemed cheerfully certain of the results of their chat: she had eased off her shoes—sandshoes from which the laces had been removed—and was flexing her toes in the sandy grass. "You were on our waiting list and a spot opened up."

"What for?" The telephone began to ring. "Do I pay for this?" asked Ruth, flustered by all the activity.

"No, love! The government pays. What a deal, huh?"

"Excuse me," said Ruth, moving into the kitchen. Frida followed her.

Ruth picked up the phone and held it to her ear without speaking.

"Ma?" said Jeffrey. "Ma? Is that you?"

"Of course it's me."

"I just wanted to check in. Make sure you hadn't been eaten in the night." Jeffrey indulged in the tolerant chuckle his father used to employ at times of loving exasperation.

"That wasn't necessary, darling. I'm absolutely fine," said Ruth. Frida began to motion in a way that Ruth interpreted as a request for a glass of water; she nodded to imply she would see to it soon. "Listen, dear, there's someone here with me right now."

Frida clattered about the kitchen, opening cupboards and the refrigerator.

"Oh! Then I'll let you go."

"No, Jeff, I wanted to tell you, she's a helper of some kind." Ruth turned to Frida. "Excuse me, but what are you, exactly? A nurse?"

"A nurse?" said Jeffrey.

"A government carer," said Frida.

Ruth preferred the sound of this. "She's a government carer, Jeff, and she says she's here to help me."

"You're kidding me," said Jeffrey. "How did she find you? How does she seem?"

"She's right here."

"Put her on."

Ruth handed the phone to Frida, who took it good-naturedly and cradled it against her shoulder. It was an old-fashioned kind of phone, a large heavy crescent, cream-coloured and attached to the wall by a particularly long white cord that meant Ruth could carry it anywhere in the house.

"Jeff," Frida said, and now Ruth could hear only the faint outlines of her son's voice. Frida said, "Frida Young." She said, "Of course," and then, "A state programme. Her name was on file, and a spot opened up." Ruth disliked hearing herself discussed in the third person. She felt like an eavesdropper. "An hour a day to start with. It's more of an assessment, just to see what's needed, and we'll take things from there. Yes, yes, I can take care of all that." Finally, "Your mother's in good hands, Jeff," and Frida handed the phone back to Ruth.

"This could be wonderful, Ma," said Jeffrey. "This could be

just exactly what we need. What a good, actually good use of taxpayers' money."

"Wait," said Ruth. The cats, curious, were sniffing at Frida's toes.

"But I want to see the paperwork, all right? Before you sign anything. Do you remember how to use Dad's fax machine?"

"Just a minute," said Ruth, to both Frida and Jeffrey, and, with bashful urgency, as if she had a pressing need to urinate, she hurried into the lounge room and stood at the window. The yellow of the taxi was still visible at the end of the drive.

"I'm alone now," she said, her voice lowered and her lips pressed to the phone. "Now, I'm not sure about this. I'm not doing badly."

Ruth didn't like talking about this with her son. It offended her and made her shy. She supposed she should feel grateful for his love and care, but it seemed too soon; she wasn't old—not too old, only seventy-five. Her own mother had been past eighty before things really began to unravel. And to have this happen today, when she felt vulnerable about calling Jeffrey in the middle of the night with all that nonsense about a tiger. She wondered if he'd mentioned any of that to Frida.

"You're doing wonderfully," said Jeffrey, and Ruth winced at this, and her back vibrated a little, so she put out her left hand to hold the windowsill. He had said exactly the same thing when, on his last visit, he mentioned retirement villages and in-home carers. "Frida's only here to assess your situation. She'll probably just take over some of the housework, and you'll relax and enjoy yourself."

"She's Fijian," said Ruth, mainly for her own reassurance.

"There you are, some familiarity. And if you hate it, if you don't like her, then we'll make other arrangements."

"Yes," said Ruth, more doubtfully than she felt; she was heartened by this, even if she knew Jeffrey was patronizing her; but she knew the extent of her independence, its precise horizons, and she knew she was neither helpless nor especially brave; she was somewhere in between; but she was still self-governing.

"I'll let Phil know. I'll tell him to call you. And we'll talk more on Sunday," said Jeffrey. Sunday was the day they usually spoke, at four in the afternoon: half an hour with Jeffrey, fifteen minutes with his wife, two minutes each with the children. They didn't time it deliberately; it just worked out that way. The children would hold the phone too close to their mouths; "Hello, Nanna," they would breathe into her ear, and it was clear they had almost forgotten her. She saw them at Christmas and they loved her; the year slid away and she was an anonymous voice, handwriting on a letter, until they arrived at her festive door again; for three or four years this pattern had continued, after the first frenzy of her husband's death. Ruth's younger son, Phillip, was different: he would spend two or three hours on the phone and was capable of making her laugh so hard she snorted. But he called only once every few weeks. He saved all the details of his merry, busy life (he taught English in Hong Kong, had boys of his own, was divorced and remarried, liked windsurfing); he poured them out over her, then vanished for another month.

Jeffrey ended this call with such warmth that for the first time Ruth worried properly for herself. The tenderness was irresistible. Ruth was a little afraid of her sons. She was afraid of being unmasked by their youthful authority. Good-looking families in which every member was vital, attractive, and socially skilled had made her nervous as a young woman, and now she was the mother of sons just like that. Their voices had a certain weight.

Ruth followed the phone cord back to the kitchen and found Frida sitting at the dining table drinking a glass of water and reading yesterday's newspaper. She had removed her grey coat and it hung lifelessly, like something shredded, over the back of a chair. Underneath it she wore white trousers and a white blouse;

not exactly a nurse's uniform, but not unlike. A handbag, previously concealed by the coat, was slung across her body, and her discarded sandshoes lay by the door. Frida's legs were stretched out beneath the table. She had hooked her bare toes onto the low rung of the opposite chair, and her arms were pressed down over the newspaper. She read the paper with a mobile frown on her broad face. Her eyebrows were plucked so thin they should have given her a look of permanent surprise; instead, they exaggerated each of her expressions with a perfect stroke. And her face was all expression: held still, it might have vanished into its own smooth surface.

"Listen to this," she said. "A man in Canada, right? In a wheelchair. They cut off his electricity one night, it's an accident, they get the wrong house, and he's frozen stiff by morning. Dead from the cold."

"Oh, dear," said Ruth, smiling vaguely. She noted that Frida's vowels were broad, but her *t*'s were crisp. "That's terrible. You found the water all right?"

Frida looked up in surprise. "Just from the tap," she said. "Who'd live in a place you could freeze overnight? I don't mind heat, but I feel the cold. Though I reckon I've never been really, truly cold. You know"—she leaned back in her chair—"I've never even seen snow. Have you?"

"Yes. Twice, in England," said Ruth. Her back trembled but she bent, nevertheless, to reach for a cat. She wasn't sure what else to do. The cat evaded her and jumped into Frida's lap. Frida didn't look at the cat or remark on it, but she stroked it expertly with the knuckles of her right hand. She wasn't wearing any rings.

"He's nice, your son," said Frida. "Got any more kids?"

"Just the two boys."

"Flown the nest." Frida folded the newspaper to frame the blurry face of the frozen Canadian and shook the cat off her lap.

"Long ago," said Ruth. "They have kids of their own."

"A grandmother!" cried Frida, with bloodless enthusiasm.

"So you see, I'm used to being alone."

Frida lowered her head over the table and looked up at Ruth so that each brown eye seemed cradled in its respective brow. There was a new gravity to her; she seemed to have absorbed it from the room's more important objects, from the newspaper and the table and the rungs of Ruth's chair. "Don't think of me as company, Mrs. Field," Frida said. "I'm not a guest. I come for an hour every morning, same time every day, I do my job, and I'm out of your hair. No surprises. No strangers showing up any time of the day or night. I'm not a stranger, and I'm not a friend— I'm your right arm. I'm the help you're giving yourself. This is you looking after you, this is you mattering. Does that make sense? I get it, Mrs. Field, I really do."

"Oh," said Ruth, who believed, at that moment, that Frida Young "got it": that she understood—how could she under-stand?—the tiger's visit, the smell in the hallway, Fiji of course, that strange, safe place, and the dream of consequence in the silly night.

But Frida broke the spell by standing up. Her bulk arranged itself quite beautifully around her; she suited her size. And her voice was cheerful now; it had lost its thrilling, tented quality. "Let's leave it at that for today," she said. "It's a lot to take in. And I've left my bag outside."

Ruth followed her into the garden. "Lovely day," Frida said, although it was a flat, pale day, and the sea lay dull against the dull sand. Frida paid no attention to the view. She stepped down the dune towards the suitcase with her elbows folded in and her hands up near her shoulders, as if afraid of falling. She was more graceful in descent; her back had so much strength that it made Ruth's ache. Having retrieved the case, Frida paused to check the state of her hair, which was dark and drawn into a no-nonsense knot at the back of her head. The suitcase was heavy and she chatted as she heaved it.

"There's nothing to worry about, Mrs. Field," she said. A rim of sweat shone on her forehead. "We'll talk duties tomorrow. I cook, clean, make sure you're taking your meds, help with exercise. Bathing? You've got that covered for the time being, is my guess. Whatever's hard on you now, I'm here for. You've got a bad back, am I right? I can see how careful you are with it. Gotta look out for your back. Here we go." Frida hoisted the suitcase over the lip of the dune, swung it across the garden and into the house, and brought it to rest next to Ruth's chair under the dining-room window.

"What's in there?" asked Ruth.

"Only about three thousand kilos. I've got to get me one of these with wheels." Frida kicked the suitcase at the same moment a car horn sounded from the front of the house, so that the suitcase appeared to have honked. "That's my ride," she said. "I'll be back tomorrow morning. Nine o'clock suit you?" She seized her coat and hunted for her sandshoes until Ruth pointed out where they lay beside the door. The car horn came again; the cats jumped and flew in giddy circles around Frida's feet. Frida didn't bend to pet them; instead, she looked around the kitchen and dining room as if surveying the goodness of her creation, and walked with confidence down the hallway to the front door.

"You have a nice house," she said. She opened the door. Ruth, following, saw the rectangle of light from outside, the shape of Frida in the light, and, dimly, the golden flank of a taxi.

"The suitcase?" Ruth asked.

"I'll leave it, if that's all right with you," said Frida. "Bye now!" She was closing the door. By the time Ruth reached the lounge-room window, there was no Frida and no taxi. The grass stood high in the winter garden, and there was no sound besides the sea.

2

Ruth's husband, Harry, used to walk, every day, to the nearby town to buy the newspaper. He undertook this exercise on the advice of his father, who retained a spry step well into his eighties and had the blood pressure of a much younger man. It was on this walk that Harry died, in the second year of his retirement. He proceeded from the front door of his house down a narrow lane (Ruth and Harry called this lane their drive), heading away from the sea. The sea disappeared; the air altered suddenly, became more dense, and smelled of insects rather than seaweed; the laneway was just wide enough for a car, and so Harry, a tall man, could stretch out his arms and touch the high grass and casuarinas on either side of the drive. Behind him was the house, the slope of the dune, the broad beach, and the beginning of the sun. This was six-thirty in the morning no matter the weather. He was in his stride by the time he reached the coastal road, which fell away down the sandy hill on which his own house stood. At the foot of this slope, a small bus stop waited in humble circumstances—a torn billboard, a splintered bench— and here Harry leaned against the black-and-yellow sign that read STOP! BUS and felt the strange movement of his active heart. Or so Ruth imagined. Harry sat on the bench with his back to the road. He wore a light blue down vest that was swollen in the back, just a little, as if designed to accommodate a minor hunch. From here he could observe the passage of seagulls over the estuary that separated the road from the beach. He had loved this beach since childhood.

Harry's noticeable height, his excessively straight posture distorted only by the swell of his down vest, the neat white brush of his hair and the startling black of his eyebrows, the soft, dishy ears that sat at a slightly odd angle from his head, and the un- usual tremble of his hands in his dignified lap: all of these things attracted the attention of a passing motorist, who drew up along- side the curb. This motorist, a young woman, leaned across the passenger seat of her car, lowered the window, and asked Harry in a loud voice if he was all right. Harry was not all right. His chest moved violently with every heartbeat, and as he turned his body away from the sea and towards the road, he began to throw up onto the sandy concrete. The motorist recalled afterwards that Harry had leaned forwards to avoid soiling his clothes, that his left hand was pressed against his ribs as if in womanly surprise, and that he made an effort to kick sand over the vomit, his head bobbing up and down in a helpless motion of agreement.

The motorist, whose name was Ellen Gibson, described these things to Phillip and Jeffrey the day after their father's death. They quizzed her, and she was forthcoming. There was a phrase Harry liked to say: "to die like a dog in the gutter." He said it of men he didn't approve of but was willing to tolerate (certain prime ministers, for example): "I don't like what he has to say for himself, but I wouldn't leave him to die like a dog in the gutter." This sentiment formed part of the expansive democ- racy of his generally approving heart. Jeffrey, with some objec- tions from his younger brother, told Ruth what Ellen had told him, and Ruth loved this Ellen who had made sure Harry didn't die like a dog in the gutter. Ellen held Harry when he began to slip from the bench and onto the ground; she assured him, again and again, that everything would be all right. He was dead when the ambulance arrived.

At Harry's funeral, a group of kindly mourners introduced Ruth to a small, tearless, hesitant woman. They called her "the young Samaritan." Until that moment Ellen Gibson had been a principle of humanity and coincidence; now Ruth must acknowl- edge her as the person who had seen Harry die. Ellen looked

young as a teenager, although she was known to have two small
sons. She would not allow Ruth to thank her; Ruth would not
allow Ellen to express regret. The women held hands for a long
time while the funeral eddied about them, as if hoping to communicate to each other a love that couldn't be justified by the
scarcity of their contact.

Now, without Harry for five years, Ruth was prepared to
accommodate the possibility that good strangers could material-
ize and love her for no reason beyond their goodness. Ellen was
proof of that; why shouldn't Frida Young be? Another sort of
woman could have convinced herself that Harry—still present
in some way—had sent Frida to look after his wife; not Ruth,
who was vaguely optimistic about the afterlife, but never fanciful. She felt similarly about the government and was ready to
accept that it might provide her with Frida after a long, sensible,
law-abiding life. Ruth and Harry had never begrudged paying
taxes. Roads! Libraries! Schools! Government carers! Of course
Harry hadn't sent Frida, but Ruth had a feeling he would approve. Her sons would approve, and their wives; so would Ellen
Gibson, who dropped in every now and then with a cake or a
new book. And Ruth liked approval. It had shored up her life. It
had made her blessedly ordinary, and now it made her want to
swear; but she still liked it.

With Frida and the taxi gone, Ruth had the day to herself.
Oh, the gentle, bewildering expanse of the day, the filling of all
those more-or-less hours. She inspected Frida's suitcase, which
was taking up audacious space in the dining room: an old-
fashioned cream-coloured case, similar to the one Ruth had carried when she first sailed to Sydney in 1954. It was heavy, and
locked. Ruth worried for a moment that it might contain a
bomb, so she nudged it with a gentle foot and thought she heard
the washing of bottled liquid. This reassured her. Obeying her
earlier contract with the number of waves seen from the window, she swept the garden path of sand. She rested her back and

watched the sea. She ate sardines on toast. She took a long shower, sitting on the plastic stool Jeffrey had bought during his last visit.

As she went about these activities, she thought about the tiger. She thought, too, about other periods of her life when she had felt something approaching this sense of personal consequence. There was her missionary childhood, during which she was told repeatedly that she was part of a chosen people, a royal priesthood, a people belonging to God. She saw it, now, as a strangely urgent life, in which her father must heal the sick and save their souls, and the flowers bloomed in useless profusion, and there was too much of everything: sun, and green, and love. Her parents were fine singers, and every night her mother played hymns on a damp piano. Ruth used to read letters from her cousins back in Sydney and feel sorry for them, with their ordinary lives. Her parents had been called to serve, and she had been called with them. She had been named for a stranger in a strange land. "How bitter is the path of joy," she would say to herself; she had read that somewhere. There was never, at that time, a moment to lose. Even as she grew older and the strong, wet light of Fiji dazzled her less, and the hymns, too, seemed less luminous, Ruth was caught up in consequence. She fell in love—of course she fell in love—with a man named Richard Porter. She was unskilled, and prudish, and baffled by love; she managed it badly. That was dreamlike, too. Every night she endured violent dreams of impossible pleasure. She received her own body, and ate a meek breakfast in the morning.

Then Ruth grew up and left Fiji. She went to Sydney, where her cousins wore the right clothes and knew the right songs; they exchanged friendly jokes about her weird, fervent childhood. And so she made, from then on, a conscious effort to live an ordinary life, like those of the people she saw around her: people who grew up where they were born, among their own kind, and made their merry, sad way through a world they understood entirely. For only one period, after coming to Sydney, did Ruth recover her sense of the extraordinary: during a childhood illness of Phillip's, a severe case of pleurisy. For four weeks, Phillip lay in bed with his chest bound. There was fever, pain, and a dry cough like sheaves of papyrus rubbing together. Ruth remembered this period of her life in more detail than any other; the sense of urgency she felt lent significance to the most trivial things. She could still recall, for example, the exact order of the books on the shelf beside Phillip's crib. His laboured breathing reminded her of a toy train ascending a mountain; she thought of it now as she washed herself in the shower, balancing on the plastic stool. She thought of that row of children's books. She could see, in the shower tiles, the faces of animals, and also the man in the moon. By then it was dark, and she had succeeded in passing the day; she had survived it. Before going to bed, Ruth closed the lounge-room door as a precaution against tigers.

She woke, just after three, to the possibility of sounds from the lounge room. The cats stirred when she did, but subsided into sleep. She listened for some time, blinking herself awake in the grainy dark, but could hear only an unusual noise of birds and insects, as if it were summer outside, or maybe a jungle. There was a whine or two that might have been a tiger, but might also have been the cats snoring; they produced so much noise for such little sleeping things. Ruth listened for him, her tiger, her consequential visitor, until her eyes drowsed shut. He was a one-off, then, she thought, on the edge of sleep and disappointed.

The following morning, a taxi pulled up in front of the house. Ruth tiptoed into the lounge room to investigate. She was sure it was the same taxi she had seen yesterday: a yellow Holden, an older make with a chariot shine and, painted on its doors, the words YOUNG LIVERY and a telephone number. Its windows were tinted a shade Harry would call illegally dark. Frida emerged from the passenger's side of the car and gave the door a firm but casual slam, as if it required such treatment to close at all. She was wearing the grey coat and, beneath it, white trousers and the same grey-white sandshoes, and her hair fell in loose curls around her face, which made her look younger. Frida walked the few steps to where Harry's car, a silver Mercedes, was parked by the side of the house. She gave the rear wheel an exploratory press with her foot and returned to the taxi; she leaned listening into the driver's opening window, laughed, and rapped the taxi's dazzling roof. It crept backwards down the drive as if fearful of causing a disturbance.

Ruth went to open the front door. The doorbell rang as she did so: an older doorbell, with a two-note chime that Ruth always thought of as actually saying "ding-dong."

"I didn't see the bell yesterday," said Frida. She was smiling, and not quite as tall as the day before, and had a string bag full of oranges hooked to her elbow; she leaned down to take Ruth's hands, a little as she had when they'd first met, and managed in this gesture to move past Ruth and into the hallway. "There I was, knocking my little heart out—no wonder you didn't hear me, when you're used to that lovely doorbell. Good morning! Good morning! I've got oranges."

She swung the bag down the hall and into the kitchen like a priest with a censer.

"You didn't need to bring anything," protested Ruth.

"I know, I know," said Frida, pouring the oranges into a bowl she took from an upper cupboard. "But I've got these beauties coming out of my ears. My brother George knows a bloke who gets 'em free. Don't know how, and I don't ask. That was my brother you saw dropping me off. It's his own taxi—he's an independent. You ever need a taxi, let me know, and I'll call George."

The oranges made a gorgeous, swollen pile.

"Thank you," said Ruth. "I have a car."

"Well," said Frida, evidently taken aback by this refusal; her eyes widened in something like disapproval.

"But sometimes you need a taxi, don't you," said Ruth. "To be honest, I hate driving."

Frida, placated, patted Ruth's arm. "Let's have the grand tour, then." She hung her grey coat on the hook behind the back door. She wore a different shirt today. It was a brighter white and matched the white trousers. She looked like a beautician.

Frida seemed to lead the tour. She marched into rooms and cupboards and corridors, announcing "The bathroom!" and "The linen press!" as if Ruth were a prospective buyer inspecting the property. No new discovery seemed to surprise her. She was tactful in Ruth's bedroom but pitiless in the guest rooms, going so far as to look under the beds, pulling up wreaths of cat hair from hidden corners and shaking her curly head. Ruth responded with an apologetic smile, at which Frida only tutted; she put her arm around Ruth's shoulders as if to say, "Don't you worry, things will be different from now on."

"These were my sons' bedrooms," explained Ruth, "when we came here on holidays. This was our holiday house."

"I see," said Frida. She ran her left forefinger along a bookshelf and examined it for dust. This was in Phillip's room, and all the books were for bright young boys. "What happened to your other house?"

"Our Sydney house? We sold it. We moved out here for retirement," said Ruth.

"We?"

"My husband and I. Harry."

Frida squeezed Ruth's shoulder again. "It really doesn't bother you to live out here all alone?"

"Not at all," said Ruth. "Why should it?"

Her mother had once warned her: loneliness is off-putting, boredom is unattractive. Ruth was convinced both sensations shone from her face. She was certain she had the odd, unexpected movements of a person used to solitude; when she watched television, for example, she mirrored the facial expressions of the actors. Sometimes she made a game of it. She did once think, while reading a newspaper article about the subject, that she might be depressed, but because Harry hadn't believed in it— "Happiness is a matter of choice," he would say—she never mentioned it to her doctor, and certainly not to her sons. She knew quite soon after Harry's death that her grief wouldn't disrupt the public order of her days. She expected, instead, a long and private season.

"Come and have a cuppa and we'll talk things over," said Frida.

Ruth worried that, if pressed, she would talk too much about Harry; she longed for the chance to and was mortified in advance.

But Frida was all business. "There's some documents you need to look at," she said, finding her suitcase in the dining room and hoisting it onto the table with a marvellous grunt. The suitcase looked smaller than Ruth remembered. It only took up the space of a bulky briefcase. Frida searched among its contents, pulled out a plastic sleeve full of papers, and, offering this to Ruth with a look of patient distaste, said, "Official paperwork."

But before Ruth could take the sleeve, Frida stepped away towards the window. "Would you look at that," she said.

The view from the back of the house often prompted reactions of this kind. There was the dune, sloping away from the garden and down to the beach; there was the wide water and the curve of the bay to the right with the distant silver of the town and, out on the headland, a white lighthouse. Harry used to stand in the garden with his hands on his hips and say, with satisfaction, "Nothing between here and South America." Since his death, it had felt to Ruth that the house was participating in a cosy continental drift, making its leisurely way on an island of its own to the open sea. Ruth liked islands. She had lived all her life on them, and they suited her.

"It's disgusting, is what it is," said Frida.

"Oh, dear," said Ruth. She had always been embarrassed by the splendour of the view, as if owning so much beauty was an admission of vanity on her part, and she wondered if Frida was the guest she'd been waiting for, the one who would rebuke her for it.

"Would you just look at this?"

Ruth looked, and saw a group of people on the beach below. There were nine or ten of them, and they were all naked, or almost naked. Some lay on the sand and others played in the water. Ruth felt a cheerful innocence rising from them; it was like standing on a mountain pass and seeing a town down in the snug valley. But Frida was unmistakably affronted, just as Harry would have been, and she loomed out into the garden. Ruth followed. So little happened at this end of the beach during winter— lone runners, a few dogs. Once, the old jetty splintered and slumped after a storm tide and over the course of a winter was washed out to sea. Skinny-dippers were a definite event, and Ruth liked the idea of them.

"Think there's no one out here, huh?" said Frida. "Think you're alone and you can do whatever you want?"

She made her way to a corner of the garden where two abandoned aluminium bins, long ago used for compost, sprang to new life in the martial gravity of Frida's intentions. She took the lids from the bins, gave them a preparatory shake, and turned to Ruth with a look of mirthful cunning. Ruth was startled by this look. Who was this stranger crossing her land and heading for the ocean with the lids of the compost bins in her firm grip? What could justify her warlike march? It was all both splendid and alarming.

Frida stood on the sandy ridge at the edge of the garden and bellowed down at the beach. She brandished the lids and commenced her descent of the dune, giving her war cry; she clashed the lids together above her head. The people on the beach—and Ruth saw now that they were very young, only teenagers—had been laughing but, noticing Frida, they lifted themselves from the sand or scrambled from the sea, their heads dark with water. They looked clumsy and beautiful from this distance. A warp in the clouds flooded sun onto their arms and backs. They jeered at Frida but swept up their possessions in anticipation of her arrival, wrapping themselves in towels and stumbling away over the wet sand.

Frida paused at the dirty line that marked high tide. Holding one lid up over her head, as if shading her eyes to see, she became a ship's captain scanning the horizon; these heroic poses came easily to her and her gallant bulk. She moved slowly towards the sea until she reached the place the children had made camp. Then she threw down the lids and began to kick at the sand so that it rose in wild flurries around her; when she finished, it fell smoothly until there was no sign anyone had ever settled on that spot. She retrieved the lids and made her way back to the house.

Ruth watched Frida's serene face float up the dune. She was hard to recognize as the woman who had laboured up this same slope the day before. It was as if she'd required only that one difficult ascent to become sure-footed; or perhaps the garbage lids were acting as ballast: she did hold them a little way out from her body, like wings.

"That's that, then," said Frida. By now she was standing beside Ruth and exhaling through her nose with an equine vigour. The incident appeared to have given her a kind of health.

Ruth, unsure of what to say, ventured, "They shouldn't swim all the way out here without lifeguards. It's not safe."

"They won't be back."

"It's just high jinks, I suppose."

Frida replaced the lids on the compost bins. "They can have their fun in front of someone else's house, then. Spoil someone else's view." And with a firm and nursery air she withdrew to the house.

Ruth remained outside long enough to watch the swimmers take the path up to the small parking lot behind the bus stop, where a Norfolk pine had once dropped during a windstorm and crushed a surfer's truck. She had expected the children to move down the beach and set up camp again, but Frida appeared to have scared them off for good. Ruth was sorry to see them go. But a ripe, wet wind was developing, a familiar sea wind which would have driven them away soon enough. Sand and salt flew up and about, into Ruth's hair and over her garden. This end of the beach was empty now. Any car taking the road to town might be full of those banished children. If I see one car in the next ten seconds, she thought, I'll tell her to go away. A white car burst from behind the hill; a dark one followed immediately behind it. Ruth hadn't had time to prepare for two cars.

"Teatime!" called Frida.

Ruth found her bustling in the kitchen among tea bags and mugs.

"How do you take it?" Frida asked. "Milk and sugar?"

"Lots of milk, one sugar."

"Milky and sweet," Frida said. The combination seemed to please her. Her own tea was strong and dark, and she wouldn't sit to drink. She leaned against the kitchen counter.

"So, tell me things," she said, peering into her steamy tea.

"What things?" Ruth's tongue stammered; she felt something like stage fright.

"I like to get a sense of my clients before we get started. Husband? Job? Family? Childhood? All that stuff."

"That's a lot of stuff."

"You can keep it simple," offered Frida. She was noncommittal; she wouldn't sit, Ruth guessed, because she didn't want this to take all day.

"All right," said Ruth. "Harry was a solicitor. He died of a pulmonary embolism five years ago. I told you about my sons. What else? I used to teach elocution lessons. I grew up in Fiji."

Ruth waited for Frida to react to the mention of Fiji, but she failed to do so. Instead, she narrowed her eyes as if trying to see farther. "You taught what? Electrocution?"

"Elocution!" said Ruth, delighted. "Speech."

"Like speech therapy?"

"No," said Ruth. "The art of speaking. Of clear, precise speech. Pronunciation, vocal production—"

"You mean you taught people how to talk posh?" It was difficult to tell if Frida was disgusted or incredulous or both.

"To speak correctly," said Ruth. "Which isn't the same thing."

"And people *paid* you?"

"I taught young people, usually, and their parents paid me."

Frida was shaking her head as if she'd been told a ludicrous but diverting story. "Is that why you sound kind of English when you talk?"

"I don't sound English," protested Ruth, but she'd been accused of this before. Once, it would have been a compliment. There had been a schoolteacher: Mrs. Mason. She was of elegant, indeterminate age, had an intriguingly absent husband, and she was English; every rounded vowel that fell from her mouth was delivered like a sweet polished fruit to her students, who were the children of sugar-company executives, engineers, missionaries, and government officials: the children of the Empire. They must be trained to speak correctly, so far from home. Mrs. Mason taught them rhymes, tongue twisters, and tricky operetta lyrics and made her students recite the days of the week, over and over, four, five, seven times on the strength of one deep breath. She discouraged the use of pidgin, slang, or Hindi; she was vigilant against the lazily dropped *t*'s of her Australian students; she pounced on the use of *would of* and *should of* and was unfailingly specific about which contractions she would and wouldn't allow. Ruth was her prize pupil.

"You sound pretty English," said Frida, scooping up Ruth's empty mug. "You sound a bit like the Queen."

Ruth had a soft spot for the Queen. "That's ridiculous," she said. "Listen: 'How now brown cow.' That's how I say it. And this is how the Queen would say it: 'How now brown cow.' Listen to her diphthongs! Completely different!"

"Dip-thongs?" Frida snorted over the sink. And suddenly it was a funny, stupid, dirty word, and Ruth was laughing, and she loved it, although it hurt her back. Frida laughed, too, and rising from her capacious chest, her laugh seemed a rare and lovely object; it seemed to spread, like wings. Her whole face was transformed: she was warm and pretty, she knocked the mugs together in the sink, and she raised a tea towel to her face to cover her widening smile. Ruth felt buoyant in her spindly chair. She smiled and sighed and thought, Yes, Ruth, silly thing, this could be good, this could be all right.

3

The house took to Frida; it opened up. Ruth sat in her chair and watched it happen. She saw the bookcases breathe easier as Frida dusted and rearranged them; she saw the study expel its years' worth of Harry-hoarded paperwork. She had never seen such perfect oranges as the ones Frida brought in her little string bag. The house and the oranges and Ruth waited every weekday morning for Frida to come in her golden taxi, and when she left, they fell into silences of relief and regret. Ruth found herself looking forward to the disruption of her days; she was a little disgusted at herself for succumbing so quickly.

But Frida was fascinating. For one thing, her hair was always different: braided, curled, lacquered, soft. Each morning, just before nine, Ruth opened the lounge-room door she had been so careful to close the night before and went to the window to watch Frida's emergence from the taxi. Frida's hair might be piled on her head or straightened to her shoulder blades. It might be a new colour. One day she arrived with hair so blond, so cloudy and insubstantial, that her head seemed an unlikely match for the capable body beneath it. She was a little bleary that morning; she made a cup of tea first thing and sat on the back step drinking it with an air of bleached glamour; the cats took pains to avoid the chemical smell she gave off. The bright blond lasted only a few days before it became brassier, more yellow; then came a softer, whitish colour, more sophisticated and at the same time more childish. After this blond period came red, and burgundy, and a glossy true black, and back to brown, ready for the cycle to start all over again. Frida accepted compliments about her hair with a dignified smile and raised one careful hand to hover near it.

"It's my hobby," she said. Ruth had never before met anyone who considered her own head a hobby.

Frida's magnificent hair never interfered with her duties. She worked in her first few weeks with a bright disposition, but was never what could be described as cheery. She had a determined efficiency about her, and at the same time a languorous quality, a slow, deliberate giving of herself. Her suitcase turned out to contain enormous bottles of eucalyptus-scented disinfectant; she cleaned the floors with this slick substance every morning, shepherding the mop with graceful movements of her tidy feet. The house at first smelled sweet and forested, and then so astringent the cats took to sleeping in elevated places, away from the scrubbed wood and tile. When Ruth drew attention to this, Frida only stood over the immaculate floors and inhaled deeply, with a nasal echo, to demonstrate the bracing bronchial qualities of her cleaning regime.

"Smell that!" she cried, and made Ruth breathe in until her throat burned. "Isn't it great? Isn't it better than seaweed and flies?"

Frida made it clear early on that she disliked the smell of the sea.

While she cleaned, Frida carried out her assessment of Ruth's "situation." She noted the absence of rails in the bath and a fence around the garden. She quizzed Ruth about her medical conditions, flexibility, hair loss, sleeping patterns, eating habits ("You're wasting away," she accused, as if she had long familiarity with the shape of Ruth's body), and frequency of social contact. She made Ruth fill out a number of questionnaires—"How often do you bathe? (a) Daily; (b) Every two to three days; (c) Sporadically; (d) On special occasions" and "Circle the box appropriate to your income in the last financial year."

At the end of her assessment, the first thing Frida announced was that Ruth wasn't eligible for public housing. "People like you usually aren't," she said with apparent pleasure. When Ruth protested that she had no interest in public housing, Frida sucked in an experienced breath and said, "Beggars can't be choosers."

"Beggars should be no choosers," said Ruth.

"*Beggars can't be* is the phrase," said crisp, corrective Frida.

"Yes, I know." Ruth laughed at herself. "I was saying the original version, it's sixteenth century, the phrase our phrase was born from. Imagine that—already a cliché four hundred years ago."

Frida's brows elevated her hairline. "Is that the kind of thing you taught your students?"

"It is, actually," said Ruth. She was proud of herself for re-membering. She felt she could have lifted her arms and recited the days of the week nine or ten times; or perhaps she would only chant, over and over, *Ineligible for public housing*.

Frida, however, was unimpressed; it showed in the delicate angle of her chin. She gave a small sniff. Ruth found it almost sisterly.

"Well, Mrs. Field," Frida said.

Ruth, not for the first time, said, "Oh, call me Ruth, please."

"One hour a day isn't going to be enough, all things consid-ered. I'm going to recommend you're increased to three. That's nine until twelve, and if you like, I'll stay another half an hour to make you lunch. That's if you can bring yourself to put up with my clichés."

Ruth was contrite now. She loved Frida's clichés; she loved the way Frida believed them; she loved how believable they were. I'm a show-off, she thought, but the lift remained in her lungs.

"All right," she said, and that was Ruth agreeing to three hours, and an extra half an hour for lunch.

"Good," said Frida. She seemed to have been made shy by something. Then she said, "I like that name. Ruth."

Frida relaxed over lunch. She made Ruth a ham sandwich and, at Ruth's insistence, boiled herself an egg and ate it from a Mickey Mouse eggcup over which Phillip and Jeffrey used to fight. As she ate, she explained the requirements of her strict diet, which was the result of her having been much heavier than she was now.

"My whole family's big," she said. "Big-boned." She sipped at the spoon with which she scooped the egg. "Mum and Dad are gone, and my sister Shelley, too—all big, though, and when Shell died, I said to myself, 'Frida, it's time to make a change.' That's when I lived in Perth. I did my training out there, in Perth. And I said, 'Frida, it's now or never.' "

These lunchtime revelations were almost boastful: Frida was like an evangelist describing her conversion from the pulpit of her born-again body. "I wrote a letter to food, telling it all the wrong it'd done me," she said. "Then I demanded a divorce. I had a certificate made up—a friend of mine, a girl I worked with, did it on the computer. Then I signed it, and that was that."

"Goodness," said Ruth.

"And look at me now!" said Frida, presenting her sizable self with a flourish of her palms.

"But you do eat?"

"Of course. You don't leave a marriage with nothing, do you? I took some things with me—healthy stuff. Everything else I was divorced from, so I just had to forget about it. There's that thing when you break up with someone and you hate him like poison but sometimes you just want to touch his shoulder, you know? Or hold his hand."

Ruth tried to imagine Frida holding someone's hand; she could just about manage it.

"But even if you want to, you can't. That's divorce," said Frida. It's death, too, thought Ruth. "And then you forget. There are things I couldn't even tell you how they taste. Ask me how something tastes."

"I don't know. Lettuce," said Ruth.

"I'm allowed lettuce. I took lettuce. Ask me something else. Ask me about ice cream."

"All right. How does ice cream taste?"

"I don't remember!" said Frida. "That's divorce."

Ruth was enchanted by Frida's divorce; she wanted to telephone everyone she knew and tell them all about it. But who was there to call? Phillip was never home, or she hadn't calculated the time difference properly; she could tell Jeffrey, but he had never quite approved of what he referred to as her "wicked sense of humour," by which he clearly meant "streak of cruelty"; he hated to hear people made fun of. So if she said to him, "This woman, Frida, divorced food," he would probably make Ruth explain the whole thing and then say, "Good for her." He was already inclined to approve of Frida. Ruth had sent him the paperwork, as promised; he also, according to Frida, sent regular e-mails with instructions on how to care for his mother, a field Frida was trained in, thank you very much, but, as you soon learn, the hardest part of this job is usually the families. Oh, the families.

Frida ate the last of her egg. "You're naturally thin, aren't you," she said, with a trace of pity in her voice.

"I've got a bit of a belly these days," said Ruth, but Frida wasn't listening. She tapped the top of her empty egg until it fell inwards.

"It's good, though, to be a big girl in this job. That's what I've noticed. I've met nurses though, tiny girls, with the strength of ten men. Never underestimate a nurse."

"I know something about nurses," said Ruth, and Frida looked at her in what seemed liked surprise. "My mother was a nurse."

"She took you to work with her, did she?" Frida asked, a little prickly, as if she had a tender bundle of children she had been instructed to leave at home.

Ruth laughed. "She had to, really. My parents were mission-aries. She was a nurse, and he was a doctor. They ran a clinic together, attached to a hospital. In Fiji."

This was the first time Ruth had mentioned Fiji in the weeks since Frida's arrival. Frida didn't respond. She seemed to be engulfed in an obscure displeasure.

"I saw how hard my mother worked, and how exhausted she always was," said Ruth, nervous now, in a bright, chatty tone. "And I suppose she was never really what you would call appre-ciated, though she was very loved. My father's work was appreci-ated, and my mother's sacrifice. That's how people put it."

"What people?" asked Frida, as if she were questioning the existence of any people, ever.

"Oh, you know," said Ruth, waving a vague hand. "Church people, hospital people, family. I've always thought of nursing as a very undervalued profession."

Frida snorted. "I wouldn't call *this* nursing," she said. Then she stood; she seemed to call on the security of her height. She raised her eggcup from the table like a chalice, passed into the kitchen, and pushed open the screen door with one hip, still with the eggcup lifted high.

"For the snails," she said, and threw the crushed eggshell into the garden.

The taxi called for her soon afterwards, and she left the house in an excellent mood.

4

Ruth often woke with a sense that something important had happened in the night. She might have dreamt a tiger again. She might have dreamt, as she used to, of Richard Porter in her bed—although surely, a dream like that should be of Harry. She did think of Richard more now that Frida was in the house, as if to have daily company reminded her of the existence of other people. Between Richard, and Frida, and this sense of curious importance, the weeks were crowded; they were also thick, Ruth noticed, with a strange hothouse heat. She shed blankets from her bed and wore light clothing—summer dresses, or cotton shorts with the small, soft T-shirts her sons had worn as boys. The cats lost their winter fur in springtime clumps, and Ruth continued to hear bird and insect sounds at night. But little happened: Frida installed bath rails and taught Ruth how to lie down and sit up with the least strain on her back; she mopped and swept; she introduced pills recommended by a naturopath friend of George's, which were supposed to help with memory and brain function and, being made of an ordinary orange kitchen spice, turned Ruth's urine bright yellow; Jeffrey and Phillip telephoned; these things filled the time, but were not extraordinary.

There was, however, the matter of the car. Ruth disliked driving and was frightened of Harry's car; she peered at it through the kitchen windows; she worried over it at night. She began to live off Frida's gifts of fruit and bulk canned goods, all sourced from some inexplicable friends of George's, so that it was no longer necessary to drive or even take the bus into town. She lost weight. She ate the last of the pumpkin seeds, and they went straight through her. Once a week, under Jeffrey's orders, she went out to sit in the car and run the engine; doing so, she experienced a busy, practical sense of renewal followed by the disquieting feeling she was about to drive herself to her own funeral.

One day, while Ruth sat in the driver's seat, Frida's head loomed at the window like a sudden policeman's. Ruth's heart jumped but she kept her hands on the wheel; she was proud of this, as if it indicated that, counter to her own belief, she was a good driver.

"You never drive this thing," said Frida. "You should sell it."

Ruth was afraid of the car, but she didn't want to sell it. That seemed so irrevocable. "I couldn't," she said.

A week later, Frida raised the matter again. "I can think of three or four people who'd buy that car off you tomorrow," she said.

"Driving means independence," said Ruth, quoting Harry, who used to make her drive at least once a week. He called this "keeping your hand in."

Frida shook her head. "Not if you don't actually drive." She promised that her brother's taxi would always be at Ruth's disposal, free of charge. "After all, you're family now," she said, with unusual gaiety.

She also offered to take over Ruth's shopping, to buy stamps and mail letters, to pay bills, and to arrange house calls from the doctor if necessary.

"You can't eat tinned sardines every night," said Frida. "If the government's paying me to do your shopping, you may as well let me do your shopping. That's what I'm here for."

Frida liked this phrase, if using it regularly indicated a preference. It seemed so adequately to sum up the melancholy importance of her willingness to serve. Still Ruth resisted the idea of selling the car. What if, alone at night, she heard an intruder and needed to get away? Or had some kind of medical emergency and the phones weren't working?

"How would you drive in a medical emergency?" asked Frida.

"It might just be a burst eardrum. Or maybe there's a problem with the cats and I need to drive them somewhere. You can't call an ambulance for a cat, can you. Can you?"

What actually worried her, she was surprised to realize, was the tiger. Which was ridiculous, of course. But what if he came back some night on which she'd forgotten to close the lounge-room door? She would hear him coming down the hallway to her bedroom, intent on his agile paws, and her only escape would be the window. Ruth pictured climbing into the garden and crouching in the bushes waiting for the tiger's superior nose to smell her out. As if, with her back, she could still climb and crouch! Or there might be a short moonlit dash over the beach with the tiger's hot breath on her heels, the car meanwhile slumbering in the comfortable driveway of a more fortunate stranger.

"I won't sell it," she said, and turned the key to kill the engine, which was the wrong gesture if her intention was to prove her resolve. The car shuddered and wheezed before falling silent, the way a much older car might.

"Suit yourself," said Frida, shrugging her round shoulders. "I'm only trying to help."

After this discussion, Frida's hair entered a dormant period of brittle French rolls. She spent more time with the floors and her eucalypt mop, and she made noises as she moved: sighs, soft grunts and groans; everything required some effort, some complaint, or, alternatively, an aggressively cheerful energy. She muttered in passing about aged drivers and overdue registration checks; she referred, more than once, to the difficulty of helping people who won't help themselves. Frida stirred the house with these perceptible struggles and satisfactions, and Ruth found it easier to stay out of her way. She withdrew to her chair. She counted ships and pretended to read the newspaper. Jeffrey called with the idea of inviting a friend from Sydney to stay for the weekend; he suggested an unmarried woman who, Ruth knew, was a discreet and grateful guest and a diligent spy for the worried children of her elderly friends. Ruth nodded and smiled into the phone. Frida mopped, and the car waited.

The following week, Ruth sat in the driver's seat facing the sea, which was level and green except in the path of the morning sun; there, it was ribbed with silver. She felt the familiar dread as she turned the ignition key, but today there was an additional terror: the car seemed to press in on her, as if it were being compacted with her inside it; the car felt so small and so heavy that it might at any moment sink into the dune, leaving her buried in a sandy hole.

"You hate this car," Ruth said aloud, and lifted her hands to those places on the steering wheel that Harry had smoothed by touching so often. He believed in buying expensive European cars that would last a long time; this car vindicated him. It was sheathed in indestructibility.

"You hate this car," said Ruth again, because she did hate it and was afraid, not just of driving it but of the expensive machinery of its European heart. Frida was right, as usual. She was probably right about everything.

But it annoyed Ruth that Frida was right, so she put the car in reverse and backed it down the long driveway with the surety that comes only from bravado. Frida came to the lounge-room window; Ruth could see hands shifting the lace of the curtains. But it was too late—Ruth was heading down the drive. Out on the road, she turned right, away from town. To her left were the hills; to her right was the sea. A low wing of cloud rolled away as she drove. It was July—the middle of the mild winter. The road was bright and grey, and the car so fast under her heated hands; the word she thought of was *quicksilver*, and that was an important word, a word for a pirate or a tomcat; her own cats had silly

athletes' names, human names she disapproved of and declined
to use; how focused her mind felt, she thought, even with all of
this in it, pirates and tomcats; she was moving towards a definite
point and would be delighted to discover what it was. She would
find it, and go home again. But her return would have to be perfect: a gesture of both surrender and magnificence. It would
have to indicate that Ruth, although willing to sell the car, was
not entirely ruled by Frida's will.

Ruth followed the broad leftward curve of a hillside until
she was a little dizzy, and there as the road straightened stood a
roadside fruit stand with space for a few cars to park beside it.
She had often wondered who stopped at fruit stands like this.
Harry always refused. Now she turned off the road, bumped up
the grassy verge, and sat for a moment in the stilled car. When
she stepped out, the air felt newly polished. It both buoyed and
stung.

A teenage boy, dark-skinned and light-haired from too much
sun, manned the stall. His blinking face was scrubbed clean by
boredom, and the surfboard propped beside him explained his
look of marine longing. His stock was almost entirely made up
of avocados, but a glorious pineapple caught Ruth's eye. It shouldn't
have been there: a pineapple, this far south, in July! She approached and laid one hand on its corrugated hide.

"Busy today?" Ruth asked. She had emptied the car's ash-
tray of coins, and now they weighed down her pockets.

"Nope," said the boy, and he shrugged and sighed and
looked towards the swelling sea. "I could of been out there for
hours."

"Could *have*," said Ruth. She produced her coins. "I don't
know how much this amounts to, but I want to spend all of it."

He was a fast counter. "Nineteen dollars and forty-five cents,"
he said. Harry would have tutted at her for not clearing out the
coins before now.

"What will that buy?"

The boy looked at the sea and then at Ruth. "Everything."

It took ten minutes to load the car with everything. The boy's chest seemed to expand with every carton; he began to chat about the weather and a shifting sandbar in the bay and finally allowed himself a luxurious scratch of his barely stubbled chin. The backseat was full of avocados, but the pineapple sat by itself in the front; Ruth was tempted to strap it in. The liberated boy waved as she drove away. The pineapple rolled a little into the coastal curves, and something about it—its swollen movement, its heavy golden smell, and the absurdity of its spiked green haircut—made Ruth feel like taking a holiday. It made her feel like driving forever and never coming back. But, she wondered, how do you take a holiday from a holiday? And by the time she wondered this, she was home.

Ruth hoped Frida might be waiting in front of the house, or at least hovering behind the front door. She wasn't, so Ruth parked the car in its usual spot. The crushing sensation was gone; the car and the ground both felt solid. She thought of a time when she was young, with young sons, and only ever looked severe while driving: she set her lips thin, her elbows strained at ballet angles from the wheel, and her face took on an expression that used to frighten her children. It couldn't be a mistake to put all that behind her.

Ruth called for Frida from the garden and the front hall; she went back and opened the car's rear doors, looked at the avocado trays, and thought about lifting them. Only then did Frida come out of the house, drying her hands on the hem of her white shirt.

"Avocados? In winter?"

"A present," said Ruth.

"Not much of a present when I have to carry them myself," said Frida, but Ruth saw that she was pleased. The quantity was what impressed her; Frida was a natural friend to bulk. She ferried and puffed until the fruit was inside, and then Ruth went to lock the car. There was the pineapple in the front seat. She lifted it out with special care: for her back, but also for the pineapple.

When Ruth reentered the house, Frida was in the dining room. She stood at the window making strange sounds in her throat: a low throaty coo that might have been a bird noise. Ruth looked, and there were magpies in the garden. Frida watched them and made her gentle throbbing calls; she stopped when Ruth said, "I've decided to sell the car."

Then Frida turned and smiled. "Yes," she said. She was lovely when she smiled, with her plump, pretty face. She held out her arms and accepted the pineapple as if she had expected it all along; had placed an order for it. Ruth put the car keys on the table. Her hands, now empty, smelled of coins.

"It's really for my own peace of mind," she said.

"George can get you a good price," said Frida, and the next day she introduced a man named Bob, who looked over the car—he insisted on calling it "the vehicle"—and was prepared to buy it for thirteen thousand dollars. The idea of freedom from the car delighted Ruth; so did the idea of selling it without consulting her sons. This satisfaction increased when Bob presented her with a cheque. Ruth noted in passing that along with his other misfortunes—Frida mentioned a traitorous wife and kidney stones—Bob bore the unusual surname of Fretweed. He returned that afternoon with a skinny assistant who maneuvered the vehicle down the drive. Ruth was reminded of the specific sound a familiar car makes, which seemed to her, almost more than any other noise—even more than the sound of Harry's voice—to have been stored inescapably in her memory. But the car was disappearing, taking its sound with it; Harry, too, went down the drive for the last time. Frida seemed sensitive to this in the quiet of the house. There was a sense of relief and exhaustion at the end of their little battle, and it manifested in small tender things: tea made, quiet maintained, and no competition over the affection of the cats. The grass beneath the car had yellowed to the colour of cereal. Frida pinned the cheque to the fridge with a magnet and told Ruth she would bank it first thing on Monday.

5

Frida took charge of Ruth's banking. She presented Ruth with statements and letters from the bank, and Ruth waved a regal arm above each one, as if in dismissal. Frida treated Ruth's bankbook like a sacred object, always requesting permission to use it and returning it with a public flourish to its proper place at the back of Harry's filing cabinet. Jeffrey had explained the function of keycards, but Ruth liked the efficient cosiness of the book; she liked how contained it felt, how manual.

Frida had no time for keycards. "Money isn't plastic," she said, although, in fact, it was.

Ruth intended to inspect all this paperwork in private, at night. She remembered her mother's lessons about managing staff: never give them any reason to believe you don't trust them. But the house at night was not the place for these daytime plans; it encouraged a different kind of resolution. After dark, the heat thickened so that every noise seemed tropical: palms rattled their spears, insects rubbed their wings in the dripping trees; the whole house shuffled and buzzed. The heat made Ruth's head itch. She listened for any hint of the tiger, but it all seemed safely herbivorous. One night she woke to the sound of a dog crying out, and it made her wonder about wild dogs—she thought she remembered a hyena in *The Jungle Book*. Her mother had read her *The Jungle Book* when she was very young, the age when her bed was moved away from the window because of nightmares; the view from her pillow was of a chest of drawers, painted green, with a glass night-light that threw pinkish shadows on a framed picture of Sydney Harbour (apparently, she was born in a place called Sydney). So she must have been six or seven.

Now she lay awake listening to the hyena, which was undoubtedly a dog on the beach. The cats fidgeted at her side, but slept again. Her sense of the extraordinary was particularly strong. She might have been seven, waiting to hear her father come home from a late night at the clinic. She might have been nineteen, waiting for Richard's voice in the hall; he came home even later than her father and stepped so carefully past her throbbing door she could easily have missed him. The consequence rose up out of the sounds she heard and those she only remembered; it met somewhere between them, and finding space there, it grew. Ruth lay and listened for it; then she grew tired of waiting. I'm too old, she thought, to be a girl waiting for important noise. Why not go out to meet it, why not prepare? She rose from her bed to run a bath and, as the greenish water filled the noisy tub, looked in Harry's study for her old address book. If I find it before the bath runs over, she thought, Richard's address will be in there. She found the book before the bath was half full; she opened it, and there under *P* for Porter was Richard's address. Just reading it felt like a summons.

Ruth lowered herself into the water with the help of Frida's railing. The water amplified the white of her legs, but it smoothed and dazzled all the folds of her skin, so that half of her body was old and actual and the other half was marine and young.

Ruth was happy and clumsy after her bath. She dressed in a new nightgown. It was sleeveless and pale and, although short, felt bridal. Frida had chosen it and dismayed Ruth with its matronly florals; now, in the night, it shone. The heat of the house made a canopy over the hallway, where the moon came in through the fanned glass in the front door. The moonlight lay on the wooden floor like a deck of cards, and Ruth could see that the hall was straight and long and empty of tigers and birds and palm trees. She crossed it with her arms held out because she was afraid of falling (Harry's mother had fallen in her old age, after a lifetime of robust health, and had never been the same again), and when she opened the door to the lounge room, the light from the windows seemed to jump at her all at once. This room felt comparatively cool and quiet, but it contained an echo of heated noise all the same. It was this noise she was looking for.

Ruth found nothing in the lounge room but the stillness of her furniture, which was either in shadow or patterned by the lace curtains that fell between it and the moon. The moon seemed to be big and full whenever Ruth looked at it, and to-night it was emphatic, as if it had blown itself to a ball in order to assure her that there was nothing unusual in her lounge room. The moon was full on the space in front of the house, but beyond that it was eaten up by the grassy drive. Anything might be lurk-ing in that drive: a tiger or a taxi. Ruth walked through the din-ing room and looked at the garden. Everything on the sea side of the house was blasted white by the moon. All this emptiness had a carved quality that made Ruth want to swear. She loved the crowded bluster of swearing, the sense of an audience; it was so humanizing. She stood at the half-open back door and said "Fuck," and wished for the comforting hot ticking singing jun-gle she had disturbed by getting out of bed. It didn't really sound like Fiji—at night in Fiji she heard cars on the road, her parents moving about, the telephone ringing in the hallway and her fa-ther leaving to see a patient, crepe myrtles rubbing at her win-dows, and the sound of hot water in the pipes when her mother ran a bath—but it sounded different enough to remind her of Fiji; it was enough to make her think of the room with the night-light and the picture of Sydney Harbour. The sound of the jungle was full, and everything here was empty.

Ruth went back to the lounge room and listened for some time. Every noise she heard was ordinary, and the cool room was stiff and airless. She lay on the sofa, turned her back from the lace of the windows, and waited. It seemed important that something might touch her, and crucial that she not open her eyes to look for whatever that thing might be. A tiger would be perfect, but anything would do; a bird, maybe, but it needn't be a bird. Just a fly. Just a frond of something, stirring in a yellow wind. Lying on the couch with her eyes closed, Ruth might feel her jungle come back; there might be yellow light, there might be a tiger to bump its broad nose against her back. The water, at least, might hammer in the pipes. Frida woke her the next morning by turning her on the sofa, peering into her face, and saying, "I nearly wet my pants, you idiot. I thought you were dead."

6

Frida gave the floors a thorough mopping that morning and, a-swim in the alluvial muck, with her bare feet depositing grey tracks no matter how long she left the floors to dry, worked herself into a black mood. She persisted with her mop, and eventually the floors were smooth and softly lit. Then she became generous and hearty. She sat at the dining-room table, gazed magnanimously out to sea, and ate dried apricots. Her hair was coiled in a complicated triple braid, and the floors were, briefly, perfect.

Ruth joined her at the table and said, "Jeffrey thinks I should invite a friend to visit."

Frida chewed her apricots.

"What he wants," said Ruth, "is Helen Simmonds, who's a sensible woman he's known forever who'll ring him up and tell him everything."

Frida clicked at the roof of her mouth with her cheerful tongue.

"So I thought I'd invite a man instead."

Frida hooted. Her whole face shone with suggestive delight. "Well, well," she said. "Just when I thought I had you figured out."

Ruth, pleased by this innuendo, nevertheless dismissed it with an airy hand.

"Who is he, then?" said Frida. "Your boyfriend?"

"I haven't seen him in fifty years."

"Ex-boyfriend?"

"No. Sort of."

"Ha!" cried Frida, triumphant. "It's always the quiet ones who're up to no good."

"Oh, Frida, it was the fifties! Nobody was up to no good. Nobody I knew. It was the fifties, and in Fiji it may as well have been 1912."

Frida snorted as if there had never been a 1912.

"I mean Fiji in the fifties, is all I mean," Ruth corrected. "I don't mean Fiji is a *backward* country."

"I could care less if Fiji is a *backward* country," said Frida. Each apricot disappeared inside her benevolent mouth. Ruth began to worry for Frida's digestive system, but counseled herself not to; Frida was the kind of woman her mother would have referred to, with approval, as having the constitution of an ox. As a child, Ruth was frightened of oxen, which rolled their eyes and ate the tops of sugarcane and were glossy flanked in the sun, but she knew now that her mother had never had those real oxen in mind when she complimented anyone's constitution.

"His name was Richard Porter," said Ruth.

"Oh, yes," said Frida, lifting one groomed eyebrow as if she'd been anticipating Richard all along. But this was Frida's way: it was impossible to surprise her. She would rather starve than be caught off guard; she had said so on more than one occasion. It was also unnecessary to ask if Frida wanted to hear about Richard, because she would only shrug or sigh or, at best, say, "Suit yourself." Much better just to begin.

"He was a doctor who came to help my father at the clinic," said Ruth. "I was nineteen. He was older."

Frida seemed to smirk at this, as if she were hearing a smutty story. But it was hard to tell what she was thinking. She sat, almost tranquillized, with her feet lifted from the floor, and looked out across the bay, where an insistent wind cleared the haze and lifted the flags over the surf club.

Richard, Ruth explained, was in Fiji as a medical humanitarian rather than a missionary, although he agreed to profess certain beliefs in order to fill the post at the clinic—it was so difficult to find trained men after the war that Ruth's father was willing to accept this compromise. Ruth's parents referred to Richard, before his arrival, as "that gifted but misguided young man" and busied themselves preparing the house, since he would be staying with them until he found accommodation of his own. He was Australian, too; Ruth's parents prayed in thankfulness to God for this provision, and Ruth prayed along with them. She was most interested in how handsome he was. He arrived during a rainstorm; Ruth stood on the verandah at the side of the house to watch him run from a taxi through the downpour. She felt a strong sense of destiny because she was nineteen and because he seemed so providential: young, Australian, a doctor, and now coming from rain into her own house. So she rounded the corner, mindful of her own effect—because she had been pretty at nineteen, a lovely pale blonde—and ready, so consciously ready, for her life to make some plausible beginning. But he was sodden and there was some concern about his bags, which the driver was carrying in through the rain. Richard seemed to want to help and was being forcibly restrained from doing so by Ruth's father, who had prepared a welcome speech and was delivering it while holding Richard in a paternal embrace. Ruth was forgotten in the confusion and then only hurriedly introduced; she went to her bedroom and moped over an impression of dark hair and a thin frame.

Later that evening, dry, Richard's hair was light and his body seemed less scarce. *Handsome* was not the right word for him; he was good-looking, but in a neat, shining, narrow way, with his combed hair and his straight nose and a paleness about the lips. It was as if his beauty had been tucked away—politely, resolutely—so that he might get on with the rest of his life, but it made itself known, just the same, in the shine of his hair and the fineness of his face. The faint lines on his forehead indicated seriousness. Ruth liked all this; she approved. Sometimes she tied up her hair too tightly to be flattering because, let loose, it was a long white-gold line, a distraction, and had nothing to do with the work of God.

They all sat together at the dinner table—Ruth, her parents, and Richard—and Ruth saw the dining room as he must have: how long and narrow it was, how dingily white, with the chipped sideboard holding family silver (a tureen, a pepperpot, a punch bowl with six glass cups, each carried lovingly from Sydney, out of the past, and rarely used; isn't it funny, thought Ruth, how some objects are destined to survive certain things, like sea voyages and war). A fan revolved in the upper air. Ruth's mother didn't believe in lamps, only in bright, antiseptic light, so the dining table was laid out, the equator in that longitudinal room, as if emergency surgery might be performed there at any moment. There were no shadows; everything blazed as if under the midday sun. Watercolour landscapes flanked a photograph of the King. When Richard bent his head for her father to say grace, Ruth saw the pale canal of white scalp where he parted his hair. The tops of his ears were red and his forehead was brown and damp. He kept his eyes open and his long, fine face still, but he mouthed *Amen*. Perhaps he could be converted. She looked at him too long, and he saw her.

They all ate with that furious attention which comes of social unease and willed good feeling. Or Ruth did, and her mother, and Richard; but her father was relaxed and happy, expanding into male medical company with obvious pleasure, as if he'd been many months at conversational sea. Ruth supposed he had. Her father dominated Richard, and she barely spoke. She hoped instead to burn with an inner intensity that would communicate itself to him secretly. Richard answered her father's questions with a politeness that suggested he was keeping his true feelings to himself. Ruth recognized and appreciated that kind of reserve. She decided, He's a moral man, but considerate. He's kind. Probably—as she admitted to herself later—he could have been utterly without principles or sensitivity and she would still have found something to admire. She was that determined to love him.

After dinner, they all sat on the verandah (which Ruth referred to, privately, as the terrace) and drank tea. The tea was never hot enough. It was like drinking the air, which pressed close around them, as if the earlier rain had finally just refused to fall any farther and remained suspended. Bats swam overhead. Richard lit a cigarette and Ruth imagined the smoke passing in and out of his lungs. Everything was a vapour—the tea, the damp air, the smoke—but Richard sat distinctly inside all of it. She rarely looked at him or spoke, but she tried to be especially graceful as she fanned her head to keep mosquitoes away; they didn't bite her, but they fussed at her face. Finally her mother grew tired and said, "I'm sure the young people have a lot to talk about," and Ruth saw her father look astonished, as if the thought that Richard and Ruth might have anything in common—even the proximity of their ages—had never occurred to him. Then the withdrawal: her mother indulgent, and her father flustered. He'd been caught midmonologue. They achieved their exit with the utmost awkwardness, and Ruth, mortified, nearly fled.

Richard sat and smoked. There was an atmosphere around him: exhaustion, relief, forced courtesy. All this just in the way he sat and smoked. Ruth liked that he held his wrist rigid. Some men, in her opinion, smoked like women; she liked that he didn't. He wore a wedding band, but not on the correct finger, and she learned much later that it belonged to his father, who was dead. Ruth, afraid of a moment's silence, asked questions. He'd come to Fiji, he said, with the hope of opening a dispensary for the treatment of Indian women.

"For the treatment of—what?" Ruth asked, surprised, because she thought he meant that Indian women suffered from some special malady, unknown to Australians and Fijians and

the English, and although she suspected it might be embarrassing, she wanted to know what it was.

"Of Indian women," he repeated. Did he think she didn't
know Indian women existed? It was a bad beginning.

"Oh," said Ruth. "I thought you were here to help us. In our
clinic."

"Your clinic?" he asked.

Ruth considered this rude of him, and enjoyed her resulting
indignation. But she was also ashamed: everything she looked at
seemed so shabby, so obvious; there was the sound of the houseboy
washing dishes in the kitchen, and no real order in the riotous
garden, and they were at once too privileged (they were not Indian women, with their mysterious afflictions) and not privileged
enough (surely, entertaining a young man on the terrace, she
shouldn't have been able to hear dishes being washed in the
kitchen). So she corrected herself by saying, "*The* clinic."

He smiled at her then, and she felt herself smiling back, unable to help it. "What I really want to do," he said—and she
leaned forward to where his smoke began; she could have dipped
her head in it—"is run my own clinic, once a month to start
with, more often if there's interest and resources. There's a man
named Carson—do you know him?"

"Yes," said Ruth with regret. Andrew Carson was a young-
ish man who worked for the South Pacific Commission. He was
suspected, in a genial way, of being a Communist, mainly because he didn't attend church. He approved of Ruth's father
because he could have been making money in Sydney as a doctor—"serious money," he called it, as if there were any other
kind—but was here instead, curing Fijians. Ruth's father disliked this secular sort of approval. The thought of Richard
and Andrew Carson becoming friends—allies—made Ruth
disconsolate.

"He thinks he's found some funds for me. I want to get out
to the villages. I want to buy a truck."

"A truck," said Ruth, with a solemnity in keeping with Richard's plans.

"And in the meantime, yes, I'm here to help in your clinic."

"I'm glad," she said, "about both things—that you're here to help my father, and Indian women." This was the most deliberate statement she had ever made to a man she wasn't related to, and she felt as if her ears were burning red.

Richard rewarded her with another smile. The smoke stood beside him without seeming to rise or fall. "Your father likes to talk, doesn't he?"

Ruth was sensitive to criticism of her father, in that tenuous and personal way in which children are anxious for the dignity of their parents. She worried a great deal for him out in the world.

"Not usually," she said. "He's happy to have you to talk to."

"I like him very much," said Richard. "I've read everything he's written on whooping cough." She waited for him to say, "But I'm sure you're not interested in all that." He didn't. His cigarette burnt right down to his fingers, and he shook them as he flicked it away. "I always smoke them down to the very end. It's a bad habit. Army days."

"Where were you?"

"Mainly New Guinea, and then for a while in Tokyo." He was obviously contemplating another cigarette; she saw him decide against it. "Is it the holidays for you? Do you go back to Sydney for school?"

Ruth stood. "You must be exhausted."

"You know, I really am," he said, standing too. "You've made me feel very welcome. Thank you."

He didn't offer his hand. He stood, holding his cigarettes, and his tea was only half finished; he had no idea of the cost of good tea in Suva. The square of the kitchen window went catastrophically dark.

"I hope you'll be happy here," said Ruth. She was moving

inside, too quickly. "I've finished school. I'm nineteen. Good night."

She ran up the stairs, thinking, Idiot, idiot.

Now she said to Frida, "I fell in love with him the very first night. What a goose. I didn't even know him."

"Usually better not to," said Frida.

"In some cases, maybe. But Richard was quite a special man."

"And you didn't marry him."

"No," said Ruth.

"Silly bugger."

"It wasn't up to me."

"I meant him," said Frida.

"Oh, he did all right. He got married before I did. We sailed back to Sydney together in 1954, and I hoped something might happen. Something definite, I mean. But it turned out he was engaged all that time. Never mentioned it, not even to my father. I went to his wedding and never saw him again."

"Really? Never again?"

"Never." Ruth liked the dramatic finality of *never*, but was compelled to admit there had been Christmas cards.

"If you ask my opinion," said Frida, who rarely waited for the solicitation of her opinion, "you're better off. What kind of bloke doesn't tell anyone he's engaged?"

"The girl he was marrying was Japanese. He met her in Japan." Ruth, defensive, saw Frida dismiss this as a reason for secrecy. "It wasn't all that long after the war. It was a sensitive subject."

Frida sent out one blind hand for an apricot. She was thoughtful; she understood sensitive subjects. She chewed her apricot before asking, "And what happened in the end?"

As if a life is a period during which things happen. I suppose it is, thought Ruth, and they do, and then at my age, at Richard's age, they've finished happening, and you can ask.

"His wife died about a year or two before Harry. She was older than him—older than Richard."

Now Frida held a hand to her dark hair and produced a sigh so bitter, so exhausted, and at the same time so sweet that Ruth was tempted to reach out and comfort her. Frida stood up from the table.

"You really want to see him again?" Her mood was shifting; she was already giving a farsighted frown.

"I think I do. Yes," said Ruth. "I do."

"It'd be a lot of work," Frida said, and she sighed and stretched as if that work were already upon her. "I hate to say it, Ruth, but I'm not sure you're up to it. And how old is this Richard now? Eighty? Ninety?" She said "Eighty? Ninety?" as if there were a negligible difference between those two ages.

"He must be over eighty," said Ruth. Richard, over eighty! That seemed so unlikely.

"You might call it irresponsible, asking a man like that to travel. Expecting to be able to look after him, at his age." Frida looked at Ruth in a way that added, "At *your* age," and swept the package of apricots up from the table.

"In last year's Christmas card he said he was in the best of health."

"The best of health for *eighty*," said Frida with a snort.

Frida believed she had a secret, Ruth saw, and it was this: that Ruth and Richard were innocents, that they were old, older than old, and that while they might still be capable of a sweet, funny romance, any physical possibility was extinguished for them both. Well, probably it was. Ruth wondered. She permitted herself to hope, and at the same time not define the thing she hoped for.

"Jeffrey will agree with you," said Ruth with a carefully blameless face, and she saw Frida consider this distasteful possibility before proceeding to the kitchen. Ruth sat still with the idea of Richard. She was surprised by how much she wanted to see him, and also by the pleasure of wanting. He would be an arrival—one that she had asked for, that she had planned.

"You know what?" called Frida from the kitchen. She often delivered good news—gave of the bounty of herself—from another room, at high volume, so she needn't be troubled by gratitude. "I could help out. You know, come over on the weekend. Not for free, mind." Now she appeared, briefly, in the archway between the rooms. "But for a reasonable price, you know, I could cook and keep an eye on things."

"Would you really?"

Frida made a clatter in the kitchen which meant "Yes, but don't you dare start thanking me."

Frida seemed to think it was decided: Ruth would ask Richard to come, and Frida would keep an eye on things. She prepared an uncharacteristically festive meal: a curryish dish, with pieces of pineapple and indecipherable meat. It tasted like the distant cousin of something Fijian.

"What do you call this?" Ruth asked as Frida fastened her grey coat and made for the front door.

"Dinner," said Frida.

Later, lying in bed with the doubtful meat in her stomach, Ruth fretted about Richard. She wanted to think only of how fine he was, of how every girl had loved him, and of how he liked her best; how she would be walking with friends and his shabby truck would roll by, his mobile dispensary, lifting dust and rattling at the seams, and he would honk his horn or stop to talk and sometimes drive her home, or take them all in the truck to the beach, and when they swam, he stayed close to her, lay beside her in the sun, gossiped about Andrew Carson, poured sand on her feet, asked her advice about some faux pas he had made with the Methodist minister's wife, told her she reminded him of a milkmaid on a biscuit tin, and finally, when the Queen visited Fiji and a ball was held in her honour at the Grand Pacific Hotel, invited Ruth to come with him—although he disapproved of queens—because he knew she wanted to go. And everyone waited for Ruth and Richard—their names were said together so often—to become an item; even when Richard began to disgrace himself by caring too much about the health of Indian women, by befriending the wrong Fijians ("agitators," Ruth's father called them), by staying at Ruth's parents' house too long ("saving money for the dispensary," he said; "staying for me," prayed Ruth), and by refusing church without even being a Communist, the women of Suva hoped to see happiness for Ruth with this "gifted but misguided" young man. She had given up the hope of converting him. She was no longer much sure of God herself. He came home late at night, and she listened for his soft walk past her door, and he never stopped. Not true: he stopped once. Her door was open. He came in to apologize; he had kissed her the night before at the Queen's ball and would never do it again. People began to wonder if he was quite normal. They wondered about Indian women and Andrew Carson; they never suspected a Japanese fiancée.

And how Ruth defended him to everyone! Because she was his favourite, his milkmaid on the biscuit tin. But that was exhausting, too. For example, he would lend her difficult books without her having asked for them and want to know her opinion; when the ocean liners docked in Suva carrying orchestras or theatre companies, he took her to see them perform. And if he didn't like what he saw or read or heard, he would call it "a bad play," "a bad book." *Bad* in his mouth was the strongest of adjectives. He always had a definite view of the play or the symphony, and he would presage it with this declamatory staccato, as if helpfully summarizing his opinion before expanding upon it: "It was bad," he would say, or "uniformly bad" if he considered it irretrievable. Or, if approved of, things were either "important" or "excellent" or "very fine." Most of the events he took her to bored her even when she enjoyed them, and she felt Richard notice this whole world of his from which she was excluded, by her own choice it seemed. She saw him observe, mournfully, her overenthusiastic applause when the thing was finally over.

He was courteous; he always withheld his opinion until it was asked for. He would wait for her to say, "What did you think?" And then he would say, "Very bad" or "Excellent," and there would be some minutes of talk about why, during which Ruth wondered how he thought of all these things to say. It astonished her that he could have such inexhaustible opinions, and that he was capable of articulating them. He's smarter than I am, she concluded, and he cares more than I do. But part of her was also suspicious of his ability to translate feeling so readily into words. She came away from music with a sense of its shape, and from plays with a suggestion of pulled threads; she had no idea how to describe shapes and threads. Richard would talk, and then he would say, "What did you think?" And she might say, "I agree" or "I liked it." She didn't have opinions, if what he had were opinions; only preferences, and these were often vague. She knew that her opinions existed—that she responded with true pleasure to the things she enjoyed—but she never found it necessary to scrutinize them. Whenever she was pressed to reveal her tastes in books or art or music, she sounded to herself as if she were discussing her favourite colours. But she shared her pleasures easily with Harry, whose delights were similarly blurry: they both loved Handel's *Messiah*, for example, but felt no need to investigate the particular sensations it aroused in them. Books were different; they were private. No one could read them along with her, reacting and looking for her reaction. Richard had tried to draw her out, and she was afraid to disappoint him with the little he found there. In comparison, the ease of Harry was a relief.

Ruth had expected her character to become more sharply defined with age, until eventually she found that it no longer mattered to her; she left off worrying about it, like a blessedly abandoned hobby. But now Richard might come with his bad books and his excellent symphonies and fill her with doubt all over again. She lay in bed with her hands on her meaty stomach and worried until the cats, from their bedposts, began to perk and stare. They were listening to something, and so she listened, but heard nothing unusual. Her heart was stiff but strong. Not now, she thought, addressing the tiger. Not with Richard coming—which meant she did want him to come. One of the cats gave a low, funny growl or produced, at least, a growl-shaped noise. When Ruth went to comfort him, he snapped at her fingers, which always made her sad and shy. She moved in the bed, unhappy, and the cats jumped and ran.

"Fine!" she called after them. She would write to Richard. Things could still happen to her. She lifted her back from the bed, went to her dressing table, and found paper and a pen.

"My dear," she wrote, "this will be a bolt from the blue, but if you can spare the time and make the journey, this old lady would like to see you again. I live by the sea, I have a very good view (there are whales), and I also have a wonderful woman called Frida whose brother George has a taxi and will collect you from the station and bring you here. We can talk Fiji and fond memories, or just snooze in the sun. Come as soon as you'd like to. The whales are migrating. Come as soon as you can."

Ruth wrote the letter, didn't reread it, sealed it in an envelope, and sent it out with Frida the following morning. There might have been spelling mistakes, and she worried afterwards about having signed off "all my love," but the important thing was that the letter existed and had been sent. Five days later there was a reply from Richard. His handwriting was lean as winter twigs. He was delighted to hear from her. He had been thinking about her lately, would you believe; and if she was old, then he was older. His next month was busy, but he would come on a Friday in four weeks' time.

7

Ruth telephoned Jeffrey a few days before Richard's arrival.

"What's wrong?" he asked when she announced herself. His midweek voice was poised for action.

"Nothing," she said. "I'm going to be busy this weekend, that's all, so I thought I'd ring you now."

"Busy doing what?"

"I've invited a friend to stay," said Ruth.

"Good on you, Ma! Anyone I know? Helen Simmonds? Gail? Barb?"

"No."

"Who, then?"

"An old friend."

"If you're going to be deliberately mysterious, I won't keep asking you about it," said Jeffrey. So like Harry it was unearthly, but Ruth supposed this happened all the time with widows and their sons, and it would be maddening to mention. She'd worked hard to maintain her belief in the distinct differences between herself and her own parents.

"I'm not being mysterious," she protested. "This is an old friend from Fiji, a man called Richard Porter."

There was that same feeling as when she'd told her school friends, "I'm taking the boat to Sydney with Richard Porter." Then, in 1954, the girls nodded and smiled at one another. Ruth blossomed in the midst of all that gentle insinuation. Her fond heart filled. Now Jeffrey said, "That's nice."

"Do you remember—we used to get Christmas cards from him? And his wife."

"Not really."

"He knew me when I was a girl. He knew your grandparents. He was quite an extraordinary man. I suppose a sort of activist, you'd call it now."

"Find out if he's got any old photos," said Jeffrey.

"I'm sure he will. I remember he had a camera when the Queen visited."

Ruth knew that Jeffrey mistook her use of the word *girl* to mean child; he imagined this Richard as a considerably older man, avuncular, and talked about him that way. He claimed to be pleased she would have company, although she should really ask Helen Simmonds up one of these days; he also worried about the extra work a visitor (who wasn't Helen Simmonds) would generate. Ruth explained that Frida was helping, for a low fee—he asked how much and approved of the answer—and she expected they would do nothing but watch whales and drink tea, which would create so little "extra work" she was almost ashamed of herself. Frida was washing the dining-room windows as Ruth spoke on the phone; she made a small noise of disgust at this talk of her fee.

Jeffrey, who was always interested in the transport arrangements of other people and spent a great deal of time planning his own, asked, "How's this Richard getting to your place?"

Ruth's answer was insufficiently detailed. The conversation persisted, and Ruth thought, What can I say that means he won't go? But when can I go? She always listened for hints that Jeffrey might be ready to finish a call, and when she identified them, she finished it for him, abruptly, as if there weren't a moment to lose. He didn't seem at all scandalized that his mother was planning to entertain a male guest, which was a relief and also, thought Ruth, something of a shame. Not that she set out to scandalize her sons. She'd never liked that obvious kind of woman.

"I hope you'll have a lovely time," said Jeffrey.

Ruth made a face into the phone. A lovely time! I carried

you under my ribs for nine months, she thought. I fed you with my body. I'm God. The phrase that occurred to her was *son of a bitch*. But then she would be the bitch.

The phone produced a small chime as Ruth replaced it, as if coughing slightly to clear Jeffrey from its throat. She considered the preprogrammed button that was supposed to conjure Phillip.

"What time is it in Hong Kong?"

Frida, with knitted brow, consulted her watch and began to count out the hours on her fingers. "It's too early to call," she sighed, as if she regretted the result of her calculations but would bear it bravely. It was always too late or too early to call Hong Kong; Ruth had begun to doubt if daytime existed in that distant place. In the last four weeks, waiting for Richard to come, she had begun to doubt the existence of any place other than this one; it seemed so unlikely that Richard might be somewhere right at this moment, living, and waiting to see her.

Returning to her windows, Frida said, "Jeff's happy with my salary, is he." It wasn't a question. The flesh of her arms shook as she rubbed at the windowpanes; the windowpanes shook, too. She had grown so attached to the house that this mutual trembling seemed a kind of conversation. Ruth found it comforting.

Now that she had told Jeffrey, Richard was definitely coming. Ruth inspected her heart: there was a leaping out, and also a drawing back. Difficulties presented themselves. The house was so hot, and there were possibly birds in the night, and almost certainly unseasonal insects. The cats threw up on the floor and the beds, and their fur seemed to sprout from the corners. For the first time in months, Ruth noticed the state of the garden: it seemed to be shrinking around the house. Harry had spent so many hours tending this garden against the sand and salt, climbing ladders and kneeling in the grass wearing soft green kneepads which gave him the look of an aged roller skater. He would be horrified to see it now. His shrubs and hedges had worn away in patches; they reminded Ruth of an abandoned colouring book. The hydrangeas looked as if enormous caterpillars had chewed them to rags; snapped frangipani branches lay across the grass; and the worn turf gave the impression of faded velvet. The soil had failed under the brittle grass—had simply blown away. Now there was sand; there was more sand than lawn; the few trees stood embattled against the sea, and the only flourishing plants were the tall native grasses that surrounded the house on three sides.

"He'll take it as he finds it," said Frida, who saw the dismay with which Ruth surveyed the garden through the dining room's soapy windows.

"Yes," said Ruth.

"It's wild. You said yourself you like it better this way."

"Yes," said Ruth.

"And inside will be pure gold."

Frida seemed very sensible of the honour of the house; it reflected her own honour, after all, and so she set about cleaning every corner in preparation for Richard's arrival. Ruth had never observed this level of zeal in her before. She wouldn't accept any help, but confined Ruth to the dining room, where she would be "less likely to cause trouble."

As Frida cleaned, Ruth told her more about Richard; talking about him made her less nervous. She may have told each story more than once. There was the green sari he'd given her for her birthday, and how embarrassed he'd been when she tried it on. There was the first time he ate a kumquat and chased her through the house trying to make her eat one, too. There was the Christmas he made her a puppet theatre out of a tea chest because she was a teaching assistant at the Girls' Grammer School. There was the royal ball.

"I had a dress made up in pale blue Chinese silk," she said airily, as if she had been in the habit of ordering silken dresses. Ruth didn't mention that Richard had kissed her at the ball and that ever since, Ruth had felt an unshakeable gratitude towards the Queen, whose dark royal head had been visible, now and then, among the people in the ballroom. She was newly crowned and not much older than Ruth. The Queen! And Richard! All in the same night. The blue silk lit Ruth's yellow hair. Richard danced with her and asked if she was tired and guided her through the crowd with his hand in the small of her back without telling her why; he led her to a corridor and kissed her there among the potted palms until Andrew Carson came and flushed them out. Andrew Carson, the maybe-Communist, the kiss-killer! It was no chaste kiss, either. Ruth had saved the dress for the daughters she might have and had no idea where it was now.

Frida encouraged these reminiscences by not objecting to them; otherwise she gave no sign that they interested her. She stayed late that Thursday, cleaning and cooking, and for the first time they ate their dinner together. Frida made a slim stir-fry, piled Ruth's plate with rice, and picked at her own vegetables.

"Still dieting?" Ruth asked.

Frida nodded, serene. "Maybe you haven't noticed," she said, "but I've lost an inch off my waist."

It was strange to have Frida at the dining table, fiddling with her food. She ate a little and a little more, and stood to clear the table.

"No hurry," she said, gathering plates, so Ruth pushed her rice away.

"I'm too nervous to eat, anyway."

"What on earth are you nervous for?" asked Frida, who was already wetting dishes in the sink. The water surged among the saucepans and plates and Frida's hands.

"There's something I'm worried about," said Ruth.

"What thing?"

"I wouldn't be so worried except that we have guests coming."

"We have one guest coming."

"Is it normal for my head to be so itchy?" Ruth held her

hand to her hair but wouldn't scratch in front of Frida. "It's driving me mad."

Frida shook the suds from her fingers and said, "How long since you last washed your hair?"

Ruth began to cry. This was unprecedented; it was terrible. But while Ruth knew this to be terrible, she let herself cry, in part because she was so horrified at forgetting to wash her hair and allowing the itch to continue without remembering. She'd worried in the night that she had lice or some parasite, or that she was imagining the itch and going insane. She woke greasily from sleep with these fears and pulled at her hair in an effort not to scratch, and now Frida was reminding her that this was simply the way hair felt when it hadn't been washed. Frida observed Ruth's tears with evident disapproval. But this mode of Frida's disapproval was usually the prelude to an act of helpful sacrifice on Frida's part, and Ruth was comforted by the thought of this assistance.

"You want me to wash your hair for you?" asked Frida, and Ruth said, gulping, "I wash every night."

"I know you do."

"I'm very particular about it."

"I'd know if you didn't, love. You'd smell," said Frida, so kindly that Ruth pressed a bashful hand to her face. Her scalp raged. It may have been weeks since she last washed it. Frida pulled the plug from the sink. She wiped her hands with a tea towel, rolled up the sleeves of her shirt, and smoothed her own hair back.

"Don't you worry," said Frida. "We'll get it washed. It'll be nice. Like going to a hairdresser."

"Oh, dear," said Ruth, feeling herself settle into a helplessness that was pleasant now, for being a little artificial. She looked forward to surrendering to the complete attention of beneficent hands. "It's a lot to ask, isn't it?"

"That's what I'm here for."

At first Frida planned to wash Ruth's hair in the bathroom basin. Ruth liked this idea. She explained that this was how her hair had been washed as a girl. She described the bathroom of the house in Fiji, with its narrow, shallow bath (her father could only squat in it, pouring a small bucket of water over his back). Her mother had hung green gauze at the windows, for privacy and also because she, like the other women she knew, considered green a cooling colour.

"Blue is the coolest colour," said Frida. And blue, when Frida said it, was the coolest colour; it simply was.

But when Ruth tried to rise from her chair to go into the bathroom, her back objected. Frida—sceptical, impatient Frida, whose reliable spine usually prevented any sympathy for Ruth's lumbar condition—decided the basin would be too much. Instead, she directed Ruth to the wingback recliner in the lounge room: a "subtle recliner," Ruth had once called it, because she didn't entirely approve of recliners, which she supposed was a very Protestant way to think about a chair. Frida filled a large bowl with water and spread towels over the chair, the floor, and Ruth. She cranked the recliner beyond any previous limits, so that Ruth could see, beyond her small stomach, the tops of her toes.

Frida was good at washing hair, which was the result, Ruth assumed, of so much practice on her own healthy head. She took great care over each of the steps: the wetting, the shampooing and conditioning and rinsing, even a head massage in the able, indifferent way of trained hairdressers. Her skill wasn't unexpected; what surprised Ruth was the way Frida, washing hair, began to talk. She started by complaining of sleepless nights, nervous headaches, and bowel trouble.

"If you could just feel my neck and shoulders," said Frida. "Like concrete."

The problem, it seemed, was her brother. More specifically, the house he and Frida owned between them. The house had belonged to Frida's mother, who died four years ago and left her property to her three children: George, Frida, and their sister, Shelley. Shelley died not long afterwards, leaving George and Frida in joint possession of the house.

"A crappy little place, really," said Frida. "Ex–housing commission. But it's home, and the view's good. The land's worth a pretty penny these days."

The house was in the nearby town. Frida's mother and Harry had, it turned out, purchased their houses in the same year. At that time, the town was functional and quiet, with an atmosphere of helpless evacuation: the canning industry that once gave it purpose had disappeared a decade before. In those quieter days, Harry and Ruth, holidaying, would drive in with the boys to buy groceries and linger only to eat slightly greasy ice cream on the waterfront. Ruth recalled streets full of neat fibro homes. They could easily have been housing commission: the cannery workers would, after all, have needed somewhere to live.

Frida's mother and Harry had bought their houses in and close to this unassuming town, and within a few years cafés and boutiques began to open among the greengrocers and news-agents of the main street, and in the old cannery buildings; a small hotel was built, and then a larger; the caravan park shrank to a third of its size to accommodate a marina. Frida's mother and Harry had inadvertently made excellent investments. They were both, as Frida put it, "sitting on a gold mine." Ruth imag-ined them congratulating each other. Frida's mother, in this im-age, was a rosy, stout Fijian woman who embraced tall, patrician Harry; Harry, never more pleased than when discovering him-self to have been astute, shook a bottle of champagne over her head.

But now this house of Frida's mother's was causing trouble. George, it seemed, was a gambler.

"Not big-league," said Frida. "Just the pokies and keno when he's at the club. But I tell you what, that's more than enough."

Ruth loved poker machines; she enjoyed the small lights and the tinny music, the complicated buttons and the promise of luck. She didn't come across them often, but she insisted on playing whenever she did and referred to this as "having a flutter," a phrase she always said in a fake Cockney accent. It had never occurred to her that a person could fall into debt from a love of poker machines, but this is what George had done. She pitied him and knew Harry wouldn't have, because Harry was so sensible, and every now and then a snob. Ruth suspected she was a snob in ways she wasn't even aware of, but felt that her sympathetic, impressionable heart made up for it.

Ruth felt sorry for George, but mostly for Frida. George had taken out two mortgages, the first to bankroll a business importing and packaging car-phone parts, and the second to establish his taxi company when the first failed. By this time he had moved into the house, and Frida joined him there soon afterwards.

"To protect my inheritance," she said. "Or he'd let it go to the piss."

Ruth didn't comment on Frida's sudden bad language. She liked it. She liked the way Frida's swift hands moved over and through her hair to prevent any water from running onto her face. It was a long time since anyone had touched her.

At first George's taxi was a success. He'd purchased two licenses from the friend of a friend, and by the time the town took off, he was in a position to franchise. There was a time when nearly every taxi in town bore the words YOUNG LIVERY. But, according to Frida, poor business sense, lack of organization, a surly manner, and a reputation for unreliability—"an arrogant prick to all and sundry, customers and employees and drivers alike, not to mention his own sister"—ruined things for unlucky George. His gambling intensified as drivers quit, cabs broke down, and insurance payments lagged. Now he was back to just the one cab, which he drove himself. Only last weekend, a lengthy love affair with one of his former telephone operators had ended in a fight with her husband, and George spent the night in hospital as a result.

In short, George was a mess. Frida had tried everything, but he didn't want to be helped. Ruth sympathized with people who "didn't want to be helped"; she felt that generally she was one of them, despite her current submission. Frida's concern now was her mother's house, which she referred to as "the house she died in." Ruth made supportive noises. She had never been to the house her mother died in, which was a rectory in country Victoria. Her mother had been visiting friends and died of a stroke in the night. Ruth's father died in hospital. And there was Harry, who didn't die in a house at all.

Frida took the bowl to the bathroom to exchange dirty water for fresh. Ruth thought Frida moved much faster than usual, but perhaps less efficiently. Soapy water splashed onto her handsome floors.

"I have no idea why I'm telling you all this," she said on her return, suddenly prim, but she relaxed again as she combed the conditioner through Ruth's hair. She held the hair at the roots so that it wouldn't tug, just as Ruth's mother had done in the green-lit bathroom. Here was the trouble: two mortgages on the house, and payments lagging. Not minding losing the house so much, except that it was "the house she died in." Government carers being paid so little these days.

"I don't need to tell *you* that," said Frida. "You know how underappreciated we are."

And George too proud to ask for help. Both of them too proud, really. Certain family members might lend a hand, for their mother's sake, and for Frida's, but pride prevented her asking.

"Once you've left home, you've left," said Frida. "You go back with your head held high, or you don't go back."

This indicated to Ruth that Frida had severed her ties with

Fiji; that her leave-taking had been dramatic and that she expected the rest of her life to live up to it. So Ruth nodded to indicate that she understood, and Frida stilled her head with strong fingers.

"I thought about taking a second job," said Frida. She paused as they both considered the noble step of taking a second job. "Then I thought, 'Excuse me? I barely have time for this one.' But it's not like I'm making millions. You know how helpful it is to have this extra work from you, cooking this weekend? It's paying my electricity bill. George leaves every light on. If it wasn't for me, he'd have the whole place lit up like a Christmas tree, all night every night. And the time he spends in the shower!"

"So wasteful," said Ruth.

"Well, who doesn't like a good, long shower?" said snippy Frida. Now she was drying Ruth's hair with a towel. "How does that feel?"

"So much better." Ruth pressed experimentally at her scalp, which responded by flaring into itch.

"What else needs doing? We want you all done up for your visitor, don't we." Ruth listened carefully for any insinuation in this, but found none. "Let's take a look at your feet."

Ruth hadn't thought about her feet in some time. She was mildly surprised to find them intact at the end of her legs; she held them out in the air with pointed toes, and Frida, Prince Charmingly, removed her slippers. Her small feet were freckled, and her brittle nails nestled in her long toes. Frida was shocked by the dryness of her heels.

"We can't have this," Frida said, and bustled to the bathroom. She returned with another bowlful of hot water, and a small grey lump of pumice stone. "You know," she said, "I once heard the best remedy for cracked heels—you won't believe this—nappy-rash cream!" Frida smirked and lowered Ruth's feet into the steaming bowl. She scrubbed with the stone, and the water went a milky white, none of which seemed to revolt her.

Ruth flexed one experimental foot. It felt heavy and boneless in the heat of the water. "You're too good to me," she said.

Frida remained quiet. The wet bowl slopped.

"My father used to do this," said Ruth. "He used to hold a foot-washing ceremony once a year. He washed all the patients' feet, then the clinic staff, the household staff, and mine, and last of all my mother's."

"What for?"

"To remind us and himself that he was there to serve us, and not the other way around."

Frida paused in her scrubbing and closed one dubious eye.

"And because it was nice," said Ruth. "It was a nice thing to do."

Ruth remembered those ceremonies as gold-lit days, brighter than usual, but there was something uncomfortable about them, a feeling of potential disaster. Her mother prepared everyone: had the patients' feet uncovered and their toenails cut and cleaned, and lined up the staff. The Fijian nurses giggled as they removed the soft white shoes Ruth's father made them wear. The hospital groundskeeper, a thin, cheerful man, rinsed his feet beneath the outdoor tap until he was beaten back from it by the nurses' cries.

"What if he sees you! What if he sees you!" they scolded.

The clinic was for the Suva poor. They came voluntarily with pains and injuries and difficulty breathing and blood in their stools and numb limbs and pregnancies and migraines and fevers, and Ruth's father repaired them or referred them or sent them home. They weren't supposed to stay overnight, but frequently they did, when the Fijian wards in the hospital were full. So on the morning of the foot washing there would be the patients who had stayed and their visiting families, and there would be the new patients, who had arrived that morning, and before seeing to any of them, Ruth's father washed their feet.

The washing took place on Good Friday: that solemn, re-

poseful day, set apart from the rest of the year (although the patients still needed tending, the floors still had to be swept, and
Ruth's mother had to arrange lunch with the help of the houseboy).
First there was church, which at that time of year, right before
Easter, was full of tense expectation. The chosen hymns were
grateful and the Bible passages subdued; the entire service was a
form of sheepish mourning. Then Ruth's family walked down
the road from the church to the clinic. Ruth's father walked in
front, his shoulders set in his church suit. He was a man of tireless industry, of easy good cheer, and he was broad over the back
the way a bricklayer is broad, or a sportsman; but his head was
small, his Adam's apple prominent, and his hair persisted in a
boyish cowlick at the back of his crown. It was fine hair, and his
eyelashes were long. He was thick and strong in the trunk, but
contradictory in his extremities: his fine ankles and long kanga-
roo's feet, his surgeon's hands, his neat head and filigree hair.
This gave him a slightly flimsy look. New mothers winced to see
their bulky babies in his slim hands. When, on the day of the Easter washing, those bony hands passed soapily over the feet of his
staff and patients and family, they felt like a woodworker's precise
tools. Ruth recalled the pressing of a knuckle against an instep,
and the two long hands held together over her foot as if in prayer.

He crawled along the floor before his staff and patients,
loose of limb and unwieldy of body; a baby elephant over the
tiles, pulling his bucket of water along with him. The palms at
the windows distributed the sun in stripes over the brown feet.
After every four sets of feet he stood to fetch new water in a small
bucket. They all watched him in silence. The nurses, before-
hand, worried they would laugh as he washed; they never did.
They stood in a bashful line. As he approached, they might hide
their smiles, but during the washing, as he knelt in humility
before them, their faces were serious and stern, and even the
youngest of them murmured and touched his head. Sometimes
they wept.

If only, Ruth would think, he could maintain his dignity as he washed: more than once he farted as he stood, and his knees clicked, especially as he grew older. By the time Ruth was a teenager she was embarrassed by the whole thing; was wrung with protective pride and fear and irritation. She began to notice some resistance among the staff or the patients, but couldn't be sure if it signified boredom or reluctance or dissent. He lost face with some. Others were grateful. Ruth felt maternal towards her father on his clumsy, wholesome knees, felt superior to his defined and allegorical world, and in her superiority broke her heart over him, whose head shrank as he grew older.

Richard refused to take part. He wouldn't wash feet, and he wouldn't allow his feet to be washed. The family stirred with this trouble; Ruth's mother was full of sensitive suggestions, and her father was thoughtful and grave. Ruth swam at the edges of this quiet consternation, indignant for her father and conscious of a mild but growing sense of rebellion. She was ashamed of the ceremony. That couldn't be helped, she decided; nevertheless she admired it. It was pure and good-hearted. Perhaps it was misjudged. But it made Richard so angry. When Ruth asked him why, he wouldn't say. There was nobility in that, too. He vacillated, unsure (she suspected) of her loyalties. She promised not to tell her father, and he said, "It isn't that."

On the evening of the ceremony they sat together on the terrace. He was quiet, and smoked, which kept the mosquitoes away. No one had seen him all day. Ruth sat beside him, desperately curious and tending towards comprehensive admiration. There wasn't a part of his body that didn't move her: his firm shoulder, the tic of his tapping foot, his calm eye. The smoke rose around their heads. Their arms weren't touching—but Ruth was conscious they were almost touching. There was that atmospheric sympathy. Wasn't he aware of all this: their arms, the moonlight, the smoke? A dog barked. After the foot-washing,

Ruth and her parents had eaten a lunch of Easter lamb imported from New Zealand. Richard's place at the table was empty, and Ruth, digging her fork among the lamb's sturdy grey fibers, couldn't bring herself to wonder where he was eating. Now she asked him.

"Where did you eat today?"

"At Andrew Carson's," said Richard.

"Why?"

"They invited me."

Ruth considered and then spoke. "Did you complain to them about my father?"

"No. No, I annoyed them all enough without mentioning your father. They all think your father's a saint. He probably is."

"How did you annoy them?"

"Oh, politics." Richard waved his hand with the cigarette in it. "All this repatriation business—get rid of the Indians, get rid of the Chinese. Send them home or give them the Marquesas, just get them out of here. Let them all kill each other somewhere else, and leave Fiji to the Fijians." He was silent for a moment. "And the English."

"You don't agree." Ruth knew he didn't agree; they had talked this through before; Ruth never cared so much as when she cared with him.

"I'm tired of controversy today," he said. "I think I'd better just go to bed."

"Not yet," said Ruth. "Not until you tell me why my father's so wrong."

Richard looked at her in a patient way, but it was enough to shake her heart. He seemed to be taking her measure. He had not yet kissed her at the ball.

"All right," he said. "All right, tell me something: When does he give them a chance to wash *his* feet? Is it that he's the greatest, the noblest servant of them all? This privilege of service! He calls himself a servant and I know he's referring to certain ideas—abasement, humility, sacrifice, the servant Christ, that whole Christian model of service—I know all that, but hasn't he ever stopped to think that he's in a country where people work and live every day as servants, for him? You have a houseboy! He doesn't wash your father's feet in a great public show—he scrubs dishes every night when no one's there to see him. I'm sorry, it infuriates me. No, but I'm not sorry—God!"

And no one spoke this way; no one grew angry. Ruth was astonished, and in her admiration became clumsy and receptive. None of what he said surprised her; she'd begun to think most of these things herself. But she had never heard a respectable man blaspheme, and this made the strongest impression. She would at that moment have ceded the Church, her family, and Fiji and fled with him in pilgrim haste to any land of his choosing—if only he would ask her. But he didn't, so she remained loyal and, as a result, defensive; it was the same impulse that made her ashamed of her father's audible knees.

"You haven't been here long enough to understand about servants," she said, but that sounded feeble (she had heard so many people say it to newcomers before), so she continued, "And what else should he do? No foot-washing at all? Just hope they all know he doesn't think he's above them?"

Ruth shifted and touched Richard's arm with her elbow, which produced no sensation. But she wanted him to put his hand on hers and agree with her, very badly.

"This morning," he said, "I drove that bloody truck over those bloody roads because somebody told somebody else who told me that a pregnant woman collapsed at Nasavu—and they wouldn't let me near her, they said the problem was caused by walking on uneven land and she'd go to the temple and be fine, and meanwhile I'd blown a tire, I rode back to Suva with a bloody monarchist, Fijians are all monarchists, and the truck's still out there, I'll have to get myself back tomorrow, and I told you I should go to bed. I really should go to bed."

And he stood and kissed her on the top of her head, which was nothing at all; she was at her most chaste when she was angry with him, or embarrassed, or particularly in love, and at this moment she was all three. Also, she felt very young.

"Can we talk about this tomorrow?" he said. And then, because he was kind: "You're absolutely right, about everything, probably, but I couldn't be fair to you tonight. I'm far too sad."

This astonished her, too. What was there for Richard to feel sad about?

There was another moment like this, Ruth remembered, without mentioning it to Frida: on the boat to Sydney. Richard was returning to Sydney to take up a position with the World Health Organization; Ruth was "going home," as her parents called it, to find work. She spent the trip in terror that nothing would happen with Richard; that nothing would happen with her whole life. She knew, foolishly, that she had counted on being her parents' daughter forever, even while she contemplated such things as university or teaching or nursing (could she be a nurse, like her mother? Would she really go back to Fiji as a teacher? She vacillated on this point daily). And the trip passed, and on a September morning she stood next to Richard on the boat's deck where schoolgirls played paddle tennis. She looked out at the heads of Sydney Harbour and said, "Apparently I'm going to have to *be* something."

"It's terrible, isn't it," said Richard, "this having to be something."

And Ruth was astonished that a man so obviously *something*—a doctor, a soldier, the saviour of Indian women—could sound so sad about it. But he had held her hand twice on the boat, once to steady her in a rough sea and once for three minutes because she'd been stupid enough to cry a little about leaving Fiji. He had sought her out with drinks and, as the weather grew colder the farther they sailed from the equator, brought rugs for her knees. They were sitting on the sundeck, and because she wore gloves, which might hide a ring, a man had smiled at them and assumed—Ruth was sure—they were married. And Richard had kissed her at the ball for the Queen, although she wondered sometimes if she had imagined that. None of it was enough, but it was the beginning—it was the passage over, and then Sydney waited, this city Ruth belonged in without knowing anything about it. Richard would show her Sydney, and she would love him, and he would love her back.

The boat entered the Harbour. The wide, bright city crowded up against the water, but drew back from its very edge; Ruth saw green parklands full of trees, with white flocks of parrots bursting out of them. The parrots surprised Ruth, who had expected Sydney to be much more like England than Fiji. And then Richard leaned forward against the railing of the deck and spoke so that she couldn't see his face, but the wind still carried every word he said, and what he said was that he was engaged to be married.

"To whom?" asked Ruth, and Richard had to turn and ask her to repeat herself.

"Her name is Kyoko," he said, which sounded to Ruth like *Coco*, and she pictured a bright blond girl with the kind of brilliant, beautiful face that produces its own light (Ruth's own face only reflected light, like the moon), and she was more surprised—at first—that Richard could love a girl called Coco than she was by the fact that Richard loved anyone at all. There was a strong gagging pulse in her throat.

"Congratulations," she said, with a stiff smile; she didn't trust herself to ask questions. They were surrounded now by the schoolgirls, waving landwards with their paddles; Ruth felt much older than all of them.

The wind was making Richard's nose run. "I met Kyoko in Japan," he said. "She's a widow. She's Japanese."

"That's nice," said Ruth, tight-lipped but dignified, she thought, which mattered most. She thought.

"She's Japanese," he said. "Which is why I didn't talk about it. I wasn't sure—well—what you'd think. All of you."

Ruth pretended not to have heard him. She shook against the railing but had no intention of crying. The main thing was to extricate herself without revealing the extent of her agony.

Now Richard turned to look at her—to properly look. He cleared his throat and squinted. "I'm sorry," he said.

"Oh, whatever for?" cried Ruth, smiling too much and taking a step away from him because she thought he was going to touch her arm. "Maybe I should go and—" She couldn't think what she should go and do; she had told him a number of times how much she was looking forward to the passage through the Harbour.

"She's going to meet the boat," said Richard. "I'd like to introduce you."

So he and Kyoko had exchanged letters with plans and arrangements: I'll be on this boat, I can't wait to see you, there'll be a child with me, a silly girl who hates opera, I'm afraid you'll have to meet her. Ruth saw the soft, admiring faces of all those girls to whom she had boasted about sailing to Sydney with Richard Porter. At that moment, those faces seemed worse than Richard's. The green and grey city tilted at the end of the boat.

"That would be lovely," lied Ruth.

She felt like stepping off the boat and walking back to Suva across the bottom of the sea. But she planned to be kind and unshakeable, an emissary from her parents, a testament to the marvellous work Richard had done among the Indian women of Fiji; she wouldn't have him think she disapproved of his marrying a Japanese widow, or that she cared about his kissing her at the ball when all the time he was engaged. Perhaps it might be possible, however, in the crowded rush to leave the boat, to meet her flustered uncle and collect her luggage, surely it might be possible to lose Richard, to look only halfheartedly for him— where *could* he have got to?—and not to meet Kyoko after all. And that turned out to be true. Richard was almost too easy to lose, as if he dreaded the meeting himself. Ruth stumbled among her luggage and in the arms of her sentimental aunt, and she was almost sure she didn't see Kyoko. There *was* a dark-haired woman waiting in a yellow dress, but she didn't look definitely Japanese. Ruth went home with her relatives to a street lined with heavy mauve jacarandas, to a borrowed bedroom warming in the mild sun, and cried into a pillow that smelled of someone else's hair.

That was a painful hour, and in the midst of it she was self-possessed enough to hope it had taught her humility. Really, her heart had been broken in the most inconspicuous way. She had never risked it (she knew this later and had moments of regret). That no one knew she was suffering was both her triumph and, in part, the cause of her torment. After a terrible week or two, it was a very governed torment. In some ways, she passed with relief from the shadow of Richard's opinions, his disapproval and his industry. She was never quite sure how he had made her a less interesting person. Was it nerves? Or did he bore her? She attended his wedding four months later with a tight heart. His imminent wife had dark hair arranged around an oblong forehead. How would it feel to walk down the aisle towards his opening face? She refused all his attempts to see her, citing busyness; and she was busy, working as a secretary for her parents' missionary society, moving into a flat with some other girls, making resolutions to be like them, to wear the shoes they did and read their magazines, to be just like every other girl in wide, clean, temperate Sydney. She suspected, at times, that Richard would disapprove, and so she made an effort to think about him less, until eventually it was no effort at all. Ruth used to overhear her mother counseling the brokenhearted nurses. "There are plenty of fish in the sea," she would say, and from her biblical mouth it sounded like wisdom literature. Now Ruth said fondly to herself, "There are bigger fish in the sea than me."

For six months she wore the right shoes and read the right magazines and went out with the right men. Then she met Harry during a work event at which she was guardian of the sandwiches. He had come with his parents, who were missionaries in the Solomons. He seemed to have a great appetite for sandwiches; he ate at least four before asking if he could see her again. And he was kind, and handsome, and effortless. It was as if they had both been raised in the same country— Missionary Childhood—and were now finding their way together in the real world. Harry liked to say, "Isn't it amazing how *normal* we are?"—which prompted a happy spasm in Ruth's grateful heart. She liked to be reassured. They kissed and courted, and Richard receded; they married, and Richard wasn't invited. Although their parents were missionaries, religion was, for both of them, a private matter; in comparison to their parents' difficult, foreign faith and the vigour with which they had pursued it, their own attempts seemed feeble and best concealed. They fell, together, out of the habit of belief. They liked the same furniture and paintings, the same music, and the same food, and this made for the easeful establishment of their household. When Ruth recalled this early period of her marriage—and she often did—the impression was of an existing happiness that had only been waiting for them to enter into it.

Frida rocked back onto her heels. "There," she said, with the same beatific look on her face as when she finished cleaning the floors. She lifted Ruth's feet from the basin and dried them with a thorough towel, and then she rubbed in moisturizer. Her hands were slick and strong. Ruth rested her head against the recliner. She closed her eyes. Frida hummed as she rubbed, and there was only safety in the world, and Richard coming tomorrow, in the best of health for eighty.

8

Ruth, stepping into the garden on the morning of Richard's arrival, was reminded of spring, as if spring were a season that took place distinctly in her part of the world. The air was sweet and dry and green. The house was clean, the cupboards were full of food, and a vase of wattle blossoms stood on the dining-room table. Frida had cut them from a tree at her mother's house; they emitted their own subtle light. Richard was due that evening.

The only flaw in all this beauty was the discovery of a sticky presence on one of the lounge cushions: cat-deposited, which inspired Frida to a brief rant about the cats' gastrointestinal hold over the house (she was convinced their messes were deliberate attacks on her own person). But after all, that was easily solved: Frida sponged the cushion, turned it over, and seemed to forget it had ever happened. She was in an exceptional mood. She was busy and in control without being domineering; she asked Ruth's opinion on everything, fluffed cushions and her currently curly hair, and fussed over Jeffrey's room, where Richard would sleep. She and Ruth made the bed together, using the best, slightly yellowed linen sheets—Frida had ironed them, and spread out and tucked in, they reminded Ruth of well-buttered bread. The entire house waited expectantly, as if the food and ironed sheets and clean windows were secrets it would be compelled to reveal by delightful means. Frida spent the afternoon cooking, so Ruth swept the garden path clean of sand. She was proud of the smooth sun over her hair and shoulders, the familiar arc of the sea, and the beauty of her house on the hilltop. Her back hurt; she thought about taking an extra pill, but chose not to; she worried the pills made her foggy at times, and she wanted clarity this weekend. She changed into a blue skirt she could belt at her becoming waist and settled to wait in her chair. Waiting was difficult under these circumstances. The sense that something important was going to happen rose in Ruth's chest as if a wind were blowing there.

Richard knocked at the door rather than ringing the bell. Because Ruth didn't hear him knock, it was a moment before she realized that Frida's bustle to the front hallway was in response to his arrival. By the time Ruth reached the front of the house, Frida had taken his bag and coat, and the sound of a car in the lane was George's taxi driving away. Ruth stepped from the door into the front garden, where Richard waited for her. He was older, yes, and he wore glasses, but he was still discernibly Richard, and her heart quickened just as it had when she'd watched him run in from a Fijian rainstorm, except that she was not nervous, or frightened, and she intended to be bold. He held his hands out to hers, and she took them. They kissed on the cheek as if they had always greeted each other this way, and as Frida passed through the door with his luggage, Richard took Ruth's arm to lead her into the house. They spoke together softly and with great happiness: it's so wonderful to see you, it's so good to be here, my goodness, you look marvellous, so do you, just like yesterday, I can't believe it.

"This is exactly how I imagined you to live," said Richard. He stood without effort in the lounge room of Ruth's house, and Ruth surveyed with him the paintings of pale cattled hillsides, the antique *masi* framed above the fireplace, and the photographs of her children and grandchildren smiling out from among green glassware. She saw evidence of comfort, happiness, and a well-lived life. Richard seemed so inevitable in that room, so welcome, that she hugged him again, and he laughed at her; they laughed together and sat holding hands on the lounge. Frida was making noises in the kitchen.

"Let me look at you properly," said Richard, and instead of hiding her face in her arm, as she might once have done, Ruth looked back; she held her breath and lengthened her neck while she did it.

His hair had thinned and whitened, but he still had a great deal of it, and perhaps for this reason he'd let it grow longish, so that it stood out from his head in an ectoplasmic cloud. His forehead was high, just as she remembered, and she felt relieved for him that his hairline had barely receded. They'd been young together, and now they were old; because there was nothing in between, this strange telescoping of time gripped Ruth's heart like vertigo. She was touched again by the flattening of his nostrils where they met his cheek, the particular tuck of his smallish chin, and the familiar way he smoothed his trousers out with the palms of his hands. It all reminded her of the night he'd criticized her father for washing feet.

"Do you smoke still?" she asked.

"Not for years."

"Good," she said, mindful of his lungs, but she was also disappointed. She wanted to see him smoke again; she had a pretty idea that young Richard would rise up out of those specific gestures—the lift of his wrist and the tap of the ash—and declare himself. Then she remembered his wife had died of lung cancer, and was mortified; she recalled giving Harry this news, and Harry's responding by talking about the low incidence of lung cancer among Japanese smokers, so that Kyoko Porter's death seemed doubly unlucky, a terrible consequence of having left Japan. Ruth sat, immobilized, while Richard told her about his journey: the traffic in Sydney, the train delayed. Perhaps he and Jeffrey would get on after all. She began to worry that he should never have come.

"Dinner is served," announced Frida, and Richard stood; Ruth saw his hand go without thinking to button a jacket he hadn't worn for decades.

"Oh, Richard, this is Frida, my dear Frida," said Ruth. She was gushing, but she pulled herself together. "Frida Young, Richard Porter."

Richard extended his hand to Frida, who took it with a so-lemnity Ruth had become accustomed to; she saw Richard's surprise at it. The two of them, shaking hands, seemed to be agreeing to a matter of national importance on which Frida had forced Richard to compromise. Ruth noticed how trim he still was as he held out his hand and was relieved by the size of her own waist, if not by the plump stomach that swelled underneath it. Richard offered her his arm, and she took it, and they walked that way to the dining table.

During dinner, Frida moved between the kitchen and din-ing room with an efficient, soundless skill. Ruth asked her to join them, but she shook her head and hands in a gracious pan-tomime. No, her smile said, softer at the corners than Ruth had ever seen, I wouldn't dream of it. Perhaps she was one of these women who behaved differently around men. Had Ruth really never seen Frida with a man? She thought of Bob Fretweed, who seemed too perfunctory to really count as a man; she thought of Frida bending into the taxi window to laugh with George. But George was her brother. Frida dished up beans and poured gravy and retreated to the kitchen, where she hummed as she went about cleaning counters that were already clean. Ruth dis-approved of this pointless industry. A triple-cleaned house, in her opinion, looked too much as if it had been licked all over by a cat's antiseptic tongue.

Ruth found it strange to eat a meal with Richard, in a din-ing room, without her parents present. Because she was deter-mined not to start out with reminiscences—she was afraid of seeming sloppy and sentimental—she was worried there would be nothing to say. Fortunately there were children to discuss. They both seemed to have raised reassuringly ordinary children;

there were no drastic prodigies among them. His eldest daughter was a doctor.

"Sometimes she reminds me of you," said Richard. "She's so stubborn, in the best way. I always thought you'd make a good doctor."

Frida was clearing the plates now, and Richard leaned over the empty table to touch Ruth's hand. His skin hadn't spotted with age, as hers had; it was a clear, folded brown. From behind him, Frida raised inquisitive eyebrows. She shook her head as she went to the kitchen, as if tut-tutting the flagrant ways of the very young.

"What made you think I'd be a good doctor?" asked Ruth.

"I watched you help in the clinic. But it's not just that. You have the right sort of mind: so clear and kind."

"Not clear anymore." Ruth shook her head as if to settle a cloudy liquid.

Richard laughed. He said, "I feel sometimes as if every part of me is different to what it was then. I feel unrecognizable."

"Oh, no," said Ruth. "You're just the same."

"Really? That's good to know." He still held her hand, which Ruth found both delightful and embarrassing. She wanted to point out that actually, as a young man, he had never touched her so readily as this. He needed something else from her now, or was more willing to demonstrate that need, or was softer and more sentimental. But he was still Richard. Ruth suggested they move to the lounge room; Richard sat beside her on the couch. Her leg touched his, so she shifted it. It was silly to be shy; she was annoyed at herself, but couldn't seem to help it. She asked questions about Sydney, and he asked questions about her house, and he didn't touch her again.

Frida came in to say good-night. She stood by the lounge-room door, demure in her grey coat, and Ruth went to her and put a hand against her cheek.

"Thank you for everything, my dear," Ruth said, and Frida nodded. She seemed bashful. Then she moved out into the hall-way and closed the door behind her.

"You're very lucky to have found her," said Richard.

"It was more the other way around," said Ruth. "She found me."

"Tell me," said Richard.

Ruth found she didn't want to. She disliked remembering the day of Frida's arrival, without being sure why. "Oh, you know, the government sent her. Isn't it marvellous? She just showed up. She's basically heaven-sent."

"A deus ex machina."

"Yes, yes." Ruth was annoyed by the flourish with which Richard produced this phrase; a phrase he had once taught her. "But really, she just came from Fiji."

"From Fiji? What an amazing coincidence. What was she doing there?"

"She's *from* Fiji," said Ruth. "She's Fijian."

Richard looked towards the door as if Frida might reappear, conveniently, to display her features for him. "She doesn't look it," he said.

"You don't think so?"

"I don't know. I suppose if you asked me where she was from, I wouldn't know where to say."

"I never wanted to be the kind of person who would say, 'I couldn't do without her,' but I think now that I am."

"These things creep up on you, don't they," said Richard.

Ruth wondered who had crept up on him. Her chest tightened—she felt for a minute as she had on the boat in Sydney Harbour, being told about a girl named Coco—and she changed the subject. "You know, you couldn't have come in a better month," she said. "You're here just in time for the whales."

At this time of the year, Southern humpbacks travelled down the coast. They lingered sportively off the headlands and fre-

quently came farther into the bay. When Ruth, younger and
subtler of spine, walked down the dune and onto the beach, it
had always felt to her that she was going out ceremoniously to
meet them. She thought they knew she was paying them court.
Phillip came one year and paddled a sea kayak out to get a better
look; Harry called to him from the shore in a forlorn monotone,
"Too close! Too close!" The whales' unearthly sounds, urgent
and high-pitched, conjured the night cries of wrecked sailors.

It had always been one of Ruth's greatest pleasures to show
her guests the whales. She liked to line visitors up on the window seat in the dining room, each of them looking with narrowed eyes out to sea; she passed around pairs of inherited
binoculars, all of which had been held to missionary faces in the
Pacific; invariably her guests became so agitated that finally,
whatever the weather, they rushed outside in an effort to get
closer to the water. Everyone shouted when a spout went up, and
Ruth felt happily responsible for the communal, mammalian
mood on the beach. She looked forward to seeing Richard see the
whales, and leaned with relief into his shoulder when they said
good-night in the hallway. He said, "I'm so glad to be here." The
visit hadn't been a mistake; it would be all right. It would be
more than all right. Ruth closed the door to the lounge room.
She slept thankfully in her bed.

But in the morning there was rain, and it obscured the view.
The sea from the windows was crooked and fogged, with no
sign of whales. There were still surfers down at the town beach,
and Ruth observed them from the dining room with unate-
teristic bitterness.

"Rain or shine, there they are," she said, peering out at the
blurry sea. She wondered if the boy who had sold her the pineapple was among them. "Don't they have jobs?"

In better weather—in better moods—she approved of their
tireless leisure.

Frida cleared the breakfast plates.

"Thanks, Frida," said Richard. "It's a long time since I ate such a good big breakfast."

Frida smiled with pleasure but said nothing.

They stayed at the dining table; Ruth sat in her chair and Richard on the long window seat. The house was peaceful in the rain. The air was comfortable and warm. Frida lit lamps against the dullness of the day, brought tea and shortbread, and worked in the kitchen preparing lunch. She was so far from the Frida of the diet and the floors; her hair was an ordinary brown and she wore it demurely, half up and half down. This placid Frida was efficient as ever, quiet, but never invisible. Her presence filled the house with calm, so that Ruth forgot the whales and relaxed into the day with Richard. He was attentive to her and to their shared past, and Ruth took great pleasure in speaking with someone who had known her as part of her family; who had known her parents, and who had seen them all together in Fiji. She could think of no other living person who was capable of remembering her in this way. They talked about her father, about his busy hopes for his clinic and the world, and the quiet, good, regretful way he left both of these places. Ruth reminded Richard about his refusal to participate in the foot washing, and he laughed and said, "I was such a snob."

"You were wonderful. At least, I thought so."

"You were quite wonderful yourself," he said. "But very young."

So, as if she were still young enough to be hurt by being accused of youth, she said, "You're much older now than my father was then." Richard gave a good-natured grimace. "I used to curse you in Hindi, you know," she said. "I thought you wouldn't understand me."

"I understood you," said Richard. "And so did your mother. She knew her Hindi from the servants."

"Oh, dear."

"We're so transparent when we're young."

Ruth was horrified for her young self. He must have known she loved him all along, just by looking—even once—at her devoted face.

"But you stopped when my Hindi improved," Richard said. "I remember the day you realized I knew more than you did. You heard me speaking to one of my patients."

Frida brought them tea, and the rain still fell over the dim, indistinguishable sea.

"Have you ever been to India?" he asked. Ruth hadn't. "I have, twice, and when I first arrived, I tried to speak what I remembered of my Fiji Hindi. They only understood every fifth word."

"I've never even been back to Fiji," said Ruth. She knew Richard had because he'd sent her a postcard, Fiji-stamped, about five years after her parents retired to Sydney. It was a photograph of the Grand Pacific Hotel, and it said, "I miss my Fijians—your mother, your dad, and you." She was a married woman, a mother, and still capable of wondering if the hotel postcard was some reference to the kiss at the ball. Overanxious, she hid the card from Harry.

"Why not?"

"At first I couldn't afford it," Ruth said. "And then, when I could—when we could—there were so many other places to go."

"There's some sense in not going back. That way, you preserve it."

"Maybe you shouldn't have come here." Ruth laughed. "You can't preserve me now."

"Oh, I can," said Richard. "I have an excellent memory of you as a teenager, and nothing will change it."

"What do you remember?"

"Let's see. I remember you reading *Ulysses* faster than anyone in the world has ever read it."

And then Ruth remembered reading *Ulysses*, which Richard treasured and had brought with him from Sydney. She was determined to read it; she'd never before worked so hard at anything. She remembered, too, that she and Richard had been young people discussing the existence of heaven (she said yes, he said no, but both admitted they had doubts—and that was the first time she realized she doubted). Oh, oh, and she remembered that in her anxiety to appreciate Bach she had found herself in love with Mozart and was ashamed of this for years, simply because Richard didn't love Mozart, until she read somewhere that Abraham Lincoln did. Then she felt herself bloom into the recognition of her own opinion. She'd read about Lincoln and Mozart in a biography of Lincoln that Harry had bought but never read. No, Jeffrey had bought it for Harry (who loved political biographies) as a Christmas present. There was also that particular passage of Auden's she had loved—Caliban's song in a long poem, she'd forgotten the name of it—and made Richard read aloud for her, and there was one line—"helplessly in love with you"—that he paused over. She was overtaken by promise. *Surely, surely,* she thought when he paused. And then he continued reading and afterwards in conversation—just a few days later—Ruth realized he'd forgotten all about it, and she was furious at the way she fell in love with small things that turned out to be meaningless. Where had all this been waiting while she worked so effortlessly to forget it? She sat trembling with gratitude for her brain, that sticky organ.

"You look very happy right now," said Richard.

She ducked her head but lifted it again to look at him. "I am happy," she said. "I'm sorry I was in such a mood this morning. I was disappointed about the weather."

"The weather is perfect."

When had she ever heard Richard describe something as perfect? He was looking back at her in a confidential way. If she'd been told, at nineteen, that it would take over fifty years to have him look at her like this, she would have been disgusted and heartbroken; now she was only a little sad, and it was both bearable and lovely. She brushed Richard's arm with her hand.

Frida was quiet in the kitchen, so perhaps she was listening. Richard was talking about the smell of molasses over the sugar mills, and Ruth told him about the time her mother took her along to a game of contract bridge with the CSR wives in a sugar town outside Suva. They sat at little tables while their children ate sausage rolls and scones, and because Ruth's father wasn't a company officer—wasn't in the company at all, and not even a government doctor—certain children didn't bother talking to her. That was the only time her mother played bridge.

"My mother would have loved all that," said Richard. "I think she would have managed very well in one of those hierarchical little sugar towns. She would have treated it like some kind of siege."

"You had to be ruthless."

"She was. Once my brother was invited to the birthday party of a school friend, but he was too sick to go. I would have been about eight, I think, and he was ten. She made me pretend to be my brother because she wanted to be on good terms with the parents of the birthday boy. She'd been waiting for an invitation to the house, was the thing, and this party was going to be the only way. So we arrived, and the other children knew I wasn't my brother, obviously, but my mother called me James and eventually they did, too."

"But why?"

"They were well-to-do, well connected, these people. It was an enormous house. I remember being impressed into submission. Invitations of that kind were very important to my mother. She could invite *them* to parties after that."

This story bothered Ruth; she wanted to swat it away. She didn't like to hear Richard compare his childhood to her own. His childhood was Sydney: liver-coloured brick, ferries on the water, leashed dogs, women pegging out washing on square lines in square gardens.

Richard leaned forward on the window seat. "It's a relief,

isn't it, not to worry about those things anymore. My wife used to complain about the casualness of everything, but I prefer it. Don't you? Kyoko ended up getting on very well with my mother."

Ruth didn't like to hear him criticize his wife, however gently. She felt that she should respond with a complaint about Harry, and couldn't. How ridiculous, she thought, to be sitting here and worrying about being unfaithful to Harry. But she laid her arm out on the table so that her small white wrist was turned up towards Richard. If he looks at it, she thought—and before she could decide what his looking might mean, he looked.

"I used to throw parties in Sydney," said Ruth, "but I was never very good at it. I used to wake up on the morning of the party and think, 'Damn it, why did I do this again?' But Harry loved parties. Then we moved out here and there was no one to throw parties for."

"How long did you live here together?"

"Just over a year," said Ruth. Really, it was such a little time. "I always planned to be one of those old women who kept very busy. You know—involved in things, taking classes, cooking elaborate dinners, visiting friends. And I was, in Sydney. I was working—well, *work* isn't the right word—I was helping at a centre for refugees. I taught elocution, did you know? I still had private students, and I taught pronunciation classes at the centre. Then we came out here, because Harry was set on it. He retired so late, which I always knew he would, and what he wanted was to rest by the sea. He'd say, 'I'm ready to put my feet up, Ruthie.' But of course when we got here, Harry spent all day gardening and walking for hours every morning and fixing things up in the house, and we would drive to this lighthouse or that historic gaol, and the boys came at Christmas and we visited the city. He could just generate busyness for himself. But I'm not like that. Especially not without him. I came out here and just sort of—stopped."

"That seems a shame," said Richard. Ruth felt, for a minute, as if he had called her a bad book or a bad play, but he was no longer that man; he was tired, she thought, and it had loosened him. He had been tired by the difficulty of having to be something.

"I don't know," said Ruth. "Everyone expected me to go back to Sydney after he died. I mourned so beautifully in every other way, they expected me to be rational about that. Or they thought I should move to be near one of my boys, or that the boys should move back home. But Phil is completely tied up in Hong Kong, and Jeffrey's father-in-law is very ill in New Zealand, and I wouldn't let them. And I turned out to be the one who wanted to rest by the sea."

The rain stopped in the afternoon. Ruth and Richard stood out on the dune with binoculars, looking for whales. Ruth was in suspense. If we see a whale, she decided, then nothing will happen between us. If we see two, then everything will happen. She was unsure what she meant by *everything*. There were no whales.

Frida had roasted a pork loin and sweet potatoes for dinner. She set it all out on the table and refused to eat, no matter how Ruth and Richard pleaded.

"No! No!" Frida insisted, and laughed as if she were being tickled; she sounded pained and unwilling.

"Then at least leave the dishes," said Ruth. "We can sort those out ourselves."

Frida objected and then acquiesced. Ruth noticed that Frida had trouble looking at Richard. Whenever he spoke to her, she looked to the left of his face and patted her neat hair. She took her coat from the hook in the kitchen, mumbled, *"Bon appétit,"* and went down the hall. The front door opened and closed.

Now Ruth was ready for something to happen. She kept her hopes vague. Richard was in the best of health. He ate with good appetite and laughed a great deal while telling her about the one and only time his daughter took him to a yoga class. He promised to cook her a Japanese meal. It grew dark on the dune, and Ruth drew the lounge-room curtains while Richard closed the seaward shutters. Neither of them made any attempt to clear the table of dishes. They moved into the lounge room, where Ruth regretted her decision to sit in an armchair and not next to him on the couch. Her nineteen-year-old self would have made the same mistake.

"I was thinking the other day about that ball we went to for the Queen," she said.

"So was I," said Richard. He sat on the end of the couch closest to her, and his hands were clenched and unnaturally still on his knees. That's how he quit smoking, thought Ruth, by forcing himself to keep his hands still. That's how he would do it.

"I still have my menu somewhere. I saved it," she said, although, now that she mentioned it, she was certain Frida had made her dispose of everything of that kind in the spring cleaning of her early employment.

"What were you thinking, about the ball?" asked Richard.

"I was thinking about you kissing me, of course. How much I liked it."

"Why were we even there? Why was I even invited?"

"All kinds of people were invited. I remember someone getting upset about it—about your being invited, and my parents left out. Do you think they minded? I thought they probably didn't care."

"And I whisked off their daughter and kissed her." Richard laughed at himself. "I thought I was so old and wise, and you were so young. I was very ashamed of myself."

"So you should have been. With your secret fiancée and everything."

"You're teasing me," said Richard. "And I think I was drinking. Was I drinking?"

"Everyone was drinking," said Ruth. "I never saw a group of people so willing to toast the Queen." Ruth felt herself lit with the pleasure of laughing with him. It was so good to flirt; it made her think that flirting should never be entrusted to the very young. "And listen—I told you a moment ago how much I liked you kissing me, and you didn't even say thank you."

"What I should have said was how much I liked kissing you." Richard bowed his head at her, courtly. It was ridiculous! And wonderful. Richard in his twenties would never have talked like this. When had he become so much less serious? Even their kiss at the ball had been serious. What we should have done, thought Ruth, was sleep together on the boat back to Sydney and then been done with it, since it would have been a mistake to marry his bad books and good plays. But this, now, was delightful.

"What made you do it?" Ruth asked.

"You were so lovely, of course. Like a milkmaid, remember? And I was thinking—well, I was drinking, but also I was thinking how sweet and straightforward it would have been to love you. You even looked like a bride, in your white dress."

"It was pale blue," said Ruth. "And why straightforward?"

"Less complicated," said Richard. He moved his hands; this movement was the first evidence of any nervousness. "It's all so long ago, it's hard to imagine. Kyoko's family disowned her, and the first house we lived in together, well—the neighbours got together and put Australian flags in their windows and refused to speak to us. We expected it, but nothing prepares you. If I'd married someone like you, they would have come to us with cakes and babies."

"So it wasn't me in particular," said Ruth. He'd kissed her to see how it felt to be simple and safe; why hadn't she thought of that?

"It was nobody else but you," he said. The room was quiet. "I really was ashamed of myself."

"I was heartbroken," said Ruth. When she saw his genuine surprise, she smiled and cried, "Let's have a drink! To toast our reunion. There's still some of Harry's Scotch."

"All right," said Richard.

"It's good Scotch."

"Lawyers always have excellent Scotch."

"Now where"—Ruth stood up with a small frown and moved towards the liquor cabinet—"has Frida put the tumblers? She's always moving things around."

"You seem to manage very well out here," said Richard.

Ruth was proud to hear this. She poured the drinks and sat down next to him on the couch. Proceedings had a promising air. The Scotch tasted shuttered and old, but golden.

"You seem very sufficient to me," said Richard.

"Self-sufficient?"

"I think you and Frida together are a sufficiency. You're like a little world, a little round globe."

"That sounds claustrophobic, actually." Ruth added the cats to the population of this little world. They sat at Richard's feet without touching him. How still they were, how like artificial cats.

"I think it sounds wonderful. I like to think of her looking out for you at any given hour."

"Not really at any given hour," said Ruth. "She goes home at night."

"Really? I just assumed she lived in."

"'Lived in'?" It's like we're discussing servants!"

"Isn't it," said Richard, mildly.

"Believe me, Frida's no servant. She's usually only here on weekdays, just for the morning. She leaves after lunch and then her brother, the mythical George, brings her back in the morning in his golden taxi. Young Livery, he calls it. I think it makes him sound like a youthful alcoholic."

"The driver who brought me here?"

"Yes, of course, you met George! What was he like?"

"He's Frida's brother? Well, *he* certainly looks Fijian. He seemed—I don't know, self-possessed. He didn't talk much. So

Frida's just staying over while I'm here, is that it? She seems very settled."

"She's not staying at all," said Ruth. "What gave you that idea?"

"Well, her bedroom." Ruth lifted her head like a wary cat; Richard paused with his glass at his mouth, as if she could hear an alarm that he, deaf but alert, still listened for. He said, with apology, "I just assumed it was her bedroom."

"Which room?"

"At the end of the hall."

"Phil's room?" asked Ruth, but Richard didn't know the rooms by the names of her sons. He had never met her sons.

He said again, "At the end of the hall."

At the end of the hall Ruth found Frida, who earlier in the night had opened the front door in her grey coat and then closed it again behind her. In Phillip's room, Frida lived among her things. The room wasn't cluttered or in any way untidy, but it was distinctly inhabited: the furniture had been rearranged, unfamiliar postcards were stuck to the otherwise denuded walls, and her suitcase was tucked neatly on top of the wardrobe. Frida sat in a chair Ruth didn't recognize, soaking her feet in a basin of water and reading a detective novel. The knowledge that Frida's feet ached and that she enjoyed detective novels was almost as shocking to Ruth as the fact of Frida's living—all the evidence suggested it—in her house. Frida laid down her book.

"What's going on?" said Ruth.

The upper half of Frida's body remained still, but she lifted her feet, one at a time, out of the basin of water and set them down on a towel that lay on the floor. She had a steadfast quality, as if she had always been in this room and would always remain; it also seemed that she would never speak. In Frida's silence, Ruth heard the sound of Richard in the kitchen, turning on the taps and shuffling dishes.

"What are you doing in here?" asked Ruth, holding tightly to the doorknob.

"What does it look like I'm doing?" said Frida. "Relaxing at the end of a long day."

"But why are you *here*?"

"Why wouldn't I be here?"

"I saw you leave," said Ruth.

"How could you see me leave when I didn't?"

"I *heard* you leave, then. I heard the front door. You came in with your coat and said good-night."

"I was taking the bins out," said Frida. "It's rubbish night."

"With your coat?"

"Yep." Then: "It's cold out there."

"I thought you were leaving."

"You assumed I was leaving, obviously. Who knows why."

"And why wouldn't I assume you were leaving? It's not as if you live here."

"Oh, dear." Frida lifted her feet from the towel, leaving two big damp marks. "Oh, dear. You knew I was staying over, to help with Richard's visit. Remember?"

"I knew you were coming over the weekend," said Ruth. "Not staying."

"And remember, we talked about George, all my trouble with George? And you said I could stay as long as I needed to. So here I am." Frida spread out her hands as if her definition of *I* included not only her body, but the objects surrounding it, and in fact the entire room.

"That isn't true, Frida, what you're saying to me now, it's not true. I'd remember." Ruth was certain; but there was a feeling of unravelling, all the same; an unwound thread. She did recognize the part about trouble with George.

"You know your memory's not what it used to be."

"I do *not* know that," said Ruth, but this felt like a confession of ignorance, an admission of something rather than an insistence upon its opposite.

Frida sat on the unfamiliar chair and looked at Ruth, impassive. Her obstinacy had a mineral quality. Ruth felt she could chip away at it with a sharp tool and reveal nothing more than the uniformity of its composition. But her own certainty that Frida was lying had a similar brilliance. Her mind felt sifted and clear; her clear and prismatic mind turned and turned over the fact that Frida was lying. To know something so definitely was gratifying, and if this was true, what else might be? What other knowledge could Ruth be sure of, with such immaculate confidence? She was hungry, suddenly, for more certainties of this kind. All her life she'd been afraid of believing something untrue. It seemed like a constant threat: the possibility, for example, of believing in error that Christ had died for her sins. She turned with horror from the unlikely thing. It was so improbable that Frida would lie; that Richard could want Ruth after all this time; that the house could really be so hot and full of jungle noises and even once a tiger. Who would believe any of it? But it was true.

"You're embarrassing yourself," said Frida, in a resigned voice. Her face was so still and blank, there seemed to be no Frida in it. Ruth wanted to make the face move again; or she wanted not to have to look at it.

"I want you to go home," said Ruth. "I want you to call George and get him to take you home. And then you can come back tomorrow morning and we'll sort it all out."

"Are you serious?" Frida's eyes, at least, opened a little wider. "Are you seriously kicking me out of your house in the middle of the night?"

"You heard me." Ruth was horrified to hear herself say this, with all its false bravado: *You heard me,* as if she were in a movie. As if she hadn't spent her adult years teaching children not to say such empty things.

"Think very carefully," said Frida. She leaned forward, her

forearms on her knees, and Ruth realized that somehow their eyes were at the same level, although Frida was sitting and Ruth was standing. How small had she become? And how large was Frida?

Frida said, "Think this through very carefully, Your Majesty, because if you make me leave now, I'm never coming back."

Then she stood. She was enormous. She seemed to have risen up from the ocean, inflated by currents and tides, furious and blue; there was no end to her. Her hair had surrendered to some force of chaos and was now massed, unstyled, around her head. This was another new thing about Frida: her hair was loose and unbrushed. It added to the impression of divine fury. Ruth's fingers were tight on the doorknob.

"I won't put up with ultimatums, Frida," she said, but she knew how tremulous she sounded, how chiming her voice was, like a small bell rung by the side of a sickbed.

"You're the one telling me to get out or else," said Frida, leaning in towards Ruth's face. Then she wheeled away and threw her hands in the air; she adopted the mystified posture she always did when appealing to the sympathy of a phantom listener, and her face became itself again. "You know what? This is one hundred percent typical. You do a good deed for a little old lady—I don't get paid extra for staying over, you know—and the old biddy kicks you out of her precious house in the middle of the night. All so she can cuddle up with her boyfriend. That's the real reason, isn't it?"

"It's not kicking you out if I never asked you to stay," said Ruth.

"So he *is* your boyfriend."

"He has nothing to do with this."

"It's just a coincidence, then, that you're kicking me out when he's here? What's he going to think of that? And who's going to look after him and you tomorrow, huh? You going to cook for him? And for that matter, how exactly do you plan to get me out of here? You going to carry me? You and whose army?"

"You wouldn't dare," said Ruth.

"Wouldn't dare *what*?"

Ruth didn't know. She pressed against the door. She wished Frida would just go quietly. That's what she hoped to do one day: go quietly.

"What I'm going to say to you right now is—get out of my room," said Frida. She began to move towards Ruth. "This isn't over, oh, no. Maybe I'll leave tomorrow, maybe I won't. But tonight you're going to get out of my room and we're both going to have a good sleep—if I *can* sleep, after this—and we'll be having words in the morning, believe me." Frida kept moving towards the door, so that Ruth was forced to step sideways to avoid collision. "All right? No more orders from you—this is my time off. Right now you're nobody's boss. Got it?"

Frida wasn't threatening, exactly; a funny, frightening smile skewed her face. Then Ruth was in the hall and the door was shut; she was unsure if she had moved into the hall and shut the door, or if Frida had done one or both things for her. She knocked on the door, but not loudly, and Frida didn't answer. Something heavy was pushed against it. Ruth didn't dare knock again, or call out; she couldn't make any more of a fuss with Richard there.

But Richard seemed relaxed in the kitchen, finishing the dishes with his shirtsleeves rolled up to his skinny elbows. He displayed the sort of sweet, studied cheerfulness he might have perfected as the father of teenage daughters. He had rubbed wet hands through his cloudy hair and revealed his architectural ears—when had his ears become so large, like an old man's? If he'd been less helpfully serene, Ruth might have wept, or at least called upon his medical expertise: "Please, Richard," she might have said, "how can I tell if I'm losing my mind? Are there definite signs? Please, is there some kind of test? What would *you* say to an old woman who heard a tiger in her house at night, who forgot to wash her hair, who didn't notice her government carer had moved in?" But his whole manner was designed to convey to her that he had noticed nothing amiss about Frida and the guest room; that he valued Ruth's dignity; that he didn't want to get involved. And so she thanked him for washing up, he deflected her thanks, and in a volley of pleasantries they said good-night and went to their respective bedrooms alone.

The cats were buried under the quilt and twisted in protest when Ruth disturbed it by sitting on her bed. The bed seemed haunted, then, by phantom lumps of Harry: one turning arm, or a twitching foot. It was macabre and awful and stupidly comforting all at once, and just thinking of it embarrassed Ruth with Richard in Jeffrey's room. And Frida in Phillip's room. When had her house become so populated? Ruth, the cats, Frida, Richard. It occurred to her that Frida might actually do what she'd threatened: that she might leave. Ruth stretched out her feet—sitting on the bed, they didn't quite touch the ground— and said, "I've done it now, haven't I." She saw her head speaking in the dresser mirror, and that was another thing she used to do: pretend to be Harry as he watched her move and speak. She turned her head away; she had no time for herself. Had she really forgotten that Frida was living in her house? But she had forgotten to wash her hair, and it was Frida who fixed it.

So the day was over, and Richard would leave tomorrow afternoon. The weekend was just like the boat to Sydney: days of promise with Richard, on which nothing definitive happened. Now she had lost him again, because of Frida. But as she lay in bed and thought this through, and considered Frida's reading a detective novel and soaking her feet, and remembered Richard's sad, smug explanation of the difficulties of having a Japanese wife and why that meant he was allowed to kiss whomever he felt like, her anger turned in his direction. Why had he come? And since he'd come, why was he only here for a weekend, when the days of the week didn't matter anymore? They were both old, and outside of time. She lay in bed, pinned by the cats, and fumed. And why had he told her Frida was in the house at night? Now she would lose Frida, thanks to him. She would lose him because of Frida, and Frida because of him; and with that thought, her last before sleep, the whole house emptied out.

9

Ruth woke late the next morning. The day was so clear that, when she went into the kitchen, she could see the town light-house from the dining-room windows. Ruth called for Frida, and Richard answered. He came from the lounge room looking like Spencer Tracy: all that bright hair and good humour, only taller.

"Frida's gone out for the morning," he said.

"Gone where?"

"She had some shopping to do. Her brother came in his taxi."

"How did she seem?"

"Fine," said Richard. He put his hands on her shoulders and kissed her cheek good morning; she was far too distracted to enjoy it.

"She's just gone to do some shopping," said Ruth. Sufficient, she thought; a little world. "It was all just a misunderstanding." She resisted the temptation to run to Phillip's room—Frida's room—to see if it was empty of Frida's possessions.

"These things happen," said Richard.

He made her a cup of tea and sat on the window seat close to her chair while she drank it. He touched her arm and her hair as they talked about the weather and the day's activities: Ruth's back was fine, the weather was fine, and they could walk on the beach with binoculars and look for whales. They might even make it as far as the northern headland. George wasn't coming for Richard until the afternoon: they had hours yet. They talked about these plans, but made no effort to execute them. Ruth couldn't help thinking about Frida.

"Just a misunderstanding," she said again. "My memory's not what it used to be."

"Your memory is fine. Think what you remember about Fiji, all those years ago."

"But that's what they say about being old, isn't it? That you'll remember things from years and years ago, and not what you ate for breakfast. And sometimes I do—you know—imagine things."

"You're not old," said Richard. "You're a girl in Fiji coming to meet the new doctor."

It was a silly and untrue thing to say, but Ruth ignored that; she inclined her head towards the pleasure of it. He was looking at her now in exactly the way she'd wanted him to when she was that girl. Time and age were a great waste laid out before her; they had also brought her here, so quickly, to Richard. But she was embarrassed by her pleasure, despite herself.

"Look at the birds," she said, and finally Richard looked away from her and out the window. White and black seabirds gathered in particular places on the bay; they seemed all at once to throw themselves at the water and then rise again. "The whales are there where the birds are—that's one way to spot them. Can you see anything? A spout? A tail?"

"No," said Richard. "But the birds are beautiful."

"Look at everyone on the beach," said Ruth. Weekend whale watchers stood motionless on the shore, and every now and then an arm would point, or someone would jump up and down. "Should we go down?"

"I predict rain," said Richard. "Rain, rain, and more rain. Best to stay indoors."

Ruth gave a small laugh and wouldn't look at him. Instead she watched the people on the beach, and when they turned and pointed in one direction, she looked there, hoping to see a whale, but only saw the slap of travelling waves. It was odd to watch this from the window without going out or taking the binoculars down. Harry would disapprove. But then Harry wasn't here. Richard leaned closer and kissed her, on the side of her face at first, and then, when she turned towards him, on her mouth. He was so exact, his hands were so dry, and he gave out such a lonely heat. With the sea and the window and the birds over the water, it was like—but at the same time not at all like—daydreams Ruth had nourished in Fiji; it was as if her youthful tending of those dreams had been so timid that only now could they bear fruit. And of course her body had been through a great deal since then—sex, and childbirth, and the effort of fifty years—and its response to Richard bore little resemblance to that girlish pulse. A dry warmth came up to meet his. And stop thinking these things, she told herself; you are being kissed. Richard is kissing you; isn't this what you invited him for? You are a chaste and vain and sentimental old woman. She faltered and Richard drew away, but she pulled him back again by catching one hand on his shoulder.

"Frida?" he said.

"We'll hear the car."

So she knew that she meant to do more kiss him. What confidence she had! In him, and in herself. She stood and said, "Come with me."

Richard took her hand and it felt as if she had lifted him from the window seat with her strength. They walked to her bedroom. Ruth didn't like seeing their reflections in the mirror, but she scolded herself: she knew it was ridiculous to be shocked by this kind of sensible sex. There was no one to ask, Can I have this? Is this allowed? It felt like swearing: something small and private she could pit against the orthodoxy of her life. But she didn't mean to sound ungrateful. She had refused a little of this, a little of that, until she found there was nothing much left to agree to; now she could agree to this.

They were both prepared to be practical. Ruth arranged the pillows on the bed the way she knew from experience would be best for her back, and Richard drew the curtains. Then, in the false twilight, they approached each other. There was no rush, and as a result no fumbling; she let him unbutton her shirt, but removed her bra herself. It was the sturdy, flesh-coloured kind that left ridges on her shoulders and torso, and her loosened breasts were powdery and white. He ran his hands over the crepe of her skin, as if he had grown old with it and knew every stage of its buckling. Then, still wearing her skirt, Ruth removed his glasses and helped him pull his shirt over his head, where it caught for a moment and submerged his face. She kissed his mouth through the cotton. Richard had a sweet, monkeyish, fluffy chest, and his breasts and stomach were puckered. It seemed important that they both be naked. They finished undressing and Richard stood as if holding his hands in his pockets while Ruth settled herself on the bed. Then he lay over her.

There was no sense of Harry in the room or in the bed; there was no sense of anything besides Ruth and Richard. There were noises, but Ruth didn't speak. Richard was tender and obliging and prudent. He would probably have been the same fifty years ago, but now there was an additional care, a familiarity, and a relief in not loving him except retrospectively. She had observed something similar about sex with Harry as they grew older: that nothing depended on it, not in the way it used to. Richard was so calm, and he was so graceful, although his frame was thin and his breath scraped over her face. He was good-humoured, too, and patient; they both were. They attempted little, so as not to be disappointed, and also because less was required, but Ruth bit the inside of her mouth because she felt more pleasure than she expected to. This made Richard kiss her on the shoulder. Richard! The cats might have been here or anywhere, and Frida might have come down the drive and walked in on them; but she didn't.

Afterwards, Richard helped her dress. They sat on the edge of her bed. He was still shirtless, and she saw moles on his lower back she'd never known were there.

"I wish I could stay," he said.

"Why don't you?"

Richard pulled on his shirt and laughed, and she shook her head in order to say, Of course not.

"It's my granddaughter's birthday tomorrow," he said. He held her hand and kissed it. "I'm not going to ask you to marry me. I think it would be unfair to our children to muddy the whole question of inheritances. I mean, at our age. Do you mind my being practical?"

Ruth said, "Not at all." And she didn't.

Then he lay his head in her lap. She brushed back his hair so she could see the upturned dish of his ear.

"How would you feel about coming to live with me?" he asked.

Ruth saw herself sitting by Richard's bed. She watched him dying. Frida had once said of Harry, "At least he spared you a sickbed," and Ruth had been appalled. Now the weight of Richard's head in her lap was both heavy and dear. She pressed the hair above his flat ear and might have bent to kiss his forehead, but he sat up and said, apologetic, "Sorry. I'm rushing things." Then he was buttoning his shirt, and she saw how thick his fingernails had become, and how his hands shook. "But you'll think about it?"

"Yes," said Ruth. She stood up, aware of her calm, her lack of surprise, and her feeling not of great luck or pleasure but of amusement, as if someone had told her a slightly sad joke. None of this seemed urgent. They had waited half a century, so why were they talking like teenagers, as if they couldn't bear to be apart? But she would think about it.

They were both dressed now, and they brushed each other down, laughing, the way their mothers might once have done. Together they walked through the house discussing possibilities. Ruth could come to Sydney in a few weeks. Richard could visit again. They could talk on the phone and write to each other.

There might have been a conquering armada of whales in the bay, and they would never have noticed. In fact they avoided the sea and sat in the lounge room, where the white light of mid-afternoon flooded through the curtains, and Richard placed his right hand on Ruth's left knee and said, "Please think about it." They heard George's taxi in the drive, which surprised them both; he wasn't due for half an hour.

Frida had been gone long enough to do more than shopping, and Ruth was afraid for a moment that George was only here to pick Richard up; that this was his last act of service before he and his sister disappeared from Ruth's life altogether. But there was a bustle in the garden, and then at the front door, of plastic bags and exaggerated breath, and then Frida announcing that George had a fare and would be back for Richard at the appointed time.

"So what's news with you two?" She wore her grey coat and looked unusually jubilant.

Ruth and Richard smiled and shrugged.

Frida, distracted, was giddily confidential among her shopping bags. "Well, *I* have news. Big news. Shark attack at the beach."

Richard and Ruth, still dazed, struggled up out of their privacy.

Richard managed, "A shark!"

"Oh, dear," said Ruth. And she made Frida tell every detail—it was years since the last attack, and the news would be in all the papers: not a local boy (not the pineapple boy, thought Ruth), but a surfer who came regularly from the city; he wasn't dead, not yet, but things were bad, loss of blood, and a leg that would most likely have to come off.

"He'll either wake up dead or one-legged," said Frida, with a small grimacing laugh.

So the visit came to an end in the commotion of this disaster. They all went out into the garden and saw a helicopter flying low over the bay.

"They're tracking him," said Frida.

"The boy?" asked Ruth.

"The shark."

The knots of whale watchers scanned the sea in frantic sweeps. Frida walked down the dune towards them, and Ruth and Richard followed. Richard, gallant, held Ruth's elbow on the slope.

It seemed natural for the whale watchers to turn to Frida and call out, as she advanced over the sand, "Is it a shark? A shark?" They gathered about her, and she answered all their questions with a festive confidence. A young girl in a wet bikini began to cry, and others took out their mobile phones to take photographs of the empty sea. There were no visible whales. There was instead a continuous scurfy roll of poststorm waves onto the shore. The helicopter produced an insectile buzz that came and went over the water. Richard held Ruth's hand as they watched it, finally, lift away from the bay; then the group on the sand disbanded.

Richard went to help Ruth climb the dune, but Frida took her arm from the other side and almost lifted her away from him. Richard walked behind them; he was like a small boy whose every attention is focused on how inessential he is. So he must make unnecessary noise, and Frida must wilfully ignore him, and Ruth must not notice, must climb the dune in Frida's arms with only the dune on her mind. But all the while she replayed the way he had put his hand on her knee and said, "Please think about it."

The taxi was waiting for Richard. Ruth even saw, for the first time, the bulky and unmediated form of mysterious George. His window was rolled down and there he sat, in shade, at the wheel, with one meaty forearm crooked into the pink of the sun. Frida made no move to speak with or introduce him. Richard's small suitcase was waiting by the front door. That was the weekend over; it had passed without Ruth's noticing. She kept waiting for something more to happen, and she supposed it had; but she was still in a state of anticipation. It was George who spoiled things; George who took people away. His taxi was waiting, so Richard must wheel his suitcase out, and Ruth must stand with Frida on the doorstep and smile.

"It's all right about last night," said Frida.

"Of course it is," said Ruth.

"What I mean is that I forgive you."

Ruth and Frida held up their hands, and Richard waved from the back of the taxi, which reversed down the drive and vanished among the yellow grasses.

10

Ruth became sick almost as soon as Richard left. She decided these things were related, because of the timing—she couldn't keep down the cup of tea Frida made her immediately after Richard's departure—and because there was nothing specific about her illness. She was heartsick, possibly. It was too much to stir up her old heart, she thought; in her less sentimental moments, she berated herself for behaving like a schoolgirl, but remained quietly pleased at this evidence of her continuing romantic sensitivity. Still, she spent a few days in bed, always tired and rarely hungry, but never with a fever or headaches or any particular pain besides her back; she took her prescriptions and assured Frida that a doctor wasn't necessary and her sons needn't be alerted. Frida thought she had simply overexerted herself with Richard; Ruth blushed, but Frida paid no attention.

Frida was a good nurse. She made soup and cleaned and checked on her patient in a sensible way, clinical rather than confiding. She exhibited no sympathy, but was never dismissive of Ruth's vague troubles. She kept Ruth's fluids up and, having quizzed Richard on the benefits of fish oil for elderly brains, introduced a large capsule fuzzily full of golden liquid. Ruth's only complaint was that Frida kept the cats from the bedroom. A new atmosphere of calm settled over the house; it was cool and clean, and noiseless in the night. Frida didn't mention George, her money troubles, or the argument about living in Phillip's room. During periods of restless confusion—when she had slept too much, or too little—Ruth would try to talk about Richard, but Frida, so serene and straightforward, only shook her head a little. She wore the plump smile of a Madonna who always looks over the head of her child, as if deciding what to cook for Joseph's dinner. Ruth, considering the possibility of going to Richard, sometimes said aloud, "Why shouldn't I? Who could stop me?" and other times argued, "Anyway, I'm not the kind of woman who would up and leave her whole life for a man." At other times, she felt she had an important decision to make, but was pleasantly unsure of what it was. Frida read detective novels and said nothing. The sun came through the window in long lines over the bed, and these lines moved throughout the day, and then it was dark again.

These were comfortable days, although swampy and forgetful. Ruth found it easy to surrender to Frida's care, and so, even when she began to feel better, she composed her face into wan expressions and pretended to sip soup. She was caught out of bed one morning preparing to smuggle one of the cats through the window, and there were recriminations.

"This is what I get, is it, for looking after you like a saint?" Frida cried. "All right, up and out. No more of this lying around with me waiting on you hand and foot."

Frida behaved as if Ruth were not only better, but in the best of health: youthful, but lazy. She shooed her charge into the garden, where Ruth was expected to sit in the sun and tail beans or polish silver.

"And don't tell me any old family stories about that silver," Frida warned.

In the garden, in the afternoons, Ruth was supposed to "take the air"—instead of an indoor nap.

"We'll have you walking on the beach in no time," said Frida, as if Ruth had been accustomed to daily canters on the sand, and whenever Ruth complained about her back, Frida tapped her temple and said, "Have you ever stopped to think it might all be in your head? What's the word for that? Jeffrey would know."

"Psychosomatic," said Ruth.

"Jeffrey would know."

One morning, Frida returned from the letterbox with a pale blue envelope. She presented it to Ruth with some ceremony and hovered to see it opened. Ruth didn't hurry. She looked at the return address: Richard Porter, and then the number and street of the house in Sydney she could live in if she wanted to. Frida shuffled and sighed beside her.

"Can you get me the letter opener?" asked Ruth. "It's on Harry's desk."

"Just open it."

"I want to slit it open. I want to keep the address."

Frida shook her head and bugged her eyes, an uncharacteristically comic face, and went inside. This gave Ruth the opportunity to smell the envelope. She pressed her fingers along the closed flap, feeling the places where Richard's hands—and maybe his tongue—must have touched. Ruth had expected to hear from him sooner, but she wasn't entirely sure how much time had passed since his visit.

Frida returned with a small, sharp knife from the kitchen.

The envelope contained a card, and the card held a sheet of that same thin paper on which Richard had written to accept her invitation to visit. The card had a photograph of a beach on it—not this beach, not Ruth's bay—and the sky in the picture was a ludicrous blue. Ruth found it hard to imagine Richard selecting the card. It said, "To dear Ruth and Frida, with thanks for a very special weekend."

Ruth passed the card to Frida, who took it with some care, as if it might be the bearer of exquisite news. Then Ruth read the note, which was addressed only to her: "Dearest Ruth, I hope you're feeling better. I would love to hear your voice and know what you're thinking. My garden is full of daylilies, all of them pink, which I want you to see—my daughter tells me I'll enjoy them for another three weeks or so. She has the family's green thumb—and all our fingers. Please telephone as soon as you're well enough, or write, or else! Or else I'll come back up there and fetch you."

Ruth wondered if she would enjoy being fetched.

Frida was watching. "Can I see?" she asked.

"It's private."

"Oh, *private*." Frida appeared to find this funny and raised her arms as if she were in a movie and a man in wacky stripes had just told her to stick 'em up.

"How does he know I've been sick?" asked Ruth. "Has he been calling?"

"He called," said Frida.

"When?"

"When you were sick." Frida stuck the card in the waist-band of her trousers.

"I don't remember."

"Do you want me to start writing everything down? I'm not your secretary." Frida shifted her weight from foot to foot. "He just wanted to tell us thank you. Like he says in his card. I don't think you missed a big chin-wag."

"If you must know," said haughty Ruth, "he wants me to go and live with him."

Frida's face registered surprise for only a moment; then she corrected it. Ruth had never seen Frida off guard, and there was something alarming about the visible motion of her thought.

"And?" Frida said.

"I haven't decided," said Ruth. She already regretted telling Frida; she remembered a phrase of Mrs. Mason's: "Trap your tongue if it tattles out of turn."

But Frida said nothing more. She evidently had further questions, but wouldn't lower herself to asking them. She flicked at the card in her waistband and rolled away into the house.

Jeffrey telephoned that evening. "I've just had a very inter-esting call from Frida," he said. "She's worried about you."

Ruth wondered when Frida had found the time; she seemed to have spent the last few hours in the bathroom, dyeing her hair.

"She actually asked me not to mention our chat," said Jeffrey. "I don't like that kind of subterfuge, though I'm sure she has her reasons."

"She usually does."

"Now, about this Richard. How old is he, exactly?"

"He's about eighty."

"Oh. He's eighty," said Jeffrey, so Ruth knew his wife was listening. "That's different. Frida made him sound like some kind of gold-digger."

"Harry isn't a gold-digger!"

"You mean Richard."

"Yes, Richard. I've known him for fifty years. He isn't after me for my money."

"But he is after you?" asked Jeffrey.

"I think, yes, he is *after me*. Is that all right with you, darling?"

"What are we talking here? Companion? Boyfriend? Husband?" There was a boyish tremor in his voice, but it seemed to stem from embarrassment rather than anxiety. He mastered it by clearing his throat.

"I think it would be unfair on you boys to drag mud over the question of inheritance, at my age," said Ruth.

"What?"

"I'm not going to marry him."

"I know you need companionship. I worry about you out there on your own, I really do."

"I have Frida."

"And thank God for Frida," said Jeffrey.

"Does Richard have your permission, then, to be after me?"

"You don't need my permission, Ma. This is about what you want. But I'd like to meet him before you make any decisions."

"The lilies only have three weeks or so," said Ruth.

"What was that?"

"He wants me to see the lilies. They're pink."

Jeffrey cleared his throat; Ruth thought she might have said something wrong.

"Pink lilies, right, okay. Where does he live?"

"In Sydney, like your father."

"Are you going to invite him for Christmas?" asked Jeffrey. "So we can all meet him? Oh—but where would he sleep?" Small, practical details of this nature always bothered him, even as a young boy; and then he seemed to realize he'd asked a more personal question than he'd intended, and he said, "I mean, with all of us staying."

"And Frida already in Phil's room," said Ruth. "Or maybe she wouldn't want to stay for Christmas."

"What do you mean?"

"She'll probably want to spend Christmas with George."

Frida appeared, without sound, at the door between the kitchen and the hall. Her hair was now a light reddish brown, rounded and shiny, like a polished apple, and her face was terribly blank.

"But why is Frida in Phil's room?" asked Jeffrey.

"Well, she lives there now," said Ruth, irritated; how many times did she have to say it?

"Is she there? Put her on."

Already Frida's hand was stretched out. Ruth offered up the receiver like a heifer to Juno. Frida's voice sounded bright when she said, "Jeff," into the phone, but her flat eyes remained on Ruth's face.

"Yes, Jeff," said Frida, with a noble weariness. "Yes, that's right. I assumed she'd told you."

Jeff's voice was so small on the other end of the line—just a pitch, really, rather than words—and this made it seem as if an

argument was already over and he had lost. Frida stood, waiting, as Jeff's voice buzzed, and her eyes flicked from Ruth's face
to her own fingernails, which she held away from the shadow of
her body.

"Look, Jeff, this is between you and your mother. Who
hasn't been well these last couple of weeks, just FYI. She didn't
want to worry you—overdoing things, is all, with Richard and
everything. She's no spring chicken. I wanted to be on hand. We
talked it through, didn't we, Ruthie?"

Frida didn't look at Ruth, who retreated into the dining
room, annoyed at her son for making a fuss. This is my house,
she thought. It isn't Phil's room; it's mine. If I want to install
one thousand Fridas in Phil's room, one thousand Richards in
Jeff's room—in *my* room—then I will. And Jeffrey didn't seem
to care one bit about the lilies, which would be long gone by
Christmas.

"Just some tiredness, loss of appetite, nothing serious," said
Frida into the phone. "And we're much better now, aren't we,
Ruthie?"

"Yes!" piped Ruth from the dining room.

"You go right ahead and do that, Jeff," said Frida. "Look, I
didn't see the need. I'm a trained nurse, and the only person
whose time I'm willing to waste is my own. All right, first thing
in the morning. You're welcome. Not at all. There's no need,
Jeff—I'm happy to do it. And she likes the company, the dear.
Don't you, Ruthie? All right, now." Frida turned and carried the
handset, on the end of its long white cord, to Ruth, who held it
with reluctance to her ear.

"Ma, if you're sick, you've got to tell me. I want you to tell
me. All right?" Jeffrey's voice was exasperated, like a boy's, as if
tired of these adult games from which he was unjustly excluded.

"Actually," she said, "I don't have to tell you anything. What
do you think of that?"

And she hung up, or tried to; but she was so far from the wall, with all that cord between them, that she succeeded only in dropping the receiver. It rolled stupidly on the floor until Frida picked it up, looked at it as if she'd never seen its like, and then replaced it in its cradle.

"Thank you," said Ruth.

The phone began to ring again, but Frida only looked at Ruth with that big, blank face and shook her head as she walked away towards Phil's room. The phone rang and rang, and Ruth didn't answer it until she heard a door slam; then she did. It was Jeffrey, of course, upset.

"Did you hang up on me?" he demanded, and Ruth, until that moment proud of her defiance, repented and said, "I dropped the phone."

Then he was warm and fatherly. "I just feel that one of us should come out there and meet this woman who's living in your house," he said.

"You'll meet her at Christmas."

"She calls you Ruthie."

"No, she doesn't," said Ruth.

"What are you paying her?"

"I told you, I'm not paying her a cent."

This wasn't true; they had worked out a small salary in return for Frida's extra services. It wasn't generous, but Frida insisted on the smallness of the amount.

"Christmas is weeks away," said Jeffrey. "Would you object to a quick visit before then?"

"Lovely," said Ruth. Was it lovely? It occurred to her that Jeffrey might be planning a visit in order to stop her from going to Richard. Would Richard come, then, and fetch her, as he threatened?

They spent some time—more than usual—saying good-night to each other, as if they were sweethearts who couldn't bear to part, until the cats came to Ruth's feet to say, "Bed! Bed!" She hung up and took them in to bed. They rolled and begged and bathed, and finally they slept. Ruth went noisily to the bathroom, washed herself with maximum fuss, and closed the lounge-room door with some force, but there was no sound at all from Frida's part of the house.

11

The tiger came back that night. At least the noise of him did; or whatever it was that produced his noise. Ruth was lying in bed thinking about Richard and what it might be like to live in the city again. Richard lived in a sunny, hilly part of Sydney, northwest of the Harbour, where the trees tended to lose their leaves in the autumn and the wide evening roads were strung with homewards traffic. The gardens up there were all rhododendrons and azaleas, as if the climate were cooler and wetter than in other parts of the city, and Ruth, who didn't know the area well, associated it with the large, heavy house of one of her elocution students whose parents had invited her to dinner and then argued with each other over the cost of her lessons. Ruth also thought about Jeffrey, how boyish he had sounded on the phone, and the way he'd said, "This is about what you want." Could that be true? Since Harry died, she'd rarely thought about wanting anything. Frida was the one who wanted. She wanted clean floors, a smaller waist, and differently coloured hair. Frida filled the world with her desires. And Ruth admired it. Why not be like that?

The cats heard the noises first. Ruth was almost asleep, but they sat up, sphinxlike, their paws folded inward and their eyes slit. They were like little emperors on fabric shipped from China to England in the eighteenth century. Their ears moved and their tails were alert. Ruth, sensing their attention, turned her head on her pillow to listen, and there it was: something moving through the lounge room, shifting the furniture; but its tread was so light, so subtle; there was a louder exhalation, the amplification of a house cat sniffing under an unaccountably closed door, and at this the cats lost their composure and fled.

Now Ruth noticed an unusual smell, which seemed to enter the room as the cats left it. This very particular smell, concentrated and rank, was quite unlike the actual jungle, although it was this childhood scent that Ruth recalled now. The smell reminded her of the warning cries of seagulls in the garden when the cats were in the grass: not a specific panic, just a general alarm. Could a smell be a seagull? Perhaps it was more like a parrot. The tiger shook his head—new breathing accompanied the shake—and padded through the lounge room. It annoyed Ruth to hear him; she was impatient with herself because there was no point to him now that she had Frida and Richard; he had prepared the way for them and was no longer needed. She listened for any modulation in the tiger's sounds, and when she heard it, she drew wild conclusions: the tiger is in the hallway, there are two tigers, the insects are eating the furniture, there may also be a wild pig. Lost in these conjectures, she fell asleep. Ruth was fortunate in this way—she always slept, no matter what her anxiety, but she suffered through the night with fretful dreams. Waking in the morning, with the cats anchoring the quilt around her feet, she concluded that her ability to sleep despite the danger indicated a lack of belief in the tiger.

"After all," she said, aloud, "there is no tiger."

The cats gave her their quizzical attention and then began to bathe. Ruth dressed. She brushed her hair. There was no tiger, not last night, not ever. Today she would telephone Richard, not to say she would come to him—not yet; just to hear his voice.

But the lounge room, when Ruth entered it, did look dishevelled. An armchair stood in closer than usual proximity to a lamp. One corner of the rug lay folded back. And were the feline hairs she found rubbed into the rug more bristly than usual, more orange? The light fell innocently through the lace curtains. Everything was calm, but each piece of furniture seemed unmoored in the flat, insipid light, as if it had been stranded in its insistence on the ordinary. Ruth had the feeling that her whole house was lying to her. How could it smell of a jungle in the night and now so strongly, so freshly, of eucalyptus? But that was Frida, mopping the floors. Ruth thought, She's hiding the evidence, whether she knows it or not. Does she know it?

"Frida!" she called.

Frida came. She came with all the Valkyric majesty of Frida in the morning, when her mood had not yet solidified for the day, and any whim might take her: to be kind, to be sullen. Capricious Frida of the milky mornings, who might eat yoghurt or deny herself dairy, who might wash Ruth's hair or kick at the cats (never striking them), and who carried with her a new kind of privacy, which also emanated from what had formerly been Phillip's room so that Ruth knew it was off-limits. The floors gleamed with water, and they threw up light so that Frida, moving over them, seemed larger than ever. How was it possible, Ruth wondered, that as Frida shrank (her diet was working), she also seemed to take up more space? It must be a trick of all that light bouncing up from the immaculate floors.

"You're up," said Frida, good-natured. "I'll call the doctor."

"What for?"

"Your son told me to—on the phone last night."

"I'm not sick anymore."

"Fine," said Frida. "No doctor." And she turned to leave.

"Frida!" cried Ruth. Frida hated to be stopped when she was busy, and she hated to hear her name called out. Ruth would do it only under special circumstances; twice in one morning was quite remarkable.

"What?" Frida asked, revolving. She seemed placid enough. Her toffee-coloured hair made her sweeter.

"Did you notice a funny smell in here this morning?"

"What d'you mean, funny?"

"I suppose a sort of animal smell."

"The cats, you mean? They're stinkers. Not much we can do about that."

"No, no, more than the cats. Stronger than that. Do they really smell so bad? Cats are clean little things, aren't they?"

"If they're clean, then I'm the Queen of Sheba."

Frida probably was the Queen of Sheba. She stood robed in magisterial light; she had just proceeded with wisdom and splendour from the court of Solomon, where she solved all manner of problems: unnecessary automobiles, impossible tigers, the melancholy of the king. Now she was here to assist Ruth. She was a golden opportunity.

"This is a golden opportunity," said Ruth.

Frida shook her head and began to move back towards the kitchen.

"Frida, wait!" Now there was urgency: when Frida shook her head, it was necessary to tell her things quickly or not at all. "What would you say if I told you a tiger walked around the house last night?"

"Walked around inside the house, or walked *around* the house?"

"Inside," Ruth said.

"What kind of tiger?"

"What kind of tigers are there?"

"A big tiger? A boy tiger?"

"Yes."

"Big or boy?" asked Frida, still reasonable.

"Big boy."

"A Tasmanian tiger? Or the ordinary kind?"

"Ordinary," said Ruth.

"And what makes you think we've got a tiger?"

"I thought I heard him."

"You didn't see him?"

"There's a smell, too. That's why I asked you about the smell."

Frida sniffed luxuriously and long. She leaned into the sniff, and her nostrils flared; her eyes narrowed; she leaned farther, as if into a fragrant wind. "A kind've hairy smell, is that it? Like a rug that needs washing?"

"Like a jungle," said Ruth. Then another possibility occurred to her. "Or maybe a zoo."

"So, what you're telling me is, even though I bust my gut daily to get this place spotless—and beach places are the hardest of all to keep clean, believe me, what with the salt and the sand— even though I work myself to the bone to keep this place spotless, you're telling me it smells like a *zoo*?"

"Oh, Frida, no!" cried Ruth. "I noticed the smell last night, but you already have everything perfect again."

"Then it's the cats, you mark my words," said Frida. Problem solved, she swiveled away on one crisp foot.

"Of course it is," said Ruth, relieved. "Or it's nothing at all. I'm imagining it. Thank you."

But Frida turned to face her again. The light that leapt up around her, off the floors and the sea, hid her face.

"And what would a tiger want with you?" she asked; she was baffled, clearly, by the possibility that a tiger might take any interest in Ruth. She propped her mop in a corner, crossed to the recliner, and sat in it. Her face was full of jovial scorn. She settled into the possibility of the tiger; she made herself comfortable.

"You think this tiger's got it in for you? Maybe you killed its mum in that jungle you grew up in, and it's here to hunt you down."

"I didn't grow up in the jungle," said Ruth. "I grew up in a town. And there are no tigers in Fiji."

"If there's jungle, there's tigers."

"That's not true. Tigers like cold weather. They live in India and China. Maybe Russia."

"There's Indians in Fiji."

"I thought you didn't know anything about Fiji."

"Everyone knows that, from the news."

"Just because there are Indians in Fiji doesn't mean there are Indian tigers. I thought everyone knew *that*."

"What I do know is, there's no tigers in Australia," said Frida. "There's no seaside bloody tigers in the local area. Unless they're on holiday."

"I know that. It was just funny noises in the night."

Frida sat on the recliner. Her face was immobile with thought. "It's the cats, then," she said.

"Yes, the cats," said Ruth. The cats were frightened of something; that was undeniable.

"I mean, it's not so surprising, when you think about it. You leave the back door open every night for the cats to come and go. That'll be how this tiger of yours got in. What if Jeff knew that, huh? What if I told Mr. Fantastic you left your back door open and a tiger walked in? I wonder what he'd say to that."

Ruth had always pictured the tiger just appearing in the lounge room, the way a ghost might; he was a haunting and required nothing so practical as a door. Now she saw him coming by road and through the high grasses of the drive; she saw him moving with intemperate speed over the beach and ascending the dune; she saw him in the dark garden, making for the open door. One of the most fanciful things Harry had ever said to her had to do with the quality of moonlight by the sea. It was brighter and bluer, he said, with the sea to reflect it. Now Ruth saw the tiger under the bright blue seaside moon, and she saw her own house high on the dune's horizon; she ran towards it alongside the tiger, and the back door lay open for both of them. But the foolishness of having left her door open at night struck Ruth as too childish to have such terrible consequences.

"Nothing to say to that, have you?" said Frida. She tilted the recliner back and her magisterial stomach arced into the air; all her neat chins folded into place, like a napkin. "Why don't you just bring the phone over here and I'll call that son of yours? Let him meddle in that."

"He already knows about the tiger." That was satisfying to say. Ruth felt as if she'd thought ahead to this moment and called Jeffrey in order to have an answer ready for Frida now. Frida regarded her from the recliner. Her legs in the air were undeniably slim, and she flexed her nimble feet in their unlaced sand-shoes.

"He does, does he?" She made a small grunt. "You told him before you told me?"

"I told him before I even knew you."

"Wait a minute. I thought you said this tiger just showed up last night."

Ruth reddened; she felt caught out in an unintentional lie. "I thought I heard it once before."

"And you told Jeffrey. Well, how about that. No son of mine would hear I had a tiger and leave me all alone to deal with it."

"I'm not alone, am I," said Ruth, but she was alone when the tiger first appeared, and Jeffrey hadn't come. He'd told her to go back to sleep and made jokes about it the next morning.

"Your own son left you alone with a man-eating bloody tiger. A woman-eating tiger. You're lucky you haven't been gobbled up in your bed."

Ruth gave her nervous laugh. She knew how transparent this laugh was, but it flew out of her regardless. She blushed. She saw herself in bed with the tiger's hot face over hers.

"It's not a tiger," she said.

"I saw a TV show once." Frida tilted her head back against the soft seat of the recliner. "Yeah, a documentary about man-eating tigers in India. You know what they say, once a tiger gets a taste of human flesh, that's all it wants to eat."

"That's only the old tigers with broken teeth," said Ruth, recalling a documentary of her own; possibly the same one. It had been intensely yellow-lit, as if the heat of India was perceptible in the shade of its sunshine. "And anyway, it's not a real tiger."

"Oh, a *ghost* tiger, is it?" Frida heaved her body forward to

right the recliner. "Here I was thinking a real tiger was dropping in for social calls. A ghost tiger is totally different. Nothing
to worry about, in that case."

"Well, obviously there's no tiger," said Ruth. "You didn't
hear it. You said you didn't smell anything."

"I said I smelled something. Like a rug that needs washing."

"That's just the rug needing washing." Ruth prodded it
with her foot.

"Don't get your knickers in a twist. I'll wash it today," said
Frida. She dragged herself up from the recliner, which shook in
alarm.

"So you see—just a silly old woman." Ruth laughed with
one coy hand at her throat. "Of course there's no tiger."

"I don't know, Ruthie." Frida headed back to the kitchen
and her mop. "Stranger things under the sun." She shook her
head, looking out at the sea as she walked, so that Ruth saw she
was taking the possibility of the tiger seriously; that the wide
spread of her thoughts was growing wider still. Frida rarely
looked at the sea.

Ruth set about scrutinizing every corner of the lounge room.
The only thing now was to find a tuft of orange fur, one frond of
a parrot's tail, or any tangible proof that her house had a habit of
turning into a jungle at night. And conversely, in the absence
of such evidence, that it didn't. She flipped the rug with her foot,
lifted the curtains, and snuck a broom from the kitchen to poke
under the sofa. Frida, with a submerged mutter, stayed out of
her way. Ruth was reminded of a period during which she had
worried over the existence of God. At that time, when she was
aged eleven or so and was reminded everywhere and at every
hour of the goodness of God's provision, she developed a horror
that she would be visited by an angel and that all of it—all that
awful good news—would be proven, absolutely, to be true. How
she longed to see that angel, and how terrified she was. She

would lie awake at night, afraid to open her eyes and afraid to sleep. It never came.

Besides the slight disarrangement of the furniture, nothing in the lounge room suggested a jungle except the carcass of a spider, cat-killed and crumpled deep under the sofa; Ruth extracted it with the assistance of the broom.

Frida, her mop rinsed and squeezed and left to dry for the day, marched into the room and, without speaking, rolled up the rug and carried it away, corpselike, over her right shoulder. Without the rug, the room appeared defenseless, and much larger. It was a long way, for example, from the window to the door. Ruth swept the dead spider through the expanse of the lounge and dining rooms, to the kitchen, and out into the garden. Frida had hung the rug over a long frangipani limb and was beating it with a wooden spoon. She pulled her arm back, holding the spoon as if it were a tennis racquet, and unleashed it with such force that dust and hair rose in grubby clouds above her shaking back.

With Frida out of the house and the living room empty of evidence, Ruth called Richard. She carried the receiver, on the end of its long white cord, down the hallway and into her bedroom, listening with pleasure to the ring of his phone in her ear and in his house. Frida was still beating the rug, and the sound of it was like a flag snapping against its pole in a high wind.

Richard's phone rang nine times before somebody answered it.

"Hello?" said a young woman. Her voice sounded harried, and out of it came the absurdity of a house in Sydney that Ruth had never seen, daughters and grandchildren related by blood to Richard and Kyoko, a whole life that had never been dismantled and moved to the sea, with no imaginary tigers, no Frida beating a rug over a frangipani branch, and Richard over eighty, herself old; and the voice, more weary this time, as if it would wait forever, firm, polite, and inconvenienced, repeated, "Hello?" Ruth, sitting on the bed where she had recently lain down and— awkwardly, optimistically, and not without pleasure—slept with a man she hadn't seen for fifty years, listened for another "Hello?" and then, holding one palm against the receiver so as not to hear anything more, hurried into the kitchen and hung up the phone.

Frida was also in the kitchen, filling a bucket with water. "Everything all right?" she asked.

Ruth nodded. They went into the garden together, Frida holding the soapy bucket against her leg, and together they washed the rug. Ruth liked the short, rough feel of the bristles under her fingernails. She liked the thin dust that coated the ground under the frangipani tree, and the soapy grey water that ran out of the rug and over the garden. Frida laid the clean rug over the hydrangea bush to dry, and for the rest of the day it fidgeted in the wind as if something trapped underneath were making halfhearted attempts to escape. Then she swept and polished the lounge-room floor, every now and then taking an exploratory sniff. There was no discernible smell in the lounge room; nothing left of the long, hairy bass note Ruth had suspected of issuing from a tiger. The animal odour had only been the rug, after all. Ruth—dirty, tired, and still hearing that "Hello? Hello?" in her inmost ear—took a long bath during which she repeatedly bit the inside of her mouth to stave off self-pity. But as she dressed afterwards—not in pyjamas, not before bedtime, that would be sloppy—she remembered that strange feline stain on the lounge right before Richard's visit and wondered about it.

Frida cooked steak for dinner—an extravagance—and when Ruth asked the occasion, she answered, mysteriously, "Red meat for strength." After the meal, she brewed a pot of strong tea, made Ruth drink two cups, and suggested they sit together in the lounge room. Frida never sat in the lounge room at night.

If she didn't go out—there were nights when George's taxi drew up, pumpkin-coloured, and carried her away—she usually stayed at the dining table, reading the newspaper or detective novels; or she went into her bedroom to soak her feet and try new hairstyles; or she occupied the bathroom for hours, dyeing and washing and drying her hair. But tonight, she said, her arms were sore from beating the rug and she wanted to sit in the lounge room, watch a little TV, and talk. She made more tea and carried it in to Ruth, who was sitting in the recliner, and who protested, "Three cups! I'll be up all night."

"That's the idea," said Frida.

"Why?"

"I want to see this tiger of yours."

Ruth sipped her too-hot tea and gave her girlish laugh, the one she hated the sound of.

"Don't be scared, Ruthie. Between you and me"—Frida flexed a savvy biceps—"your Frida is a match for any old tiger."

"Stop it," said Ruth. "Turn on the television."

Frida didn't move. Her face was agile with anticipation. "We'll be bait. Lure him out, then *kapow*! Though maybe that's not the best idea. Wouldn't want to hand you to him like a meat tray in a raffle." Ruth eased herself out of the recliner. "Where are you off to?"

"If you're going to be ridiculous, I'm going to bed."

"Tiger on the loose, chances are it's a man-eater," said Frida. "We should check the news for zoo escapes."

"I don't intend to be laughed at in my own home."

"I wish you'd told me about this before, Ruthie. For one thing, I might have run into it on the way to the loo one night. Couldn't have it see me without my hair all done." Frida laughed, and her belly shook.

"Good night, Frida," said Ruth, and the cats, only just settled on the sofa, followed her to her bedroom, where she took her pills before lying on the bed and remembering the voice at the end of Richard's phone number saying, again and again, "Hello?"

Frida turned on the television and the sound of it comforted Ruth, like a light under a door. She lay on her bed, still dressed and without even her lamp lit: she wanted the dark to cool her burning face. The television continued to buzz until late, and every now and then Frida laughed from the lounge room.

When she woke early the next morning, Ruth couldn't remember falling asleep. More than this, she couldn't remember her own body; it seemed to be missing. Nevertheless, she was able to move. She got out of bed in the slow, deliberate way Frida had taught her: bend your legs, roll onto your side, keep the spine intact, think of it as a steel rod, let gravity do the work, stay relaxed, sit up, don't twist, move the spine as a unit, rest, stretch as tall as you can, bend forward and lift, straighten your legs, and then you're standing, Ruth was standing, without ever quite knowing how she came to be on her feet. She felt nothing. This might be the true weight of age, she thought, without feeling her thought; it was weightless, everything was, but not in a light way. That might be pleasant. This weightlessness was all absence. Her back should hurt and her legs should be shaking. And she wanted Richard, but her heart didn't ache. Then there was a noise in the room, which finally she recognized as her own voice—she wasn't sure what her voice was saying, but the existence of it, and its definite sound, returned sensation to her back and legs. Her skin was dirtily damp. There she was in the mirror, and the cats had found her and were running in and out of the door pleading for breakfast. It wasn't long past dawn, the sea was outside; it was audible, and so were her feet on the floor, so she called to the cats just to hear her voice again. "Kit! Kit!" she called. Her tongue was sticky in her mouth.

Out in the lounge room, Frida was asleep on the sofa. She woke when Ruth came in, starting up with a hand to her hair and rubbing her bleary face. Ruth couldn't think what to say.

Her body had returned to her, but she was still unsure of her control over it.

"Whatsa time?" enquired Frida, but Ruth didn't know. They looked at each other, Frida from the sofa and Ruth standing by the window, and after a moment of this, Frida shook her head and stood up. The ease with which she stood was awe-inspiring. She was like a wave. But strands of her hair were stuck to the sweaty sides of her face.

"It didn't come," she said, stretching her arms behind her head and walking towards the kitchen. Her hair had flattened in the back. "The tiger."

Ruth made a small sound of disgust. It was childish of Frida to persist in teasing. But she saw, without wanting to, evidence of Frida's seriousness: her crushed hair, the displaced sofa cushions, and the cups of tea. Now Frida came back into the lounge room with pills and a glass of water; Ruth accepted them; she put the pills in her mouth, swallowed, and felt safer for knowing she was able to do so.

Ruth wanted to telephone Richard while Frida was making breakfast, but it was far too early. So she called him later, while Frida was in the shower, and this time he answered.

"Ruth!" he cried, obviously delighted. "Ruth, Ruth, Ruth!"

She wanted to hear his dear voice settle down into a slow, happy rhythm, but he was excited to hear from her, and he talked too much and too quickly: about his garden and the local council, who were sending men to remove a tree that afternoon, an old juniper that was threatening the neighbour's roof but gave him such pleasure because of the way the cockatoos ate the berries and rolled around drunk on the grass, and about his great-granddaughter who had just gotten a part in the school play, she would play a pirate with a wooden parrot, and he was in charge of finding an eye patch and a scarf fringed with gold coins, and also, and this was sad news, but Andrew Carson—did she remember him?—his son had died last week, very unexpected, a stroke, and Richard would be at the funeral tomorrow; of course, Andrew was long gone himself—this phrase *long gone* dismayed Ruth—but he would pass on Ruth's sympathies to the rest of the family.

Ruth listened and asked questions and made appropriate noises; she was reminded of the old Richard with too much to say after a play or a film, except that now his talk was full of people and events and objects, and not the abstract things that used to frighten her. But she found herself missing them, or missing the man who had waited for her to talk about them with him, because she couldn't contribute to the pirate play, the juniper tree, or even Andrew Carson's son, who had been born not long after the kiss at the ball, and consequently quite soon before Ruth left Fiji. Was it that Richard remembered her as only being capable of this sort of low-level gossip? Or was it that she was exhausted and saddened by this evidence of the vitality of Richard's life, which failed to appeal to her? So she ended their chat without saying any of the things she wanted to: that she missed him, for example, and that she thought every day about their morning in her bedroom. It was only as they said goodbye that Richard said, "I've rattled on, I'm sorry, I get nervous on the phone," and she was ashamed for him—Richard, nervous! Ruth promised to call him again soon, but thought she would write him a letter instead.

That night, Frida joined Ruth in the lounge room after dinner. She brought two of her detective novels with her and dropped one into Ruth's reclining lap. It was called *The Term of Her Natural Life*.

"I heard you were a big reader," Frida said, before positioning herself on the cat-abandoned sofa and opening her own novel.

So Ruth read along with Frida. She liked the book: it was set in Australia, which charmed her, as if it had never occurred to her that ingenious crimes might be committed and solved in

her own country. The harsh cries of native birds frequently interrupted the musings of the plucky protagonist, and the seasons were all in the right places. Frida didn't speak, but the
sound of turning pages and the light of the lamps produced a
mood so confidential and snug that Ruth found she wanted
her to. She cleared her throat and asked, "What will you do for
Christmas?"

"I'll be gone by Christmas," said Frida, still reading.

"What do you mean, gone?"

Now Frida raised her head. She kept one finger on her place
in the book. "I'll take a holiday, is what I mean. I'll be out of your
hair."

"I might take a holiday myself," said Ruth.

"Ah. Richard."

"Yes."

"Good for you." Frida bent her head over her book, then
lifted it once more, with a wise expression, as if she couldn't help
herself. "It's best to take these things slow, though, isn't it. I always preach caution—look at poor George. You don't want any
nasty surprises."

Ruth remained quiet. She was unsure of what nasty surprises George might illustrate.

"What's that machine for, for one thing?" asked Frida.

"What machine?"

"The one he sleeps with. The mask over his face."

Ruth looked back at her book. She had no idea Richard slept
with a mask over his face.

"And it's not as if he hasn't surprised you before," said Frida,
with a sympathetic chuckle. "The Japanese girlfriend! Better
make sure he doesn't have another one of those up his sleeve."

Ruth's chest fell inward and her ribs felt tight against her
lungs. She made a show of reading so that Frida would stop talking. But Ruth couldn't turn the page. She read the same sentence
again and again: "Leaning warily into the burnt car, Jaqui swept

the fibres into a small transparent bag." Stiff tears stood in her eyes, and she blinked them back.

"Did you hear that?" asked Frida.

Ruth's jumping heart jumped faster. "What?"

Frida didn't answer for a few long beats. "I thought I heard something outside."

She stood. Her arms were bare and her face was flushed with red; she was in a marvellous mood. It was a cool spring evening, but the house, Ruth noticed now, was jungle hot. Here he comes, she thought, without meaning to. She was reminded of a poem she'd made her students recite: "Here comes the tiger, riding, riding, up to the old inn door."

"You go to bed," said Frida, heading into the dining room. She stood tense at the window, baring her equatorial arms, still wearing her whitish uniform.

"I'm not tired," said Ruth. But she was gathering her things— her teacup and book—and preparing to stand.

Frida was so still. "Hear that?" she said, cocking her head. "I'm going out there."

Ruth listened. "There's nothing," she said. But Frida was already outside and had closed the back door; Ruth watched her from the dining-room window. Frida stood on the grass in the window's light, her nose lifted and her head moving from side to side. The beach was empty under the spring moon, with that bare, blanched look of a seashore at night. Frida waved Ruth away from the window, and when Ruth didn't move, she waved again. The cats sniffed and howled at the closed door.

"Quiet," Ruth ordered; she shepherded them into the bedroom and turned on her bedside lamp. "She can't scare me," she said, still to the cats. She sat on her bed, and among the ordinary stirrings outside she heard Frida stepping through the brush by her window. There were three taps on the glass, and Ruth, unsure of how to respond, turned her lamp off and then on again.

Or, because it was a touch lamp—a gift from Jeffrey—she turned it dim, dimmer, off, and back to bright again. Frida moved on. She circled the house for at least the next half hour and, for the first few rounds, tapped at the window as she went; Ruth responded with her lamp, so that she imagined her window as a lighthouse over the bay: off and on, on and off, signaling both safety and danger. It was like being a girl and singing hymns with her parents; on those nights, it was as if her family sang together not towards God but against death, which pressed up at the windows but knew better than to expect an invitation. The brighter the light in the house, the safer they were, and the singing doubled and then tripled the light; the house was so luminous with the song and with the presence of her parents that it must shine out over the garden, the town, the island, all of Fiji, and the entire Pacific. This, she had understood, was how to be a light in the world. Frida stopped tapping, but Ruth continued to operate the light. After this tense half hour Frida came inside and said, "Enough with the lamp. Go to sleep."

"How could I possibly sleep?" protested Ruth. She propped up her pillows and sat unbending in the dark listening for Frida's footsteps outside her window. The cats curled at the hinges of her arms and legs. She slept and woke and slept again, still listening for Frida. An hour might have passed, or six, when she heard a cry—Frida screaming, was that possible?—and the back door rocking shut. She tapped the lamp and checked to see if the light had disturbed Harry. Of course not. There was no Harry.

"Ruth! Ruthie!" Frida called, and when she swung on the door into Ruth's room, her face was pale and her torso shook. "Thank God you're all right!"

"What is it? What happened?"

Frida collapsed onto the bed and over Ruth's legs. "Look at this!" She presented her left forearm, where three long scratches already brimmed with blood.

"What is it?" Ruth felt at that moment more curious than concerned, but she made herself lift her hands, in horror, to her mouth.

"He may have hurt me, but I scared the bejesus out of him."

"Who?"

"Who do you think?" snapped Frida.

Ruth couldn't think. George? Richard? She gathered blankets into her hands.

"I don't know how he got in," said Frida, "but I sure as hell know how he got out. I opened the door and he bolted right through. Knocked me arse up on the sand, as a matter of fact, and I'm lucky I've still got all my parts. But he gave me a good swipe. A parting gift."

Ruth sat up as best she could and looked at the curtained window. She half expected to hear three taps against it. Frida was crushing Ruth's legs, and Ruth's heart pumped a strong, slow beat. "There's no tiger," she said.

"You think I clawed my own arm?"

"He's not real."

"He's real, all right, but he's also gone, and he won't be back in a hurry. Scared him right off."

"The cats?" Ruth asked in a small voice.

"Don't you want to know how I scared him off?" Frida propped herself up with her uninjured arm and made a terrible face at Ruth: she bared her teeth and gave out a noise somewhere between a growl and a hiss, and her face was so human that Ruth was frightened. "He ran off with his tail between his legs. Ha! Some tiger." Frida lay back on the bed and laughed, as if it were typical of Ruth to have been harbouring such a timid tiger. "But"—Frida raised her wounded arm so that it waved above her like a cautionary stalk—"that doesn't mean the danger has passed."

"Let me see your arm," said Ruth. She tried to shift her legs. Frida was a set stone.

"Don't you worry about my arm. It's seen worse than a few fingernails, believe me. Stop wriggling!"

Ruth stopped. Frida, completely horizontal, shrank in on herself; her belly flattened, and her breasts. Her delicate ankles jutted out over the floor. Her hair looked black, as if she'd chosen this colour specifically for the advantage of nocturnal camouflage, and was pulled back into a jaunty ponytail. She shook her sandshoes off and fanned her toes like a peacock's tail.

"You actually saw it?" asked Ruth, whose legs were beginning to fall asleep. She could feel her buzzing blood. Frida didn't answer. "Frida?"

Frida smiled. She closed her eyes. "Oh, Ruthie," she sighed. "What on earth would you do without me?"

Ruth had no idea.

12

Frida spent the next morning building tiger traps around the house.

"I thought you scared him off," said Ruth.

"Scared him off *for now*," said Frida. "Tigers can be patient. They know all about lying in wait."

She invested most of the morning on the largest trap: a hole halfway down the dune, in the middle of the rough grassy path to the beach. When the hole was deep enough to satisfy her, she walked along the shore gathering fallen pine boughs and brought them back to fill it with. Her left forearm was bandaged to cover last night's tiger scratches, and she stretched it out to look at it from time to time, as if inspecting an engagement ring; otherwise, her arms seemed normal, capable, as she carried the branches with the sprightly bustle of a nesting bird.

"Don't walk there," Frida said, pointing out the pit.

No tiger will fall for that, thought Ruth. Already the dune was subsiding into the hole. Ruth went inside and wrote her letter to Richard. It was only supposed to be a short note, designed to seem casual and pretty, in which she would suggest they start out by having her visit for a weekend, to see the lilies, at least. "At least the lilies," she wrote, noticing, as she did so, that her handwriting was not what it once was. It was quite inexpertly square now; Mrs. Mason would be disappointed.

George's taxi rolled up to the front of the house. Ruth watched from the lounge room as Frida chattered through his open window before hauling a bundle of barbed wire from the boot. George reversed the car expertly down the drive; only then did Ruth go outside.

"Did you say anything about the tiger?"

"What do you take me for, an idiot?" said Frida, but she wasn't angry. She was genially indignant, which was one of her best moods.

"Then what does he think all this is for?" Ruth asked, indicating the wire.

"I told him it was to stop erosion." Frida smiled, as if the gulling of George was one of life's simple pleasures. She took the wire out onto the dune and wrestled with it in the grasses. Ruth worried about cats caught on hidden barbs, but Frida dismissed her fears.

"Look at them watching every move I make," she said. "They know what's going on."

The cats did sit in watchful poses, very still, which they occasionally animated with the urgent bathing of a paw.

"So the tiger is biding its time, is that it?" Ruth asked.

Frida nodded. She wore thick gardening gloves—Harry's—and they seemed to require a strict rigidity in her arms and shoulders. Only her head could move freely.

"How will we know when the time is up?"

"We won't," said Frida. "He'll just show up."

"Like a thief in the night."

"Exactly," said Frida. "Therefore: traps. I'd love to rig up a whole video system, like I bet they have in zoos." She explained to Ruth that surveillance was a hobby of George's; she looked philosophically out to sea. "A cabbie can't be too careful, you realize. Poor Georgie." Ruth felt a shiver of jealousy at this affectionate name. "He's no green thumb when it comes to growing money."

Frida was finished with her traps by early afternoon. The sky had clouded over.

"That's good," said Ruth, looking out at the garden from the dining room. "Clouds mean a warmer night."

Frida shook her head. "Tigers need shelter from the rain, just like the rest of us."

The tiger was Frida's now; and not just this tiger, but the entire species. She was proud of him, and of her arm; the heroics of the night before seemed to give her precedence in all household matters. She took milk in her tea, which she drank in front of the mirror in Ruth's bedroom—she preferred the light in there, she said, for arranging her hair—and closed the door so that Ruth knew not to follow her. When Frida reemerged, she wore her grey coat and a green scarf over her hair; under the influence of the green, her hair verged on a dark, distinguished red.

"Chilly this arvo," she said, tilting her head towards the back door, which was open and admitting a stiff wind. "Let's close this, shall we?"

"The cats are still out," said Ruth, who was a little cold herself; she was wearing a thin summer dress. She sat with her chair pulled up to the dining table, reading *The Term of Her Natural Life*. The letter to Richard lay at her elbow, snug in an envelope, addressed, and awaiting a stamp.

Frida smothered a cough. "I have a weak chest." Frida had a chest like the hull of a ship. She stood at the back door and called, without conviction, "Here, kitty kitty." Then something approximating a miaow.

"You'll scare them," said Ruth.

"All this fuss over cats, for God's sake." Frida began to gather things into her handbag. "They're not sheep, are they—now sheep are *dumb*." She swayed through the kitchen, gathering, gathering. She plucked the spare keys from the top of the fridge. "And I have plans this afternoon. I am going O.U.T." And on that final, plosive *T*, she pulled the door shut, flung its bolts home, and deadlocked it.

"I want it open," said Ruth.

"I know you do, but I can't leave you here all alone with the door open and a tiger on the loose, can I?" said Frida. "What's

this? A letter for Prince Charming? Shall I post it, Your High-
ness? Yes, no? Shall I?"

Frida swept the letter up into her quick brown fingers and
tucked it inside her coat, somewhere in the busty vicinity of her
heart.

"Give that back and open the door."

A car horn sounded from the drive.

"That'll be George," said Frida. She adjusted her green
scarf. "Don't wait up! See you soon, Bonnydoon!" She waltzed
to the front door while Ruth called, "Frida! Frida!" and there
was her merry voice greeting George, the door closing, and the
sound of the taxi driving away.

Then Ruth was alone in the house. "Shit," she said.

The front and back doors were bolted tight, and all the keys
were gone: the set in Ruth's purse, the fridge set, and even the
last-chance spare key, gummed to the bottom of one of Harry's
desk drawers. Ruth went to some trouble to look for that one;
bent and stiff-backed in Harry's study she swore again, with
greater pleasure this time, as if the word *fuck* could increase in
beauty the more care she took to say it. The cats battered the
back door in frantic longing.

"Shoosh, chickens," she crooned, pressed against the door,
which only sent them into wilder spasms; they howled like hungry babies. Ruth retreated. She was furious with Frida for locking her in and the cats out, for making fun of her with this tiger
nonsense, for taking the letter, for waltzing and teasing and acting as if she owned the place. In her anger, Ruth kicked a pile of
detective novels in the lounge room; the skidding of the books
lifted one corner of the rug, much, she imagined, as the tiger's
tail might. If he were really a tiger. If he were really a tiger, she
thought, he would be as long as the rug. He would turn the corner behind the recliner and in doing so bump the lamp; Ruth
bumped the lamp, and it fell to the floor. His tail might sweep

over the coffee table and send all the television remotes flying; they went flying, and one set of batteries rolled out. Ruth considered the mess she had made. She liked it. If I were a tiger, she thought, I wouldn't be frightened of Phil's room. Of Frida's room. This realization sent her down the hallway on soft feet.

Ruth pushed open Frida's door. She stood in the hallway and listened for the return of George's taxi, but heard only a little tick, which seemed to be coming from the room itself but was, after all, only the tiny sound of her heart behind her ears. Ruth inhaled the room's new beauty-parlour smell. Frida had turned the top of the chest-high bookshelf into a vanity: it was covered in creams, mousses, hair spray, combs of different widths, and all the other hardware of her glorious hair. Above this cache, on the wall that used to display a poster of Halley's Comet, hung an oval mirror. Ruth had trouble looking into the mirror; she suspected Frida might look back at her out of it, like a fairy-tale queen. Instead Ruth saw her own pale face and the reversed room behind it. The bed was made. Phillip's children's books were still lined up on the shelf.

Ruth opened the wardrobe and slid Frida's clothes off their hangers. They pooled at her feet. Most of them were white or off-white, the assorted parts of her daily uniform, but there were other intriguing items: a pink blouse, dark purple pants of impressive circumference, and a black dress with gold sequins stitched into the sleeves. Frida in sequins! Ruth smiled and swam among the clothes, pulling at sleeves and skirts and shuffling in the faint eucalypt odour. Touching the fabrics lifted the hair on her forearms, but she persisted until every item either lay in the bottom of the wardrobe or spilled into the room. She sifted through drawers, too. Frida's underwear seemed to fly from Ruth's fingers. The bras were particularly aerodynamic and made a lovely soft clatter as they floated to the floor. So this, thought Ruth, is what a tiger feels like, bumping and brawling; but I am not a tiger, she reminded herself. I can use tools.

Ruth fetched a broom from the kitchen and used its handle to poke at the underside of Frida's suitcase, which sat on top of the wardrobe like a long-neglected household pet. She shook and battered the case, and it made a maraca sound as it fell; bursting open, it spread a rainbow of pills and capsules over the bedroom. They crunched underfoot, except where they were caught up in Frida's clothes. Ruth recognized most of them as her own pills; she was delighted to see their picturesque array, the prescription ones all blue and sweet pale yellow, and the thick turmeric ones, and then of course the golden vials of fish oil. Those glowing capsules were the most satisfying to step on because when Ruth pressed them they resisted and bounced and then they popped.

She hadn't finished with the broom; she used it to fish under the bed, and with it she caught two boxes. The first looked official: it contained bank statements in orderly manila files. The names on these files were unfamiliar, except for one: Shelley, the name of Frida's dead sister. Shelley's surname wasn't Young, so she must have been married, and the thought of Frida at a wedding—as a bridesmaid—made Ruth feel a little guilty. So she pushed the box under the bed with one foot.

The second box was old, shoe-sized, and made of a dull, thick cardboard. Ruth, bending to pick it up, felt her back seize and burn, as if a wheel under her ribs were turning a long, hot cord up her spine. Nausea welled in her throat, her mouth filled with spit, and she threw up onto Frida's bed: a dryish welt which looked like something the cats might produce and made her laugh, but sheepishly. Before leaving the room with the box under her arm, Ruth made one last valiant plunge to the floor for a handful of pills. Most of them were the blue ones she took for her back, and she swallowed a couple down, waterless. The rest she pushed deep into the pockets of her dress.

Ruth opened the box out at the dining table. It was full of rocks and bottles of sand; small sections of glass and rock gleamed from the greasy dust. Each object was tied with twine and identified by a small shipping label. One rock was marked *Coral, various*. Another: *Brimstone fr. Volcano, 4000 ft*. Another: *Shell of the Cowrie type*. She looked more closely at this rock, wiping at it with her fingers, and a patterned shell did emerge. Ruth recognized its glossy freckles. She knew these things, and this box—she looked again at the lid and remembered the image on it, an advertisement for boot polish; she cried out and her hands trembled in the air. This box had belonged to her father.

Now Ruth went under the sink for cloths and cleaners. Her back throbbed and stung, but she ignored it; she pictured the tiny blue pills dropping down her long, dry throat into her waiting stomach. She removed every object from the box, one by one, and knew all of them. Small explosions flared in her brain; she felt them in specific places, and she could visualize them, too, as if watching a map on the evening news that identified the locations of burgeoning bushfires. Her kindling mind; the good pleasure of cleaning; every moment of discovery: all this was thrilling, was so deeply satisfying that Ruth found herself tapping her foot the way she would to music. She set to cleaning every item with a singleness of purpose she recognized as belonging to an earlier part of her life; she felt her attention as something laserlike and constant, which she could turn with great pleasure onto any item in the box and watch it emerge, minutes later, from its own ruin. Each item required specific care. The coral clung to its dust; when Ruth tried to scrub it, it disintegrated in her hands. She breathed on it gently instead, and pinched the fibrous dirt between her fingernails—how long they were, she noticed, and still sturdy, just as they'd been when she was a girl. She fetched a toothbrush to clean with, and a jar of water. Shells shone out of their grime, and Ruth listened at each one to hear the irretrievable sea. There it was—and gone—and there. She recognized the distant roar of her own blood.

In the bottom of the box, dust and bits of rock and broken shell all mingled in a filthy glitter. Ruth nudged the wastepaper basket down the hall from Harry's study to the dining room. She loaded it up with dirty cloths and papers and shook the box out over it. Then she replaced the lid, from which a dark, happy shoeshining boy smiled up with oversized teeth. She lay the box down next to her chair.

"Now look," said Ruth, to nobody; to herself. She had forgotten Frida, and even the cats.

Everything was clean. Everything was laid out on the table, orderly and labelled; nothing touched anything else. Small bottles of brown and blue glass looked as if they'd been fished, moments before, from the sea. Inside each one, mysterious substances settled and slept. The shells were now pink and purple again, flesh-coloured, immodest. They nestled into themselves like ears.

Ruth wanted to share all this with someone. It should, she thought, have been Harry; she called Richard's number. It rang four times and then clicked and popped; there was Richard's voice, but with a mechanical buzz to it, as if he were still a smoker. I can't come to the phone right now, he said, and his was an old man's voice, an ending.

"Richard?" she said. "It's Ruth."

The line exploded with sound—there was that same young woman's voice saying "Hello? Ruth?" and Ruth was sure she heard laughter in the background, and one laugh in particular: she rarely heard it, but when she did, it was a golden, bouncing swell, a brass ring, and unmistakable. It was—Ruth was quite sure—Frida. What could Frida be doing at Richard's house? And in fright she hung up the telephone. It rang again, naturally; Ruth lost track of the number of times. She sat in her chair and watched a strange yellow haze pass over her eyes, as if a cloud, in crossing the sun, had been half burnt away by its light. Bright circles formed in this fog, and they pulsed in time with the ringing of the telephone. Ruth watched them even with her eyes closed; they seemed to stick to her eyelids, so she took another pill to make them go away. The phone stopped, finally, and she might have been asleep; her sleep was dusty and angular, punctuated by swimming light. Somewhere in it, she saw the sea running up and over the dune, muddying the carpets and rising and rising, until strange shelled animals clung to the lower walls and fronds that were either worms or the homes of worms beckoned from the skirting boards. Then there was nothing but wreckage and ruin. She saw herself and Frida floating on a raft fashioned from the back door. Frida used the broom as a pole and punted them, like a Venetian gondolier, towards the triumphant pennants of the surf club.

This vague sleep broke when Frida returned; Ruth heard her coming through the front door, and she noticed the end of the day's light hanging reflected in the east.

"Ruthie?" Frida called, and she bustled into the dining room in a tremendous mood, unwrapping the green scarf from her hair. She looked browner than she had when she left, and her hair seemed a different shade of flattering bronze.

"What a day!" she sang.

She gave a girlish laugh and claimed to have gained two pounds, and she patted Ruth's arm as she passed by on her way to the kitchen. It was as if she'd been away for three weeks. In her arms, she carried a load of pink lilies wrapped in Christmas paper. She dumped them on the countertop before fishing in the fridge for her yoghurt, which she ate straight from the container while leaning against the wall and explaining that George had taken her to a beach far away, "so I could sun myself like a frog on a log." On some days Frida was furious with George; on other days he was inviolate. This was one of those saintly days. "It's so necessary to be with family," said Frida, her spoon dripping with yoghurt. "You know I'm crazy about you, Ruthie, but it's not the same thing. And time away gives you a chance to think about what you want from life. Believe me, you'll see some changes."

"Those are beautiful lilies," said Ruth. "Where are they from?"

"Mum's house. What's all this junk?"

"It's my father's. It isn't junk."

"Are they antiques?" Frida butted the table with one curious hip; a blue bottle began to roll. Ruth caught it with the tips of her fingers. Her head felt a little clearer now, but everything she saw was strangely luminous.

"I suppose they're old. They've survived war and shipwreck, these things. Well, not shipwreck. But they did survive. Even just the sea they survived—the shells."

"Are they worth anything?"

"Oh, now, Frida—goodness!" Ruth gave a miniature laugh. The lilies burned on the countertop; it was easier not to look at them. "I doubt any of it's worth anything. Just personal value."

"But you could take it to someone, couldn't you, and find out? George'll know. He knows about this stuff."

"I wouldn't sell my father's things."

Frida prodded a glittering rock. "This looks valuable. It looks like silver."

"It's only mica," said Ruth. "Look at the label. Your mother grew lilies?"

"And then there's the insurance. Think of that! What if the house burned down—this stuff might be worth millions."

Frida touched the curve of a shell with her finger and watched it vibrate against the table.

"That's pretty," said Ruth. "Shell music."

Frida touched another. It was a spotted shell, but she wasn't really looking at it; something else had occurred to her. "Ruthie," she said, "where did you find all this?"

"There used to be other shells, too—big ones. What do you call those big ones? Starts with a *c*? Not conches. Cowries."

"Cowries aren't that big."

"We had some big ones with island scenes etched in. They must be around somewhere."

Frida bent to the floor; the action seemed so effortless, so well-oiled. When she stood again, she had the box in her hand; she rubbed its sides with her big thumbs and looked into its empty corners. The expression on her face was one of recognition, as if she, too, remembered the box from childhood.

"That's my father's," said Ruth. "It's mine."

Frida didn't speak. She held the box to her chin to inspect it further; then she turned into the hallway, towards her room, and Ruth began to recall what she would find there.

"You locked me in!" Ruth called. She rose from her chair and hurried to the lilies—it was easy, when she had taken multiple pills, to rise and hurry. The lilies were still damp. Ruth tore the wrapping paper away in order to be closer to them. Each petal was flooded with pink, but the centres paled out to blond, and the stamens, which shook as Ruth held them to her face, were loaded with dusty yellow. Frida bellowed from her room; Ruth fenced herself in with lilies. They smelled both clean and definite. They smelled of a saltless garden.

Frida was quiet coming back down the hallway. Still holding the box, she stepped into the kitchen as if walking out onto a rickety jetty. Her shoulders were drawn back and her chest was full of air, as if she were about to recite the days of the week; but she didn't. She didn't even shout. She looked at Ruth among her flowers and said, "Those aren't yours."

Ruth held tighter to the lilies. "They're from Richard," she said.

"Poor dear crazy. Give them here."

"I'm not crazy."

"Confused, then. As usual, poor Ruthie's just a bit confused."

"No," said Ruth, but she recognized the word *confused* as approaching what she was, after her sticky, bright dream.

"All right," said Frida. "Let's see. How old are you?"

"Seventy-five."

"What colour are my eyes?"

"Brown."

"And what's the capital of Fiji?"

"Suva."

"No it isn't."

"It is," said Ruth. "I lived there. I should know."

"You *don't* know," said Frida. "You only *think* you do. That's what I'm talking about—confused! Now that's cleared up, maybe you can tell me what you were doing in my room."

"It's my room. My lilies."

"Give them to me. I'll put them in some water."

"No."

Frida came no closer to Ruth. She held her arm out with the box at the end of it, as if it might be the perfect receptacle for flowers; then she turned and threw it into the wastepaper basket that sat beside Ruth's chair.

Ruth winced. "I know you were at Richard's house. Why? Why was my box under your bed?"

"What were you doing looking under my bed?"

"You locked me in."

"I didn't lock anybody in!" Frida cried. She was in the kitchen now, tearing at the wrapping paper, which was wet from the lilies and stuck to her angry fingers. She shook it off into the wastepaper bin. "I closed the door so you wouldn't go wandering out there with all the traps in the grass. The bloody doors weren't locked."

But Ruth had tried the doors. She had tried them. "What do you want?" she asked, because it occurred to her that Frida wanted something from her—was always wanting, wanting, without ever quite admitting it.

"I want you to apologize for trashing my room," said Frida. "For wrecking my stuff and for disrespecting my privacy. I want you to give me those lilies, and I want you to admit Suva isn't the capital of Fiji."

Ruth shook her head.

"All right then," Frida said, and, her face expressionless, used her forearm to sweep the objects across the dining table. They clattered over the surface, catching and dragging, and the bottles tipped and rolled to the left and right, but they were all carried by Frida's arm to the table's edge, and then they fell into the wastepaper bin. None of the glass shattered; everything fell neatly and quietly, almost as if the objects were taking up their original places, snug in the bin as they had been in the box. It was like a magic trick. Then Frida lifted the bin and held it on her hip like an awkward baby; she opened the door with one quick hand and, still matronly, marched into the garden.

Ruth couldn't understand how the door had opened; but she was safe behind her lilies. She followed and watched as Frida shook the contents of the bin out over the edge of the dune. Some of the shells and coral bounced a little before rolling, and all the grit and dust swarmed up in a grubby cloud before puffing away, abruptly, as if with a specific destination in mind. The box flew from the bin and caught a little in the coastal wind; it only subsided among the grasses after a short, desperate flight. Then Frida threw her arms out, so that the wastepaper basket swung high into the low sun and spun onto the beach.

Ruth stood beside Frida at the crest of the dune. The lilies were growing heavier in her arms. Down the slope, the coral and shells were beginning their primordial crawl back to the sea.

"Those things belong to my family," Ruth said.

"A little life lesson for you, Ruthie," said Frida. "Don't get attached to *things*."

Ruth began to test out the slope of the dune with one foot. Frida was grinning into the salt of the wind. There was a tremendous well-being about her, and she lifted her face to the sky

as if feeling the sun for the first time in months. Frida often gave
off an impression of posthibernation. She was a great brown
bear, a slumbering hazard, both dozy and vigilant. And Ruth
was used to her slow surety of movement; but now she had woken up.

"You're an awful woman," said Ruth, and Frida gave a
gnomic titter. The chalky sand rubbed at Ruth's bare feet. "A savage woman." Frida laughed harder, with that same round gong
Ruth had heard on the telephone. Ruth pointed down the dune
with her lilies. "I want everything back."

Frida dusted her hands and emitted the sigh she often did
immediately before standing up. "Two things," she said. "First of
all, apologize. Second, tell me Suva isn't the capital of Fiji. Then
I'll pick it all up for you. Otherwise, you can do it yourself."

Ruth began to descend. She still clung to the lilies. This was
the very worst request to make of her back: to walk down a
steep slope with her arms full. She bent into the dune and it fell
away beneath her; she kicked up whirlwinds of sand.

Frida watched from above. "Mind your step," she said.

Ruth moved forward and the grass collapsed; she felt her feet
slide, and then she was lying on the ground with the lilies scattered over and around her. She wriggled them off. She didn't
think she was hurt; it didn't even feel like a fall. It was as if the
dune had scooped her up, and she was caught in a shallow,
sandy bowl.

"Oh, Ruthie," said Frida from above.

"What is it?" asked Ruth from among the grasses, but she
knew she had fallen into the tiger trap. It had filled considerably
in the hours since its construction; now it cradled Ruth. It was
fragrant with lilies. She closed her eyes and opened them again,
and the world bumped up against her and tilted away. She was
lying on her side. Ants moved among the sand, over and under
each grain, and all of this was too close to Ruth's nose. Above

her she saw the very edge of the lawn, or what remained of it. It was a frayed rug of green. It was the only kind of civilized grass that consented to grow here—a tough, shiny species with strenuous roots. Harry never liked it; it wasn't soft enough, he said, and it contrasted too much with the sand. Ruth was able to roll onto her back, and then the sky appeared, a dark, blank blue. She felt a dizzy sting behind her eyes.

"Any bones broken?" called Frida.

Ruth looked to every bone for information, and each reassured her. But her back was burning. She felt around in the sand for some kind of handhold and found a small mineral lump with string still attached. A flurry of sand from above suggested Frida might be coming down the dune.

"Don't!" Ruth cried.

"Please yourself." Frida sighed again, and the sound was both resigned and happy. The sand settled. "You know, this is exactly what I said to Jeff. I said to him, it just isn't safe to have an old girl like your mother living in this kind of environment. She walks in the garden, and what do you know, she slips and falls. I've seen a fall do someone in—never the same again. And that's why I'm here twenty-four hours a day." The sea sounded close, and something tickled in Ruth's ear. "But does Jeff ever thank me? Does he ever ring me up and say, 'Frida, you're the ant's pants'?"

Some sand scattered across Ruth's forehead. She wasn't sure if the wind was at fault, or Frida. She tried to sit up and found that she couldn't. "I can't get up," she said, but not to Frida; to herself.

"Not with that attitude, you can't."

"I really can't," said Ruth, still to herself. She would have liked to see one cloud in the sky. That would have been fluffy and merry and in some way comforting. If I see a cloud, she thought, it means I'll get up again. It means I haven't fallen.

"Take me, for instance," said Frida. "If I went around all day saying, 'I can't, I can't,' I'd get nowhere. What you need is some positive thinking. Say to yourself, 'I *will* get up.' Then do it."

Ruth moved one foot experimentally.

"Too many people in this country are old before their time," Frida sighed.

"Frida." Ruth heard the bleat in her voice. Her body wouldn't move. "I think I'm paralysed."

Ruth felt something tickle at her forehead, like a handful of thrown grass; she knocked it away with her right hand.

"Not paralysed," said Frida. "See? So negative. You know, this might be good for you. Give you a bit of a challenge, break you out of your can't can't can't and show you your actions have consequences. I'll be inside, Ruthie, tidying your mess. And one day you'll thank me for this." Frida inhaled loudly, as if she were filling her lungs with the sea, and then she was gone. Sand rose in her wake and settled over other sand. The back door opened and closed again.

Now the cats emerged from wherever they had been hiding. They sniffed at Ruth's cheeks and shoulders. One of them curled against her side. The dune had shifted to accommodate her, and it was pleasant to think—or at least less frightening to think— that eventually this hollow would shape itself around her and be perfectly moulded to her back and bones. Then she would sleep the way she had as a child, when everything was supple and new and it was possible to abandon her body entirely, night after night, without ever knowing how lucky that was. Something whirred in the grasses near her head, some insect, and it occurred to Ruth that Frida's tiger might be nearby. He might come as night fell and find her. Frida might make him come; she might make him a real tiger, with real teeth. This alarmed Ruth into action. She would have to make her way back to the house, even if it took her all night, and then she would run. She would go to Richard: find his address on the envelope she had saved, take the bus into town, catch the train to Sydney. Ruth felt around with her hands and caught at the grasses; the grass cut into her palms, little quick slits, as she pulled herself into a half-sitting position. The cat at her side leapt away, indignant. Her hips were a faulty hinge, and she fell to the sand again.

Ruth's back objected to all of this. She often imagined her back as an instrument; that way she could decide if the pain was playing in the upper or lower registers. Sometimes it was just a long, low note, and sometimes it was insistent and shrill. To Ruth, lying in the sand, it was both. It was a whole brassy, windy ensemble. She cried out, but there was no one to hear her. The lifesavers would be sitting in their flagged turrets down at the surf club, scanning the sun and the sea, ready to pack up for the day; they didn't know she was drowning. The wind was a little cold. Perhaps, if she lay still enough, it would make her a coverlet of sand.

The cats watched her from the grasses. They seemed to be encouraging her with their dumbstruck eyes. This is what you get, she thought, for living on a beach, not a road; and that was Harry's fault, since Harry had insisted on this isolation and then killed them both with it. Because now she felt she was in danger of dying out on the dune, and that Frida had been trying, all along, to bring her to this point—had sent a tiger, and built traps, and now was trying to kill her. And Ruth was sure, too, that if Harry had stayed in Sydney and walked every day beside the Harbour the way he used to, he would still be alive; he would have been whisked to a state-of-the-art hospital, where the business of saving the lives of stupid old men happened every day. Not that she blamed the girl who picked him up from the gutter. What was her name? Ellen something. Jeffrey had told her this Ellen Something had held Harry's head as he died. What a stupid old isolated head. Now Ruth lay dying in a tiger trap, and no one was there—not even Frida—to cradle any part of her.

She might have cried, but one of the cats had climbed onto her chest and was clawing lovingly at it. She felt the fraying of her thin skin. In shifting to shake the cat off, Ruth managed to lift herself onto her elbows. This presented new possibilities. She saw her feet now, and that thin sickle was the edge of the sea. If she pushed her feet towards the water and kept her elbows propped underneath her, she could manage a slow backwards shuffle up the dune. She reversed an experimental inch and her back didn't make any special objection. At first this filled her with wild energy. She thought of the grim joy of mountaineers trapped on glaciers, who realize they can cut off their own crushed arms. An inch later, she lay back in the sand, exhausted, and slid a little way towards the beach. She wasn't overly disheartened, because she had accepted that this would take hours. Part of her welcomed the effort of it; it was so allegorical. The fight for life! Ruth was quick to feel sorry for herself, and quick to congratulate. This was deliberate on her part; a lifelong mechanism which in her opinion had served her well. She lifted her elbows and began her backwards crawl.

Everything was millimetres away, particularly the sea and the ending sun, but the house was impossibly far. Whenever she paused, she slipped down the dune, and those were precious millimetres lost; but if she didn't rest, her eyes filled with the pain of her back, and her arms seemed to melt away. Then she had to lie back in the sand and stretch her arms out on either side of her, like wings; or she stretched them down over her body, to touch her thighs. She felt lumps in her skirt, fished in her pockets, and found pills. One more can't hurt, she thought, and she swallowed a pill dry, gagging on her own sandy spit. Then she raised herself up and started again. This may have happened more than once. She learned to turn her feet outward to brace herself against the sand, and to hold on to the roots of the grass, which helped slow her slide. Her rests grew longer and the cats lost interest. Ruth felt the way she did on plane rides: empty, suspended, and consumed by the inconvenience of urination. She knew she had kicked free of the tiger trap when there were no longer any lilies around her feet.

The sun dropped before Ruth reached the edge of the garden. She was moving faster now; the grass was thicker, and she rarely slid. She rested half on the dune and half on the lawn and wondered if, summoning her strength, she might make one magnificent final burst for the house. This summoning of her strength took some time. A bright star came out—or was it Venus? Harry knew the constellations. He had taught her some way to look at Venus and figure out the direction of the pole. Or was that in the northern hemisphere? The sky was still bluer than the sea, but the lights were coming on in the town across the water, the Milky Way was scattering, and soon Frida's tiger might run along the beach under the stars of that galaxy.

There was no sign of life from the house until the sky grew darker; then one window was lit, and another, so that half of Ruth's body lay in shadow and the other half in a yellow square. Whose hand lit those lamps? Ruth couldn't be sure. Frida's, of course; but it might also have been Harry's, and maybe her own. Until now she had never experienced vertigo while lying down. She thought she heard a male voice inside the house, but it might be the television. The cats were nearby begging for their dinner, but Ruth refused to join their chorus. She would never cry out. She lifted herself again and now was almost walking on her elbows, dragging her feet along; she made it to the house. She used the wall to reach a full sitting position, and she rested with her head against it, by the back door.

It was peaceful in the garden. It was so separate. The evening seemed to be stalling, to only reluctantly be growing dark. Ruth lay against the wall and thought of Frida inside the house, waiting for her arrival, but at the same time she was inside with Frida, sitting in her chair and being tended to. She was both in and out of the house; she was away from Frida, but bound to her; she was hungry. The cats cried out again—what a noise they could make, those tiny things—and finally somebody opened the door and stood above Ruth without speaking; all she could see was the light. Arms attempted to lift her, but she resisted them. She let her body go limp and drag, and eventually the arms gave up. Then the door closed. Someone was moving in the kitchen, feeding the cats and singing and cooking sausages. The fat smell of the sausages cleared Ruth's mind. It came to her that the box hadn't belonged to her father. It was Harry's—it had come from his family, from the Solomon Islands, and it had nothing to do with her. How was it possible to forget a thing like that?

If the box wasn't her father's and the doors hadn't been locked, then maybe Suva wasn't the capital of Fiji. And what did that matter? There was so little of Fiji left to remember. There was only this feeling, which everyone must have about their childhood, that it was extraordinary in some way. But she had been to a royal ball. Ruth saw the small figure that was the Queen at the ball. It was funny to watch a queen grow old; it made Ruth feel as if she hadn't grown at all. But of course they both had. They had expanded, as they must, into their responsibilities. She wondered if that was the point of a queen, if you had to have one: that she should help you mark the passage of time, because you saw every year how her profile on the backs of coins became softer with age, but at the same time she stopped you from noticing time at all, in the sense that she seemed fixed and immovable on her distant throne. How unlikely she appeared from here, on the ground, in the night, on the other side of the world. But there was something to knowing that one day, in 1953, they had been in the same place at the same time. So Ruth felt proprietary when Phillip talked about how unnecessary the Queen was, how anachronistic, and when she protested, citing the Queen's dignity and suffering, Jeffrey was always careful to say, "We have nothing against her personally, Ma."

"Yeah," Phillip would say, "I'm sure she's the salt of the earth."

But didn't salt stop the earth from producing greenery? Didn't crops never again grow in fields sown with salt? So who would want to be the salt of the earth? And didn't salt come from the sea? The salt of the earth, then, was sand. And Frida hated sand. Ruth thought she would wake up one morning and find that Frida had swept all of it into the sea. She imagined Frida with a great broom sweeping at the sea, and the obedient waves swallowed everything she threw at them. The beach would lie empty and open: rock and fossil, the immodest bones of dinosaurs, great petrified sea monsters, the ashy ends of ancient fires. After Frida, everything would be clean, white, and extinct. She would soap it all up with eucalyptus, and only then would she be happy. Ruth couldn't tell if she wanted Frida to be happy. This seemed to be something Ruth had once—perhaps quite recently—held a position on. Frida, Frida, Queen of Sheba. And there, with the Queen in attendance, was Richard kissing Ruth—but all the time loving someone else. The thought of this—Richard's loving someone else, loving her, or perhaps both, or perhaps it was the same thing—became, then, more exhausting than climbing the dune. It became juniper trees and pirate granddaughters and funerals, when she, Ruth, wasn't even sure how she would stand up again.

There was a noise from behind her, a creaking, and then arms lifted Ruth out of the garden. She was too tired to oppose them. No one said a word, but doors opened and closed, and then she was lying on her bed. She drank water and swallowed some pills; after that, no one fussed. Ruth lay and lay and became hungry and restless, but because no one came to her, she fell asleep. Her back didn't hurt her in the morning, and the sun

was inviting in the grass. Ruth felt she was the only one awake in
the house: no husbands, no boys, no one else stirring. She rolled
up from the bed and found her handbag in Harry's study; her
coin purse was inside it. Ruth knew, without quite understanding why, that she must act quickly and make no sound. The
front door did squeal a little as she closed it behind her.

The grasses in the shaded drive were so tall! It must be a
good harvest. This was the way Harry walked in the mornings,
out into the drive and onto the road, and so Ruth walked to the
road and looked down the hill. She was surprised to see people
at the bus stop. They crowded around it as if something dramatic were taking place. She made her careful way down the
hill. What a spread the sea made from here, finer somehow with
the road running alongside it. A particular glassy quality to its
surface meant it lacked colour and was only shine; but by the
shore it turned green. Ruth remembered explaining to her children that the glitter on the water was the reflection of a thousand thousand suns off each new angle made by the waves;
every point of light was the sun, repeated. She must walk this
way more often.

The people at the bus stop, it seemed, were not gathered for
a disaster, but for the bus. They had come sandily from the
beach—the sky in that direction suggested rain. The thought of
rain worried Ruth, but she felt strangely placid, at a remove
from the particulars of her life, and simultaneously at one with
the pleasurable fates of the people around her, as if they were all
waiting together at the gates of heaven. The bus arrived. She
fumbled with her coins and had to be helped; the driver selected
the correct change out of her palm, a bird after worms. A courteous young boy vacated his seat for her. She sat, feeling sentimental towards herself, feeling beloved and assisted, and
watched as the displaced boy swayed farther up the bus. The
rear windows depicted, like a painting, a heavyset woman

descending the hill. Grey clouds fell into the sea. The windows were moving away from the woman. Oh, but she would be left behind! Ruth cried out, although she felt no distress. The man across the aisle cast a sceptical look in her direction, and Ruth smiled. Together they had all crested the next hill by the time Frida reached the bus stop.

13

The bus deposited Ruth on a hillside street where she expected shops and the railway station—and found only houses. Their tiled roofs were deep orange; they flared up against the colour of the sea like a warning against tidal wave or flood. The horizon felt higher than it ought to, so that the sea tilted dizzily down over the houses and Ruth found it necessary to walk with her hand touching their low brick fences. She remembered this street after all. She'd walked here once with Jeffrey, when he was a boy. He dropped a coin and it rolled beneath a parked car; she risked her back to recover it for him. He didn't cry, but stood with his fists tight and an expression of unbearable suspense on his face. When she returned the coin, he thanked her so formally, and with such solemn grace, that he seemed like a foreign child accepting some attention from a tourist. Then he spent it, minutes later, on a tea bun, and was his sticky, happy self again.

A large red dog walked down the middle of the street. It moved its head from side to side, attentive, as if it were hunting. Ruth stayed pressed against the fences. She admired the houses, which were neat and unassuming, with white-framed windows sheltered by awnings and brick fences the same red as the dog. One of these houses might belong to Frida's mother. Ruth's shoulders had begun to ache, as if she'd been lifting heavy objects all night long.

She turned a corner and found herself on the main street of town. The shops nestled together in tidy rows; it felt like Christmas because lights were strung up across the road. Perhaps there were always lights now, to make shopping feel festive. She remembered the merriness of the butcher, who displayed annual signs declaring him the South Coast Sausage King. This was an official title, apparently, won year after year and jealously guarded. A taxi drove down the street and Ruth hid from it in the shade of the butcher's doorway. That meant she blocked the opening door, and she and the door and the person behind it were forced to do a sprightly little dance, and the person, a woman, turned out to know her.

"Mrs. Field! Ruth!" cried this woman. She was so very small—"petite," Ruth's mother would have called her—that she made Ruth think of a little toy prised from behind the door of an expensive Advent calendar. Ruth tried to arrange her face into an expression of recognition; she must have failed because the woman said, with a hopeful smile, "It's Ellen?"

"Oh, Ellen!" said Ruth, and in saying the name aloud did remember her as Ellen Gibson. "But how funny! Do you live here, too?"

"Yes. Yes, of course," said Ellen. "I've been meaning to call you. It's so nice to see you again."

Ruth beamed. Yes, it was *nice*—what a true word that was, how fine and underrated. It meant more than kindness; it meant a fastidious effort to be thoughtful and good. To be nice in this world, thought Ruth, was to be considered—what? Milky and feeble, she thought; fragile. But Ruth valued niceness, and so did Ellen Gibson. This was their bond; this was why Ellen would stop her car to ask after an elderly man of distinguished bearing, breathing strangely on the side of the road.

"And how are you doing these days?" asked Ellen.

"I'm doing very well, my dear. And of course I have Frida to help me." Ruth recognized Frida, then, as a shield of some kind; she seemed to be wielding her. "Frida cooks everything and cleans. She's my right arm."

"I'm so pleased," said Ellen. "What brings you into town this morning? Some shopping?"

At this moment, Ruth was unsure what had brought her into town. She had an idea that her business would eventually lead in the direction of the railway station.

"Can I drive you somewhere?" Ellen was asking. "I'd be happy to take you home. I love driving out that way."

Ruth wanted to accept because it would please Ellen so much. Wasn't it wonderful to please people? But that was impossible. "I don't want to go home," she said.

"All right," said Ellen. She wore sunglasses pushed up into her hair; that was why light flashed from the top of her head. "Can I take you somewhere else?"

"I have some shopping." Ruth looked in her purse for her to-do list. She always brought a to-do list to town with her, and today it was missing—wasn't that just typical? But she was there at the butcher's. "Sausages," she said, and the butcher's door sang as she opened it; inside, the shop had a cold, bloody smell. Ellen remained for a moment in the street with a look of surprise on her face, but Ruth refused to let that worry her. The South Coast Sausage King stood behind the counter, chatting and joking, while his courtiers ordered lamb chops and steak. He knew her name, too; did everybody?

"Mrs. Field!" he called.

She felt quite famous. This might have been why he won that prize, year after year; not for his sausages, but for his memory. Ruth used to know the name of the Sausage King. He used to hold a barbecue for his "favourite customers" in the New Year, when Ruth and her family were always at the coast for the summer; she had been to his house. He barbecued with fierce pride and made people taste everything. He winked at her now, which was his way of saying, "I don't want to serve this woman, I want to serve you; I can't wait to serve you," and flattered, Ruth waited her turn. She and Harry used to laugh about the jolly flirtations of the Sausage King. They never offended any husband. She had known this man for nearly forty years.

"Mrs. Field," he said now, turning towards her. He was tall and merry and trim. She remembered there had been some heartbreak over a son who didn't want to be a butcher; or maybe the trouble was that he did. The Sausage King wore a striped apron and seemed to have absolutely no hair on his arms. His hands were big and pink, and youthful from the handling of all that meat.

"We haven't seen you in town for months," he said, twinkling. "Tell me where you've been hiding."

That was another thing she remembered: he always used the royal plural, as if speaking for both himself and his sausages. But what was his name?

"Nowhere, nowhere," she said, bashful. He always made her blush, and she supposed this was how she knew his attentions were harmless. "I have someone to shop for me now."

Frida bought all their meat in styrofoam and plastic from the supermarket, but he didn't know that. Still, Ruth felt the guilt as a new heat on her face.

"It's just a treat to see you," he said, and turned to the other people in the shop—people younger than Ruth and the Sausage King. "Mrs. Field is one of my oldest and most loyal customers. We've known each other since before you were all born."

Ruth blushed further. No one in the shop was that young, but she might have been that old.

"And what can I get for you today?" he asked. "The lamb is a miracle, the spring lamb."

"Oh, yes, lamb. From New Zealand."

"Australian lamb, Mrs. Field! Always! Now—a roast? Chops?"

"Oh, dear," said Ruth. The other customers began to stir with polite exasperation. Many of them had been in the shop before the arrival of the steadfast Mrs. Field. "Chops," she said, because Frida would scold about a roast. Frida, returning home from the supermarket, talked at great length about the expense of groceries in this day and age.

"Chops it is. How many? How many?" sang the Sausage King. His busy pink hands worked over the lamb chops, selecting good specimens and shifting the plastic parsley. "Five ninety-nine a kilo, five-fifty for you." The customers shook their heads at the lovable favouritism of the Sausage King.

"Five-fifty," said Ruth.

"One kilo it is. Anything else I can do for you today?" He wrapped the lamb in waxy white paper. Ruth loved the cool weight of butchers' bundles; they reminded her of babies.

"That's all," she said, wishing she could be sure it really was.

"No sausages? I tell you what, I'll throw a couple in, on the house." Now the shop threatened mutiny. The door opened and the bell rang; someone was leaving. The Sausage King swaddled the sausages in white paper. Ruth saw him wink at another woman; he would serve her next. "And that's five-fifty for Mrs. Field."

Ruth nodded. She opened her purse and there was no money in it, except for the few coins she had left after the bus fare. The only other thing in there was a library card. "Goodness," she said. "I've forgotten my purse."

The Sausage King looked at the purse in her hands.

"I mean, it's empty. What a duffer!"

He was poised with the smooth white packages. "Not to worry, not to worry," he reassured, but he grinned now at the other customers. His grin said, "Silly old bird." It said, "Stupid, stupid, and old, old, old." Once, when he was still young, he had presented her sons with hats folded out of butcher's paper; they had loved them for a whole afternoon.

"I can't think—" began Ruth, but the woman who had been winked at stepped up, businesslike, although determinedly kind, and passed six dollars to the Sausage King.

"There now!" he cried, as if a spring-lamb miracle truly had come to pass. How he trusted and loved the world; it was everywhere on his face. He patted the woman's hand. She would be invited to the New Year's barbecue.

"Oh, thank you, thank you so much," said Ruth, taking possession of her packages and their smooth infant weight. She had some idea of sending Frida to her saviour's house with six dollars, but the woman was ordering now—a complicated order, designed for a family, which called on all the skills of the delighted butcher. Her expression was resolutely against interruption or further gratitude.

"Goodbye, Mrs. Field!" the Sausage King called, and Ruth waved from among her parcels and empty purse, and a woman opened the door for her. The bell shook. When she passed into the street, the customers laughed at some joke he made. Ruth hated him and his lusty courtesies. Harry was truly kind; truly chivalrous. None of it was for show. She would tell him that, when she got home, and she would also conceal the embarrassing free meat from Frida, who frequently expressed her contempt for handouts, freeloaders, and anyone who didn't perform honest hard labour for her money. Frida would never hear about the empty purse or the helpful, mortifying woman or the temptation of the lamb roast, and she wouldn't be angry. To believe this filled Ruth with busy purpose. Where to next? The street was lined with conveniences. Next door was the chemist, across the road was the bakery, and farther down was the bank. She wondered why she didn't come to town more often. Where had she parked the car? She was always forgetting that. No—she had caught the bus. And at the end of the street was the railway station, where the trains pulled out for Sydney every three hours. Why should that be such a comforting thought? Her arms still ached.

Two boys waited outside the chemist with that particular alert boredom of boys who have been promised a reward for their patience. They watched every passing car with interest; whenever the street was empty, their shoulders fell; their feet stepped over each other, shifting their bantam weights, like newly foaled giraffes. They had boyish faces, choral and virtuous, as if cast in a Nativity play, and long light hair which they threw out of their eyes with a beautiful backwards motion of the head. They were maybe nine and eleven. The older boy was sure of his gestures—the movement of his head, the stepping of his feet— and the younger one copied him, so their resemblance seemed less genetic and more an act of desperate study. Ruth's heart was burdened with love for these boys, who waited outside the chemist and cancelled out the Sausage King. They wore blue-and-grey school uniforms. In the shadow of the striped awning they waited and slouched, and because they had been so patient, she would buy them a milk shake each, or an ice cream if they wanted it. Surely she had enough coins for that.

Ruth hurried to them with her hands outspread; her purse dropped right at their feet, and the oldest boy picked it up for her. He was nearly as tall as she was and handed her the purse with a bashful elegance, almost feminine, which drew his features into a courtly mask.

"Thank you, my darling!" cried Ruth, and embraced him.

"S'all right," he said, in that gulping growl of boys on the very verge of change, and she released his rigid shoulders.

"You're such good boys for waiting so quietly. How about a milk shake?" Ruth held her hand out to the youngest boy, who hung back behind his brother and looked at her as if she had committed some fascinating faux pas, right there on the street. But Ruth knew the way boys could behave when they reached a certain age; she knew to ignore the discouraging twinge it produced in her throat. She shook her hand at him again, cheerfully. "What do you say? A milk shake, or do you want ice cream? You've certainly earned it."

"Mum," he said, and he seemed startled and perhaps a little

afraid, and he looked past her at a woman who was leaving the chemist.

"Hello again!" said the woman; she was Ellen Gibson. "Have you met my boys? This is Brett, and this is Jamie. Boys, this is Mrs. Field."

The boys nodded their blond heads, and their bodies seemed to dip in brief curtsies. They had the same shy smile. Their names were Brett and Jamie. They seemed to have agreed to conceal some residual awkwardness from their mother.

"You've got your meat, Ruth? Can I take you home now?"

Ruth looked towards the railway station. How would she pay for a train, with only a library card? And also—the meat would spoil.

The boys were already walking; Ellen was walking. So was Ruth. She was being led. The sea retreated, as if it had been winched down to its proper level, and that was a kind of surrender.

"This way. Mine's the red car." Ellen smiled and nodded, that same curtsey of the head her sons made. "I'll drop the boys at school first, if that's all right? They're late today, they've been to the dentist."

The boys, already belted into the back of the car, groaned on cue, as if appalled to have had their dentistry made public. Ruth sensed an injustice; she suspected her seat had been promised to one of them for the ride, and now she'd usurped it.

"Oh, dear," she said, because she couldn't manage her own seat belt. Ellen snapped it into place while Ruth held her hands, as if at gunpoint, on either side of her downcast face.

The school wasn't far away; the boys ran towards the entrance and seemed to fall into it. Ruth was amazed they could do anything at all on those long feet. "They're going to be very tall, aren't they," she said.

Ellen smiled and nodded. "Just like their father." She was proud of them; she watched until they were out of sight.

"Isn't it funny to watch children grow."

Ellen said, "It's a privilege."

Ruth scrutinized this possibility. No, she thought; it's melancholy and strange. Children were so temporary. When Jeffrey was born, Harry stroked his son's nose and said, "What's amazing is that this is *forever*." But it wasn't forever; it wasn't even a month. In a few weeks Jeffrey was different, and the blind, bumping, waterlogged Jeffrey was gone; he was rosy and plump; he butted at her face the way the cats did. It came to her that she missed her children, not as they were now, with their own children, but as they had been when they were young. She would never see them again. Jeffrey on the beach when the house was still for holidays; Phillip's failing breath; their small hands. She wanted—very badly—to say "Fuck."

"Now let's get you home," said Ellen.

"Do you know the way?" asked Ruth, because she herself was unsure.

"Yes. But you might have to remind me where to turn in."

Ruth tried to picture where to turn in and saw only grass—long, pale grass with a tiger in it. She smiled vaguely. She was so comfortable in the car, which Ellen handled with such confidence. The town passed, and the sea. The suggestion of rain had vanished now, and the pale sky tended cloudlessly towards white. Ellen wanted to know what Ruth had been up to; if she'd had visitors; if she'd been getting out and enjoying the weather. "How are your sons?" she asked, and Ruth said, "They're going to be very tall."

"How often do you come into town?"

"Not nearly enough. You know how it is. Busy busy busy."

"Oh, yes," said Ellen.

"You know how it is. You're a mother."

"And you have someone looking after you?"

"I'm very well cared for," said Ruth. The car advanced so easily. "Not only that, I'm *defended*."

"Defended? Against what?"

Ruth noted the wonder in Ellen's voice—these small currents of response were important to her now, they were signposts for behaviour, and they alerted her to the possibility that she must rethink her previous comments—so she answered, "Against the slings and arrows of fortune."

"Of outrageous fortune," said Ellen, laughing.

And Ruth was grateful to her, and also to Frida, who had worn herself out with constant care on behalf of the house and the cats and herself, and who had driven out the tiger. But she was aware of a sense of misgiving, as if she had done something to make Frida angry; why was she frightened of Frida? The fear came and went. She remembered, then, something about making a mess in the house yesterday: throwing pills on the floor and flowers on the dune. Of course Frida was angry.

The sea was different when travelled along at speed. The sun shone from every part of the sky and water: bright light arrived from everywhere. Ruth closed her eyes and saw strong pink. She could feel the car climbing the hill and said, "It's just on the right here." Then, opening her eyes, it was like arriving at her house for the first time. She saw the grasses and tangled scrub that needed beating back from the drive, and the riot of the ruined garden, and among all this frenzy was the neat house with its scrubbed windows. It radiated a tidy quiet, but there was something unusual about it nonetheless; a faint fog seemed to rise from behind it, dimly grey and almost invisible against the water. Ellen brought the car to a stop.

Frida was sitting on the low step across the front door of the house. She looked wearily up at the car, her face resigned to disaster, and her arms fell across her knees so that her wrists turned out, as if expecting handcuffs. But when she saw the unfamiliar car, she raised herself from the step with a slow concentration that recalled her mythically fatter past. Ellen leaned over Ruth to open the passenger door, and Ruth found herself wanting it closed again; she wanted it shut against Frida. But it was too late now: Ellen was out of the car, Frida was moving. Ruth swung in the seat and her legs came sticking out into the air like a child's. This seemed to prompt Frida to hastier action. She held out her arms for Ruth to run into, and so Ruth did; she was closer to Frida's body at this moment than she had ever been. It gave out an agitated heat. She recognized this embrace; it was the way she'd hugged Jeffrey the day she came home from the hospital with his baby brother. Perhaps Frida wasn't angry after all. Ellen had averted her eyes and was studying the foggy house.

"Where in God's name have you been?" Frida cried, but Ruth, remembering her manners, drew back and turned to Ellen.

"This is Ellen," she said. "Frida, this is *Ellen*."

"Hello," said Ellen. "You're Ruth's nurse?"

"I'm her carer." Frida released Ruth from her arms.

"Frida, can I ask what's happened here?" Ellen sounded terse and assured. She sounded almost detective-like, until Frida took a terrible step towards her; then the difference in their sizes was frightening.

"What's happened here," snapped Frida, and then she seemed to reconsider her position and soften her voice, "is that I've been worried sick about Ruthie vanishing like that. I've been waiting for my brother to help me find her."

The tone was soft, but also efficient and proud. Ruth waited by the front door, cradling her bundles of meat and her purse, concerned that Ellen and Frida's meeting was going badly. She noticed a bitterness in the air, a smell of old bushfire.

"You didn't know she'd left the house?"

"Not till she was halfway to the bus. Listen, you," said Frida, addressing Ruth now, "that was quite a stunt you pulled." She stepped backwards and drew Ruth into a huddle under her arm. Ellen rattled her keys and looked towards the car.

"You better say thank you to your friend for bringing you

home safe," Frida said, and Ruth, who knew this was unnecessary, smiled at Ellen. Ellen smiled back. There was an understanding between them.

"How often does this happen?" Ellen asked, looking at
Ruth.

"Never before," said Frida. "But that's just the way it is with
these old dears. They get it in their heads to do something, and
off they go."

Ellen continued to address Ruth. "If you'd ever like to go
into town again, please give me a call. I'd love to take you out to
lunch one day. You have my number, don't you?" She looked at
Frida. "She has my number. Ellen Gibson. I'm the one who—
helped when—"

Frida nodded in a businesslike way. Of course she knew all
the details of Harry's death, but this nod seemed to indicate that
she considered her own work—the daily drudgery of care for the
widow—much meatier than Ellen's glamourous part in proceedings.

"All right then," said Ellen, and her body turned towards
the car, but she seemed to be waiting for something—some reassurance, possibly, that it was all right to go. Frida didn't move
towards Ellen or the house. She gave the impression that she had
grown on this spot, from tender root to woody trunk, and would
never be persuaded to leave it; nor would she, for that matter,
release Ruth.

"Drive safely, won't you," said Frida, in a tone indicative of
her merry indifference to Ellen's well-being.

"Goodbye, Ruth," Ellen said, and although she hesitated
again, with one leg in the car and the other foot on the ground,
she still sat down and drove away and was swallowed up by the
grasses.

With Ellen gone, Frida's bravado vanished. She wept. Could
this be true—Frida weeping? Ruth held her—was really held *by*

her, but in a clinging way—and she watched Frida the way Harry used to watch a fire he was building: with a feeling that he had no real control over proceedings but should probably be on hand for emergencies.

"I thought I'd lost you," Frida sniffed. "I thought you were gone for good. How long have you been planning this?"

Now she mastered herself and held Ruth at arm's length. Her eyes were a damp, foggy red, and her face had puffed into a new and compassionate shape, but she shook Ruth a little at the shoulders and pulled her close into another airless clinch. "Come on," she said. "What were you up to?"

Ruth, smothered, only shook her head.

"Who did you see in town, hey?" Now Frida was walking them into the house. "Did you plan to meet Ellen? Who else were you chatting to?"

When they reached the front hall, Frida released Ruth against the coatrack before locking the door and leaning against it with small exhalations that still managed to lift her chest to her chins.

"No one," said Ruth. She stood nestled among the winter coats, which hung all year in the hall and gave off a stale, resentful smell. There was the vaguest odour, too, of Harry—just a fugitive whiff. Ruth thought she might have stood among the coats after he died, searching out that smell. "Only Ellen. I bumped into her outside the chemist. Wasn't that a lovely piece of luck?"

"Just lovely," said Frida. "Just absolutely darling."

Frida seized Ruth's purse and reviewed it in a business-like way.

"Oh! And the Sausage King," said Ruth, proffering the white parcels. She anticipated a scolding for omitting the Sausage King, but Frida only straightened her shoulders as if she needed to reassert her own majesty.

"Now listen," she said, "I'm going to get this over with. There's been a small accident while you were out, but don't worry. Hardly any damage done. This way—it's the kitchen."

Ruth followed her down the hall.

There had been a fire in the kitchen: a small, blackish, crawling kind of fire, apparently, because the kitchen hadn't burned. Instead it seemed to have expired, having first given up on something—some former dignity, some presumed usefulness—before slumping into despair. Dark streaks spread up the wall from the oven as if painted by a brush of smoke, and the smell was intense—the comforting fug of a house fire, mingled with something bitter and almost salty. Sooty water puddled the floor.

"Oh," said Ruth.

"I'm sorry," said Frida. She didn't seem to be apologizing so much as imparting information. "I went crazy when I couldn't find you—I forgot I had oil on the stove."

Ruth considered the stubbed kitchen. "What do I do?"

"What d'you mean?"

"How do I fix it?" Ruth supposed she would have to fix it.

"You *don't* fix it. I fix it. Like I fix everything."

"That's what you're here for," said Ruth.

"Yeah, yeah," said Frida. "Now take a seat. I can't believe you, running off like that. What am I going to do with you?"

She began to bustle in the kitchen. Ruth sat in her chair and felt weighed down by gratitude for Frida, who fixed everything. It was as if something heavy and warm had been placed on her lap. Then a thought came to her, and she said, "But what were you cooking?"

"What now?" called Frida, as if her head were buried at the bottom of some inconvenient cupboard, among linens, when in fact she was only putting the butcher's parcels in the fridge.

"What were you cooking when the oil caught fire?"

Frida sighed and stalled behind the fridge door. "Fish fingers," she said.

"Oh."

"Why, Sherlock, do you want to see the box? Do you want to check the garbage?"

Ruth laughed. "I only wondered."

Frida ran into the dining room, sat at the table, and surprised Ruth—seemed to surprise herself—by beginning to cry again. What a fragile Frida she was today. Ruth felt so sad for her.

"This is too much for me," Frida said in a voice entirely unaffected by the weeping; but Ruth could see the tears on her face and the despairing lift to her shoulders.

"Oh, no, no," Ruth said. "Don't cry, dear. Everything's lovely. Everything's fine."

Then Frida lowered her head onto the table. Her hairstyle seemed perfectly designed for this maneuver because it remained fixed in a rigid bun. Ruth could undertake a detailed inspection of the back of Frida's neck. It was smooth, except for one thick fold that traversed it like a defensive moat. Her skin was paler than Ruth remembered it, which worried her momentarily; she scrutinized Frida's arms, which were pale, too, and sallow; then she remembered that winter was barely over. Everyone paled in the winter. Ruth saw that Frida's hair was currently a nutty brown, a rich yuletide colour, which matched her lighter shade perfectly. How clever she was, and how farseeing. But fish fingers? In oil? And in the morning?

Frida looked out at Ruth from the cradle of her pastel arms. "You're too good to me. Last night—"

"Now listen, my dear," said Ruth, who had an idea that a kind severity was called for in response to such statements. "There's no need to cry. There are plenty more fish in the deep blue sea."

Ruth found it easy to say these things from the safety of her chair. It was a little like recovering a language she'd forgotten she knew and still wasn't entirely sure of the sense of.

Frida lifted her head from the humid table; her face was blotted and wet, but she had stopped crying. "You're a funny old thing."

Ruth didn't feel funny, but she smiled and smiled.

14

Later that day the telephone rang. The noise startled Ruth, who was dozing in her chair, half aware of Frida's cleaning the kitchen. Ruth was pulled from a dream about a trapeze and a public swimming pool; she was hoisted in the air, on the trapeze, and the water glinted below, dangerous in some indefinable, chlorinated way.

Frida answered the phone. "Yes, Jeff," she said. "A little adventure, yes. She's fine, the silly duck. She probably won't remember any of it tomorrow."

And then: "Now, Jeff, it's not exactly—"

And finally: "Sure, sure, here she is."

Frida presented the phone to Ruth, then returned to scrubbing the brown kitchen. Ruth held the receiver to her ear.

"Ma? I just had a phone call from Ellen Gibson." Jeffrey's voice came at Ruth from around a suspicious corner.

"Lovely Ellen!" said Ruth.

"I hear you went into town today. What was that for?"

"I felt like it," said Ruth. She suspected she was in trouble, but couldn't decide how to feel about it. "I'm allowed, aren't I?"

Jeffrey was quiet for a moment. "I was thinking I might come out for a visit soon, see how you're getting on. What do you think of that idea?"

"That sounds nice," said Ruth. She had not yet considered it an idea, nice or otherwise.

"You don't sound so sure."

"There's a problem." She was filled with sudden anxiety; but what was the problem?

"There is!" Jeffrey pounced as if he had lured her into a con-fidential trap.

"I know!" she cried. "I can't get to the railway station."

"You don't need to pick me up from the station, Ma. I'll take a cab."

"Oh, that's marvellous! That's just as well. I've lost your father's car."

"What do you mean, you've lost Dad's car?"

"It's not lost, of course not. It's sold."

"You didn't tell me you were selling Dad's car."

"I'm not selling it," said Ruth. "It's sold."

"When was this?"

"Frida arranged it."

"She did, did she?" Jeffrey used Harry's lawyerly voice—ruminating, withholding, sure of some hidden possibility that ticked over in his mathematical mind. "Listen, how about this coming weekend? I'll have to check flights, but if I come on Friday night, how's that?"

"Yes, all right, yes," said Ruth. Then the proximity of Friday startled her. "This Friday? So soon?"

Frida stopped scrubbing and looked over her shoulder.

"The sooner the better," said Jeffrey, and this seemed to de-cide it. Yes, the sooner the better. "Friday, then. You don't have any more mysterious visitors coming, do you? No more boy-friends? We'll have a great time. We'll play Scrabble and look for whales."

So Jeffrey didn't care about the trip to town; not the way Frida cared. He was her good and generous son, her forgiving son. How kind and clement he was. He was just, as his father had been—he was unyielding, but also compassionate. He was the law. Ruth called Frida over to hang up the phone. There was nothing to be afraid of.

But Frida's face was a cliff under a cloud. "What's happen-

ing on Friday?" she asked, leaning against the wall as if she had
been washed up, just like that, on the beach. There was a general look of wreckage about everything surrounding her, but the
dark streaks on the kitchen wall did look cosier after their
scrubbing; almost old-fashioned.

"Jeffrey's coming," said Ruth.

"Why? What did you say to him?"

"Nothing," said Ruth. She felt as if she'd been caught up in
a procession of events over which she had no control; but she was
calm.

"First Ellen, now Jeff. Those two stickybeaks are in it together." Frida said *Ellen* with a specific spite. She walked from
the table to the window and back again, and when she reached
the window for a second time, she tapped it with one calculating
hand. "There are a couple of things we might not mention to
good old Jeff," she said.

"What things?"

Frida was coaxing and deferential. "Obviously the tiger."

"I thought you were proud of the tiger."

Frida failed to look proud. She seemed to have failed, generally, in some important way. She gave an impression of pending
collapse that she warded off only by tapping the window.

"If Jeff knew everything I do for you, he'd only worry. He'd
put you in a home, and you know what that means: no more
house. No more sea views. No more picking and choosing what
you want for dinner. No more Frida."

Ruth sat with this possibility. It seemed quite soothing to
her, at that moment.

"And he'll never let you go to Richard—you know that,
don't you? No one's going to let you do that. They'll say you're too
old and he's too old, and you can't look after each other. They'll
say it's not in your best interests."

"Who'll say that?" asked Ruth, startled, not just by the

thought of being stopped, but by hearing Richard's name, which had been important to her last night, or even this morning. She had, hadn't she, wanted to go to him?

"Jeff will," said Frida.

"Jeffrey can't stop me."

"But the law can stop you, if Jeff wants it to. The government can stop you."

"You're the government," said Ruth.

"Well, I quit."

"When?"

"Right now," said Frida. "But I can help you, Ruthie, if you help me."

Ruth nodded. She needed time to think; also, she was hungry. Why did her shoulders still hurt?

"So that's decided. Now I'm going to use the phone," said Frida. "I'm going to call George."

"Maybe George can sort out the garden." Ruth was worried about the state of the garden; Jeffrey wouldn't like it.

"I'm going to call him from my room. In private."

Ruth nodded again. It felt good to nod, so she continued to do so; yes, she said with her pendulous head, and yes and yes again; she was a clock, she thought; she was generous and wise. Frida left, and Ruth went into the lounge room. She went looking for Richard—not because she thought he would be there, but because she might find evidence of him. There might be something to tell her he really had put his hand on her knee and said, "Please think about it." But the only unusual thing in the lounge room was a dent in the lampshade, which Ruth attempted to smooth and only deepened. Lifting her arms towards the light, she noticed funny yellow patches on her skin.

The cats had followed Frida to Phil's room and were probing at the closed door with their adventurous noses; they gave out little cries, and Ruth called for them to come. At the same time, Frida raised her voice. She must be shouting at George. Ruth supposed he didn't want to come and sort out the garden. A new idea came to her: that George, and not the cats, was responsible for its wreckage. Possibly George was responsible for everything. He assumed a new shape for her then: sinister and godlike. Then Frida must have let fly with her foot or her arm; something crashed. The cats baulked and blinked and turned to Ruth for comfort. She coaxed them onto the lounge, where they stretched and sat in funny bundles.

"I don't think I want an angry man in the house," she told them, but she wasn't sure exactly which man she meant. Maybe Jeffrey? But why was he angry? Maybe George. She couldn't mean Richard, who wanted her to go to *his* house. Frida's voice rose, indecipherable, from her bedroom.

Ruth sat among the cats. They bumped their heads against her and their claws needled her lap. Every window was open, and the front and back doors, because of the smell of the fire. Still the house was hot, and the smell had only intensified. It was a sharp, unmistakably burnt smell, but it reminded Ruth of the night jungle; it had the same colour. The lounge-room clock sounded five times, and with each chime the cats twitched and sank.

Frida appeared in the lounge-room doorway. She looked undone. Her hair had strayed from its style, her mascara was smudged, and her white beautician's pants were soiled with ash. "I have some bad news," she said. "It's George."

"What's George?"

"It's really bad."

"Oh, Frida," sighed Ruth. She thought she knew. She saw George dead in the road, entombed in his taxi. She saw him prone in the grass, maybe a heart attack. Possibly in the sea— buoyant, with burst lungs. There were so many possibilities. Maybe smoking one day, alone in the dunes, and then—the tiger. Yes, she could see that: the water sprawling below his feet, the smoke near his face, a view of her house from where he sat, and also the town—the rigid flag over the surf club—and the tiger, downwind, stalking unfortunate George. She would say to Frida, "I'm sure it was all over quickly. I'm sure he felt no pain." She would say, "I wish I'd known him better." But she had no wish to know him better. She preferred him as a dark shape in the front of a taxi.

"I'm so sorry," she said, but Frida said, "What for?" so quickly that Ruth knew to be quiet.

"Right then," continued Frida. "George has stolen all my money and lost the house and ruined me." She calmly announced this deadpan disaster.

"No!" cried Ruth. Panic and horror were a handkerchief at her throat. "But you just spoke to him!" Frida just spoke to George, so he couldn't be dead in the taxi or from the tiger; he couldn't have stolen all her money.

"That's how I know," said Frida.

"But how?"

"Because he told me, is how," said Frida, defensive, as if she suspected Ruth of not believing her.

"But how did he steal all your money?" This genuinely puzzled Ruth, who had never considered stealing anyone's money and wondered how to go about it.

"It's to do with Mum's house."

"The house she died in," said Ruth.

"Yes, yes," said Frida, impatient. "I've been giving him my salary and he hasn't kept up with the mortgage and they're going to take the house."

"Who are?"

"The bank," said Frida. "Unless I can pay them right away. And the worst thing is, I can't just catch up on the mortgage. It's still legally half George's house. So I need to get the mortgage up-to-date *and* buy half the house from George. Otherwise I'll lose it."

"That doesn't seem fair," said Ruth. "You just keep giving George money? That can't be right."

"It doesn't matter, because I don't have any money to give."

"I know what we'll do," said Ruth, and Frida raised her head with a quick, sharp look. "We'll talk to Harry. He'll know how to sort all this out."

"Jesus," said Frida.

"He's a very good lawyer."

Frida sank into the catless end of the couch. "Ruthie," she said, with unexpected softness, "Harry's dead."

"I know that," snapped Ruth, and she did know it; she had even known it a moment ago when she suggested they consult him. And she was disgusted with him, because nobody could be really, truly dead; nobody could stand it. It was one thing, maybe, to die—and Ruth held his head as Harry died, she remembered that now, she saw the sand on the pavement at the bus stop and Harry's shaking dying head—but it was quite another to go on being dead. That was obstinate; it was unkind.

Frida buried one hand in the yielding fur of the nearest cat. "I do have an idea," she said. "We might be able to help each other."

The cat twitched under her fingers, stood and yawned, and trotted onto Ruth's lap.

"Richard," Frida said. "I can help you with Richard, and you can help me with George."

"Do I need your help with Richard?"

"You need me on your side if you're going to convince Jeffrey. You need me to say, 'In my professional opinion, your mother should go live with Richard.'"

"Should I?"

"I went to see his house yesterday. I wanted to see the setup there, whether or not it'd be good for you."

"And?" A tiredness came over Ruth; it felt like a blanket, suddenly pulled. She thought she might have done the pulling.

"It's a really nice place. All on one level, a huge kitchen, even a spa bath. It's too deep for you right now, he doesn't even use it, but I could put railings in and—bingo!"

"What about the garden?"

"Very pretty. His daughter looks after it. Jacaranda tree, big herb garden, brick patio."

"Lilies?"

"He picked the last of them for you. And he has this one fat palm tree that looks exactly like a pineapple."

"Good for the cats."

"Well, that's one downside. His daughter's allergic to cats. I thought about not mentioning that, by the way, just for the record. But you just lock them up when she visits. Easy fixed. The other thing is that he sleeps with this mask at night, it's for his breathing, and it's loud."

Ruth closed her eyes at the thought of these loud nights. "I can't believe you went there without me," she said from her lidded darkness. She saw the garden: green, with a fence, and other fenced greens at its edges. She saw that ear of Richard's again, horizontal against his head, and his head lying still: his sickbed. And no more sea.

"Now, if I help you with Richard, maybe you can help me with George."

Ruth opened her eyes. "Where are the lilies he picked for me?" She thought perhaps she knew where they were; she thought they might be related to the yellow stains on her skin. But she couldn't recall.

"They're gone," said Frida, and Ruth closed her eyes again; she had been waiting for that answer. If the lilies are gone, she said to herself, if they're finished and I never saw them, it means—what? The cat squirmed on her lap and couldn't get comfortable, so she pedaled her knees until it jumped away. There were lumps in her lap—they were the leftover pills from yesterday, still in her pockets. Then she remembered where the lilies were. She remembered falling into the tiger trap. She was wearing the same dress she'd climbed the dune in; she'd slept since then and been to town, with pollen on her arms and dirt in her shoes. Now her gritty grey skin declared itself, and the sand at the roots of her sticky hair. No wonder Ellen had called Jeffrey.

"I'm a wreck," Ruth said.

"We'll both be, soon enough," said Frida. "Unless we act quickly."

"Why do you want me to go to Richard?"

"I want you to be happy," said Frida. Ruth suspected her of telling the truth. "You don't know what it's meant to me, living here with you these last few weeks. You're like the mother I—"

"No," said Ruth.

"No?"

"I won't go to Richard." That was easy enough: the lilies are over, don't go to Richard. Ruth was irritated at herself, actually, for almost falling for it: that version of leaving her house, of ending her life, as if she might scrub out the disappointment of fifty years ago and step, bridal, over Richard's door. "If he wants me, he can come here. I hope he comes. I'll invite him."

"But—"

"You can still help me. You can go away," said Ruth, and that was easy too. "You leave me alone, and I'll help you. I'll lend you the money for your mother's house. I have plenty of money. I'll pay the bank—tell them that."

"I can't tell them that," said Frida. She was very still at her end of the couch, but Ruth could see the tick of her temple.

"Why not?"

"It's too much money."

"You took care of my house, and now I'll take care of yours. It's like a poem."

"What are you talking about?"

"It rhymes," Ruth said, explanatory.

Frida sighed. "Do you know how much money that would be?" She shook her head. Something was amazing her.

"I have plenty of money," said Ruth. "Harry sold the Sydney house. That was a big house."

"I don't know what to say," said Frida. She seemed caught up in a kind of sad, disbelieving relief.

"But you have to leave. You can't live here anymore. You should live in your mother's house and leave me alone."

"I'll go," said Frida. "I'm already going. But I want to make you happy, you understand? I don't want to leave you all alone in this horrible house."

"There's nothing wrong with this house," said Ruth. "Only I worry—isn't it silly? I do worry about that tiger."

"Really? The one thing you're worried about is the tiger?"

Ruth nodded, embarrassed.

"We can't have that," said Frida. "You leave the tiger to me."

"What will you do?" asked Ruth, a little fearful.

"What needs to be done." Now Frida sat upright. "How do I know you won't forget all this tomorrow?"

"I might," admitted Ruth, trying to smooth out the lumps in her skirt. "So I'll write myself a note. Isn't that what people do?"

This prompted Frida into action. She rolled up from the couch and into the dining room; the first writable surface she found was Ruth's detective novel, which she opened to the first page and settled on Ruth's lap.

"Write it here." Frida produced a pen from about her person.

Ruth felt as if she were signing a book she'd written. She tested the pen with a little flourish at the top of the page, then wrote, under the title, "TRUST FRIDA."

"What's the date?" she asked.

"I don't know," said Frida. "Tuesday night."

So Ruth wrote, in brackets, "Tuesday night."

"How do we do this?" she asked, blowing lightly on the

book. The pen's ink had blotted on the cheap paper. "Do we go
to the bank?"

"Yes," said Frida. "But! But! You can't just go into a bank
and say you're buying a house. We need George, we need a solicitor, we need all kinds of things. I *told* him we couldn't rush
this."

Ruth, knowing Frida would find a way around these problems, remained silent and waited for it.

"But," said Frida. "But! How about this? You transfer the
money to George, I get a written agreement from him—we sort
out the details later. The main thing is to get this done before
they take the house."

"When do they take the house?"

"Friday."

"I'll write a cheque," said Ruth. "Bring me my book." Ruth
had always enjoyed writing cheques. They were so businesslike.

"A cheque'll take days to clear," said Frida.

"Not really, not these days." Ruth remembered Harry's explaining this. "It's only about three business days, these days."
And she laughed, because having said *days* three times made it
feel as if those days had already passed.

Frida zigzagged up and down the living room. This was her
thinking walk. "Three days is too long," she said. "All right, all
right. This is what we're going to do. If it's okay by you." She
tapped at her forehead as if coaxing her brain. "We'll go into
town tomorrow and go to the bank. They know you in the
bank, don't they?"

"Some of them might know me. I haven't been to town for a
long time."

"Yeah, not for *ages*." Frida shook her head. "And you can
buy cheques that clear quickly. There's a name for that—what
is it?"

The word dropped into Ruth's head. *"Expedite,"* she said.

"That's it!" Frida raised her jubilant arms. "Is that how you say it? Say it again."

Ruth cleared her throat. "Expedite." In her mind's eye, she saw \ek-spə-dīt\.

"Expedite!" cried Frida. "And that's what we're going to do. Now what about Jeffrey?"

"What does he have to do with any of this?" Ruth asked, surprised.

"He's coming on Friday."

"So let him come!" cried Ruth. "Let them all come! We'll have a party. If Jeffrey's coming, and Richard's coming, I'll invite Ellen."

"Richard's coming?"

"Yes, of course. I told you about Richard, didn't I—a man I knew in Fiji?" Frida walked impatiently to the lounge-room window. "He's coming for the weekend. He's coming for Christmas."

Frida stood at the window, and because the lights were on and the curtains were open, Frida stood in the window looking back. Her face was so severe; probably she didn't approve of Richard. She was such a prude, really. She drove those naked children off the beach.

"Are you really frightened of the tiger?" she asked.

Ruth only laughed. "Of course, Phil should come, too, if Jeffrey's coming. I'll call him, shall I?"

"By all means," said Frida, magnanimous. "Call Phil, call everyone. Call the Queen, my love. Why the hell not."

"I saw the Queen," said Ruth, and they both said together, "In Fiji."

"Jesus, Ruthie," said Frida in the window.

15

That was the night Frida fought the tiger. He came earlier than he had the other nights: Frida was in the bathroom and Ruth sat up in bed with the lamp still lit. She was thinking about calling Richard, but couldn't be sure of what she wanted to say: something about an invitation to Christmas, and also about hating Sydney because of bad junipers and good pirate plays. She was aware of being very tired and thought she would probably make a fool of herself. So she sank down into the bed and, as she did so, heard the first suggestions of the tiger: the footfalls in the lounge room, the moving lamps and chairs. He had come without the jungle, although Ruth could feel that it was nearby, outside the windows, in a way that reminded her of Fiji. It was like night in their wide, hot house beside the hospital, where the moths knocked up against the windows and the gardens dripped in the dark. The light around her bed stirred like the mosquito netting she had slept under as a girl. Then the tiger: softly at first, his usual nosing and breathing, which was all so quiet that Ruth was inclined to ignore this evidence and assume he was still banished to the beach. The cats, however, stiffened and stared—a bad sign, a tiger sign—and shortly after this, the tiger began to make a sharp whine, as if he was hungry. Then he was unmistakably the tiger.

Frida was still in the bathroom. Ruth's door was ajar, and she could see light falling across the hall in a way that meant the lounge-room door was open. The tiger was there, in that light! What would it mean to actually see him? Would it hurt? The jungle pressed against the windows, not insistent; only present.

Ruth got out of bed. She felt lately as if she were always

heroically rising from bed, mainly because of her back. Tonight it hadn't had the chance to freeze in sleep; it still had the day's limited elasticity. The cats watched her. They were in no hurry to leave the bed. Ruth shook her head at them to say "Quiet!" She crossed the floor and leaned into the hallway. It was empty. Then Frida was at the end of it, and running towards her.

"Did you hear it?" called Frida.

"Quick!" cried Ruth, and she pulled Frida into her room. Frida wore a white towelling dressing gown. She was soft and without shape. "Close the door!"

Frida closed the door. "Did you hear it?"

"Yes," said Ruth. "I think—yes, I did."

They both stilled and listened. He had come into the hallway, Ruth was sure of it. He must have heard Frida, or seen or smelled her, and now he knew with certainty they were there. Now he nosed at the door.

Frida flew against it. "All right, all right," she said. "Think."

They both thought. There was nothing to think. Ruth's mind was blank of everything but the tiger. Frida pressed against the door. Finally she said, "I'm going out there."

"You can't!" cried Ruth. But she was certain Frida would; there was no alternative.

"I can and I will." Frida's face was resolved above the white fluff of her dressing gown. She pressed one ear against the door, listening, but there was silence in the hallway. Ruth waited for a hungry howl.

"Promise me you won't come out, no matter what you hear," Frida said. "And if something happens, promise me you'll call George and tell him about it yourself."

"Frida!"

"Promise me."

"How do I call him?"

"Look him up in the phone book. Look up his taxi. Young Livery. Can you do that?"

Ruth nodded.

Then Frida turned to face the door. She adjusted her robe, took a deep scuba breath, opened the door, and disappeared into the hallway. The door closed behind her. Then it was definite: Frida was going to fight the tiger.

"Can you see him?" Ruth asked through the door.

"Not yet. I'm going to find a weapon."

"Get a broom."

"All right, a broom," said Frida. "And maybe a knife."

Ruth heard Frida run into the kitchen in search of a broom and a knife; then came the sound of the tiger's paws on the floor of the hallway. This sound reminded Ruth of the soft rhythm of a particular trolley on the floor of the clinic in Fiji; she heard it passing up and down while she waited in her father's consulting room. The tiger was following Frida, but without hurrying; he was a cat in long grasses; he was hunting. Pressed against the door, Ruth could hear her busy heart, the hunting tiger, and the hospital trolley; then the sound of Frida's finding a broom.

"Frida!" Ruth called. "He's behind you!"

The broom cupboard was stiff with equipment, mops and brooms and buckets all piled in together, and they fell out on the floor as Frida selected her weapon—Ruth heard all this from her room.

The cats jumped from the bed and clamoured at Ruth's feet. They wanted to get out. Frida was swearing in the kitchen now, among the mops and buckets, but she stopped when she saw the tiger and cried "Aha!" The tiger answered with a crisp, proud puff from his nostrils. Then he sprang onto the table— Ruth heard the table scrape over the floor. Frida was in the knife drawer now. Its metals rang. Frida would carve the tiger! But he was ready to pounce.

The house was hotter than ever before. Ruth pressed her sticky hand against the door, as if checking for fire. The kitchen had burned today! Frida was facing the tiger! Did she really stand in the Sausage King's with an empty purse only this morning? Was there such a thing as a bus, a town, a mortgage? The cats clawed at Ruth's legs. Whose side were they on? They were wild with panic and fear, and Ruth could barely recognize them.

Frida wielded her broom—she was trying to herd the tiger out the back door. But he wouldn't run tonight. Frida commanded, "Out! Out!" The broom battered the shutters and walls, but he stayed put. Ruth had seen the cats hunting birds in the garden; she knew the tiger's whole rusty front would be still and low, and his back paws would be lifting, lifting, beneath his undulant tail. Then—the table moved again, sharp against the floor—he flew at Frida. She lifted her broom, which cracked against something hard. They were both so quiet; Ruth marvelled at it. Every now and then, Frida produced an "Oof," but there were no shouts of pain or whimpers from the tiger; only the noise of furniture shifting, and periodically a shatter of glass. Ruth closed her eyes. The tiger was stronger than Frida and determined to fight.

But Frida was fearless. She didn't give up any ground or lose hold of her weapons. She struck! And now the tiger gave out a high squawk. The cats went mad at the door, and Ruth—her eyes still closed—opened it for them, quickly, and closed it again. They ran through the kitchen, through Frida and the tiger, and outside. Their flight was enough to distract him; Frida struck again. Now he ran. All through the hospital the tiger fled, into the house and the hallway and through the clinic, and as he ran, the patients sat up in their beds, even those that couldn't sit, as if the trumpets of the resurrection had sounded and their souls were rising from perpetual sleep. Someone began to ring a bell, which might summon the fire brigade; it might wake the doctor with his canny, flimsy hands and bring him running in expectation of surgery. It might wake the whole town, the whole island; it might bring the sea to a halt, waiting, waiting to see the tiger run by. He ran into Phillip's room and out of it again, and everywhere he ran, Frida followed him with her broom and her knife and her battle cry. Ruth heard, along with the bell, a new sound—the beating together of the compost-bin lids, sailing across the sand. Children fled from the beach. Children in the wards began to cry out, but not in alarm; they called "Frida! Frida!" Lights came on in every room. The bell rang. Lights disappeared and came on again in every room. The tiger ran blindly into furniture. His claws skidded over the floors.

"Oh, no you don't!" called Frida, and Ruth called—everyone called—"No you don't!" along with her.

The tiger was trapped in the hallway. Ruth pressed against her door; her heart struck again and again. There he was in the hallway, there was his snarl and the fury of his breath. The cats cried out in the garden. Now Frida began to roar; she was magnificent. The tiger answered—he roared, and his roar was a stone flying over water. Then Frida struck. The speed of her striking arm lifted a wind in the house. The tiger yelped in surprise—a startled domestic little yelp—and then he was in the jungle again, or of the jungle, and enraged. Ruth felt for a moment on the verge of understanding exactly what the tiger was saying when he roared. He wasn't concerned for his safety, but for his dignity. There was a sense of enormous injustice, not quite conceivable to him. But you must take Frida seriously, thought Ruth. She found herself pitying the tiger. He was fighting to save his territory, but Frida meant to finish him off. Then he roared again, a war cry, and she stopped trembling for him. She was never afraid for Frida.

Something heavy fell against the door; it was unclear which of them it was. But the tiger must have struck because Frida cried out in rage and pain. She fought back. There had been no beginning to Frida and the tiger, and now there would be no end. They both snarled and bared their teeth. Frida called out the strange syllables of a warlike alphabet. Her voice grew louder, but the tiger's slowed. He still roared, but his roar seemed full of static, like the roar of a tiger on television. It came and went. Frida's broom rattled. The bell stopped and all the lights went out. There was no hospital and no house; only Frida and the tiger. Ruth leaned, terrified, against the door.

Now the jungle began, sudden and synchronized: insects tucked in trees, and a high peal of hidden birds. The wind died out among the foliage and became instead a hot, damp gag, barely moving, and carrying something wet whenever it did. Frida had the tiger down near the coatrack now, and she was holding her ground. Probably his ears were flat against his head. His tail moved to and fro. There was the scrape of his claws on the wood of the floor.

"Frida!" cried Ruth, and when she did, there was the sound of falling bodies, more cries, more knocks of the broom on the wall, but it was as if nothing more serious than a scuffle were taking place, a closing-time fracas, until there came at last a screech—the sound of a cat whose tail has been trampled. Frida grunted; she was pushing something hard. She called out, and then her body—or his body—a heavy body—fell. The hallway was quiet. Then light came in under the bedroom door.

"Frida?" said Ruth. Frida groaned. "Are you hurt?" Frida rapped on the door with the end of the broom. "Can I come out? Are you all right?"

"Stay where you are," said Frida. The words heaved out of her. The light disappeared. "Open the door," she said. "Don't look out here."

Ruth opened the door. The wet smell of the tiger was every-where. Frida came in carrying the broom, but not the knife.

"It's finished," she said, and accepted Ruth into her arms. There was blood on her white robe and on her face; tiger blood.

16

Ruth rose early the next morning. She crept by Frida's bedroom door as high on the tips of her toes as her back would allow. The house was in disarray. Sand lay in banks and eddies all over the floor. Ruth decided to sweep it, but it seemed to be sticky at the bottom, as if soaked in liquid—each clump had the long, damp foot of a mollusc—and sweeping only thickened the bristles of the broom with mud. Her back hurt. Her chair lay shipwrecked on the sandy floor. Ruth kept walking over hard objects that she worried were teeth and tiger claws but turned out to be miscellaneous grit. Frida's broom, or the tiger's tail, had knocked glass to the floor, and the lamp tilted drunkenly in the lounge room. But the tiger's body was gone.

Frida had covered the area by the front door with a tarpaulin, and she had weighed this tarpaulin down with buckets of water. The water smelled rusty, and it was a rust colour when Ruth dipped her finger in it. She couldn't lift the buckets to see under the tarpaulin, and when she opened the front door, she could see only that something large had been dragged to the grass at the edge of the drive. The ground was muddy. Frida had spent hours in the night filling buckets with water and throwing them out over the path she had made with the body of the tiger. She wouldn't allow Ruth to leave her room.

When Frida emerged, fully dressed—in her white uniform, with her hair pulled so tight into a bun she looked more like a beautician than ever—Ruth was dozing in the lounge-room recliner, still wearing her nightgown.

"Come on, lazybones," said Frida. "The bus is due at quarter past ten."

"What bus?" Ruth blinked and squinted.

"To take us to town? To the bank?"

"Isn't George going to drive us?"

"I told you, darling heart, George's run off. Now get a move on, or we'll miss it."

"We're going to the bank?"

Frida flourished a book in front of Ruth's face. The book had writing in it—it said "TRUST FRIDA."

"I know, I know," said Ruth, a little crankily.

"Chop chop!" cried Frida, clapping her hands. She hauled Ruth out of the recliner, marched her into the bedroom, and took charge of dressing her. Ruth sat mute on the end of her bed. Frida's hair was so severe, and her uniform so white, that it would have been impossible to conjure the bloody Frida of the night before except that bruises were beginning to bloom on her forearms.

Frida muttered at Ruth's open wardrobe. "Something sensible, something sensible. Try this." She pulled out a neat grey skirt suit.

"It's very formal," said Ruth.

"Just try it. Can you manage?" Frida advanced on Ruth and began tugging at her nightgown.

"I can manage!" The thought of being naked in front of Frida was terrible: proud, firm Frida of the lacquered hair, who had killed the tiger.

Frida threw up her hands. "Then hurry," she said. She turned her back to Ruth, but stayed in the room.

Ruth struggled with the skirt. When had she last worn this suit? Years ago, surely, and it was a little big for her. When she managed to button the skirt, she was so pleased with herself that she mustered the courage to ask, "Frida, where's the tiger?"

"You don't need to worry about that anymore," said Frida.

"I only want to know where he is. I thought there could be something—some kind of ceremony. A funeral?"

"I killed him for you, and you want a funeral?" Frida used her most incredulous voice. "Now get a wriggle on. It's nine fifty-five."

"I need stockings," said Ruth. Frida turned, appraising. Ruth hated to wear those thick flesh-coloured stockings she saw on other old women. For formal, suit-wearing occasions, she liked thin black ones. "They're in the top drawer."

"You look just fine," said Frida. "Get some shoes. Quick, quick! Or we'll miss the bus."

"We could call a taxi," said Ruth, despairing, but Frida blocked the way to the chest of drawers and tapped her wrist as if she wore a watch there.

"How many times do I have to tell you," said Frida, guiding Ruth to the door now, "George has run off?"

"There are other taxis in the whole wide world."

In the hallway, Frida had a glass of water and Ruth's pills; Ruth swallowed these expertly. She took her purse from the coat hook it hung on.

"Watch the buckets," said Frida. "Watch your step."

She hurried Ruth into the front garden and towards the drive, where Ruth dawdled looking for evidence of the tiger. By the time she reached the road, Frida was already partway down the hill, waiting for her.

"What do you want me to do, give you a piggyback?" Frida called. Ruth didn't answer. Frida began walking again. She called out, "What you need is a wheelchair."

Ruth wasn't happy at the thought of a wheelchair. She made little, tripping steps to catch up. If only Frida wouldn't walk quite so fast; if only this skirt didn't restrict her movement. How typical of me, she thought—of me and of any *old person*—not to want a wheelchair. When really, what could be so bad about being pushed around? Right now she would have liked to be piggybacked down the hill. She half hoped Frida might offer again.

"Wheelchairs," Ruth said, "are for people whose legs don't work."

"And backs!" cried Frida. "People with bad backs!"

There was no one at the bus stop. It loomed up before them, unaccountably familiar. The day was that wet, pressed sort on which no one would make an effort to come to this part of the beach. In weather like this, the beach was revealed as both dangerous and dirty. The sea was oppressive, and the sky was bright and colourless and dragged down upon its surface. Frida fretted at the bus stop, as if it might be a trick of some kind; no bus would come, and they would be left waiting forever. She always seemed so angry at the possibility she might have been made a fool of. Ruth sat on the bench, which felt harder than any other hard material she had previously encountered. A car slowed and then moved off again. Ruth didn't like having her back to the sea or the road, so she sat in a nervous silence, as if by being completely still she might ward off a possible ambush. Frida was silent, too. In fact they might never have met; they might have come together by chance at this bus stop, and Frida out of courtesy would allow Ruth to board the bus first, and she might even smile at her, and that would be the extent of their dealings. Then another life would take place, riskier, in which each would never know about the other.

"The bus is coming," said Ruth, although that was perfectly obvious.

Frida boarded first and paid for them both. Ruth recognized the bus driver. He had the thick, high hair of a young man, but it was completely grey. He smiled at her and said, "Out and about again, eh?" The smile pleated his forehead up into his verdant hair.

Frida took Ruth's hand. "Come on now, Ruthie," she said.

Frida's palm felt like a steak wrapped in baking paper.

The bus was emptier today. The few passengers sat in studied silence, as if the grim weather wouldn't permit sociability of any kind. Frida walked down the aisle with a maritime stride, and she dragged Ruth along with her.

"Isn't this nice," said Ruth, settling in beside Frida, and a woman of about Ruth's age, two seats down, with her remnant hairs united in a Frau-ish scarf, scowled as if Ruth had spoken in a movie theatre. Frida said nothing. Ruth's back snapped with every shake of the bus. With so little room on the seat, she was forced to hold firmly to the rail in front of her at any suggestion of a left turn for fear of being tipped into the aisle. She adjusted her position until Frida said, in a low voice, "Stop pressing into me, would you?"

Town seemed different today: more grey, and emptier. It hadn't rained, but the houses and gardens huddled in expectation of bad weather. The bus paused at a stop sign, and looking down the side of a house, Ruth saw a woman taking towels off a clothesline with frequent glances at the untrustworthy sky. The line swung in the gathering wind, and the woman's arms became heavier and heavier with towels. She had no Frida to do her laundry for her. Ruth felt a wild disdain for this anxious woman and her cradled laundry. If only the sky would break open at this very moment so Ruth could witness the unfortunate flurry of woman and towels. But the bus moved on, and no drops flattened against the windowpanes.

"Here's our stop," said Frida, and she began to stand, so Ruth stood; the bus lurched as it stopped, and Ruth nearly fell; Frida caught her and sighed aloud, while other passengers—all but the severe scarfed woman—half lifted from their seats to help.

"You're making a scene," said Frida, guiding Ruth down the aisle, and then they were on the main street of town with people pushing out of the bus behind them. "Out of the way, out of the way," Frida urged, pulling Ruth to one side of the pavement. Ruth held her purse tight against her hip. Her jacket had skewed a little to the right. Frida was walking, and Ruth, adjusting her suit, followed. "I'll never know," said Frida over her shoulder, "how you managed this on your own."

Men from a construction site crossed the road among the traffic. They had broad, happy faces, and Ruth watched them fearfully because they were courting bad luck. A woman with very red hair stopped and smiled at Ruth, talking; Ruth knew she should recognize her, but didn't.

"We're going to the bank," said Ruth, indicating Frida, who waited under the Sausage King's awning.

"Don't let me keep you!" cried the woman, and moved on.

"Do you know *everyone*?" snapped Frida, so Ruth kept her head down. When she caught up with Frida under the awning, she turned her face away from the butcher's window. She opened her purse and peered inside: she saw banknotes, and her cards were back in their slots. Perhaps they'd been there yesterday, under the watchful eye of the Sausage King. Frida was fiddling with papers she had drawn from her bag, smoothing them down and looking them over. Her bag hung open, and for some reason that book Ruth had written in was wedged inside.

Ruth was interested to notice that Frida's size diminished when compared to the doors and cars and letterboxes of the world; she was still, however, the most conspicuous thing on the street. What else was there to look at? Her hair shone out in the grey light of the skyless day, and her shoulders were as broad as the construction workers'.

"You ready, Ruthie?" Frida almost held her hand out to Ruth; Ruth almost took it.

"I want to see the tiger," said Ruth. She knew how sulky she sounded.

"You can't," said Frida. "He's in the sea."

"How did you get him down there?" People stepped around them to enter the butcher shop, and the bell chimed sweetly. Ruth crowded closer to Frida.

"I started out dragging him and then I used the wheelbarrow. I made a mess of him, Ruthie. You didn't want to see that."

"How much of a mess?"

On closer inspection, Frida looked exhausted. With her hair off her face, she was older and sadder, and the rings under her eyes were more obviously plum-coloured. She had been awake most of the night taking the tiger to the sea.

"I cut open his stomach," she said. "Do you really want to know? His guts came spilling out. And then, to kill him, I slit his throat. There was a lot of blood."

"I'm all right with blood. I practically grew up in a hospital."

"Didn't we all." Frida zipped up her bag and set her square shoulders. "You ready for the bank?"

"But how did you get him right into the sea?" Ruth insisted. "What if he washes up again?"

"What I did," said Frida tonelessly, "is I crammed him into the wheelbarrow good and tight. His tail, his paws, his head on top."

"Was he heavy?"

"Bloody heavy. Then I pushed the wheelbarrow down to the water, which was tough going, let me tell you. The tide was out. The sun was just thinking about coming up. And I pushed the wheelbarrow out into the ocean as far as I could go, until he started floating."

"In your dressing gown?"

"I took it off."

So Ruth saw Frida down in the lightening sea, naked, straining at the wheelbarrow; she saw the water lift the tiger and carry him away. He would be smaller and darker while wet and knife-slit, but still a tiger.

Frida put her hand on Ruth's arm and squeezed it. "Are we doing this, Ruthie? Should we go save my house?"

"The house she died in," said Ruth.

The bank was a safe and scrupulous place, although Ruth didn't quite approve of a seaside bank. She had lived by the sea for years, but there was still a holiday air to the sound of the gulls and the palms among the pine trees. A bank in this place should be issuing money for the buying of ice creams and beach towels and surely had no business with the solemnity of mortgages. Harry and Ruth had taken out a mortgage to buy the holiday house. Harry spoke of this mortgage as if it were an aged relative, slowly convalescent but sure to mend. When it was paid, they came out for a weekend—the boys were adults now—and Harry said, "I think we should move here permanently when I retire."

"Oh, no," said Ruth, without thinking. "Really? What would we do all day?"

Harry retired, and they moved, and all day they were Ruth and Harry.

"You go first," said Frida. The automatic doors were opening and closing, a little wildly, with no customers to prompt them, and a few ordinary pavement pieces of paper and plastic were gusting in and out. Frida prodded Ruth a little in the back. "Smile," she said.

Ruth smiled. She would have liked to hold Frida's hand. A woman in a red suit sang, "Good morning!" and Ruth sang back, "Good morning!" It was like being in church. What would the woman say next? What would Ruth reply?

"How can we help you today?" the woman asked. She was pretty and young and held a clipboard; Ruth was unsure how a woman like that could help her, although she was receptive to the idea of being helped.

"We're right, thanks," said Frida, steering Ruth towards the queue, which was made up of more pretty young women, many of them strung with children.

"If you let me know what you're here for, I might be able to speed things up for you," said the woman, following them with high-heeled steps. Her hair was frosted into a surf of blond, and she wore a small name tag: JENNY CONNELL, CUSTOMER SERVICE ASSISTANT.

"Your doors are haunted," said Ruth.

"Haunted!" Jenny Connell smiled. "I like that. They always act up on windy days. I'm so sorry." She wasn't sorry at all, which Ruth appreciated. The doors opened, and the paper and plastic blew in, then settled as the doors closed; the doors opened again, and the papers were sucked out. It was tidal.

Frida pressed close at Ruth's back the way Phillip used to as a boy.

"So what can we help you with today?" asked Jenny, but she was looking at Frida now.

"We're here to save the house," said Ruth, and Jenny's smile widened, but she continued to look at Frida.

"We're here to transfer some money," said Frida.

"Wonderful!" cried Jenny, and Ruth was delighted. "Did you know you could do that from the convenience of your own home using Internet banking?"

"It's a lot of money," said Frida.

Jenny nodded appreciatively. "Our daily online limit is five thousand dollars," she said.

"It's more than that," said Frida.

The woman in front of them in the queue turned to look, and Frida shuffled on her white-clad feet.

"Much more," said Ruth.

Jenny continued to nod. "Then you're in the right place," she said. "Our daily transfer limit in the branch is twenty thousand dollars."

"We have a cheque," said Frida.

"So it's not a transfer, then." Jenny seemed relieved. "We have a cheque deposit station right over there." She gestured towards a helpful-looking wall.

"I was asked to have Mrs. Field come in herself to verify the cheque," Frida said, without looking at the wall. She repeated, dully, "It's a lot of money."

The bank doors opened and closed, admitting paper and wind and more customers. Jenny looked at these newcomers, anxious, as if they had tugged on her sleeve. "Just go ahead and wait in line," she said, "and someone will be right with you."

Frida rolled her eyes.

"We have a cheque?" said Ruth.

Frida exhaled loudly. "No," she said.

"Why did you say we did?"

"We need to buy a cheque."

"I have cheques at home," said Ruth.

"This is a special cheque. Remember? Expedite. A fast cheque. Don't worry about it, Ruthie. I've got it under control."

Frida didn't look as if she had it under control. She seemed to be brimming with a scarcely concealed fury. The line in the bank was long, and the wind that came through the doors was cold for November. Children cried and were shushed and continued to cry, but mutedly. Ruth leaned into Frida to manage standing for all this time. The woman in front of them turned again and said, "There are chairs by the window," and both Ruth and Frida looked at her, not smiling, as if she had spoken in an unfamiliar language. "If you want to rest," she added, but Ruth only leaned farther into Frida and nodded her head one time. The woman jogged a baby on her hip. She turned away with a shrug, but the baby continued to watch Ruth until Ruth made a face at it. It regarded her with a jaded expression before hiding its round head.

Frida adopted a new vigilance when they reached the front of the queue. She clutched her handbag and watched for a teller to become available, and when the signal finally came—a flashing gold number and a cheerful chime—she walked with such brisk purpose that Ruth, who was still leaning against her, stumbled to keep upright. So Frida paused and took her arm, not roughly, but without patience. She steered Ruth towards the counter with the pulsing number and presented her to the woman behind it as if she were a piece of evidence.

This woman, also dressed in a red suit, was unlike Jenny Connell. She was older, with broad shoulders, as if she had evolved to move quickly through water, and girlishly cut hair. She wore a wedding ring but bit her fingernails. Her name, according to her badge, was Gail, and then something complicated and Greek.

"Good morning," Gail said from behind a wall of glass. Her voice issued from a small microphone, as if it needed great assistance to travel so far.

"This is Mrs. Field," said Frida, and she began to produce items from her handbag: Ruth's bankbook, some documents, and a piece of paper with numbers written on it.

"Good morning," said Ruth.

"I'm Mrs. Field's carer, and I'm here to help her write a cheque."

"I don't have a cheque," said Ruth conversationally.

"We need to purchase an expedited cheque," explained Frida.

Gail looked between Ruth and Frida as each one spoke, and her face was calm and dispassionate.

"That's very fast, isn't it?" asked Ruth. "An expedited cheque?" She liked the sound of the word *expedited*. It sounded risky and important.

"It's not immediate," said Gail. "But it does clear in one business day."

"One day, Frida!" said Ruth. "Usually it's three."

"The fee is eleven dollars," said Gail.

Frida produced eleven dollars like a magic trick from her handbag.

"Thank you," said Gail. What a polite woman! She began to consult Ruth's bankbook and then the computer, typing quickly with her bitten fingers, but the rest of her movements were unhurried. Frida gripped her handbag as if she would have liked to vault the counter and manage everything herself.

"Would you like to fill the cheque in right now, Mrs. Field?" asked Gail.

"Oh, yes," said Ruth.

Then the cheque seemed to swim up to the glass as if Gail could only just contain it; it had a life of its own. It flew through the gap between the glass and the counter, and Gail pushed a pen behind it. Now everyone was looking at Ruth.

"Would you like me to help you with that, Ruthie?" asked Frida.

Ruth peered at the cheque. Her name was printed on it already, and a series of numbers she recognized as belonging to her bank account. Her memory for numbers was good.

"This is for George," said Ruth.

"For George Young," said Frida. "That goes right on this line." She put her finger on the cheque.

"Young Livery," said Ruth.

"George Young. You write it just here." Frida looked at Gail again. "I'm her carer."

Gail nodded. "I believe we have you right here on the account. Technically you could write the cheque yourself."

"Not for this amount of money." Frida sounded aggrieved. "I was told Mrs. Field would need to authorize that herself."

Ruth wrote *George Young* on the line. She wondered why Frida's name was on her account.

"Excuse me for one moment," said Gail. A telephone was ringing—had been ringing for some time, Ruth now realized—and Gail went to answer it. She was taller than Ruth expected.

"Concentrate," hissed Frida. "Here." She took the pen from Ruth, paused for a moment, then wrote *seven hundred thousand dollars* in an elegant cursive.

"That's beautiful!" said Ruth.

When Frida wrote the amount in numeral form, however,

all those 0's crammed into one box reminded Ruth of schoolgirl writing, floaty and skewwiff.

"Now sign," Frida said. She gave Ruth the pen, and when Ruth hesitated, still looking at the crooked zeros on the crowded cheque, Frida flicked open her bag and produced the book.

"Look! Look!" she said, holding it open to the title page; there was writing there, but it was shaking too much for Ruth to read. Why was Frida making such a fuss?

Gail returned to her place behind the glass. Other golden numbers were flashing over other counters, and the line grew longer, and Jenny Connell greeted each gusty new arrival.

"Banks are so friendly these days," said Ruth, and she smiled at Gail, who failed to smile back.

"We're holding people up," said Frida, sliding the book away.

Ruth signed the cheque. Something seemed to deflate in Frida; she shrank a little, as if she'd been standing on the tips of her toes and holding her breath. Ruth passed the cheque under the glass. She waited to see Gail respond to the amount; she was proud to think she could sign a cheque for so much. But Gail made no acknowledgment of Ruth's generosity. What kind of bank was this, then? Did millionaires wander in every day, passing enormous cheques into the care of indifferent Gail?

"Do you have some form of identification, Mrs. Field?" asked Gail, and Frida gave an impatient whinny.

"Let me see." Ruth began to dig in her purse. "What kind of identification?"

"A driver's licence, for example."

Ruth remembered keeping her driver's licence in the glove box of Harry's car. She heard the car, once again, make its final journey down the drive.

"Or a passport," said Gail.

"A cheque is a cheque," said Frida. She leaned towards the hole in the glass, and her breath smudged its outer edges.

"My passport is at home," said Ruth.

"She's clearly who she says she is," said Frida. "You have her bankbook."

"We need photo identification for any large withdrawal," said Gail, immaculate behind her Frida-proof glass.

"We'll come back tomorrow," said Ruth. "I know exactly where my passport is. It's in the top drawer of Harry's desk."

"We don't have time," said Frida.

"This afternoon!" said Ruth. "We'll take the bus."

"What about your Senior's Card, Mrs. Field?" Gail seemed to have withheld this possibility and now to enjoy suggesting it.

Frida took the purse from Ruth and began to shuffle cards.

"They really get stuck in there," said Ruth, and she looked to Gail for commiseration, but Gail was watching Frida's hands. The wind came in and around the edges of Ruth's suit. She remembered that she wasn't wearing stockings and was embarrassed. Frida passed Ruth's Senior's Card under the glass, and Gail checked it and nodded and typed. Jenny Connell greeted a new customer. "Good afternoon!" she sang. Ruth pressed her knees together. She looked at the clock and saw that it was right on twelve.

17

Frida hailed a taxi to drive them home and paid for it herself. The taxidriver knew her; he was boisterous and nostalgic, describing George at work and play, so Ruth assumed he must once have been part of the ill-fated Young Livery. Frida stayed tight-lipped. No doubt she was maintaining her dignity by protecting George, but Ruth wanted to tell this driver every bad thing she knew.

Ruth was surprised by the state of the house. It was littered and muddy and smelled of salty dirt, as if the tide had washed through it. This was the tiger's doing, she remembered; it made her tired. She wanted to rest her back in bed. Frida was courteous: she removed Ruth's shoes, and then her jacket. She offered to bring water or tea.

"I'll just stay on top of the covers," said Ruth. "I'll just stay dressed. I need to be ready."

"Ready for what?"

"For Richard. Didn't I tell you I invited him for Christmas?"

Frida lifted Ruth's legs to help her onto the bed.

"My feet are cold," Ruth said.

Frida put the jacket over them. She placed one hand over the jacket and said, "You sing out if you need anything." Then she left, closing the door behind her.

Ruth didn't sleep. Her bedroom was bright and there were no shadows. Frida was busy in the hallway clearing the buckets and the tarpaulin, and she hummed a little as she worked. At one point the telephone rang and Frida answered it. Ruth heard talking for a minute or two, considered picking up the receiver

next to her bed, and decided it would require too much effort.
The talking stopped. The house grew so quiet it became possible to hear someone whistling to his dog on the beach; Frida
went outside as if summoned by this whistle, but returned almost immediately. The waves were high and loud in the wind.
Ruth felt childishly convalescent. She lay in her bed all afternoon, and when she sat up, only two hours had passed.

"Frida!" she called. She coaxed her back with the breathing
exercises Frida had taught her, and when she stood, it rewarded
her by not hurting.

"Frida!" she called. The hallway was clear. Frida had mopped
the area by the front door, and it shone a rich woody red. She
wasn't in her bedroom, the lounge, or the bathroom; but all of
these places had been cleared of the worst of their tiger mess.
Some small piles of broken glass remained in the hallway, swept
up together in a little archipelago that looked vaguely like Fiji.

Frida was in the kitchen washing vegetables in the sink.
When she saw Ruth, she dried her hands and said, gently,
"Afternoon, Sleeping Beauty." Then she stepped forward and
kissed the top of Ruth's head.

"What was that for?" asked Ruth.

"Let's get you ready."

"Ready for what?"

"For your visitors." Frida took Ruth's shoulders and steered
her into the bathroom. "Richard for Christmas, and Jeff on
Friday. We'll do your hair."

"Wash it again?"

"Better than that. Into the shower." Frida tugged at Ruth's
skirt until it came loose from her hips. Ruth stepped out of it.
She raised her arms, and Frida lifted the shirt over her head
without unfastening a single button. Ruth removed her bra herself; she was proud of that little operation.

"Don't turn the shower on," said Frida, heading into the
hallway.

Ruth stepped into the shower with the aid of the railings. She had failed to remove her underpants, but didn't let that small slip upset her. She sat on the shower stool and waited for Frida, who returned with a comb and a vigorously shaken bottle. Frida was humming. She wrapped a towel around Ruth's shoulders, instructed her to close her eyes, and then Ruth felt a line of cool liquid on her scalp.

"What is it?"

"Sh," said Frida. "Close your eyes."

A sharp, bitter smell came next, pressing against Ruth's eyelids. Frida combed and smoothed and soaked Ruth's hair in this awful smell, but its pungency felt powerful, like some kind of protection. Ruth recognized it as the scent of Frida's hair when she had just dyed it.

Opening her eyes, Ruth saw deep brown stains on her skin where the dye had splashed and fallen. "It's so dark!"

"Don't worry," said Frida. "I've done a lovely ash blond, very subtle. You'll be so pretty when Richard comes. Can you sit like this for a while?"

Ruth thought she could. From her perch in the shower, she heard Frida moving through the house; she heard her in Phillip's bedroom, shifting things around. She was packing, then. She was leaving. And I told her to go, Ruth thought, and with that thought she became frightened of what she had done. She was in a bell, swinging outwards; she could feel the dome of the bell above her, and also the darkness under her feet where there was nobody, nobody; the fear struck and struck. It echoed, so that every time it came—it came in pulses—it left some of itself behind, and all of that leftover fear gathered under the dome with her. The tiger had never terrified her so much; not even the man on the telephone who told her Harry was dead. She remembered his saying, "Come to the hospital to see your dead husband," but of course he couldn't have said that. She swung out over the darkness, holding on to something—was it Richard? It might have been Richard—and didn't drop, but the fear only grew, and then Frida was behind her.

"Stop crying," Frida said, so Ruth knew she was crying. The shower stall amplified the sound. "What's wrong?"

"I'm so frightened," said Ruth. She held out her hands as if she expected to see something in her palms. "Look how I'm shaking." But she wasn't shaking.

"What are you scared of? I killed the tiger. The tiger's dead."

"Long live the tiger."

"No, you ninny," said Frida. "Death to tigers, remember?"

"Death to tigers," said Ruth to Frida the tiger killer, and then the fear—which had stilled for a moment—came back again, and now she understood why: it was because Frida was leaving. All the safety she had ever relied on flew away from her, out from under her feet, away over the garden and the sea; that was how it felt.

Frida had turned on the shower, and soft water ran in dark brown lines over Ruth's pale skin.

"Close your eyes," ordered Frida. "Close your mouth." But she said it gently.

Ruth closed her eyes and mouth, but a terrible noise was still coming from somewhere; possibly her own throat.

"I was going to blow-dry your hair, too," scolded sad, sweet Frida. "But all you're good for is bed."

The water ran clear and Ruth was no longer in the shower. She was in the bedroom, and Frida was dressing her in a nightgown. Ruth called out that her face was hot, so Frida left and returned with a wet cloth to wipe it.

"I don't know what all this fuss is for," said Frida, which Ruth considered cruel, and when she cried harder—her chest rose and sucked and fell—Frida swatted at her face, without touching her. "Oh, shut up, Ruthie. You've taken your pills. You'll be all right. You want me to go, and Jeffrey's coming on Friday." Frida settled Ruth into bed, looked once about the room, and left it, closing the door behind her. Ruth's cries became deep breaths. She was aware of falling asleep because the childhood feeling of doing so with tears on her face was familiar, but she didn't believe it would ever happen.

Ruth woke in the night, hungry. When she looked at her clock, it was only eleven. She called out for Frida, but there was no response, and because her stomach was making eager sounds, she sat up and stood up and was out of bed. Her back was calm. It hadn't felt so soft in months. She saw herself in her dressing-room mirror and gave a small wave—in the dark, she was only a blur of greyish white. Her hair felt damp at the back but otherwise dry. She wasn't afraid to walk into the hallway. The house was cool and quiet. Frida had left a plate of grilled lamb chops in the fridge, and the fruit bowl was filled with dimpled apples that reminded Ruth of the green-skinned mandarins she had eaten as a child. She stood at the kitchen counter eating the cold, greasy chops with her fingers and looking across the bay through a gap in the shutters. There were no lights in the town; there was not a lamp on for miles. No ships out at sea, either, and no moon. The foil that covered the lamb was the brightest thing in the world, and the loudest. The cats didn't come into the kitchen, not even with the smell of meat. Ruth felt as she had, younger, when her feet were more steadily planted on the floor, and her children and husband slept; that feeling was like an address she'd returned to, wondering why she'd been away so long. Even the taste of food was younger. The back door was closed, the house was cool, and the tiger was dead. Her head felt rinsed of everything.

"What a tantrum," she said, scolding herself.

Ruth knew Frida's bedroom would be empty, but she looked all the same, just to confirm her own instincts. She was surprised, nevertheless, to see it arranged as it had been before Frida moved in: as if Phillip, seventeen, had just walked out and left it for some nobler destiny. Frida had changed the sheets and swept up the crushed pills. She'd removed her mirror and all her grooming equipment, and Halley's Comet had returned to the sky of the mirrorless wall.

Ruth looked through the rest of the house for signs of Frida, but she could find none beyond those that were her enduring legacy: the twilight gleam of the floors, for example, and the new order of the books on the shelf above the television. Otherwise she might never have come. The clocks ticked louder. The furniture was lifeless without the tiger or the birds or Frida, and so it reverted to its previous function, which was to provide comfortable familiarity. The lace was lit grey at the windows, and Ruth crossed to it and looked out at the front garden. An unexpected shape occupied the front step: it was Frida. She sat completely still, but intent. She was stone that had been carved into life. She had her suitcase, and she was waiting for someone. It must be George; whom else did she ever wait for? But George had stolen her money and the house her mother died in. Why wait for George?

Ruth was calm. She felt no desire to cry out, to rap the window, or to open the front door. She knew Frida was leaving her, and not because she had demanded it; after all, she had ordered Frida to leave before, with no results. Frida only ever did what she wanted. Ruth knew that, just as she knew that Frida was not honest and had fooled her in some important way. The clocks ticked louder. Ruth went to her bedroom, where she didn't bother to check for her shape in the mirror. There was no one in the mirror: not Frida, not Harry, not even Richard. The cats followed on their springy feet, and they slept the rest of the night the way she did: motionless, undreaming, and without making any sound. In the morning, when she woke, Ruth returned to the lounge room and looked out the window. Frida was still sitting on the doorstep.

18

That morning was spare and bright. The sun had risen clear, the whole sea was visible and without shine, and there was no wind in the grass. It was springtime still; it was only November. Ruth knocked at the window, moved the lace curtain, and continued knocking until Frida turned to face her. Frida looked very young, sitting on the doorstep and staring up at Ruth, as if staying out all night had wiped her face clear of everything she had collected on it, and now she was only tired and childish. She was smooth, like delivered milk. Then she turned away, and although Ruth knocked again, and called "Frida!" through the glass, loudly, with her hands cupped at her round mouth as if that might help the sound travel, Frida remained on the step for another twenty minutes; then she came in.

"I just need to make a phone call," she said heavily, and she walked heavily to the kitchen, where she eyed the phone as if it were a disguised enemy. She said, "Aren't I allowed one call, Officer?"—and then she laughed.

Ruth stayed in the lounge room and looked out at the doorstep again. Frida's suitcase still sat in the sandy grass. It could convincingly have grown from a stalk into a grey-white fruit.

"Your suitcase, Frida!" called Ruth, but Frida didn't respond. She was pacing in the kitchen, cradling the phone, and she wrapped the cord around and around her arm until she could no longer pace and had wound herself to the wall. She was waiting and listening. Then she hung up and tried another number; then another. Only once did a voice respond at the other end of the line, but even at this distance—Ruth hovered at the end of the dining table, leaning on it for support—the voice was obviously recorded. Ruth went into the kitchen. Frida took a deep breath, replaced the receiver, and pressed her head gently against the wall.

Then she turned and looked at Ruth. "George is gone," she said.

"I know," said Ruth.

"No, I mean, this time he really is. This time it's real. And he's taken all my money. Which means he's taken your money, too, my darling. He's taken everything."

How could this mean anything? It meant very little.

"He's done it now," said Frida. She leaned against the windowsill. She was so amazed that her face looked slightly happy. "He's actually gone and done it."

It began to mean something. Frida was no longer in control; Frida was frightened. She had fought the tiger, but now she was leaning, pale in the face, against the windowsill because she couldn't trust her legs to hold her.

How could he have taken everything? Everything was still here: the house, the cats, the sea, Ruth, Frida.

"He's taken us both for a bloody ride," said Frida, still with that note of wonder in her voice. "A bloody joyride." Now her voice rose. "That bastard has ruined everything, and I have worked *so hard*. Look at this!" She flung one arm out. "I've washed these floors a thousand times or more, I've cooked and cleaned, I've *lived here* because he said we could save on rent, we could get more done, he said, we could worm our way in—I've lived and breathed this house and you, Ruthie, you! For months! All he did was say, 'You've earned it, just you wait, you deserve it,' and drive around in that bloody taxi, and now he's taken everything."

Frida looked at Ruth as if she might be in a position to right things; as if she might be in a position, at least, to acknowledge Frida's misfortune. Ruth gave her a small smile. She wanted to say it would be all right, but she seemed to be having trouble breathing; some part of her, she thought, was furious; but which part? She was supposed to be angry at George, and so she was.

"I told him we needed to wait for a man!" raged Frida. She stood now. "There's no use with a woman. I *told* him how much harder it would be. People always fuss over a woman. A woman with sons! Sons always fuss. But oh, no, not a minute to lose, this is the one, Frida, this is it. What I should have done"—she spun to look at the telephone, as if it connected her to George in some mystical way—"what I should have done is make *him* come along and do it all. *I* could be the one running off into the sunset, and then where would he be?"

"Oh, Frida, I couldn't have had a man in the house," said Ruth. "What would people think?"

"Exactly!" cried Frida. "The two of you would be married by now, my love. Oh, yes, you would. Don't look at me like that, so innocent! And George would have driven Richard off with a stick."

"I don't even know George," objected Ruth.

"But *I* do," said Frida. "Jesus, do I know George. He'd screw a goldfish if he thought it had any money." She stood at the window and beat it with one flat hand, so that the glass and the sea all shook, and she stamped one foot as if it were chained to the table. There was a quiet minute in which Ruth tried to determine whether Frida was weeping. Then Frida turned suddenly and cried, "What now, what now?" and there were no tears, but her face was so fierce and so abandoned; suddenly she doubled over as if in pain. Her buried head said, softer, "What do I do now?"

"Stand up," said Ruth. "I can't bend." She tried, anyway, to bend, and Frida held out one hand to stop her.

"No," Frida said, and righted herself, but as she did so she gathered Ruth in her arms and lifted her a little way off the floor. Frida's face was softly creased. Her body vibrated. "He's left me, Ruthie," she said. "I've got nothing. What do I do?"

"Put me down," said Ruth, although she wasn't sure if that was what she wanted, and Frida set her back on her feet.

"I had this dream that the sea came right up to meet us, up here on our hill." Frida was looking out the window at the water, and the wondering expression had returned to her reddening face. "And there were all these boats on the waves—old-time boats, you know, like they have on TV, some with sails, some with clouds of steam and huge chimneys. They were heading straight for us up on the hill, and the people in all of them were waving like crazy. I couldn't tell if they were waving hello or telling us to get out of the way."

"What did you do?" asked Ruth. It seemed like a comforting vision; it would be like the boats on the water at Suva, and in one of the boats would be the Queen. The Queen had sailed away in a boat with Richard, all the way to Sydney.

"I woke up," said Frida.

"I suppose that's best," said Ruth, disappointed.

Now Frida walked to the back door. She wore her sandshoes and coat, but under the coat, Ruth noticed, were brown trousers. Ruth had never seen Frida in brown. She must have changed clothes in the night.

"What should we do, Ruthie?" Frida asked in a considering voice. "Because this is the thing—we can do anything. You know that? Should we go out in the garden? Should we go down to the beach? No, not yet. There's things to do first. What things? What things?" Frida was talking to herself. She backed into the kitchen. "What's today?" she asked herself. "Thursday? Thursday! Do you understand, Ruthie, that George has left me and stolen all our money?" And she went out of the kitchen and down the hallway towards the front door.

So George had taken everybody's money. Ruth clapped her hands once, twice. It was what she did when the cats were brawling, or her children misbehaved. The sharp sound appeased her. Her back didn't hurt; it was perfect. But still: all our money! She remembered her empty purse in the butcher's, and the patient, pompous look on the Sausage King's face, and she wondered exactly when George had done it. They were so worried about the tiger, and all along the real danger was George. Ruth felt most sorry for Harry, because he was proud and careful and wouldn't, for example, have let her keep the door open at night. It was an embarrassment for Harry and would hurt him if he were here. Where was he? All our money! Frida came back with her suitcase.

"I want you to know that if it came to choosing—you or George—I'd always choose you. I want you to know that." Frida was very serious. She had her suitcase on the dining table, unlocked, and was removing things from it; things made of glass and silver and gold, which Ruth thought she recognized. "If I'd known how everything would work out, is what I'm saying," said Frida, still explaining. "If I'd known what a bastard he was."

Ruth peered at the objects on the table.

"Look at me," said Frida, and Ruth looked, and then back at the table, and then at Frida again, because Frida took her chin and made her. "Tell me you know I would choose you." What was clear on Frida's face was neither love nor hate but conviction.

"What's all this?" asked Ruth, pulling her head away.

"Presents."

"For me?"

"They *were* for me," said Frida. "But you can have them, now. May as well."

One of them looked like Ruth's mother's engagement ring. Ruth stretched her hand out, and Frida passed her the ring. It was gold with a nest of diamonds; it was her mother's ring.

"It's beautiful, isn't it," said Frida, who had never said the word *beautiful* in Ruth's hearing, and so Ruth was filled with pride. She put the ring on her finger, where it spun above her other well-fitted rings. Frida gave a small humph and said, "Too

big." Then she took Ruth's hand, tapped Ruth's own engagement and wedding rings, and said, "I told him I wasn't going to
take those. They're yours forever."

Ruth made a fist with her hand. "They *are* mine. Harry
gave them to me."

"That's what I told him. Now there's something I need to
show you."

"Can you spare the time?" asked Ruth.

"It's only Thursday."

Frida went to look for something in the study; when she returned, she held a letter on thin blue paper and shook it in the
air like a thin blue flag. "You may as well see this now," she said.
"What difference does it make?" She passed the paper to Ruth
with delicate fingers.

The letter was from Richard.

"This is the latest one," said Frida. "There are others. He
wrote nearly every day after he left. I'll get them all for you if
you want."

"Oh." Ruth felt squeezed inside, a great clenching, and then
release. She looked at the letter, which began, "My dearest
Ruth"—but couldn't bring herself to read any more.

"You trusted me, didn't you," said Frida. It wasn't a question.

"There are no guarantees," said Ruth. She considered it
likely that she had never trusted Frida. But then she didn't trust
herself.

"You said it." Frida was writing something on a piece of
paper and taping it to the telephone. "This is Jeff's number,
right here on the phone."

"You press star and then one to call Jeff," said Ruth.

"Forget that. I wiped that weeks ago. You need to call this
number—see it on the phone? You remember how to work the
phone? That's something else—sometimes I turned the ringer
down low, so you wouldn't hear it."

"Why did you do that?"

"To stop you from talking to people. I couldn't stop Jeff, though. A guy like Jeff fusses. Do you love me, Ruthie?"

"Yes," said Ruth, without thinking, which meant she did love.

"I knew it," said Frida. She lifted Ruth into her arms, like a baby.

Ruth still held the letter. "Where are we going?"

"Just outside."

"Do you know what you're going to do?"

Frida shook her head. "I have no idea what I'm going to do."

Ruth didn't believe her. As they passed out of the house, Ruth saw herself reflected in the dining-room windows: high in Frida's arms, with different hair.

Frida carried Ruth to a shady part of the garden and set her down so she stood on the uneven grass. Her back was partially propped by the bending limb of the frangipani tree.

"I'll be right back," Frida said.

Ruth watched Frida walk to the house. Something about her was different, but what? Her hair was still dark and straight, she was still tall and wide; she was still Frida. Because Ruth held Richard's letter, she looked at it again: "My dearest Ruth, Frida tells me you're beginning to feel better, which is such good news, it calls for a celebration." And lower on the page: "Will it embarrass you to hear you are the best of the lovely things?" She remembered his handwriting; once, she used to hoard every example of it she could find. She liked the long, adult forward tilt of his *t*'s and *h*'s and *l*'s. He had kissed her at the ball and then in the bedroom. Would he be a good husband? Had he been a good husband? Or was that someone else? Harry was the husband—but he was missing.

"Harry?" she said into the wind. Where was he? Here in the garden, maybe. She listened for sounds of him. "Harry? Darling?"

The garden was empty. There were no cats and no plants; it

was bare and scrubbed. The trees were leafless, as if someone had plucked every branch clean. There was also no sun. Only the dune, greyish, and the sky, greyish, and at some distance the white-and-black sea.

"Here I am!" cried Frida. She had come out into the garden carrying Ruth's chair; she found level ground for it near the frangipani tree. Then she came to Ruth and held her shoulders, something like the way she had when Ruth had arrived home with Ellen from town.

"Here *I* am," said Ruth. She looked about, still, for Harry. He was probably kneeling in some garden bed, possibly among the hydrangeas. Hydrangea flowers don't fall off. They go brown, don't they, and they stay; but really they should fall. In the past, Harry must have cut them. Maybe she could help him. There must be some worm that wanted to come and eat the flower-heads. Ruth stamped her feet to call the worms up out of the ground. The sound of her feet travelled through the dune, and other sounds joined it: the shooting of new roots, maybe, and busy crabs and insects burrowing in the sand. Frida held her tighter, to keep her still.

"Now, what's this?" said Frida, and she began to sing a low lullaby; Ruth recognized the tune, but not the words, which didn't seem quite English. Then she recognized them, without understanding. It was a Fijian song. She and Frida rocked on the dune, the words fell over and around them, and the lullaby inhabited some interior place of Ruth's, where it greeted other things—the shape of her mother's mouth and a dog she saw killed on the street in Suva. There was a reunion there, in that place. Ruth attended to it, and to the subtle movement of Frida's big body, and to the feel of the air on her arms as they moved. The nurses sang sometimes as they worked in the clinic. New mothers sang to their babies. Her mother and father sang hymns. Her father read to them in the evening while the houseboy sang in the kitchen: "Consider the lilies of the field," read her father, and Ruth considered them. "How they grow; they toil not, neither do they spin." I neither toil nor spin, thought Ruth. She leaned into Frida's belly and felt herself arrayed in glory.

What could this song be for? To send babies to sleep. Phillip slept fitfully in his crib. Isn't *pleurisy* a lovely word? Beside his crib: *The Cat in the Hat. I Am a Bunny. Go, Dog. Go!* Ruth rested and sang. It was humid in the hollow of Frida's arm, and Ruth's hair clung to her cheek. She remembered then that Harry was dead. I remember that I remember that, she thought. Thank God that fact was sticky enough; she wanted to honour it. Every future minute announced itself, broad and without Harry. And then her life, her whole past, crowded up against this minute— entirely filled this minute, it was over so quickly. It all insisted so busily on something Ruth could not identify, something that had to do with happiness. How disappointing it was not to have been happy, thought Ruth, at every moment you expected to be. Now, here, she might be happy, but it was unlikely.

Frida bent her knees to the ground and took Ruth with her. She still sang, but there were no longer any words; Frida was only a tune, and warm breath, taking Ruth towards the ground. The grass was smooth and rough, and Frida laid her out on it. Frida kissed Ruth's forehead; she lifted her free hand to keep the sun from Ruth's eyes. She still sang, but she paused to say, "This won't do," and she moved Ruth a little farther into the shade, or what shade there was under the thick grey lace of the frangipani, with no flowers on it yet, and few leaves, so early in November. A gull sat at the top of the tree, not watching, not sleeping, not anything but a gull.

"How's that?" asked Frida, and she lifted Ruth's head and laid it on something soft.

"My back doesn't hurt," said Ruth, as if delivering a weather report. "It's very fine."

"That's the way," said Frida. She stood over Ruth and was no longer wearing her coat. She held a glass of water, which she gave to Ruth, and a blue pill, and another, and then—hesitating a moment—another. Frida helped Ruth swallow each one. "Now you'll be comfy. You just rest there for a little while, and when you're ready, I want you to call Jeff and tell him right away about George. All right? You promise me?"

"I promise," said Ruth. The ground was more elastic than she remembered.

"What will you tell him about George?"

"Young Livery."

"That's right, that's his taxi," said Frida, patient. "But what has he done? What bad thing has George done?"

"George has run off with everyone's money."

"Good. Tell Jeff I've left papers on the table for him to give to the police. All right?"

"Frida," said Ruth, smiling, "I can't call Jeff from out here."

"I know. You'll need to get yourself inside—just like that day when you were out here on your own and you got back in all by yourself. But this time your back won't hurt you, because of the pills, and also I put your chair out here to help you get up. You just hold on to your chair, and it'll be easy. I'm going in a minute, and then, when you're ready, you start heading for the phone. Call Jeff as soon as you can. All you need to do is give me some time. Got it?"

"What do you need time for?"

"I don't know yet."

Ruth still smiled. Frida was kneeling beside her now, wearing a pink T-shirt. Pink! Her whole face was lit with the colour.

"The back door is open," said Frida, stroking Ruth's face, "and the cats are in your bedroom with food and water. You just go in there when you want to find them. Nothing to worry about, all right?"

"All right," Ruth said. Frida stayed still, looking at her. "All right," Ruth said again, and she squeezed Frida's hand, which she noticed was holding hers. The squeezing produced little effect—Ruth couldn't feel her hand tightening, and she didn't know if Frida squeezed back. Harry always squeezed back. One, two, three squeezes meant "I love you." In her other hand, Ruth held Richard's letter.

"I'm going now," said Frida, but she still didn't move. She had a terrible look on her face, calm but terrible; it was resolved, and patient. The sand and grass would ruin her pretty trousers.

"You should wear pink more often," said Ruth, and Frida let go of Ruth's hand and stood. Now her face was gone completely. She stood there for a moment—Ruth could see her legs, and her trousers were a little crushed from the kneeling, but not stained; she had a rim of hair at her ankle, and a small mole. Frida turned and walked into the house. The gull still sat in the frangipani.

19

The empty garden was quiet. There was a lull in everything: the wind, the sound of the sea, and even the light, as if a thin cloud was passing over the sun. Ruth settled her head into the pillow Frida had given her and rested for some time, in order to gather the strength she would require to reach the telephone. She thought of Harry as she lay there in the garden because she knew he was dead, and she knew she had forgotten he was dead. That seemed the same as forgetting he had lived. Mainly she thought of how his face looked beside hers in bed. Ruth thought of Harry and squeezed her own hand. She rubbed her feet together the way happy babies do, but she couldn't feel them. It was as if a soft coat had risen over her legs—something soft and heavy, also warm, but not a fabric. It took her some time to decide what this blanket might be, and eventually it occurred to her—since she couldn't seem to lift her head from where it lay on the pillow—that Frida might have covered her feet with the skin of the tiger. Then she saw herself under the tree under the tiger skin, and what would Harry say? He would say, George, George, George. Young George stole everyone's livery money. Ruth couldn't tell if she had stopped rubbing her feet. She thought Frida should have brought the telephone out here if she wanted her to call George so badly. She thought Frida should have done many things differently. Something was cutting into her hand as she squeezed it, and after she had squeezed some more, she realized it was her mother's engagement ring.

Soon she would have to get to the house to find the telephone. It would be wound in white cord. Ruth couldn't feel her feet, but she thought she could feel her elbows. She tried to lift

herself on them the way she had the day she was caught in the
tiger trap. They wouldn't lift; nothing would. When she lay in
the tiger trap, there was only the wide sky, but here there was the
green slant of the sun in the frangipani. Ruth knew the size of
that sun, and all of its properties: it was moving now down the
length of her spine, burning some things away and dulling others. Its heat rolled, but subtly. She imagined her spine as a rough
shaft, crusted and frayed, like underwater wood. She needed to
find this shaft of wood where it splintered underwater; she
seized hold of it with her hands; she tugged and the wood came
free. Then Ruth came out of the sea. She tasted the salt on her
lips to check that it was the sea; she had no memory of getting
there. Also she was holding this piece of clammy wood, which
was easy enough to throw out over the sand, so that it flew above
the dunes and up and into the long-distance wind. The wind
made a high piping sound before leaving pinkish traces behind.
The sky reddened a little—the tiniest drop of blood stirred in
water—which was the strangest weather. A storm might be
coming, or leaving; this might be the centre of it. It rattled the
windowpanes like a herald, as if to say, "Prepare! Prepare!"
Someone must take the chair into the house before it was ruined.
No one could move the gull away from the frangipani, but he
might fly off with the first piece of rain. The whales would
sound deeper, where there was no storm, and the boy might
speed out across the water in his boat to look for them. Then
Harry, that necessary man, would call out from the shoreline,
"Prepare! Prepare!" He was too busy to take the chair in from
the garden, so it would have to be bound with white cord and
pulled, the way the wood was pulled from under the sea. Harry
ran along the shore, calling out, and the boat was a narrow yellow spill on the bay. The waves rose up and sent spray out over
the dunes. The spray fell across the frangipani tree, but the gull
stayed; it only turned one curious eye. The cord was too heavy to
lift from the floor, so the chair shook, but couldn't be moved.

The sun was gone now; it was no longer the sun. There was no name for it because it wouldn't come again. A papery blue shape fell from somewhere and gusted up into the tree. It wasn't terribly important. The chair would have to stay outside, and so would the man calling below the dunes. The windows could rattle and rattle, and no one and nothing would be inside.

Then the rub of the storm over the trees. There was no rain; only sound. First the birds, objecting, as if morning had come in the middle of the night, and then every insect. A bell rang to call a doctor out of sleep. "Not in this weather," said a woman, a mother, but the father went out into the sound nevertheless. He went down to the beach, where people stood with binoculars. He waded there among the people and it was as if a god had come among them; an old, pastoral god, driving sheep. The mother's ring spanned her finger. She had lost her husband, too, and was inconsolable; she said, "There's no marriage in heaven." Now the volume of the jungle increased, but it wasn't quite right: there were monkeys and macaws, all the wrong objects, great opening lilies that sent out a smell of rain. Nothing is so loud as the sound of insects. And on the faint sea: a yellow shape that wasn't a boat. It was long and walking out of the water. It paused to inspect items on the beach; it turned every now and then when it heard someone crying out, but at a distance. It stayed in the rough edge of the waves, and it came closer and was recognizable. The tiger was there in the water. His throat wasn't cut, and he wore his own seared skin. Tigers can be patient; they know how to wait.

He was also fast; he was coming. He seemed to know there was nothing to stop him. Now he was out of the water and on the sand; now at the bottom of the dune where the end of the trap lay. His breath came in evenly over the sound of the birds, his ears lay back against his head, and his claws in the sand made a sound of rolling rock. He was the colour of the gone sun. And he sang! He sang a low hymn as he ran, which came out with his breath over his irregular tongue. Now he came singing up the dune, and all the birds flew screaming behind him, except the one gull in the frangipani tree. That tree swam in and out of the green light. It was bound around with a long white cord that couldn't be lifted from the ground, and a sound intermittently rang out from it. Could it really be so loud under this tree, after all that quiet? Here he was at the beginning of the grass. His heavy head was so familiar, and he still sang in a low, familiar voice. What a large gold space he filled at the edge of the garden. His face flared out from itself, and every black line was only a moving away, so he seemed to be retreating even when he stood his ground. And he was totally unharmed; someone had lied about this tiger. A woman as large as he was, and real as he was, had lied. When he came forward over the lawn, the hydrangeas shook and the dune grass blew back from the greener grass. He stopped at the chair and reached forward—all that length of him, reaching forward—and sharpened his claws on its wooden leg. Then he leant back on his hind legs, and paused, and leapt onto the chair. It tipped to the left. He didn't sing, after all, but his breath was melodic, and he sat up tall with his paws together, like a circus tiger. He began to groom his symmetrical sides.

"Now," said Ruth. Ruth was her name. It had been promised to her and had remained faithful. "Now!" she called out, but the tiger didn't move. She noticed she was in the process of standing only because she was no longer on the ground. Weren't those oil tankers high in the water? Her wooden spine was burned away, and she could stand. There wasn't even any need to hold on to the white cord, which was just as well, because where would it lead her? Standing, as she was now, she was as tall as the tiger. He didn't watch her, only licked and smoothed. Ruth held her hands out to him. She crossed the fine, dusty lawn, and every step seemed to sweep it away. All the grass flew down the dune, and only the barest, brownest white showed through.

"Now," she said to the tiger, but he only swung his lazy head to his other flank and licked it down. He defined his stripes. He fastened them with his tongue.

So Ruth stepped closer. "Kit, kit, kit!" she said. She reached out with her arms and gripped the rough, warm fur on his shoulders. Now the bird in the tree began to sing out for the first time. It sang "Prepare! Prepare!" But there was no reason to be afraid of this calm tiger. He smelled like dirty water. She leaned her head into his soft chest, where his great heart ticked.

20

The cats found a home with Ellen Gibson. She learned of their plight because her sister was a receptionist at the veterinary surgery Jeffrey called to ask for details about the nearest cat shelter. He was apologetic on the phone, Ellen's sister reported, but there were dogs and international flights and allergies to consider, and his tone was both guilty and defensive. Ellen knew that when Jeffrey called the surgery he had just come from the bank—various people had seen him there and witnessed his rage with the bank manager and with Gail Talitsikas, and they all talked about him in those fresh, suspenseful days, so that everywhere Ellen went she heard new details: that Frida's surname was not Young, for example, and that the government had never sent her.

Ellen drove in her small red car to the top of the hill, parked it on the coastal road, and made her way to the house on foot. Her intention had been to arrive without fuss and with no air of judgment, but she was forced to battle with the scrub that had overtaken the drive. Low, stunted trees caught at her legs and in her hair, and the dune grasses shook off a seedy substance that made her sneeze. Jeffrey was waiting for her when she emerged by the house.

"It's like a fairy-tale castle, isn't it," he said. He wore old clothes that might have been his father's, and gardening kneepads.

"A little." Ellen sneezed again and gave a small laugh; she felt both intrusive and self-righteous. She felt silly.

"It's much better in a car," said Jeffrey. "You just nose your way through and push everything out of the way."

Ellen thought Jeffrey should be ashamed of having, among other things, allowed his mother's property to reach this state; but she also remembered the condition of the drive only a week ago, which hadn't struck her as nearly this impassable. It was as if the garden had deliberately grown up to hide the house. She gave Jeffrey a small, awkward hug, and he patted her shoulder lightly, as if to say, "There, there."

"You seem to be the guardian angel of our family," he said.

The angel of death, thought Ellen. She had thought about this. She was a bad omen; a bird circling overhead asking, "Are you all right?"—when no one was ever all right.

"I'm so sorry about—everything," said Ellen; but that sounded like an apology and there was nothing, really, to apologize for. The part of Ellen that considered it Jeffrey's place to cancel her apology and make one of his own was hushed by another, more sympathetic part. He was leaner than he'd been at his father's funeral, as if that death had surprised him into cardiovascular diligence. But he also stood with one fist balled into the small of his back, stretching it out, as if he'd inherited Ruth's back and was only just feeling it now. Maybe a family's troubles, thought Ellen, are always with them, and they just pass among the members with every death. Of course—silly—that's genetics, isn't it.

"We're very grateful to you."

"Oh, there's no need. I wish I could have done more." She wished, actually, that she could have done less.

"We all wish we could have done more," said Jeffrey, which was intolerable; for a minute Ellen let her full disgust at Jeffrey rise up from some bottomless place. If Ruth had been *my* mother, she thought, as she had thought so many times before; but she gave her head a compassionate tilt. It was difficult to think what to say. Jeffrey had a strange convalescent look, like a man recovering from a dreamlike illness, and all his movements had a submarine quality: he stepped over to a wheelbarrow that lay by

the side of the house and half lifted it, then let it drop again. So
he was suffering, which Ellen realized she required from him,
and then she was afraid she would cry.

Phillip erupted from the house.

"Ellen!" he called. He looked like his mother, with that
same light-haired, dairy-fed roundness of cheek, and he had her
expansive smile. He was the baby of his family and had never
quite abandoned the undignified safety of that position. His duty
to be sweetly jovial was, under the circumstances, a great burden; he enfolded Ellen and held her for some time. He smelled
of fresh laundry. When he released her, he was smiling—but
sadly, lovably. He held her hand. Phillip was much easier to forgive than his brother.

"I feel like you're part of the family," he said as Jeffrey
walked away from them around the side of the house. "Like
you're a sister." Ellen preferred this to being an angel. She
squeezed his hand in hers.

"I can't imagine—" she began, but she could imagine, so she
stopped.

They went inside to find the cats.

The house was tidy, but important objects were missing—
the lounge, for example, and then, in the kitchen, the oven. The
wall behind it was stained a deep, frazzled brown, as if there
had been a fire. There were no longer any paintings or photographs on the walls, and the lounge room was full of funeral
flowers. Ellen had sent hers ahead to the funeral parlour and
now regretted it. Ruth's favourite chair stood where the lounge
should have been; it looked battered and bleached, as if it had sat
outside for many days in strong temperatures. The dining table
was covered in papers; Phillip swept his arm over them and said,
"Everything the police didn't want. You'll have a cup of tea,
won't you?"

Through the windows, Ellen could see Jeffrey in the garden.
He seemed to be pulling weeds out of the dune grass with some

difficulty; or perhaps he was pulling up the grass itself. The sea behind him was a drenched green.

"Are you selling the house?"

"Absolutely." Then, as if to temper the finality of this, Phillip said, "Yes." He called for the cats by name but without conviction, and they didn't come.

He was obviously adrift in the kitchen. He opened cupboards and closed them again, looking for cups and tea and sugar in a slow slapstick. Ellen sat in one of the dining chairs and made an effort not to look at the papers on the table. When the water began to rattle in the kettle, she said, "I hear they found Frida's brother. That's good news."

"He was her boyfriend," said Phillip, fussing with milk.

"Oh. For some reason I thought brother. I suppose that makes more sense."

"More sense of what?"

"Of why she would just—give up. She didn't strike me as the type."

Then Ellen felt nervous at having raised the topic of Frida; at having said her name like a bad spell in this emptying house.

But Phillip didn't seem to mind. "You met her, didn't you?"

"Once," said Ellen. She remembered the way Ruth and Frida had run together like lovers, and how embarrassed she was by that intimacy, and, later, how unsettled. A great deal of time seemed to have passed since the day she saw Ruth in town.

Phillip brought mugs to the table and cleared space among the papers with his elbow. He looked out at his brother in the garden. "I just got here yesterday," he said. Then he went to the door and called out, "Jeff! Tea?" Jeffrey stood up from the grass with his arm pressed against his forehead and shook his whole torso to say no. He seemed to be holding a bundle of barbed wire.

Phillip turned to Ellen, who dutifully sipped her tea, and said, "I took the first flight out of Hong Kong. Jeff's been here since Friday."

"I wish I'd known. I could have brought food out."

Now Phillip sat. "You know what we found among all this?" he said, indicating the papers. "Letters from a man she knew in Fiji. Love letters, all recent, most of them unopened. Did you know she lived in Fiji? We wondered if that's why she dyed her hair. So Jeff called and told him, and he'll be at the funeral. You're coming, yes? Richard, his name is. He came out here to see her, and of course he met Frida. Everyone met her but us." He blew on his tea. "What was she like?"

"It was so brief," said Ellen. "She was very tall."

"Her mother contacted us through the police. She's English, apparently. The father was from New Zealand—half Maori. He's been dead for years, and there was a sister, too, also dead, cancer. But this mother—she's really something. She wants to come to the funeral."

"Goodness," said Ellen. "Is she local?"

"She lives in Perth, but she flew out. So that's something else we have to decide."

"I only talked to Frida for a few minutes," said Ellen. "But I got the impression she really loved your mum."

Phillip remained quiet for a moment. Then he said, "She was a cleaner, you know, at that nursing home. Seawind? Seacrest?"

"Seacrest Court."

"We assume that's how she got Mum's details. Jeff rang them earlier this year when Mum seemed a bit wobbly, calling in the middle of the night with bad dreams, that kind of thing. The police think Frida and George were waiting for some opportunity or other, and there she was." Phillip seemed so serene as he said all this, but Ellen suspected he wasn't the kind of man to have complicated regrets. He was filled, instead, with a dulling, puzzling grief, which occupied everything. He rubbed one finger over the edge of his mug of tea, and outside his brother pulled weeds. Jeffrey had found Ruth lying under a tree in the garden, everyone knew, but Ellen didn't think this accounted for his industry; he was probably just getting the house ready to sell. Some people in town disapproved of this haste, and others supported it.

Because the town, of course, was electric with all this news, with these events and fears and speculations. Some were sure they had seen George Young's taxi parked at the end of the Field drive late at night or early in the morning; others had seen Frida arguing over cheques in the supermarket. Everyone called their aging parents or dropped in on them at nursing homes. For the couple of days after Ruth was found, when no one knew where Frida and George might be, Ellen, like everyone else, double-checked the locks on her doors and windows, as if anything might come creeping through in the night. And then on Sunday afternoon a fisherman discovered Frida's body where it had been swept among the lighthouse rocks, and there was some disappointment in town; they wanted her brought to justice. She was too heavy for one man to lift out of the water, and by the time the requisite emergency services arrived, a crowd had gathered to watch. For two days, everyone had wanted this woman, and now she was hoisted from the sea. Then the danger seemed to have passed, but the flag stayed at half-mast on the surf club.

Now the cats came in from the garden, but they lingered at the door, unwilling, so Ellen leaned down and made kissing noises; then they approached with caution.

"You really are a lifesaver," Phillip said, and that was awkward because—in the case of the cats, at least—it may have been true.

The cats wore imbecile expressions; they jumped superstitiously at their own tails, trimmed their tidy claws, and sniffed at Ellen's offered fingers with mild curiosity. Phillip told her they weren't eating a thing.

"In the spirit of full disclosure," he said, "the tabby, the boy, throws up at least once a day."

The tweedy boy cat looked vacantly at Ellen. He allowed

himself to be handled into a carrier she had bought specially, and the tortoiseshell girl was similarly docile. They were fragile bundles beneath their important fur. They made no noise as they were carried from the house or were settled into the backseat, but they howled as the car descended the hill, with plaintive, inconsolable cries. As she drove past the bus stop, Ellen saw a cloud of seagulls rise in a body from the sea. They lunged for the sky, then fell back.

THE
Fall Guy

also by **James Lasdun**

FICTION

Delirium Eclipse

Three Evenings and Other Stories

Besieged (selected stories)

The Horned Man

Seven Lies

It's Beginning to Hurt

POETRY

A Jump Start

After Ovid: New Metamorphoses (coedited with
Michael Hofmann)

Woman Police Officer in Elevator

Landscape with Chainsaw

Bluestone: New and Selected Poems

MEMOIR

Give Me Everything You Have: On Being Stalked

W. W. NORTON & COMPANY

INDEPENDENT PUBLISHERS SINCE 1923

NEW YORK | LONDON

Fall Guy

A NOVEL

James Lasdun

For information about permission to reproduce selections from this book, write to Permissions, W. W. Norton & Company, Inc., 500 Fifth Avenue, New York, NY 10110

For information about special discounts for bulk purchases, please contact W. W. Norton Special Sales at specialsales@wwnorton.com or 800-233-4830

Manufacturing by Quad Graphics, Fairfield
Book design by Fearn Cutler de Vicq
Production manager: Anna Oler

Library of Congress Cataloging-in-Publication Data
Names: Lasdun, James, author.
Title: The fall guy : a novel / James Lasdun.
Description: First Edition. | New York : W. W. Norton & Company, [2016]
Identifiers: LCCN 2016018259 | ISBN 9780393292329 (hardcover)
Classification: LCC PR6062.A735 F35 2016 | DDC 823/.914—dc23 LC record available at https://lccn.loc.gov/2016018259

W. W. Norton & Company, Inc.
500 Fifth Avenue, New York, N.Y. 10110
www.wwnorton.com

W. W. Norton & Company Ltd.
Castle House, 75/76 Wells Street, London W1T 3QT

1 2 3 4 5 6 7 8 9 0

For S., in memory

THE
Fall Guy

one

They'd arranged to leave late so as to avoid the traffic. Matthew, trundling his suitcase from the subway, arrived at Charlie's house in Cobble Hill at seven and helped load Charlie's bags into the back of the Lexus. It was a humid evening, and by the time they were done his shirt was soaked in sweat.

They took the tunnel out of Brooklyn and headed up the West Side Highway, Charlie slowing the heavy vehicle at every intersection to avoid the speed cameras and accelerating hard for the next stretch. All the way through Midtown the lights cooperated with his progress, spreading green welcomes as if waving some dignitary through checkpoints. Not that Charlie noticed, of course, Matthew observed to himself; Charlie would never deign to notice such a trivial piece of luck.

In Harlem they exited to stock up at Fairway, filling a cart with cheeses, olives, artichokes, caper berries. At the last minute Charlie threw in some tins of Osetra caviar.

"Best thing on earth for late-night munchies . . ."

Matthew shrugged: Charlie was paying, after all.

A few minutes later they were crossing the George Washington Bridge.

"Why don't you find some music?" Charlie said.

Matthew had thought they might talk, but did as his cousin asked, selecting Gieseking's Debussy on the iPod.

"Good choice."

After a minute, though, Charlie said:

"Actually, could you find something by Plan B?"

Matthew scrolled to Plan B. Hard beats and aggressive voices replaced the rippling piano.

Oi! I said Oi! What you looking at you little rich boy?

"What do you think?" Charlie said. "Great, aren't they?"

Matthew glanced over to see if his cousin was joking, but he didn't appear to be.

"Not bad."

"Needs to be louder, though."

Matthew turned up the volume.

They drove down the Palisades and onto the Thruway. As they passed the Suffern exit Charlie motioned with his hand that he wanted the music turned back down.

"You know that feeling when you've forgotten something?"

"Yes . . ."

"I'm getting waves of it."

"Uh-oh."

"But I'm not getting a fix on what it is."

"Someone you're supposed to've called?"

"No."

"Something to do with work?"

"Nope."

"Family?"

"I don't think so."

"Maybe it's just a phantom version of the feeling."

"Let's hope."

Twenty minutes later, Charlie slowed down and pulled onto the shoulder.

"It's Chloe's anniversary present. I bought her a bracelet. I left the fucking thing behind."

"Shit."

"Shit is it."

"Can you get it when you next go down?"

Charlie shook his head.

"No. Our anniversary's this Sunday. I can't not have a gift for her. It's our tenth."

"Well, okay. Let's go back."

"So much for dinner at the Millstream."

Chloe had left that morning to drop off their daughter, Lily, at music camp in Connecticut before heading back west into New York State to meet Charlie and Matthew. The plan had been to rendezvous at the Millstream Inn in Aurelia for a late dinner before going on to the house.

"We won't get in till two or three a.m. Chloe doesn't like being there alone at night. She'll be deeply pissed and I won't be able to explain why it happened without ruining the surprise."

"Why don't I go back?" Matthew offered. "I can get the train from Harriman and catch the late bus up to Aurelia."

"No, no. No. Anyway, there isn't a late bus."

"Well, I could stay in the city. Come up tomorrow morning."

"No, this is my screwup. *I'll* get the train down and you can drive on up and meet Chloe. That's what we'll do."

"That's ridiculous, Charlie. Let me go back. You need to open up the house, deal with the pool. Chloe'll be much more upset if I show up without you than if you show up without me."

"No, that wouldn't be right. I couldn't let you do that."

"Don't be silly. Plus this way you won't need to invent a reason for being late. You can just tell her I had some last-minute hitch and couldn't come till tomorrow."

Charlie went on protesting, but Matthew knew he'd given his cousin what he wanted: an excuse to let Matthew fetch the bracelet without it looking too much like he, Charlie, was taking advantage. It would be a matter of purely practical necessity. In due course he agreed to the plan.

At the train station he gave Matthew his Amex card.

"Don't stint on taxis. And get a decent dinner. Rucola should still be open, or go somewhere fancier. Anywhere's fine."

"I like Rucola."

"Also you can sleep at the house if you like. Lupa'll be there in the morning, so you can just leave everything for her."

"Well, I have no choice. My subletter's moved in for the summer."

Charlie looked surprised.

"Your subletter? I didn't know you'd sublet."

"I can't afford not to, Charlie."

"Oh. Well, great. That's great."

"I hope so!"

"The bracelet's in the safe, which is probably why I forgot the damn thing. I never use it."

Charlie wrote down the burglar alarm code for the house and the combination numbers for the safe.

"I'll have to kill you, obviously, as soon as you get back tomorrow," he said, handing Matthew the scrap of paper.

"Obviously."

"Seriously, though, tear this up when you leave the house."

"I'll swallow it."

"And be careful at the Port Authority tomorrow. We don't want you getting mugged with a ten-thousand-dollar bracelet."

"Maybe I should swallow that too."

"That's gross, Matty. I'll see you tomorrow."

• • •

There was an hour's wait for the train. Matthew had a book—his father's old copy of Pascal's *Pensées*—as well as the summer issue of *Vanity Fair*. But he was distracted. After a while he realized he was actually a little upset. Not about having to go back for the bracelet, but about Charlie's apparent surprise at the news that he'd sublet his apartment.

Hadn't Charlie meant what he said when he'd invited him to stay for the summer? He could remember Charlie's words exactly: "Come up to Aurelia with us. You can have the guesthouse. We have plenty of room for other visitors. Stay as long as you like. Stay the whole summer, bro . . ." Matthew had thanked him noncommittally, not wanting to snatch too eagerly at the

offer in case Charlie should have second thoughts. But a week later Charlie had repeated it, more firmly: "Chloe and I would love to have you stay for the summer. I'm going to have to be in the city quite a bit and it'll be good for Chloe to have someone around. We thought we could appoint you official cook and grillmeister . . ." Matthew had taken him at his word, appreciating the tact of the little quid pro quo. And since he had no reason to come back down to the city for the period, he'd found a subtenant to stay in his apartment until Labor Day.

Now he had to wonder if he'd misunderstood Charlie's invitation. Had his "stay the whole summer, bro" not been meant to be taken literally? Was it what his father would have called just a *façon de parler*?

Well, there wasn't much he could do about it if it was. He'd advertised his apartment two months ago and the subtenant had arrived this morning: a Norwegian art historian who wanted to spend her summer exploring Brooklyn and looking at paintings in the Met. Anyway, Matthew told himself, Charlie hadn't seemed upset or put out, exactly; more just surprised.

They were first cousins, he and Charlie; their mothers sisters from Providence, Rhode Island. Charlie's mother had died when Charlie was thirteen. His father, at that time posted at the Dubai office of his bank, had sent Charlie to live with Matthew's family in London. The two of them had gone to the same London private school as day boys, and for a while they'd been close: brothers in all but name. Charlie's return to the States for college five years later would have been a wrench for both of them if things had continued as expected, but that had not been the case. Instead, calamity had struck. Matthew's father,

a well-to-do solicitor who'd become a member of Lloyd's, had lost almost everything when the insurance giant collapsed in the late eighties. A man of unstained character until then, he'd emptied the accounts of several of his clients and disappeared out of the country, vanishing without trace and leaving a pall of bewildered shame and grief hanging like a gaseous wake over his abandoned family. In under a year, Matthew, acting out in his own singular fashion, had been expelled from school after admitting to selling drugs. As for Charlie, rather than remain in the blighted Dannecker home, he had asked his father to enroll him as a boarder for the remainder of his time at the school, and with Matthew continuing his education at a series of crammers in increasingly obscure corners of London, the boys had soon lost touch with each other. A reprisal of the friendship had never been something Matthew had considered remotely in the cards, or even especially desirable. But ten years later, circumstances had brought Matthew himself to live in the States, and after some initial reluctance he had contacted his cousin. Charlie, at that time freshly separated from his first wife and still raw from the experience, had responded with unexpected warmth, and the two had become friends again.

Still, it wasn't the same as if they'd never had a breach. And it didn't take much for Matthew to start wondering how dependable this newfound relationship really was.

He made an effort to shrug off Charlie's surprise about the sublet, telling himself he was being oversensitive, and started reading an article in *Vanity Fair* about gourmet food trucks, a subject that happened to interest him.

The train, when it finally came, crawled morosely toward

New York as if in protest at having to work at this ungodly hour. Just outside Secaucus Junction it seemed to realize it was about to relinquish any further chance of inconveniencing its passengers, and came to a complete halt for forty minutes. It was past midnight by the time Matthew arrived at Charlie's house in Cobble Hill. Rucola would be closed. He was too tired to look for somewhere still open, let alone cook for himself. He was fastidious about food, and preferred to go to bed hungry than eat poorly.

He chained the door, kicked off his shoes, and went upstairs. It felt a bit strange, climbing the three flights to the guest room with no one else there. He'd never been alone in the house before, and had only been in the upstairs quarters once, when Charlie had first bought the place and was showing it off to him. The sleek fifties furnishings that Chloe collected seemed to look at him askance from their blond frames and Naugahyde upholstery. A baby grand in a second-floor room stood with its double-hinged lid half open, baring its antique teeth in a cringing grin.

Charlie had said they always kept the guest bed made up, but in fact it just had a folded comforter on a bare mattress. Matthew didn't feel like hunting up a set of sheets, and went to look for somewhere else to sleep. Lily's bed, on the floor below, was made up, but it didn't seem right to sleep in a young girl's bed, surrounded by dolls and furry toys. He went on down to Charlie and Chloe's bedroom. The king-sized bed stood with its gold chenille cover and rumpled satin sheets flung back. It would do.

There was a gray marble bathroom en suite, with two sinks and a brass showerhead the size of a gong in the shower. He undressed and slid open the glass door, standing under the deluge of hot rain until he felt the grime of his journey cleansed from him.

Books on global finance, climate change, Zen and Tibetan Buddhism were stacked on one side of the bed; photography magazines and paperback novels on the other. Naked, he climbed in next to the paperbacks and magazines. As he laid his head on the pillow, he caught the smell of Chloe's perfume. He breathed it in deeply. As always, it stirred a very specific emotion inside him; unnameable, but powerfully evocative of its wearer. A short, sheer nightdress with thin shoulder straps lay crumpled on the carpet below the mattress. He picked it up and held it against the light. A strand of Chloe's dark hair glinted on the cream-colored silk. He let the garment slide down softly against his cheek, and filled his lungs again with the delicately scented fragrance.

In the morning he woke early and went down to the kitchen to retrieve the bracelet. The safe was in the wall behind the refrigerator. Unlocking the castors as Charlie had instructed, he hauled the appliance out of its berth. The safe's dial protruded at eye-level from a metal door in the wall. He turned it to the numbers on the notepaper Charlie had given him. The last four digits were 1985, and when he looked again at the other numbers he realized they formed the date Charlie's mother had died. He knew Charlie had this tender, vulnerable side, but it wasn't always visible, and his feelings toward his cousin, which could sometimes be harsh, softened whenever he was reminded of it. The steel door clicked open, spilling cold air onto his forearm. Inside, in front of some stacked blocks of cash and four bottles of Cipro, was a flat Tiffany's jewel box. He took it out and closed the safe, replacing the refrigerator and relocking the castors.

Curious to see what ten thousand dollars could buy, he opened the box. The bracelet was a thick cuff of gold, with *Tif-*

fany & Co inscribed along one edge. An utterly bland piece of jewelry, in Matthew's opinion. He felt bad for Chloe, about to receive something that, with her taste, she could only find banal, but which she would obviously have to pretend to like.

He put the box in his pack and left, resetting the burglar alarm.

It was another day of clinging heat in New York. The Port Authority smelled like a dumpster. But the bus was cool inside and not too crowded, and as it headed north, the foliage along the Thruway glittered promisingly.

He picked up the article he'd been reading the evening before, on gourmet food trucks. It was a business he'd been thinking of getting into himself, some day, if he could raise the money. In London, when he was eighteen, a friend of his mother's had taken him on at the trattoria she owned in Fulham, and taught him the rudiments of the restaurant business. Later, an acquaintance of the same woman had offered him a job in New York, where he'd learned to cook professionally, and one way or another food had been his livelihood ever since. A somewhat lean one in recent years, it had to be said. A curious lassitude had taken hold of him lately; a feeling of being adrift, and of not quite having the willpower to do anything about it. He'd had a share in a farm-to-table restaurant in Greenpoint that he'd sold three years earlier for a small profit, and he'd planned to reinvest the money in another, more promising venture, but he'd hesitated at the last moment; stayed home in a state of peculiar inertia on the morning of the final round of discussions, and the opportunity had passed. Since then, as if in obedience to some mysterious but inflexible organic law, his field of operations

had been steadily dwindling. He blogged about food and made a little money off ads. A friend at a TV production company sometimes called him up to consult. He was registered with an agency that sent out chefs for private dinners, and occasionally he got a gig. But it was all beginning to feel rather remote— and not just the food business but other things too. Recently, he'd come across the coinage "meatspace," meaning the real, as opposed to the virtual, world, and had found himself adopting it as his own private expression for what he seemed to be steadily, unaccountably, withdrawing from. Or what seemed to be with- drawing from him. Meatspace of worldly accomplishment. Meatspace of relationships. Meatspace of money. At thirty-nine he was close, in fact, to living off pure fumes of just about every- thing. It wasn't something he experienced as a great hardship, but he was aware that the moment was approaching when even the fumes would run out.

· · ·

The bus stopped by the village green in Aurelia, opposite the hardware store. The place was thronged: teens playing Hacky Sack, gardeners at work on the riotously blooming plantings, tourists milling around with cameras and ice creams. Behind the clapboard and brick buildings rose the round-topped mountains of the Catskills. They weren't majestic, exactly, but they were big enough to suggest the idea of a wilderness, and to confer a bucolic air on the bustling little town. Matthew sat on a bench with his bag, waiting for Charlie.

He'd been to Aurelia several times before: weekend visits, and once over Thanksgiving. A century ago an arts colony had

been founded there, and the town had been a haven for artists and musicians ever since. In their wake, these bohemians had brought an unusual combination of ragged drifters and well-heeled New York weekenders who mingled together in a curious symbiosis of mutual flattery. The weekenders were of the type who liked to think of themselves as successful members of the counterculture, and the drifters clearly enjoyed the boosted status they got from being the real thing. Some of the stores along Tailor Street—the main thoroughfare —were head shops selling tie-dyed T-shirts and drug paraphernalia, but there were also upscale realtors' offices advertising two-million-dollar homes, as well as a couple of cafés where you could get a decent macchiato, and one good restaurant, the Millstream Inn.

After ten minutes Charlie pulled up on the road behind the green, stopping in front of the white-spired Dutch Reformed church. He was driving the convertible now, a cream-colored BMW that Chloe had driven up the day before. He was dressed in a white tennis shirt and shorts. His handsome, regular features were already a little sunburned.

"I brought you something from the juice bar," he called out, waving a tall cup at Matthew.

Matthew took the drink and got in the car. It was a watermelon juice; cold and not too sweet.

"Thank you."

"Thank *you*, man. You saved my ass. Everything go okay?"

"Everything was fine." He gave Charlie the bracelet.

"Thanks, Matt. Really appreciated."

"No problem."

Charlie grinned at him in the mirror:

"Were you surprised to see all that moolah in the safe?"

"I didn't really look," Matthew said. A momentary disappointment crossed Charlie's face, and it occurred to Matthew that his cousin had wanted him to be impressed by the money.

"I mean, it looked like a good amount..."

"One and a half mill," Charlie said. "Everyone was doing it after 9/11. Then the Cipro after the anthrax scare. To be honest, it seemed irresponsible not to."

"Totally irresponsible."

"Hey, don't mock!"

"Sorry."

"If the big one drops, you'll know where to come, right?"

"Thanks, Charlie."

"I mean it."

Leaving town, they wound up into the mountains. The warm air rushing over Matthew's face smelled of summer. At Charlie's road they began climbing more steeply. The road, with its hairpin twists, had been cut into the mountain in the nineties when the town first began attracting the so-called "little millionaires" of the Clinton era. The houses along it were sleek and modern, with irregular-angled decks jutting out to take advantage of the view, stone-bordered swimming pools flashing turquoise in their grounds.

Charlie's house, on a parcel of twenty acres near the top, was an almost invisible structure in which bluestone, cedar and glass mingled with the surrounding rocks, woods and sky in an ingenious way that made you unsure, as you approached, which part of what you were looking at was natural, which man-made.

From the front there was a tremendous view all the way to the Hudson River, across what looked like virgin forest, at least in summer when the billowing foliage swallowed everything but the odd church spire.

As Charlie opened the front door, Fu, their enormous black chow, bounded over. Matthew found the dog's slobbering friendliness hard to take, though he did his best to conceal it, letting the creature jump up against his chest in his usual overfriendly greeting, without betraying too much distaste. Charlie tried to calm the animal but Fu ignored him, mashing his wet nose and bluish-black tongue into Matthew's chin.

"We're having some issues with Fu," Charlie said apologetically.

Stone floors and walls kept the air cool inside. Rawhide sofas and armchairs were grouped in the sunken living room around a carved wooden coffee table laden with Chloe's photography books.

Off to the side, the open-plan dining room and kitchen looked out onto the terrace and lawn through a Japanese wall in which glass doors, paper panels and wood-framed bug screens could be arranged in combinations to let in different amounts of light and air. On the far side of the lawn was the pool, flanked by the pool house, with the guesthouse perched on a rock beyond.

"I'm going to take a shower," Charlie said. "Go say hello to Chloe. She's by the pool. Your bag's in the guesthouse. Everything's ready for you."

two

Matthew hadn't seen Chloe for a couple of months, but even if he'd seen her just a day ago, or only an hour, it would not have been a neutral event for him to see her now. It never was.

He had been trying hard, lately, to come to an accurate understanding of his feelings for her. A year or so after his father's disappearance, his mother had sent him to a therapist: a large, somber Australian named Dr. McCubbin. The sessions at Dr. McCubbin's office overlooking Hampstead Heath had done little to alleviate the effect on Matthew of his father's actions, but in their own way they had been instructive. McCubbin had taught Matthew how to analyze his emotions by instilling in him the habit of asking himself: What does this feel like? Where else have I experienced this particular shade of joy or sadness? What specific associations does it have for me? He'd also taught him

not to be afraid of any desire or impulse he might discover by this process. The psyche, McCubbin had shown him, was autonomous. You couldn't alter its inclinations, however much you might want to, so there was no point in trying. You could, however, avoid being tyrannized by them, and the better you understood them, the easier this would be.

In the case of Chloe, Matthew had teased out a large number of disparate components in the general feeling of enchantment he experienced in her presence. Being several years older than her, he had to acknowledge something paternal in his attitude; a kind of protective, delightedly disapproving fondness that he imagined he might feel toward a daughter if he should ever have one. At the same time, as Charlie's cousin and honorary brother, he felt related to her on a more equal, sibling- or in-law-like footing. Then, in the tacit arrangement by which it was always as the beneficiary of her and Charlie's hospitality that he saw her (there was never any question of them visiting him in his dismal little one-bedroom in Bushwick), there was also something of the dependent child in his feeling toward her; or at least a projection of something parental onto her. Then too, there was that very precisely defined and circumscribed amatory interest that the medieval poets understood so well: the attraction of the squire to his master's lady; a matter of devotion on one side, and infinite kindness on the other, with the mutual understanding that any favors granted must be of a purely symbolic nature. More prosaically, he'd always felt a simple, friendly affection for her. She'd been a food photographer before marrying Charlie, and knew some of the people Matthew had worked with in the restaurant business in New York. She liked art and literature in the same

unintellectual way as Matthew did, and shared his weakness for low-end celebrity gossip. The soft peal of her laughter as the two of them worked their way through the love lives of Lindsay Lohan and the Kardashians, often to the accompaniment of Charlie's snores, was a sound Matthew had come to associate with his evenings at their home in Cobble Hill, and it formed a significant part of the picture he'd imagined as he looked forward to their summer together in Aurelia. And then finally there was that sense of almost supernatural kinship that exists often between people who seem on the surface quite unalike but whom life conspires to link by a succession of small affinities, creating a bond that exists in a world of its own, requiring neither comment nor confirmation in this world.

He'd felt this bond since first meeting her, a decade earlier. Charlie and she had just started dating, and Charlie, whose disastrous first marriage had left him distrustful of his own judgment, had wanted to know what Matthew thought of her. The three of them met at Charlie's old apartment in the Village. Right away Matthew could see she was in another class from the women Charlie had introduced him to previously. Her clear, structural attractiveness, her good taste in clothing that came across as a natural elegance completely unlike the overgroomed glamour of her predecessors, her quiet curiosity and absolute lack of pretension, made him extremely happy on Charlie's behalf. Charlie, who was redecorating his apartment, had just bought some Basquiat drawings, and the three of them had started talking about art. At one point Charlie had asked Chloe what her all-time favorite painting was. She'd thought for a moment, and then, as she began to speak, Matthew had known with a strange certainty

that she was going to name the one and only Old Master painting that had ever meant anything to him: Bellini's *Madonna with
Saints*, which his father had brought him to see in the Church of
San Zaccaria when they went to Venice on a trip around Europe
the year before he disappeared. "That would have to be Bellini's *Madonna with Saints*," she'd said, and the hairs had stood up
on the back of Matthew's neck. It had seemed to bring him back
through the years to the moment when he'd entered the church
with his father, both of them weary and surfeited from their
day of sightseeing, and stood together, bound suddenly close in
their silent mutual amazement at the monumental slabs of color
arrayed across the painting in the form of the saints' robes, each
figure in its dissonant brilliance engulfing the two of them like
some tumultuous, intensely differentiated type of joy. "We won't
forget that in a hurry," his father had said when they finally ran
out of coins for the illumination, "will we?"

Not wanting to upstage Charlie, who hadn't heard of the picture, Matthew had restrained his reaction, merely nodding to
show that he approved of Chloe's choice. But as Charlie's friend
he'd felt overjoyed that the woman who was so obviously the
right woman for Charlie was also, so to speak, the right woman
for himself.

So now, as he went out through the glass doors across the
bluestone terrace with its glazed urns of pink geraniums, over
the freshly cut lawn and through the lines of young apple trees
planted to conceal the chain-link pool fence, he was in some
fantastical sense approaching an idealized composite in whom
daughter, sister, cousin, mother, mistress, friend and mystical
other half were all miraculously commingled.

At any rate, that was the best he could do to account for the trance-like state he seemed to enter when he was with her, in which he felt simultaneously hyper-alert—as if some benign force were commanding every resource of wit, charm, sensitivity and brilliance he possessed to stand at attention—and dazed to a point of happy unselfconsciousness.

• • •

She was sunbathing on a deck chair at the far end of the pool. As Matthew opened the gate she sat up and waved to him.

"Hello, Matt."

"Hi, Chloe."

She stood, putting a shirt on over her swimsuit and sliding her sunglasses up over her dark hair, which she had knotted on top: imperfectly, so that strands fell over her face.

It was a highly expressive face, constantly in subtle motion. Her large, very dark eyes seemed to register every passing nuance of feeling with warmly mirthful intelligence.

"I'm so sorry about last night," she was saying as she came toward him, her white shirt catching flares of light from the pool.

"Oh, no problem—all my fault anyway," he bluffed, realizing he'd forgotten to ask Charlie what reason he'd invented for Matthew's return to New York.

They kissed on the cheek, and he caught her scent again; its bittersweet notes that seemed to him so precisely emotional he barely noticed their physical qualities at all.

"Make yourself at home," she said, motioning to the guesthouse. "Then come have a swim."

A second gate led to a path that climbed the outcropping of

rock on which the guesthouse stood, an octagonal wooden aerie with towering black pines behind and the abyss of the vast valley dropping almost sheerly in front.

He'd stayed there before when they'd had other guests in the main house. He loved the place. Often, when things got too much for him in New York, he fantasized about asking Charlie to let him live there full-time as his caretaker. The wide-board floors scavenged from an old sawmill, the rustic wooden walls, the assortment of furniture Chloe had picked out—spindle-backed Shaker chair, bird's-eye maple dresser, cedar blanket chest, the modern rug of overlapping green and gray squares—all appealed to him as if they'd been chosen expressly with his own tastes in mind.

He could see the pool through the window above the dresser as he unpacked his clothes. Charlie came through the far gate in his trunks, carrying an iPad. He went over to Chloe, who tilted her lips up to receive a kiss, placing her hand on his thigh. Despite his own feelings, Matthew enjoyed witnessing the flow of affection between Chloe and Charlie. He had no actual designs on Chloe, and in fact believed in her and Charlie's marriage almost as an article of religious faith. It was something he considered absolutely right and absolutely fixed. Its very solidity was precisely the reason why he was able, as Dr. McCubbin would have put it, to "experience" his own feelings for Chloe with as much pleasure as he did, with as little guilt, and with no sense of rejection whatsoever. It was actually a very comfortable arrangement, as far as he was concerned.

Charlie sat at a table in the shade of the pool house and began working on his iPad. He'd recently been let go from a hedge

fund when it was bought by a company that wasn't interested in keeping the Green Energy Equities Division Charlie had been managing, and he was currently in the process of trying to reposition himself as some kind of ethical investing consultant. One of the things he'd told Matthew he was planning to do over the summer was write a document—an article or possibly even a short book—that would address contemporary culture from the point of view of the socially responsible investor. "I'll be requiring your input, bro," he'd said, and Matthew had felt flattered, and wanted.

· · ·

At breakfast the next morning, Chloe was wearing the bracelet. She held out her wrist as Matthew joined her and Charlie under the grape arbor that shaded the stone terrace.

"Look what Charlie gave me."

He feigned the surprise expected of him.

"Isn't it nice?" she asked.

"It's gorgeous."

"Tiffany's. Look." She pointed at the edge of the cuff where the name was engraved. He nodded, glancing up into her eyes and then quickly away, not wanting to be complicit in anything even gently ironic at Charlie's expense.

"What's the occasion?" he asked Charlie.

"Oh. It's our wedding anniversary," Charlie answered, pouring himself a cup of coffee.

"You should have told me. I'd have brought you breakfast in bed."

Charlie gave a vague smile and turned to his iPad, apparently

uninterested in extending the harmless charade. It didn't surprise Matthew: playfulness had never been his cousin's strong suit.

"Well, happy anniversary," he said, raising a cup of coffee.

Later, by the pool, it occurred to him that the two of them might want to celebrate alone.

"You two should go out tonight. I mean for a romantic dinner, by yourselves."

"Huh . . ." Charlie said, looking over at Chloe.

"No, let's just stay here," Chloe said, not opening her eyes. "It's so much more relaxing. Matthew can cook us all something special for dinner. Right, Matthew? We can have some nice drinks and just . . . relax. Don't you think, Charlie?"

"Actually, I do."

"I'll tell you what," Matthew said. "I'll check out the Millstream's specials and give you what you would have had if you'd gone there."

"Great," Chloe called out from the raft she was floating on, smiling dreamily. "Only it'll be ten times better."

"Nice thought, Matty," Charlie said.

They kept a pickup truck at the house, an old Dodge, for winter storms when the steep road became too icy for even the Lexus's four-wheel drive. Charlie had offered it to Matthew for the summer when he invited him, and he gave him the keys when they went back inside for lunch. It had minimal suspension— every dent in the road jolted up through the seat like a mule kick—but Matthew enjoyed driving around in it. It made him feel like a soldier bouncing around on some important mission in a jeep.

In this particular instance the mission, diligently transcribed from the Millstream's website, entailed hunting down guajillo chilies, fresh Gulf shrimp, mesquite chunks for the grill, trevisano radicchio, baby artichokes and a butcher who knew how to cut flat iron steaks or would let Matthew cut his own. It took all afternoon, but between a farm stand twelve miles away in Klostville, the new All Natural Meats and Smokehouse on the road to East Deerfield, the surprisingly well run fish counter at Morelli's Market in East Deerfield itself and a bodega off the Thruway near Poughkeepsie that Matthew had discovered on a previous visit, he managed to get what he needed.

The evening was a notable success. Charlie opened a 1973 La Lagune, and even though Matthew wasn't much of a wine connoisseur, he had a good enough palate to appreciate the simple grandeur of the bottle. Remembering it in later days, he made the connection he'd never made before, between the word "claret" and the idea of clarity it had originally been adopted to express. It seemed to sum up the evening. Clear evening sky. Simple perfection of the dinner as he served the appetizers and then, after a pause to let the mesquite chunks burn down, the flat-iron steaks. These, though not actually from Wagyu beef, were as good as any he'd eaten, their seared crimson flesh branchingly marbled by the infraspinatus fascia that offset the fire-and-blood carnality of the shoulder muscle itself, sweetening it with rich oils. Clear, untainted friendship between the three of them: their easy happiness together as they sat around the stone table with the citronella candles flickering in silver buckets between the terra-cotta herb pots beside them, and the stars coming out in the cloudless sky.

The conversation flowed, gaining just enough of a charge from the slight tension between Charlie's stubborn high-mindedness and the more bantering style of Matthew and Chloe to feel both relaxed and interesting. Charlie mentioned a video clip he'd watched that afternoon, of Noam Chomsky talking about the Occupy movement. Chloe rolled her eyes good-naturedly. Placing her hand over Charlie's, she asked what Noam Chomsky had had to say about the Occupy movement, and she smiled sweetly up at him as he embarked on a long answer in which the professor's opinions became inextricably entangled with Charlie's somewhat rambling commentary.

"He used the word 'dyad,' I remember. I had to look that up."

"What about it?"

"Oh, something about how from the point of view of corporate power the perfect social unit is the dyad consisting of you and your screen. Pretty accurate, wouldn't you say?"

"It certainly describes you, darling," Chloe said affectionately. She was still wearing the bracelet, swiveling it in the candlelight as if to stave off any suspicion that she might not have liked it. And maybe she really did like it after all, Matthew found himself magnanimously conceding. It was entirely possible that the aesthetic fastidiousness he attributed to her was purely a figment of his own imagination. A side effect of the unspoken sympathy between them was a frequent sense of "knowing" things about her that he couldn't objectively vouch for, and he was quite prepared to admit that they weren't always strictly accurate, and moreover that they tended to skew in the direction of certain qualities, such as "reserve" and "tastefulness," that certainly oversimplified her and possibly idealized her too. The

gift she'd given Charlie, for example, was neither reserved nor especially tasteful: it was a Givenchy shark T-shirt, which Charlie was wearing under one of his white linen shirts, the top three buttons open so that it looked as though a shark were breaching up out of his chest. But it was certainly more interesting than the bland gold manacle he'd given her.

Charlie went on talking about Occupy for a while. The movement, which at that time was still gaining in strength, had interested him from the start. Once, when Matthew had gone to meet him at his old office, Charlie had insisted on dragging him off to the Zuccotti Park encampment. For two hours they'd ducked in and out of the tarp shelters and nylon tents, listening to teach-ins and strategy meetings, watching the "human microphone" in action. Charlie was taking pictures on his phone and earnestly questioning the protesters, who'd been roughing it for several weeks by then and were easily distinguishable from the tourists and visitors by their dirty clothes. The little oblong park was like a raft thrown together after some great shipwreck, Matthew had thought, with its makeshift dwellings lashed down every possible way. For him the whole phenomenon existed in a realm he had long ago placed off-limits to himself, a realm of faith in human betterment that he considered himself too tainted by experience to enter. His duty, he felt in an obscure way, was to preserve that realm from his own limitless skepticism.

Charlie, however, had no such inhibitions. The visit had made a deep impression on him, and he'd brought it up many times since, often wanting to show Matthew articles or YouTube clips on his iPad, frowning into the screen as he asked Mat-

thew what he thought, or used him as a sounding board for his attempts to articulate what *he* thought.

As a banker, it had seemed necessary to him to formulate a position in regard to this movement. He seemed to want to find arguments that would place it and himself in a sympathetic relation to each other. At the same time Matthew sensed that he wanted to be able to set it in a larger context that would allow him to demonstrate its flaws and contradictions, and thereby, presumably, diminish the anxiety it seemed to arouse in him.

"I was forever trying to persuade Chloe to photograph the different encampments around the country, wasn't I?" Charlie said now. He'd been going on about the movement for quite a while by this point. Drink made him long-winded, and he'd drunk a fair amount. "I thought it would make a great project for her. Go round the country photographing all those tent cities. Right, Chlo?"

"Right."

"How come you weren't interested?"

Chloe shrugged. Seeing the quick shadow of impatience cross her brow, Matthew mentioned something he had noticed earlier that day. He did it purely to change the subject, not wanting the atmosphere to be even momentarily spoiled.

"Speaking of photographic projects," he said, "I was noticing the mailboxes up here as I drove around today. They're so full of character, the way people decorate them with all those little hand-painted stars and flowers. I was thinking they were a kind of folk art almost . . . It crossed my mind that they might actually make a worthwhile project for a photographer."

Chloe turned to him.

"That's interesting."

"What mailboxes?" Charlie asked. "I've never seen any deco-rated mailboxes."

"They seem to be all over the place. Especially down the smaller roads."

"Yes. They're everywhere," Chloe said.

"I hadn't noticed." Charlie poured himself another glass of wine.

"Sometimes you see a whole cluster of them."

Chloe nodded. "Right. At the corner of shared driveways. The mail vans don't go down private roads."

"I saw a row of about fifteen all tilted together. They looked like a sort of drunken chorus line."

Chloe laughed.

"Huh?" Charlie muttered.

"You know, I think you're right, Matthew," Chloe continued, looking thoughtful. "That *could* make an interesting project."

She smiled warmly at Matthew. He wiped his lips with his napkin, trying to conceal the pleasure her reaction had roused in him. Actually, he was a little surprised at her enthusiasm. Having given up commercial photography after marrying Charlie, she'd become serious about pursuing it as an art, exhibiting her work in downtown galleries, and he didn't think she'd really be tempted by that kind of purely coffee table material. He'd only raised the subject to steer the conversation away from Zuc-cotti Park, which had seemed to be boring her, and he'd frankly expected the idea to be politely rejected. But she appeared to be genuinely interested.

"I'll take a drive around tomorrow," she said. "Thanks, Matt. That was a great suggestion."

After they'd finished eating, Chloe insisted on helping Matthew clear up. Charlie, promising he'd do it next time, sprawled into one of the Adirondack chairs with a cognac, feet up on the footstool.

"I'd like to make a toast, though," he announced, reaching for his glass. Matthew put down the dishes he'd been about to carry in. Another effect of drink on Charlie was a tendency to make toasts and speeches that could ramble on indefinitely.

"To Chloe," Charlie began, his voice a little slurred. "To Chloe, whom I love more than anything under the stars, I want to say . . . I want to say *thank you*. I want to say thank you for ten years of unwavering love. I want to say thank you for your . . . for your support . . . for your *patience*." He paused, nodding slightly as if in private satisfaction at something unexpectedly judicious in the choice of word. "I want to say thank you for the ten happiest years of my life so far. Look, I don't . . . I've never claimed to be a saint, but I think I'm a better person than I was, and if I am, if I've made any . . . if I've grown in any way as a human being I owe it to you, Chloe. You have a way of bringing out the best in people. Maybe in my case even making them better than they . . . better than their best. So here's to you, my beloved wife . . . Here's to the next ten years, and all the . . . all the next decades ahead of us. May they all be as happy as this, and full of love, and adventure, and . . . well, you know . . ." He raised his glass and drained it, and then sank back against the slats of green-painted wood.

After a moment, Chloe stepped over and leaned down, kissing him tenderly.

"I love you too, Charlie," she said.

A look of immense contentment spread over Charlie's

sleek features. He closed his eyes. Pretty soon he started snoring. In sleep, he looked older than he did when he was awake. You noticed the thick, tawny eyebrows over the closed lids, the slight lugubrious prominence of his lower jaw, the extravagant sprawl of his limbs. You could see he was destined to become one of those kingly, leonine old men who appear in ads for golfing resorts and upscale retirement communities. Without envy, with a kind of amused inner candor, Matthew often thought of himself as a member of some troll-like, inferior species when he was in his cousin's presence.

In the kitchen, Chloe told him Charlie had complained of feeling under the weather the previous afternoon, after taking Fu for a walk in the woods.

"I hope he didn't get a Lyme tick," she said, glancing out at the terrace.

"Probably just a touch of rabies," Matthew answered. After a moment, Chloe gave a soft peal of laughter.

He loved making her laugh. It was the one bodily pleasure he was permitted with her; a harmless physical trespass. And since they seemed to find the same things funny, he did it fairly often.

"I'm going to have a swim," she said when they'd finished the dishes. She didn't ask Matthew to join her. He assumed she didn't think he needed to be asked, but even if she had, he would have declined. He wouldn't have wanted Charlie to wake from his slumber on the terrace to find him and Chloe having a midnight swim together. Not that Charlie would have thought anything of it, but he himself would have, and he was dimly conscious of a need to keep himself well back from any realm in which feelings of desire or guilt might proliferate.

He said good night and went on up the rocky path to the guesthouse, navigating the last yards by the light of the moon that had risen above the valley.

From his octagonal room he could see the still-undisturbed surface of the pool, and then the dark figure of Chloe in her white T-shirt coming to the gate. Lightning bugs flashed in the apple trees as she passed through them, making the small apples gleam. As she opened the gate he closed the curtains. He thought she might swim naked and he didn't want there to be any suggestion in her mind, ever, that he could be spying on her. Still, his guess was that even alone, at night, she probably would have worn her swimsuit. She was rather American and modest in that way.

But closing the curtain had the effect of opening his imagination to the thought of her undressing at the pool's edge with the moonlight on her supple body, and as he heard her plunge into the water he felt again, more strongly than ever, the sensation of lovely clarity that had pervaded the whole evening.

three

The summer thickened around them. Soon it reached
that point of miraculous equilibrium where it felt at once as if
it had been going on forever and as if it would never end. The
heat merged with the constant sounds of insects and red-winged
blackbirds, to form its own throbbing, hypnotic medium. It
made you feel as if you were inside some green-lit womb, full of
soft pulsations.

After breakfasting, the three of them would go their separate
ways. Charlie drove off early in the convertible to play tennis.
Afterward he'd take Fu for a walk in the woods, returning as
often as not looking exhausted and a bit chagrined, with some
tale of the ungovernable animal thundering off after a deer, or
attacking a porcupine, only to get a muzzle full of quills.

In the afternoon he'd sit in the shade of the pool house with

James Lasdun

his iPad, reading articles and watching YouTube clips. If Matthew was around he'd try to interest him in whatever he was
looking at. "There's something authentic there," was his typical
opening comment, or "That's the real thing, don't you think?"
After which, having secured Matthew's agreement, he would
come out with some deeper-level objection.

On one occasion he showed Matthew some video footage of
the students on the Davis campus being pepper-sprayed by cops
as they sat stoically on the ground, refusing to move.

"You can't question their authenticity," he said, prodding his finger at the screen. "I mean, you don't see that kind of courage without some authentic moral conviction underwriting it. Do you?"

Matthew made his usual murmur of assent.

"But what is it?" Charlie asked. "What do they actually
believe in? What do they even want? How come we don't remember what they were protesting or demanding? Did we ever in fact
know?"

Sometimes in the early evening he'd sit in his meditation garden—a small, enclosed lawn with a stone Buddha at one end—
or drive up to a sitting at the nearby Zen monastery, returning
for dinner looking serene and smelling of sandalwood. Now and
then he had to go into New York for meetings connected with
the consultancy group he was trying to set up. He left early in the
morning and it was understood that Chloe and Matthew would
wait to eat until he got back, which was often not before eleven
or midnight. Whatever the time, he'd want to talk and drink for
a couple of hours before going to bed, and they'd sit with him
on the terrace listening to his analysis of the day's meetings. He
seemed eager to discuss these meetings, whether they'd gone

well or badly. It seemed to bolster his sense of their importance, and with that, his belief that he was making his way back into the game he'd been ousted from earlier that year. He'd never admitted to any feelings of rejection or failure after being "let go" from his hedge fund, but Matthew knew him well enough to know it must have been a blow to his ego. Being without a recognized position in the world would have felt highly uncomfortable to him. There was nothing of the natural maverick or outsider about Charlie: he wasn't the type to base his self-esteem on his own judgment. He needed official recognition and approval. Whether that was a sign of virtue or weakness, Matthew wasn't sure, but he was certainly doing all he could to rebuild his career, and Matthew couldn't help comparing himself—bogged down in this peculiar inertia of his—unfavorably with his cousin, at least in this respect.

Chloe's routines were less predictable. Some days she did nothing but lie by the pool with a pile of magazines and her phone, ignoring both as she steeped herself in sunlight. She'd signed up for yoga and Zumba classes in town and some mornings she went off with her rolled-up mat and water canister, but often she didn't bother. Even when she did go off for a class she was capable of changing her mind, as Matthew discovered on one occasion when Charlie, who'd left his favorite tennis racket in the Lexus, asked Matthew to grab it from the car on his way back from town, and the car had turned out not to be in the yoga studio parking lot. She'd succumbed to her own laziness as she approached the studio, she confessed later, and spent her yoga hour in a café drinking a triple latte, from which she was still visibly sparkling with caffeinated good humor.

She did seem to be pursuing the mailbox idea, however, and would drift off with her cameras, usually in the late afternoon, to catch them at magic hour.

"That was such a good idea of yours, Matt," she said, returning from one of these expeditions.

"Well, I can't wait to see the results."

He thought of her driving around the country roads, making her judgments, setting up her cameras, filling her memory cards and rolls of film, all because he had casually suggested she might find these harmless things interesting, and this was as satisfying to him as if he had actually been driving around with her. The project had become another instance of that action-at-a-distance that his feelings for her thrived on, and that seemed to be all they required by way of sustenance.

As for his own routines, he took his role as chef seriously and spent much of his time driving around to farmers' markets or checking out little specialty stores hidden on rural roads or in the immigrant neighborhoods of nearby towns. Whenever he set off he made a point of offering to do any errands that needed running. Charlie asked him to pick up some stones he'd ordered for an outdoor pizza oven he planned to build. One time Chloe asked him to get a copy of an entertainment magazine at the Barnes & Noble in East Deerfield. Occasionally she put in a request for kumquats and chocolate, her favorite snack. Otherwise it was mostly just dropping off dry-cleaning or taking the garbage to the town dump. A cleaning lady did their laundry at the house.

When he wasn't marketing he was usually swimming or sunbathing—mostly at the pool but sometimes at one of the swimming holes in the creek, the Millstream, that ran along the back of town.

The clear, cold water fell into a series of pools defined by smooth-edged boulders that grew immensely warm by midmorning. He would park the truck in the gravel lot by the bridge that connected the main part of town with some quieter residential roads. Stone steps led down under the bridge to the first of the pools and you could pick your way along the shelving stone banks to a half dozen other pools running under the backyards of the private homes on the road that ran parallel with the creek. Trees at the top of the bank made it easy enough to find shade. He'd set up with a towel and his copy of Pascal or a magazine and watch the world go by.

There were packs of noisy high schoolers, young couples staying in the nearby bed-and-breakfasts, elderly retirees with wrinkled white bodies. There was also a steady stream of Rainbow people and Deadheads who gravitated around Aurelia in the summer, camping in the woods behind the public meadow known locally as Paradise. On weekends they held late-night drumming sessions that you could hear all the way up at the house, and there were more low-key sessions, audible from the stream, that seemed to run pretty much continuously, adding their own frequency to that of the insects and birds, the pulsating dial tone of summer.

He found this latter group—the Rainbows and Deadheads—especially fascinating. They'd drift down to the water in the late afternoon in their beads and leather vests, trailing clouds of patchouli, often carrying their drums. Settling in groups on the smooth rocks, they'd preen and horse around with a mixture of childlike unselfconsciousness and highly self-conscious theatrical self-display.

He'd always had conflicting feelings about these hedonistic types. To live in that blaze of color, scent and music, moving

everywhere in loose tribal groups with everyone looking out for each other (at least in theory) appealed to a deep instinct in him. In his teens, after being expelled from school, he'd hung around on the fringes of an English version of the same subculture—travelers, hippies, "freaks" as they called themselves. He had become, in a kind of perverse, retroactive justification for his expulsion, a small-scale dealer of pot and acid, and those were his customers. For a while he'd dreamed of leaving home, what remained of home, and becoming a fully fledged member of one or other of the groups. But something always held him back; some lingering attachment to respectability, but also a growing impatience with their constant petty criminality. These American counterparts struck him as more idealistic, or anyway less obviously out to rip each other off, though by this stage in his life he was too much himself to think, even jokingly, about joining them. But they interested him to observe.

One day a wizened old guy with gray hair in a red bandanna, who'd perched on the rocks next to Matthew and begun darning an embroidered shoulder bag, treated him to a rambling monologue about himself.

"I'm what we call an Early," he said, taking Matthew's vague nod as an invitation to talk.

"An Early?"

"Early to the vision."

He'd joined the Rainbow Family of Living Light in the early seventies, he told Matthew, right after the first "Gathering of the Tribes," and had been "dogging it" across the country from gathering to gathering ever since. Now, he said, he was an official "hipstorian" of the group.

)esignated vibeswatcher too," he added with a gummy
. "And Shanti Sena. That's a peacekeeper."

Matthew smiled back:

"I like the lingo!"

"Yep. See, when you quit Babylon you gotta make your own
language for your own values. I'm saying, like Babylon talks
about the *e*-conomy and the *e*-go, whereas we're all about the
we-conomy and the *we*-go."

"Nice."

Two girls came by.

"Hey, now, Pike," they said.

"Hey, now."

They squatted down on the rock. One of them had pale green
hair and a face like a kitten. The other had a lot of metal in her
eyebrows and nose. They looked about eighteen. The air around
them filled with a candylike fragrance.

Pike (that seemed to be the old guy's name) told them that he
and Matthew had been talking about the Family.

"I'm interested in it," Matthew said encouragingly.

"Cool," the one with the piercings said.

Her friend said, "Fantastic."

Both eyed Matthew warmly, as if excited to be sitting down
with some obvious Babylonian.

"I'm explaining the lingo," Pike said, chuckling softly. His
thin old legs looked awfully hairy next to the smooth limbs of
the girls in their very short cut-off jeans.

"You mean like Zuzus and Wahwahs?" the green-haired girl
said.

"What are those?" Matthew asked.

"Different types of tasty morsels, you could say," Pike offered.

"Drainbows," the other girl offered, "Hohners, Snifters."

"All different types you find at the gatherings," Pike put in.

"Heil Holies, Blissninnies."

"Blissninnies!" Matthew repeated with a laugh. He was enjoying the little interlude, as much for its unexpectedness as anything else. He was about to ask the girls how they had come to join the Rainbows, when a tall, shirtless guy in a pair of ragged shorts walked barefoot slowly across their rock and the girls fell silent. He had long ringleted hair with gold glints in it, well-defined muscles and strong features that made Matthew think of Dürer's famous self-portrait. As he passed by, Matthew saw that he had 99% inked on his left shoulder. He didn't say anything, but a few paces beyond their rock he turned around and, looking at the girls, made a laconic beckoning motion with one hand, turning again and continuing on his way: confident, apparently, that they would get up and follow him. They did.

Pike, glancing at Matthew, gave a sort of chuckle and busied himself with his darning.

It wasn't much of an incident, but it made an unpleasant impression on Matthew. He assumed the girls must have known the guy. But even so, that casually proprietorial gesture rankled with him. It seemed consciously insulting. The guy's physical appearance, which had struck Matthew as extremely calculated, also rankled. No shoes, no pack or bag, no clutter of any kind; as if he were proclaiming the utter self-sufficiency of the human animal, at least in his own fine case.

It occurred to Matthew that although he'd always been

drawn to these types, he'd always been slightly irked by them too, regarding their rejection of "Babylon" as a tacit admission that they lacked what it took to succeed there, but that, unlike him, they refused to accept its judgment against them. So that for one of them to present himself as somehow, a priori, a superior being was like a challenge that ought to have been answered.

"Who was that guy?" he asked.

Pike looked up from his bag.

"That's Torssen. He just showed up last week. We call him the Prince."

"Why's that?"

"He likes to organize shit, I guess."

"You mean he's political?"

"Yeah, kinda."

"I noticed the tatt."

"Right."

"Is there much of a connection between you guys and Occupy?"

Pike knitted his brows.

"See, we're historically more a spiritual thing than a political thing. It's like a different movie, dig? Our movie's not about protest so much as, what do you give some kid who works minimum wage at a convenience store with no hope of getting out? They gotta have something to be *for*, not just against."

Matthew nodded. He had detected a definite lack of enthusiasm on Pike's part for the "Prince," and this endeared the old guy to him.

He smiled, suddenly amused at his own foolishness for letting something so trivial get to him. He went over the funny

words in his mind, making an effort to commit them to memory. It would be something to talk about at dinner. Chloe would appreciate it. He could see that guileless involuntary smile of hers already in his mind's eye; feel in advance the appreciative brush of her hand on his arm.

• • •

Toward the middle of July the weather grew hotter, and with the heat came a muggy humidity that made it hard to be outside, even up on the mountain.

Chloe, when she wasn't out photographing or at one of her classes, sat in the living room with the AC on high. Charlie also went out less. It was too hot for tennis and he spent most of his time working or meditating in the pool house, which was also air-conditioned.

Then the temperatures soared even higher, spiking into the high nineties.

The three of them sat in the living room one morning playing scrabble. Matthew's family had been avid scrabble players and Charlie had been introduced to the game when he'd gone to live with them as a teenager. He hadn't much liked it—it hadn't accorded with his sense of what was "cool": a novel concept in Matthew's old-fashioned home, but extremely important to the adolescent Charlie—and he hadn't been very good at it either. And yet as an adult he'd incorporated it into his own household rituals when Lily learned to read. The game seemed to have a significant emotional resonance for him, and Matthew was always touched when he suggested playing. It was as if his cousin were acknowledging the ancient bond between them.

Someone had managed "sioux" and as a joke Matthew put a *p* at the end of it.

After a moment Chloe burst into laughter.

"I don't get it," Charlie said.

Chloe explained:

"Soup. He's spelling 'soup.'"

Matthew made to take the *p* away but Chloe said to leave it.

"It's hilarious."

"Well. I'm not scoring the *i* or the *x*," Charlie said.

"Don't be a spoilsport, Charlie," Chloe told him quietly.

A frown crossed Charlie's face, but he said nothing.

After the game he left for New York, where he had a late afternoon meeting. A little later Chloe said she had to go out too.

"Anything interesting?" Matthew asked.

"Oh, I need to buy a present for Charlie," she said vaguely, and then added, "I've been feeling guilty about that T-shirt I bought him. It was so ungenerous compared with the bracelet he gave me. I want to get him something else."

Matthew wished her luck. He had no idea what their financial arrangements were, but he assumed the money was all from Charlie's side and it amused him to think of Chloe feeling guilty about underspending Charlie's money on a present for Charlie and then assuaging that guilt by spending more. At the same time he was touched, as always, by her quietly scrupulous devotion to her husband.

Later, lying on his bed in the guesthouse, he found himself thinking about the many different ways in which you can know a person, and the many kinds of knowledge that might not help you know them at all.

In Charlie's case, it seemed to him that the résumé more or less evoked the man. He was pretty sure that if he knew only that Charlie had become head prefect at the school they went to in London, had gone on to Dartmouth as a legacy student, had worked in banking and then hedge fund management, was currently writing a screed on socially responsible investing, played tennis avidly, and practiced some form of Zen Buddhism, the picture that would form in his mind would be pretty close to the actual Charlie he knew. But in Chloe's case nothing he ever learned about her in the biographical sense—that she'd grown up in suburban Indianapolis, the daughter of an engineer and a music teacher, that her boyfriend before Charlie had been a medical researcher for the World Health Organization, that she had once been one of Condé Nast's go-to photographers for fruits and berries—seemed to have any bearing at all on his actual knowledge of her.

She wasn't secretive, exactly, but the essential elements of her nature did seem stowed in deep pockets hidden from public view—hidden even from each other, somehow.

Once, when he was up for a weekend visit, staying in the main house, he'd come down to an early breakfast to find her just returning from somewhere in the car. It turned out she'd been at Sunday mass in East Deerfield. He'd had no idea she was religious, or for that matter that she was Catholic. Their daughter had been at the house that weekend but Chloe hadn't brought her along, which had seemed to further emphasize the very private nature of the thing.

Music too. He knew she was a discerning listener—early on they'd discovered a shared enthusiasm for the voice of Beth Gibbons, its strange vacillations between sweetness and caustic harsh-

ness. But Chloe turned out to be more than just a consumer of music. He'd happened to be passing their street in Cobble Hill one evening, just as Charlie was arriving home from work, and Charlie had invited him in for a drink. Piano music came from upstairs as they stepped in. A Beethoven sonata, he'd guessed, played by Ashkenazi or some other master of the Romantic. But the music stopped dead in the middle of a passage of complex glissandi, starting again a moment later, and he'd realized there was someone up there actually playing it. He'd asked Charlie who it was. "Oh, that's Chlo," he'd said, without great interest. "She's good!" Matthew had exclaimed. Charlie had shrugged. "I think she wanted to be a pro at some time but she wasn't quite up to it. She only plays now when there's no one around. Or when she thinks there isn't."

And then, just a couple of days ago, Matthew had discovered another of these secret pockets of Chloe's personality.

It had been a baking, breezeless afternoon. The three of them had been lazing by the pool, when he saw that Chloe was looking closely at some of the flowering shrubs that ran along one side of the fence. Beyond enjoying the occasional scent of lavender wafting from them, Matthew hadn't taken any notice of these plantings. But as Chloe gazed steadily and purposefully along them, raising a pair of binoculars to her eyes from time to time even though the bed was only a few yards away, he'd started gazing at them too.

"What are you looking at?"

"The butterflies."

Only then had he become conscious of the mass of wings in as many bright colors as the flowers themselves, trembling on the blossoms or hovering in the air above them.

It turned out Chloe had had the bed put in that spring and had selected the plantings specifically to attract butterflies. Handing Matthew the binoculars, she'd told him what the different plants were and which species each one attracted. Yellow potentilla for the coppers, hackberry for the checked fritillaries, purple swamp milkweed for the monarchs. At this proximity the heavy Zeiss binoculars organized the space into a succession of flat, richly lit planes in which everything looked, paradoxically, more three-dimensional than it did to the naked eye. The effect was somewhat hallucinatory, and in fact, as he lost himself among the enormously magnified wings and velvety petals in which, alongside the butterflies, huge bumblebees with bulging gold bags of pollen at their thighs were cruising, Matthew remembered long summer afternoons in his teens when he would lie in the Kyoto Garden in Holland Park, tripping on Green Emeralds or some other species of acid left unsold from his morning jaunts down to the flyover at the bottom of the Portobello Road and would seem to cross from his drab existence into some realm of fantastical enchantment.

That was Chloe; full of little surprises: pockets and recesses, inlets and oubliettes, with music in them, and Sunday mass, and a garden full of butterflies.

four

The temperature fell a little. It was still too hot to eat meat, but at dinner, after three days of chilled soups and composed salads, Charlie said he needed something to get his teeth into. The next morning Matthew called the fish counter at Morelli's to see what they had in fresh. It turned out they'd just had a delivery of line-caught striped bass from Nantucket.

"It'll go fast," the man said.

Charlie and Chloe had gone off a few minutes earlier; Charlie in the convertible to an early sitting at the monastery, Chloe in the Lexus to her yoga class in Aurelia. Matthew had told them he was going to spend the morning by the pool, but when he found out about the bass he fired up the pickup and set off for East Deerfield, a half-hour drive.

The striped bass had been laid out on the counter when he

got there. It looked superb, the flesh a gleaming alabaster white, the thin, stippled stripe down its length a dark reddish color, as if a wounded bird had hopped across a field of snow. Nantucket striped bass fed on the sweet-fleshed baby squid that spawned off the eastern end of the island, rather than on mackerel or other oily creatures, which gave them an incomparably delicate flavor. Matthew bought two large slabs and for good measure some oysters and scallops, and had them packed in ice. Charlie had given him a credit card for buying provisions.

He was driving along the strip of gas stations and fast-food joints that led out of town when he saw a silver Lexus peel off to the right at the stoplight fifty yards ahead. As it climbed the steep access road to the mall, Chloe's head appeared in profile at the wheel. She'd changed out of the black tank top that she'd been wearing when she left the house, into a white blouse with short puffy sleeves, but it was definitely her.

He was confused, seeing her here in East Deerfield when she'd said she was going to her yoga class in Aurelia. He supposed she must have remembered some chore she had to do in East Deerfield. But even as he articulated the thought, he was aware that it didn't account for the change of clothing.

He was planning a stop at the mall himself to buy razors and toothpaste, and he kept his eye on the Lexus as he made the same turn. Actually there was a whole complex of malls and big-box stores up there above the town, with parking lots around them and a labyrinth of branch roads looping in between.

At the top of the access road, where Lowe's and Walmart were signed off to the left, Chloe turned right, and although Matthew had planned to do his shopping at Walmart, he turned

right also. Jumbled together in his mind as he made the turn were the thought that he could just as easily do his shopping at Target, which was in this direction, and the memory of a brief exchange he'd had with Chloe a few days ago when he'd asked if she'd found another anniversary present for Charlie and she hadn't seemed to know what he was talking about until he reminded her that she'd felt guilty about the T-shirt. "Oh," she'd said with a sort of brusque vagueness, "no, I didn't find anything." He'd dropped the subject but her obtuseness had seemed odd, and it came back to him now.

Keeping well behind, he followed Chloe past the sprawling, polygonal fortress that housed Target, Best Buy, Sears and Dick's Sporting Goods. He was just curious, was what he told himself, though he was aware of that not being entirely the truth. If he'd stopped to analyze himself more exactingly, he would have realized that he was amusing himself with a kind of playacting of husbandly suspicion. Beyond the Sears entrance, she branched off onto a subsidiary road that led back downhill past a Wendy's and around a hairpin bend. As Matthew rounded the bend, he saw that she'd turned off into the parking lot of a large horseshoe-shaped building.

He drove on past, pulling in to a Laundromat a hundred yards farther on, and doubling back. Driving slowly past the turnoff, he realized it was the rear entrance to the East Deerfield Inn, a motel you would normally access from the main road down below.

She was getting out of the Lexus as he passed. In place of the yoga pants she'd been wearing when she left the house, she had on a summer skirt. She must have changed her clothing on the

way here, he thought, glimpsing her in his mirror. She'd known in advance she was coming, which meant that the business about going to yoga was a premeditated lie.

The playacting sensation had worn off by now, giving way to the less amusing knowledge that he was in fact spying on her. He considered going home and forcing himself not to think about it. But he doubted whether that would be possible, and anyway it occurred to him that, however distasteful it might be, he was under an obligation of friendship to stick around. A double obligation, in fact: one to Chloe in case her presence here turned out to have an innocent explanation, and one to Charlie in case it didn't.

He had an idea that he might be able to see down into the motel court from the Wendy's parking lot on the road above it, beyond the hairpin turn, but when he got there he saw that there was a guardrail around the lot that made it impossible to get close enough to the embankment. All he could see was a slice of the building's flat roof with its bric-a-brac of vents and turban-like fans.

He had no choice but to get out of the truck. Assuming the confident air of someone on legitimate business, he climbed over the guardrail. A stand of thin trees beyond it led to the edge of the embankment, which fell away steeply, giving a view into the motel parking lot. The ground under the trees was littered with old wrappings of burgers and fries. Truck-sized blocks of yellowish stone formed a retaining wall at the bottom of the slope.

Chloe was walking across the parking lot, carrying a canvas bag. Reaching a door on the left arm of the building, with some

kind of vintage maroon car parked outside it, she knocked once. The door opened, and she stepped inside.

. . .

The day was already stifling. Even in the shade of the little trees where Matthew was standing, it was intensely hot. He stared at the distant door, not knowing what else to do. From time to time he looked briefly away, as if to rest his eyes from a glare.

Twenty minutes passed; half an hour. As the sun climbed higher in the sky the saplings gave less shade. Beads of sweat began trickling down Matthew's face and neck and under his shirt. He stood there, motionless. It seemed to him he had a responsibility to remain in sight of the door. At the same time, however, he couldn't bear to think what might be going on behind it, so that even as he studiously faced out in that direction, his mind was just as studiously avoiding it.

A few crickets, day-shift replacements for the katydids that chorused at night, chirped in the foliage. Traffic exhaust mingled with fumes of hot grease. He heard a couple of people pause behind him as they crossed the parking lot. He didn't turn and they continued on their way. He was barely sheltered now from the midmorning blaze.

Almost an hour had passed by the time the door opened and Chloe came out. Her hair looked damp. She was wearing her yoga pants again, and the black tank top. The sandals were back on too. She climbed into the silver Lexus, and Matthew watched her drive away.

He turned to leave, but then changed his mind. What if there really was an innocent explanation for the visit? He tried to come

James Lasdun

up with a possible scenario. Nothing he could think of seemed terribly likely, but if anyone was capable of secretly pursuing some unexpected but completely benign activity, it was Chloe.

After about fifteen minutes the door opened again and a man came out, carrying a leather duffel bag. He had a wide head, framed in collar-length hair, and a triangle of pointed beard. A stout, if firm-looking, belly swelled under his billowing blue shirt. Sturdy knees and stocky calves narrowed from his cargo shorts into a pair of blue deck shoes.

He unlocked the maroon car, threw in his bag, and drove away.

Matthew turned and climbed back over the guardrail. He felt as though he had been briefly concussed. Spots drifted on his vision; nausea swayed in his stomach.

Opening the door of the pickup, he was hit with a blast of fishy-smelling heat. In his rush earlier, he'd neglected to leave a window open and now the fish was half cooked. He threw it out and went back to Morelli's, where the same man served him the same quantities of striped bass and shellfish as he had ordered before. From the man's sly expression, he seemed to imagine Matthew had absentmindedly forgotten that he'd already made this exact purchase an hour and a half earlier.

• • •

Charlie was at the house when he got back, excavating a Brillat-Savarin cheese he'd brought from the city on his last visit. He had a weakness for pungent cheeses and a habit of gorging on them in private, scooping out the soft centers and leaving the hollowed rind.

"No tennis?" Matthew asked, putting the Morelli's bag in the fridge. He was so uncomfortable he could barely bring himself to look at his cousin. His intention, to the extent that he'd formed one, had been to tell Charlie everything he'd seen at the motel, as soon as he could find a suitable moment. It was just an emergency response at this stage, not a considered plan. The urge to rid himself of the incident, obliterate it from his mind, was overwhelming, and telling Charlie seemed the best hope of accomplishing this.

Charlie yawned.

"Too hot."

Chloe's car crunched on the gravel outside a few minutes later—she must have been killing time so as not to be home from "yoga" too early—and she came in to the kitchen, smiling absently and waggling her fingers as she passed through into the sunken living room, where she collapsed in one of the sofas with a copy of the *Aurelia Gazette*.

She'd made the same kind of entrance numerous times and there hadn't seemed anything remarkable about it. It was just a natural way of observing basic courtesies while asserting her wish to remain in her own private space. But now it seemed to Matthew steeped in guile.

"How was yoga?" he asked.

She didn't seem to hear the question.

"Chlo—Matt's asking how yoga was," Charlie said.

"Oh, sorry, Matt. It was great, thanks."

She flashed him her lovely smile and resumed her reading.

He had to admire her poise, but to have betrayed that smile of hers, which had always seemed to him the ultimate expression of

her intense and innocent capacity for joy, to have sent that smile out on a mission so perfidious, was strangely upsetting.

Into his mind came another memory: the time her car hadn't been in the yoga parking lot when Charlie had asked him to get his tennis racket, and she'd claimed to have been in some café instead, drinking a triple latte. He saw her again in his mind's eye as she recounted it, making fun of her own enervated laziness with the same sparkling smile as she wore now, and the treachery seemed to spread like a crack into the past.

In the afternoon Charlie went out on some errand and Chloe disappeared upstairs. When Charlie came back he went up to join her, and the two of them stayed up there the rest of the day.

Matthew lay by the pool, watching the butterflies. Fu yelped periodically, wanting his walk, but Matthew was damned if he was going to offer to take him. He was going over the events of the morning, retracing the sequence from the moment he'd spotted Chloe ahead of him on the road below the mall, to her exit from the motel, and the man's emergence a little later. The discomfort provoked by the memory of the events was as sharp as it had been during their actual occurrence, and he wished he could think about something else—his own problems, for instance; the question of how to get himself out of his rut, jump-start his career, find a less grim apartment—which were after all the things he'd come up here to address—but it appeared to be impossible. Again in his mind the events revolved: Chloe at the wheel in her white blouse; the blunt little jolt inside him as he'd realized something suspicious was going on; the hot vigil at the edge of the Wendy's parking lot; Chloe in her summer skirt entering the motel . . . It seemed to him he had been presented with

some difficult problem to which he alone could provide the solution, and which he was under an obligation to solve as quickly as possible. But instead of formulating an answer, or even groping in the direction of an answer, his mind simply repeated the little sequence yet again, so that once more he was turning up onto the access road behind Chloe, following her past Target and Dick's Sporting Goods, climbing over the curved metal guardrail, and standing motionless under the thin trees, staring at the motel door with its glinting handle, while the fume-filled air grew hotter and hotter.

• • •

Around six, he started on the dinner. He'd intended to cook a version of a Catalan seafood dish that matches a firm white fish with a mixture of blood sausage and sea urchin roe, seasoned with chorizo. He had some decent chorizo from Fairway and he'd bought some Morcilla blood sausage at the place near Poughkeepsie. It wasn't the same as Catalan Botifarra Negra, which tended to be lighter on the cloves and cinnamon, but it was the only type you could get in the States and it gave the palate the same kind of womby, cave-like background from which to fall on the sweet flesh of the bass. In place of the sea urchin roe he planned to butter-fry the oysters and scallops.

Charlie and Chloe usually drifted into the kitchen for a drink well before dinner, but they were still upstairs by the time everything was ready. Once or twice during previous visits, Matthew had heard discreet sounds of lovemaking come down through the ceiling, and he'd been vaguely listening out for them, but he hadn't heard anything, and he supposed that was less disturbing

than it would have been if he had, all things considered, though it didn't do much to alleviate the tension inside him. The thought of telling Charlie what he'd seen that morning, while still presenting itself as his only option, had been filling him with dread. He'd have to find some way of doing it as soon as possible; preferably tonight. He didn't want it lingering over him.

He called up but there was no reply. Feeling awkward, he went to the bottom of the stairs and called again. After a while Charlie answered groggily, "Yeah?" and Matthew told him dinner was ready.

They both made an effort to be sociable when they finally came down, but he could tell they hadn't wanted to be disturbed, and that neither of them much wanted to eat. They sat out on the terrace with the usual candlelight and katydid chorus, but it was a lackluster affair. Charlie explained apologetically that he'd eaten too much cheese earlier, and barely picked at his food. Chloe at least made an effort but she was obviously distracted by her own thoughts.

"How's Lily getting on at camp?" Matthew asked her.

She gave some vague answer, and he felt a bit malicious for raising the subject. Soon afterward she stood up and asked if they'd mind if she went to bed.

"Everything okay?" Charlie said.

"Yes. I'm just tired."

She yawned and waved good night.

"Another delicious dinner, Matt. Thank you."

"You're welcome," he said, pleasure rising in him, in spite of himself.

Alone with Charlie, he decided he might as well get the

unpleasant task over. He was racking his brains to think of some appropriate way to introduce the subject, when Charlie gave a loud yawn and said that he also was feeling tired.

"Would you mind if I hit the hay?"

"Of course not," Matthew said, relieved.

• • •

The bulk of summer still lay ahead of him, he reflected later, in bed. All year he'd been looking forward to the long hot weeks up here. He needed them badly. He'd been counting on them to restore him, bring him out of the strange funk he'd drifted into. Was he really going to have to spoil these precious days? Because one way or another that would surely be the effect if he spilled the beans on Chloe. He hadn't thought it through earlier, but now that he did he could see that telling Charlie was going to wreck the summer—for all three of them.

But how the hell could he *not* tell Charlie? Wasn't he obliged to? Obviously it would be easier not to—just to go on as if nothing had happened—but the very fact that it *would* be easier seemed to confirm that what he needed to do was precisely the difficult thing. Wasn't that his responsibility as Charlie's cousin and friend? And would it be possible, anyway, to salvage the summer by pretending nothing had happened?

Briefly, as he posed these questions, he became aware of something minutely false in presenting the problem to himself in terms of friendship and cousinly duty: a sheen of spuriousness overlaying the formula. It wasn't how he'd seen it this morning, after all, but somehow an emergency measure conceived purely to expunge the intolerable reality from his own mind had mor-

ɔhed into something more altruistic, a "duty," and he didn't trust altruism, or not when it fronted his own impulses. His mind stalled, overcome by the complexity of the situation. On top of the question of whether or not to tell Charlie, there was the question—possibly even more unsettling—of how this new knowledge was going to affect his own relationship with Chloe; a whole dense layer of potential damage that he hadn't yet been able to bring himself to inspect.

He thought of Charlie over at the Zendo that morning; pictured him in the lotus position, pinched fingers on his sunburned knees: being "in the moment" while Chloe was doing whatever she'd been doing back in that motel room . . . It occurred to him that *he* had actually been the one in Charlie's "moment," and that, far from being a state of bliss, it had been extremely painful.

It was somewhat typical of Charlie, he found himself thinking, to arrange for someone else to feel his pain.

five

Several days passed. The same routines filled them as before. But their regularity no longer had the same agreeably lulling effect on Matthew. When Chloe set off to take pictures or attend one of her classes, it was impossible to avoid the question of whether she was in fact going off to meet the man from the motel, and the thought would leave him jangling with useless emotions. Meanwhile the sight of Charlie working or meditating, or driving off in his tennis gear, formed an image of increasingly irritating innocence. Even his own pleasantly mindless activities were losing their charm, their soothing rhythms broken by gusts of crackling interference from a situation that had nothing to do with the problems he was trying to sort out.

But what was he supposed to do? The feeling that he ought to tell Charlie about the motel remained undiminished despite

recurrences of that sense of something false about it, or at least something glossed-over. Yet he was finding it vastly more difficult to tell Charlie than he had foreseen. Whenever he tried, a curious, contradictory impulse would take over. Cornering Charlie in his meditation garden or down in the wine cellar, he would begin by steering the conversation to the closeness and longevity of their friendship, meaning to prepare Charlie for the necessary blow. But within moments another part of his mind would send out torrents of diversionary chatter; meaningless blather about his own life and plans—the food truck idea, or his hope of being able to afford a bigger apartment before long, or any other topic besides the one he'd intended to raise. Charlie would look at him strangely at these moments, and Matthew knew he risked appearing a little crazy, but it was always a relief to come away from him with the secret intact, the blow still undelivered.

Who wants to be the bearer of such tidings? If Charlie believed him he'd be devastated. If he didn't—and that was obviously a possibility—he would think Matthew was deliberately stirring up trouble. Either way he would almost certainly resent him. And it wasn't just the summer that stood to be ruined as a result, but their whole, precariously reconstructed friendship, which for all its stresses and imbalances had become as important to Matthew this time around as it had been the first time.

So he prevaricated: told himself he needed more evidence before doing something so potentially destructive; that he'd perhaps misconstrued the episode at the motel; that Chloe and the man might have been transacting some perfectly legitimate business in his room; that even the seemingly undeniable element

of deception—claiming she was going to yoga, changing her clothes—had some innocent explanation. He tried to convince himself that even if he found rock solid evidence of an affair, his duty was actually to protect Charlie rather than inflict pain on him. Or else that it was to find some way of quietly bringing the affair to an end: confronting Chloe, dropping a hint or just somehow making her feel he was watching her . . . All of which seemed to him equally impossible and repugnant.

What he settled on, in the end, was the formula that it was simply none of his business. *None of my business,* he would tell himself firmly as Chloe left the house, and the agitation started up in his heart. *None of my business,* as the unruffled contentment of Charlie's demeanor prompted that sudden sharp urge to shatter it. *None of my business* . . . And after a while a fragile calm would descend on him.

• • •

One morning he was at the Greenmarket in Aurelia, waiting to pay, when he became aware of a presence at the next register. Before even turning he caught a familiar signal on his antennae. A direct glance confirmed it. There was the beefily built figure, the Vandyke beard, the gray-streaked dark hair falling in wiry clusters on either side of the broad, sharp-tipped chin. The untucked shirt, pink this time, was worn in the same billowing style, over knee-length breeches. It was the man from the motel.

He stared, unable to stop himself.

The man looked solidly in his forties; hale and undimmed, but with no trace of the youthful uncertainty men in their thirties still project. His blocky nose jutted. His eyes were small but

lively, glancing around the store with a ready-to-be-entertained look. It didn't surprise Matthew to hear him comment on what a gorgeous day it was to the sales clerk when his turn at the register came. What did come as a surprise was the accent: it was the self-delighting twang of a Southerner used to being found charming in the North. As his purchases crossed the scanner, Matthew observed them closely, and with growing consternation: bread, milk, coffee, olive oil, eggs, sea salt: not the purchases of someone staying in a motel. A bag of kumquats and some bars of chocolate appeared; still more disconcerting.

"Paper or plastic?" the clerk asked.

"Oh, I think I'll take the paper, miss. A day like this makes you want to save the planet, dudn' it?"

He left, carrying the bag against his stomach. Matthew, who was still waiting in line, considered jettisoning his own shopping so as to drive after him, but resisted, not wanting to draw attention to himself.

As it happened the man was walking, not driving. Leaving the store, Matthew saw him at the upper exit of the parking lot. Matthew put his own shopping into the truck, and walked after him, keeping well back. After crossing Tailor Street the man cut through a passageway next to the hardware store into a quiet back alley that led past a communal vegetable garden to the bridge across the Millstream creek. Matthew followed him over the bridge, where he turned left along Veery Road, the street that ran parallel with the creek. It was a residential street of houses in large private yards with tall hedges and fruit trees and rustic split-rail fences. There was no sidewalk. The houses on the left backed onto the high bank of the creek, and it was into the

driveway of one of these—a simple whitewashed A-frame with a screened-in porch—that the man now entered. He was lifting the domed black lid off a Weber grill with his free hand as Matthew reached the driveway. The same hand a moment later stuck a key in the front door of the A-frame, opening it. The maroon vintage car Matthew had seen outside the motel was parked in the driveway. It was a Chrysler LeBaron.

Matthew walked on to the end of the road, which eventually curved around to intersect with the county road, and made a left onto Tailor Street. From there he crossed to the Greenmarket parking lot and climbed back into his truck.

So, he was here. Not ten miles away in an East Deerfield motel this time, but right here in Aurelia. Staying here, it appeared; renting or borrowing that A-frame. Buying supplies for himself. Stocking up (the thought sent its own painful reverberation through Matthew) on Chloe's favorite snack.

All of which implied what, exactly? Was there any difference between a lover who lived far away and had to rent a motel room to visit, and a lover who moved right in under the husband's nose? No. Infidelity was infidelity.

But as he drove back up the mountain he felt the encroachment of new disturbances. He found himself imagining the progression of feelings between the two lovers that must have taken place in order to bring about this development: tender exchanges about missing each other; increasingly bold proposals for how to be together more often. It seemed to him he could hear, almost as if it were taking place right there in the car, the conversation the lovers must have had, breathless with the thrill of illicit passion: *I want to be with you all the time . . . I want that too . . . What if*

I had a place of my own up here . . . ? What if I found you somewhere in the listings . . . ? None of his business, he repeated mechanically to himself, and yet it seemed to him he could feel, on his own senses, the mounting excitement at the new intensities of passion, intimacy, danger, that such a move would bring about. And by the time he got back to the house there was no doubt in his mind that things had taken a serious turn for the worse.

The next day at breakfast, Chloe asked Charlie what he was planning to do that morning.

"I have a conference call. Why?"

"There's a preview for an estate sale at one of those mansions across the river. I thought you might want to help me pick out some things."

"Sorry, Chlo. I have the call scheduled. I did tell you about it."

"Did you? I forgot. Anyway, it doesn't matter. The preview's on all week." She yawned. "I think I'll go to yoga, in that case."

She cleared a few things off the table and called goodbye from the kitchen.

"Are you coming right back?" Charlie asked.

"Yes?"

"Grab me a watermelon juice, would you?"

"Sure."

She left in the Lexus. The sense of something catastrophic arising inside him gripped Matthew. Some explosive force seemed to be coming at him from within. He stood up, staggering a little as he pushed back the chair. Charlie glanced up from his iPad.

"You okay?"

"Yeah. I'm actually going to head off too. Do the shopping before it gets too hot."

"All right, Matt."

He drove straight to the Yoga Center, a barnlike wooden building down a cul-de-sac at the back of town. The Lexus wasn't in the parking lot. He'd predicted it wouldn't be, and yet its absence genuinely shocked him. He couldn't quite connect Chloe with the blatantness of her lie.

He drove straight to Veery Road, slowing as he approached the short driveway to the A-frame. The LeBaron was in the driveway, but not the Lexus. But the comfort its absence afforded was short-lived: he found the car less than a hundred yards away, hidden behind a small commercial strip with office buildings and a wine store, where Veery Road intersected with the county road leading out of town. Evidently Chloe had decided it wasn't safe to park right in her lover's driveway.

Well, and so what to do? The explosive feeling had passed, leaving a kind of murkily ruminant confusion. In a dim way he'd assumed that the possession of unequivocal knowledge would spur him into some equally unequivocal action. But in fact he felt less clear than ever. The idea of going back to the house and telling Charlie he could catch his wife *in flagrante* if he hurried down to Veery Road was too grotesque to countenance. But to go back and say nothing seemed just as awful. Telling himself he needed to think, he circled back through town and went down to the creek, leaving the truck in the parking lot by the bridge.

The rocks near the bridge were crowded with the usual idlers and vacationers. Downstream the numbers thinned out. He spotted a promising ledge on the other side of the creek. The fast-flowing water was too wide to jump, and he rolled up the legs of his pants to cross. From the rock, looking downstream,

he saw the blue-trimmed white apex of the A-frame, standing out above hedges on the other side. If he walked another fifty yards and climbed up the steep bank, he would be standing in its backyard.

Had he come here in order to do that? He hadn't been conscious of it, but what other reason would there have been to come? And yet what could possibly be gained by placing himself there?

What do I want? he wondered. What am I looking for? Did he need to see Chloe in the house, with the man, in order to satisfy himself that his appraisal of the situation was correct? Surely that wasn't necessary. What, then? Baffled by his own actions, he climbed off the rock and walked back upstream.

A group of Rainbows was settling in on a flat reddish slab where the water fell in combs from one level to another. At their center, unmistakable with his Dürer ringlets and the cobble-like muscles of his arms and torso, was Mr 99%. Torssen. The "Prince." He had a baguette in his hands and was breaking off pieces to share out. He was laughing, his teeth gleaming in the morning sun, and the others were laughing too, their silver- and leather-bangled arms stretched out toward him. Some of them were pretending to plead for their morsel of bread like children, adding further to that sense they always gave off as a group, of staging and performing their own busy merriment for the benefit of others: the Babylonians, presumably, whom of course they affected at the same time not to notice. It was striking, but even more so was the almost—no, it had to be fully—conscious manner in which this charismatic breaker of bread was reproducing in his own gestures those of Christ from a thousand illustrations

of the miracle of the Loaves and Fishes. You had to hand it to the guy, Matthew thought; he had a gift for striking a pose. His long, sinewy arms made their motion of breaking and offering the glazed loaf (it looked like one of the over-aerated "French Sticks" that the local bakery, Early to Bread, sold) with an ease and grace that seemed to source the action in some utterly natural impulse of generosity.

Matthew passed on, wondering why he felt so irritated by these harmless people, and so ill-disposed toward the ringleted man in particular.

When he drove back behind the wine store the Lexus was gone. He looked at his watch: an hour had passed since the beginning of Chloe's "yoga." She'd be on her way home, he realized; with Charlie's juice. Watermelon juice! Cynical amusement brought a smile to his lips as he thought of the thin, astringent flavor of this decoction that Charlie was so fond of. It seemed a fitting gift, somehow, from his unfaithful wife.

He was such a funny mixture of weakness and strength, Charlie. Or softness and hardness. He could be ruthless, that was for sure; selfish in the extreme. But there was that hurt, vulnerable side to him too. Whenever Matthew found himself thinking too harshly of him, he would remind himself of this.

He remembered an incident from the evenings he and Charlie had shared when Matthew first came to the States. They'd been in one of the bottle-service clubs on Twenty-seventh Street that Charlie had frequented for a brief period, where he would pay five hundred dollars for a bottle of vodka and, when he was drunk enough, invite women to their table. They'd just sat down, when a silver-haired man had come over to say hello to Char-

lie. Charlie had seemed guarded, and when the man left, he'd downed his drink in a single gulp, baring his teeth at the burn.

"Have you ever been fucked in the ass?" he'd asked. "Because that's what that guy did to me." The incident he'd recounted to Matthew had occurred when Charlie was working as an analyst. The bank had been doing an IPO for a telecom equipment company, and the silver-haired man—a senior manager—had been pressing Charlie to join him on a junket in Las Vegas, where the company was giving a presentation to potential investors. Analysts weren't supposed to go near these presentations, and Charlie had asked his boss to shield him from the improper pressure coming from the silver-haired guy. But instead of shielding him, the boss had made it clear that Charlie would lose a chunk of his bonus if he didn't go. It wasn't the bonus itself that he cared about, Charlie had said, but the year-end review. If that was bad, as it would be if he held out, he'd be finished in the business. So he'd gone to Vegas, accepted the courtesy suite at the Bellagio, the limitless Pol Roger champagne, the hospitality bag stuffed full of Hermès ties and Zegna cuff links, and in return had written a report that smoothed over the company's liquidity problems and minimized the threats to its long-term market share posed by its rivals, and in short had let himself, as he repeated with morbid self-disgust, be "royally fucked in the ass."

He'd never mentioned the episode again, and Matthew had forgotten it until now. It must have been the humiliation Charlie was undergoing at the moment, albeit unwittingly this time, that had brought it back.

six

In the period that followed, Matthew found himself heading off into town several times a day on some pretext or other—invented as much for his own benefit as anyone else's—and driving around in the vague hope (or was it dread? he wasn't quite sure) of glimpsing Chloe's lover.

It seemed important to get some sense of the guy: some idea, as he put it to himself, of what he was "up against." There was also the fact that being in motion like this offered the sensation of doing something about the problem without committing him to the irreversible course of actually breaking the news to Charlie. At a certain level of consciousness he was aware of something unnecessary, and possibly even a little unhealthy, in what he was doing. What difference could it make, after all, even if he did pick up some nugget of information about the guy? And yet that

awareness was peculiarly thin and ineffectual. Indulging in these meandering little expeditions seemed to satisfy some sharp craving in him. He almost felt as if he were at work, in some obscure way, on the recalcitrant stuff of his *own* existence.

He would cruise slowly past the A-frame, and, if the LeBaron wasn't there, would look through the parking lots around town in search of its distinctive boxy maroon outline. He saw it outside the FedEx office on one occasion, in the Millstream Inn's parking lot on another. Twice, he saw the man himself in the Greenmarket. The second time he followed him from there to the movie rental store next door and stood behind him as he returned a DVD. His neck was sunburned reddish at the back. He wore a beige canvas cap from which his hair bunched out in wiry curls. Dark stains showed at the armpits of his faded blue T-shirt, the sweat-smell partly masked by a coriander-scented deodorant. He wasn't obviously good-looking in the way Charlie was, but he had a certain dynamism about him, Matthew had to admit; an unrefined if not quite crude forcefulness even when he stood still, that reminded Matthew of a statue he'd seen on his trip to Europe with his father, of some artistic colossus portrayed stark-naked, with a jovial grin. His calf muscles, big as hams, were palely furred below his cargo shorts. He engaged the clerk in friendly conversation, his voice quiet but commanding, with a pleasant buzzing edge. "It's a great little movie, you should see it," he told her, exiting the store.

Matthew watched him cross the parking lot back to his car, before leaving the place himself. What had he learned? In terms of hard information, nothing. Yet for some reason he drove away with a sense of having accomplished something, and for the rest

of the afternoon he found himself reliving the little sequence: following the man once again in his mind's eye from the Greenmarket to the rental place, standing behind him at the register, watching him return the movie. The memory of the statue he'd seen became clearer in his mind. It seemed to superimpose itself on his image of the man, supplanting his features and figure with its own more archetypal embodiment of stout-bellied vigor, striding the earth with jovially arrogant confidence. Was that how Chloe saw him? It seemed to him, in that close proximity he often felt to the current of Chloe's feelings, that it was, and that for precisely this reason it absolved her, at least in her own mind, of hypocrisy. She had her own code of conduct: he'd always sensed that. For all her churchgoing sweetness and compassion, what motivated her wasn't the ambition to be a "good person" in any conventional sense (Charlie was the conventional one in that respect), but simply a desire to engage with whatever offered the promise of life, energy, vitality. It was, he realized with a sort of gloomy clarity, one of the things he most admired about her.

A few days later, after he'd been puttering around town for the better part of the morning, he caught sight of the man again, approaching on foot from the far end of Veery Road. He continued driving toward him, aware of the black hemlocks and green laurel hedges flowing backward around him as the distance closed between them. He'd been mentally planning a dinner of scallops and pork belly with a parmesan espuma as he drove around, and had realized he'd forgotten to bring any spare cartridges for his foamer when the man's stocky figure had appeared in the distance. He was walking on Matthew's side of the road, sensibly facing the oncoming traffic, and carrying a shiny white

shopping bag with a bottle in it: champagne, Matthew saw as he drew closer and the foil top glittered. He found himself simultaneously wondering where he might be able to get hold of nitrous oxide cartridges for the espuma, picturing the man pouring a foaming glass of champagne for Chloe as they lay in bed and realizing with a sudden gush of aggression that with nothing more than a quick jerk of the steering wheel he could knock him down, run right over his thick neck and be gone before anyone knew what had happened.

Instead, he slowed down politely and swung wide of him, receiving an appreciative nod in return.

He felt shaken after that. He hadn't realized he bore the guy actual hostility. The "incident," purely imaginary as it had been, made him aware he was getting a little overwrought about the whole business.

It seemed to him he had been given a warning: to pull back, or at least formulate a more rational, practical plan of action than this rather aimless to-ing and fro-ing.

But a plan to do what, exactly? Aside from the desire for things to be restored to their original condition, which was hardly a realistic aim, he had no clear objective around which to build a plan.

· · ·

That afternoon Chloe announced she was going out to photograph some more mailboxes. There was one in particular, she said, that would make a good cover for a book if she ever collected them.

"Where's that?" Matthew asked, adding quickly, so as to

cover the tone of suspicion he'd caught in his own voice: "I mean, I was wondering if I'd seen it."

She smiled, gathering up her car keys.

"Probably not. It's on a road that doesn't really lead anywhere."

Charlie, who was on his iPad at the kitchen table and hadn't seemed to be following the conversation, said, without looking up:

"Which road?"

"Fletcher," Chloe answered without hesitation. "Just past the place that sells ducks' eggs. Why don't you come with me and take a look? It's very pretty. You too, Matthew, if you'd like ..."

Charlie grunted, "Maybe another time," and Matthew, realizing he'd been outmaneuvered, muttered that he was a little tired.

"Well, come down later, if you feel like it," Chloe said, smiling at each of them. "I'll be there till sunset."

As she left, Matthew saw Charlie glancing after her, and thought he caught something uneasy in his expression. He had in fact considered the possibility that Charlie had some inkling of what was going on. He happened to know that his cousin had a problem with jealousy. In those candid talks they'd had during the first months of their reunion in New York, when Charlie was still hurting from the breakup of his first marriage and glad of a willing listener, he'd confided in Matthew that one of the reasons for the breakup was that he'd driven Nikki, his wife, crazy with his suspicions. He'd wanted a kid, and when she'd said she wasn't ready he'd taken that—by his own shamefaced admission—as evidence that she wanted to go on,

in his words, "fooling around with other guys." He'd changed since then, obviously. Under Chloe's steadying influence the anguished, self-flagellating Charlie of those days had given way to the contented husband and father that now formed the image he presented to the world, and presumably he'd learned to ignore the tremors of his hypervigilant instincts. But those instincts were surely still alive in him somewhere, however much he might wish to suppress what they were telling him. And if that was the case, might he not, at some level, be actually grateful for an opportunity to talk?

True, he'd shown no sign of interest in Matthew's attempts so far to open the subject, but then those attempts had been so indirect that it was entirely possible Charlie hadn't even realized what they were.

All of which seemed to argue for a more direct approach, or at least (caution intervening once again as the decision formed to broach the topic) a less oblique one.

"You seem," Matthew said, perching on a kitchen stool, "really happy, you and Chloe."

Charlie looked up at him.

"I'd say we're pretty happy."

"You seem to have a great balance between togetherness and ... independence."

"Uh-huh."

"I admire that."

"Well, Chloe's always been totally her own person."

"I know."

Charlie continued looking at him, as if his curiosity had been piqued, and Matthew felt he could safely develop the point.

"Unusually so, I'd say, compared with what I've noticed in other married couples."

Charlie seemed to mull this over.

"What do you mean?"

"Oh, just that she seems to have these very strongly demarcated areas of her life that she keeps . . . private."

"Such as?"

"I suppose I'm thinking of the way she goes off for her classes, or the photography. I mean, I think it's good to have that kind of separation in a relationship. I think it's a real strength."

"It seems pretty normal to me."

"Absolutely. Absolutely."

Now he was afraid he'd misjudged Charlie's mood after all, or else scared him off.

"I guess I'm comparing it to the way you described your relationship with Nikki."

Charlie's jaw muscle clenched a moment.

"Yeah, well, it's definitely very different from that."

"You used to get suspicious whenever she went out alone, right?"

"I was an idiot."

"Though you did always, I mean . . ."

Matthew faltered, sensing danger.

"I did what?"

"Well, you did always maintain that your suspicions were probably justified . . ."

A frown crossed Charlie's features. He was silent for a moment.

"I've evolved since then," he said finally. "I think it's import-

ant to take responsibility for your own character defects. I've tried to."

He looked at his watch.

"Listen, Matt, I'm thinking I might head up to Hudson. There's a burgundy tasting I sort of want to go to."

"That sounds fun."

Charlie stood up. "Well . . . you're welcome to join me."

Matthew hesitated; a car ride together might be just the thing to force him to bring this distasteful business to an end. He glanced back over at Charlie, intending to accept the invitation, but was stalled by an expression in Charlie's eyes. They seemed to be regarding him with an odd neutrality.

"I mean, it's kind of an invitation thing," Charlie said, looking away. "But I'm sure it'll be fine if you come along as my guest."

Reflexively, though with a dim sense of being a little cowardly, Matthew grasped at the excuse to delay action once again.

"Oh. Thanks. Actually, maybe I'll stay here. Work on my tan . . ."

Charlie nodded.

"I'll see you later, then."

He left, grabbing his keys from the countertop.

Matthew sat down at the table where Charlie had been. It struck him that it might have been tactless to mention Nikki. Not that he'd had any reason to suspect Charlie was still sore about his ex after all these years, but he did know it was a mistake to underestimate Charlie's sensitivity in general. *Stupid of me*, he thought. Next time he'd go straight to the point. Say what he'd seen at the mall and let Charlie take it or leave it. No more beating about the bush.

It was five o'clock. He stood up, wondering what to do with himself. Two or three hours of solitude lay ahead of him. It should have been an appealing prospect, but it was filling him with curious apprehensiveness, as if the blank stretch of time were mined with strange perils. It seemed to him, oddly, that he was capable of doing something he might regret if he wasn't careful, though he couldn't imagine what form any such action might take. He considered his options.

Really he ought to get started on the project of taking stock of himself that he'd managed to avoid so far. He could have a swim, a skinny-dip even, since he had the pool to himself, and then lie in a deck chair and do some good hard thinking.

It occurred to him that, for that matter, he had the whole house to himself. He was standing by the staircase now, a flight of polished planks that seemed held in their curving succession by pure air. He'd had no occasion to go up them on this visit, but there was no particular sense that the upstairs was off-limits. He began climbing.

The air up there was different: warmer, sweeter, redolent of soaps and lotions and Chloe's scent rather than the cooking smells and faint rawhide odor that permeated the downstairs spaces.

He didn't have anything specific in mind. "I'll see if they've done anything different to the spare room," he said to himself, opening the first door. The blond wood sleigh bed still dominated the room but there was a new dresser next to it: deco, he guessed from its simple lines. Some fifties-looking ceramic vases had been arranged along the windowsill. Not that interesting, he thought, articulating the words as if to supply himself with some kind of harmless official motivation for moving on along the corridor.

The guest bathroom didn't tempt him. Nor did Lily's room, though the door was open and he was briefly nonplussed by a pair of eyes glittering in its curtained darkness: a rocking horse. The room Charlie used for an office had even less allure; almost a kind of antimagnetism, as though walled in the aura of faint tedium that Charlie's existence, rich and privileged as it was, often seemed to give off. The master bedroom was next. He paused before opening the door, frowning. Further justification seemed required by some scrupulous inner agency before he could allow himself to proceed. *Evidence*, he found himself thinking. Some vital evidence that might, in spite of all indications to the contrary, exonerate Chloe, could be lying around somewhere. What if he was wrong about everything after all, and was at the point of jeopardizing, possibly even sacrificing, his two most precious relationships because of some absurd misreading of the situation? Didn't he owe it to himself—to everyone, in fact—to go forward?

Dubious as he felt it to be, the formula enabled him to lift the old-fashioned black iron latch. Pushing the door open, he seemed to step into a tumult of scents, colors, emotions, too overwhelming to allow any action to occur other than a kind of stupefied swaying, and any observation other than that of his own reeling dizziness. The question of a search, methodical or otherwise, was gone from his mind, utterly eradicated, as if it had never been present. He took in the fact that the bed was unmade, the floor either side of it strewn with books, magazines, disheveled bathrobes and pajamas. Laundry spilled from a basket in the adjoining walk-in closet, under racks of jackets and skirts. His eye skimmed it and in his hand a moment later was a pair

of silken underwear, insubstantial as a mist-net but charged with forces that had set his heart slamming in his chest. Jesus Christ, he thought. This was not what he wanted to want. He remembered an exchange with his father: one of their very last, as it happened. Charlie, recently arrived in their household, had been overheard somewhere using the phrase "jerking off," not at that time a common expression in the British lexicon. Later, in private, Matthew's father had asked Matthew what it meant. Embarrassed, Matthew had explained, and his father, taken aback, had reacted with the words, "That's something I hope you'll never do"; an injunction that might have been forgotten had he not disappeared so soon after, but that, by virtue of its timing, had taken on the gravity of a biblical commandment, forever conjoining the activity it proscribed with a feeling of burning shame. Even allowing for the more relaxed and modern attitude Matthew had absorbed over time from more enlightened sources (and which he guessed his father himself, had he been caught less off his guard, might well have professed), the exchange had infected Matthew with an irrational disgust for the act, which, one way or another, all too often took the form of self-disgust. He tossed the garment back into the froth of Turnbull & Asser shirts and Lanvin yoga pants and walked quickly out of the room, thoroughly unnerved at the devious machinations of his own mind in bringing him up there in the first place.

Downstairs he went immediately outside to the truck and drove into town, heading straight for Veery Road. This, he realized, was what he had really been wanting to do all along.

The LeBaron was in the driveway of the A-frame. The Lexus was behind the office buildings at the end of the road. So much

for the photographic expedition to Fletcher Road. It was exactly as he had foreseen. And yet, again, it gave him a jolting shock to see the imagined act made literal.

Evidently Chloe had gambled on no one taking her up on her invitation to join her out at the mailbox. Or else she'd just counted on being able to brazen it out, somehow, if they did and found she wasn't there.

He drove back to the house—what else was there to do?— and started on the dinner. Having failed to find cartridges for his foamer that morning, he'd put white beans in a Crock-Pot of stock with two heads of garlic and a half pint of olive oil and managed to find a leg of lamb that didn't look as if it had spent the last decade on the high seas in a refrigerated shipping container. What he had in mind was a simple gigot d'agneau aux haricots, the leg hot-roasted country-style to make the fats run gold under the crisped parchment of skin while the meat stayed tender and pink. He'd first tasted the dish at the Trumilou in Paris when he and his father had taken their trip around Europe. The combination of the tongue-thick slices of succulent meat, with the soft beans in their creamy juices, had made a powerful impression on him; both elements so robust his mouth had felt as if it were at the confluence of two big rivers of flavor, and it was one of the first dishes he had set out to master when he became a chef.

He studded the joint with rosemary sprigs and rubbed it in lemon juice (in Iceland they glazed it with coffee, something he'd always meant to try), and started to prepare a fricassee of oyster mushrooms for the appetizer. The previous day he'd given a ride to a hitchhiker, a barefoot young guy who reeked of pot and was trying to sell wild mushrooms to the local stores. Matthew

had asked what he had, and he'd opened the sack he was carrying, filling the truck cabin with the loamy pungency of what he assured Matthew were chanterelles, something he called "chicken of the woods," and oyster mushrooms. The latter had looked safely unambiguous and Matthew had bought the lot.

He got a vegetable bouillon going and went down to the cellar: the recipe called for some muscadet. Being in the basement, which was very much Charlie's domain, got him thinking of their discussion earlier, or rather of his failure, once again, to open the real subject he'd wanted to discuss. He wondered if he'd just been plain wrong about Charlie seeming uneasy when Chloe left. Either way, it was pretty obvious he wasn't ready to hear that his wife was cheating on him, and as Matthew found what he was looking for—a 2008 Domaine de l'Ecu—and carried it back upstairs, he found himself reversing his earlier resolution to take a more direct approach, deciding once and for all (or so he hoped; he knew from past experience that these mental circlings of his had a way of defying all efforts to stop them once they started) to ignore things and just enjoy the summer.

None of my business, he told himself as he diced the shallots and began wiping clean the shelved clumps of oyster mushrooms. *None of my business*, as he debated whether to run out in the truck again on what would almost certainly be a fool's errand to track down some real cane sugar in the "ethnic" aisle at the grocery store or stay put and hope the so-called brown sugar in Charlie's pantry, which would almost certainly be white sugar sprayed with molasses, would make a not-too-calamitous substitute for cassonade.

He was aware that he could get a little obsessive at times

about the finer points of his recipes. It was his own kind of Zen practice, in a sense. What all the niceties of bamboo breathing, positive versus absolute *samadhi* and so on were for Charlie, balanced flavors and correct technique were for him. The patient pursuit of culinary perfection was his way of escaping his own "wandering thoughts" and achieving the no-mind state of *mushin*. At any rate, the little mantra, *None of my business*, seemed to be working, and as he assembled the fricassee he felt a welcome blankness descend.

But it didn't last long. Without warning his calm was shattered by one of those waves of apprehension that render entirely futile any notion one might have of being able to master one's own mind. With it came an image of Chloe and her lover fucking in the A-frame, and the realization that however much he might wish to ignore what she was doing, it was going to be impossible.

Yes, it was none of his business, it was Charlie and Chloe's business alone. And yet it was his own sense of reality that was being threatened. The geometry of his relationship with Charlie and Chloe might shift as one of them drew closer or further away, but it was permanently and excusively triangular. Inconceivable, somehow, had been the possibility of a fourth figure breaking open this shape altogether, and the intrusion of such a figure was proving remarkably difficult to accept. It was like having to believe, suddenly, in a fourth prime color, or a second moon.

• • •

Charlie returned from his wine tasting a little before eight. He came into the kitchen carrying a mixed case of burgundies and looking much happier than he had before.

"Let's open one of these babies, shall we? What's for dinner?"

"Gigot d'agneau."

"Aha!"

Charlie selected a bottle from the box and uncorked it.

"I love your gigot d'agneau."

"Thanks."

"Here." Charlie poured him a glass. "Cheers."

"First time I had it," Matthew said, "was with my dad, on our trip across Europe. It made an indelible impression on me."

"Oh?" Charlie composed his features into a look of polite interest. It always seemed to make him nervous to hear Matthew talking about his father. Usually Matthew avoided the subject, but occasionally he felt a perverse desire to bring it up, unfurl it like an old rug and waft its mildewy odors in Charlie's direction. He wasn't sure why. Certainly he didn't regard Charlie as implicated in any way in his father's misfortunes. Not even Charlie's father, Uncle Graham, could really be held responsible for them. True, in his informal capacity as the family's financial advisor he had talked Matthew's father into taking advantage of the new terms by which Lloyd's was making it possible for middle-class investors to join its hitherto exclusively super-rich club of "names." But there was never any suggestion that he had any inkling of the Armageddon of claims about to descend on the company, or that he stood to profit by recruiting his brother-in-law. And even if privately, irrationally, Matthew's father did accuse his brother-in-law of all kinds of heinous treacheries and deceptions, obviously Charlie himself, a boy at the time like Matthew, had nothing to do with it.

Still, as Matthew knew from his own experience, a father's deeds have a way of lingering in the psychic atmosphere of

their offspring. Which was perhaps why Charlie was looking so uncomfortable right now. The contented air he'd come home with had left him. He gave the impression that he would have liked to remove himself from Matthew's presence, and yet he seemed at the same time transfixed, his wine glass stalling in the air as he waited, head bowed, to hear what else Matthew might be about to bring up from the past.

But in fact Matthew had had no clear motive in bringing up his father in the first place, and, seeing Charlie's discomfort, was as eager to move away from the subject as Charlie was.

"Anyway, it should be ready in about twenty minutes," he said.

Charlie's tension seemed to lessen.

"Sounds good."

"I assume Chloe'll be back by then . . . ?"

"I would think. Magic hour's pretty much over." Charlie checked his watch and looked out at the sky, from which the pink evening light had almost drained.

"I think I'll sit outside for a bit," he said.

He crossed the terrace and turned toward his meditation garden. Passing between tall viburnum bushes, he checked his watch again, and disappeared from view.

He was very attached to that watch, a Patek Philippe Calatrava that had belonged to his father. It had a loud tick and Matthew had often wondered how Charlie could get into any serious *samadhi* state with that racket going on.

• • •

Chloe came home as Matthew was putting the finishing touches to the dinner. She seemed at once fragile and elated: full of

smiles and clearly wanting to share her joy, though just as clearly at a loss how to do so without giving herself away. Her solution seemed to be an exaggerated all-round friendliness. She watched Matthew with a fond smile as he finished the fricassee.

"We're so lucky," she said, "to know someone who cooks as well as you do, Matt."

His heart swelled helplessly. Fu waddled in, and instead of ignoring him as she usually did, Chloe knelt down and hugged him. Rolling onto his side, he made a quiet crooning that sounded like the expression of feelings remarkably similar to Matthew's own at that moment: a grief-suffused love.

"Did you get what you were looking for?" he asked.

Her look of joy faded, and he immediately regretted forcing her back into her lie.

"I think so," she said.

He thought of asking her if he could see some of the pictures, but he didn't quite have the nerve. Besides, he assumed she'd fob him off with some story about not having taken any digital photos, even though he knew for a fact that she always shot on both digital and film.

But a few minutes later, when Charlie came in, she took one of her digital cameras out of its case.

"Here, Charlie." She turned on the monitor. "This is where I was." She glanced at Matthew, and it seemed to him she must have sensed his suspicions.

Charlie scrolled through the pictures.

"Very pretty," he commented.

"Take a look, Matt," Chloe said. "This was your idea, don't forget."

She held the monitor up to Matthew. His heart gave a brief lurch, as if there might be a reason to expect anything other than what she showed him. It was just a mailbox on a country road by a cornfield, with a red and white Dutch barn in the background. The mailbox itself was an old-fashioned grooved metal canister painted in bright enamels with a picture of baby turkeys following their mother past a simple rendering of the same cornfield and barn. On the rustic wooden stand to which it was fastened, a clay flowerpot with a midnight-blue petunia plant had been set. Low sunlight, coming in gold across the cornfield, made the tangled flowers glow above the little scene, and the whole image was given an extra, jewel-like gleam by the monitor's liquid crystal display.

"There," she said, smiling gently at Matthew, and he felt like a jealous husband who has just been offered an acceptable alibi and finds himself pathetically grateful for it, even though he knows perfectly well he is still being lied to.

It really was as if he had become Charlie's stand-in; a kind of surrogate cuckold, condemned to feel all the injury but deprived of any means of doing anything about it, even protesting.

The pictures had all been taken in the same light. Chloe must have dashed out after her assignation at the A-frame to snap them before coming home.

seven

At the beginning of August Chloe's cousin Jana and her husband Bill rented a house on Lake Classon, a half hour's drive from Aurelia. They arranged to visit one afternoon, along with another couple who were staying with them.

It was a hot, clear day. They brought their swim things and everyone splashed around in the pool for a while, drinking cocktails.

Jana taught psychology at a college in New Jersey. She had a round face, nothing like Chloe's, and plump thighs that she wrapped in a towel as soon as she got out of the water. She seemed in awe of her beautiful cousin, nodding enthusiastically at everything she said. Chloe, smiling her hostess smile, asked after family members.

Bill, gray-haired, with a small snub of a nose that looked like

a baby's, was a political consultant. He and Charlie floated off on inflatable armchairs into a corner, where Matthew heard them comparing different news networks' coverage of the Libor scandal.

The couple they'd brought along turned out to be English. Hugh was a writer of some kind, teaching for a term at Jana's college. He seemed good-natured if somewhat abstracted, his eyes partially obscured by thick round glasses. Not shy exactly, but quiet, and rather serious, and apparently oblivious to the heat, judging from the thick tweed jacket he'd arrived in. George, as the woman called herself, owned a vintage clothing shop in London. She was tall and bony, with blades of straight black hair, and spoke in what seemed a cultivated cockney accent, her thin mouth accentuated by bright lipstick. For a while the two of them and Matthew gravitated together, swapping stories of the expat life.

"I was going out of my effing box by about March this year," George said. "I thought winter was finally ending. And then the blizzards began! It was fun for about fourteen seconds, then you realize all it is is just piles of useless white gunk that just sit there getting covered in dog shit and soggy fags."

"That's why people go to Florida," Hugh said. "Snowbirds, I believe they call them."

"Yuck. Florida? Yuck."

"Or the Caribbean," Matthew said, pronouncing it in the American way.

"*Caribb*ean?" George mimicked. "Don't give me that! You're as bloody English as I am!"

"All right, Caribb*ean*."

"Do you know it?" Hugh asked.

"A little."

I'm curious to go there but I'm told it's mostly been ruined."

"We used to go to one of the smaller islands when I was a boy," Matthew said. "Apparently it hasn't been developed much even now. There's still no airport."

"Oh, yes? Which one is that?"

Matthew hesitated.

George immediately splashed water at him.

"You don't want to tell us, do you! He doesn't want to tell us. Thinks we'll cause an airport to be built and fill the place with Eurotrash."

Matthew, who had been thinking exactly that, grinned and told them the name.

"Never heard of it," George said. "Must be crap!"

She swam off, laughing.

"I should start the grill," Matthew said, not wanting Hugh to feel obliged to linger. To his surprise, Hugh said he'd help.

"I think I'll get dressed, though, first."

Matthew waited while Hugh changed in the pool house, emerging in his jacket and trousers and a pair of heavy brown brogues.

A silence fell on them as they went out through the pool gate and crossed the lawn toward the grill. Matthew, feeling he was in some sense the host, decided it was up to him to break it. He asked Hugh what books he'd written.

"You're not supposed to ask writers that," Hugh said, smiling.

"Oh. Why not?"

"Because nine times out of ten you won't have heard of any of them, which leaves you feeling like an idiot and the writer feeling like a failure."

Matthew laughed. "Sorry!"

"But the answer is books on social history. I wrote one on the British slave trade. One on the Sheffield radicals."

"I'm not sure I—"

"Oh, no one's heard of them. They were part of the working-class anti-slavery movement at the end of the eighteenth century."

"Interesting."

"Another one on Chartist strikes and insurrections..."

They reached the grill area, off to the side of the terrace. Matthew opened a sack of charcoal and tipped the lumps into an aluminum chimney. Hugh sat down on the pile of flat stones Charlie was planning to use for his pizza oven. (They'd lain there untouched since Matthew had carried them over from the truck two weeks ago.)

"So... revolution," Matthew said cautiously. "That's your basic subject?"

"Well, exploitation, primarily. I think it's a more complex phenomenon than people realize. But yes, revolt also. What about you? What's your—"

"Restaurant business," Matthew said. But, not wanting to get into a conversation about his ailing career, he added quickly, "Am I allowed to ask if you're working on something now?"

Hugh shrugged, his large shoulders conveying a sort of burdened but stolid patience. He was surprisingly—considering his sensitive-looking eyes—thickset and stocky. His steel-tinged brown hair hung in a pudding bowl and looked as if it had been hacked into that shape by a pair of blunt gardening shears. His skin was mealy and pale.

"Oh, I always have a few little projects on the go. There's a more

cultural-historical sort of book I'm thinking of calling *The Last Taboo*, about money—how it affects the consciousness of people who have it, or work with it."

"Like my cousin Charlie?" Matthew said, lighting the paper under the charcoal.

Hugh nodded. "I was certainly curious to meet him."

"Not that he's your average money person, though," Matthew put in, a little defensively. He'd formed the idea that Hugh must be some kind of rearguard Marxist. He had a vague sense of the glamour socialism still possessed among the more cultured of his former compatriots; that it was far from being a dirty word, as it was in America.

"In fact he sees himself pretty much in opposition to the archetype."

Hugh smiled—amiably enough:

"That's good."

"Where does the taboo part come in?"

Hugh thought for a moment.

"Put it this way, it's the only subject left that celebrities don't talk about in their memoirs. Their *own* money, I mean. They'll come clean about all the things that used to be taboo—sexual proclivities, drug habits, petty crime—brag about them, in fact. But they don't talk about their money and we don't expect it of them. It's the one subject that's still off-limits. Probably because unlike sex and drugs it's inextricably connected to the one source of guilt and shame that actually has some objective validity, namely the sense that you've stolen another person's labor—cheated them out of their own bodily and mental exertions. All those other forms of shame are basically just masks for this one, in my view: ways of

James Lasdun

not thinking about the one thing we all know in our hearts to be unequivocally wrong."

Matthew nodded, fanning the chimney with an old copy of the *Aurelia Gazette*. He wasn't sure he understood what Hugh was getting at, but he was enjoying the sensation, rare these days, of being taken for an educated man of the world. It wasn't how he thought of himself, exactly. His shambles of an education had seen to that, and he tended to be on his guard whenever the talk took an intellectual turn. But this thoughtful compatriot, with his worn old jacket and out-of-season shoes, put him at his ease.

They chatted on until the others came over from the pool, and for the next hour Matthew was in and out of the kitchen, busy with the dinner. Charlie and Chloe had made it clear they wanted a casual, no-frills barbecue, which was fine with him, but he was damned if he was going to serve up store-bought hamburger buns or ketchup, so there was all that to see to as well as getting the grill rack brushed and oiled and heated to the right temperature. As he was taking the brioche dough out of the fridge, George appeared in the kitchen.

"So what exactly is your gig here, then?" She perched tipsily on a stool. "Are you the English butler or something?"

Matthew explained that he was here as Charlie's cousin and old friend but also happened to be the designated chef.

She chuckled.

"So democratic, the American class system. Right?"

He made a noncommittal sound and began shaping the brioche buns.

"No, but seriously, what is your racket?"

"You mean in general?"

"Yeah, whatever . . ."

"Not much right now," Matthew said. Then, not wanting to come off as a complete nonentity, he told her about his plan for a gourmet food truck.

"How Brooklyn! What would you make?"

"I'm thinking maybe pupusas."

"What the *fuck* is a pupusa?"

Matthew explained, adding, "It probably wouldn't work in England."

"You'd have to call it a pupusa buttie . . ."

He smiled. "Anyway, it's strictly a pipe dream till I figure out how to get my hands on a truck."

"And how much would that set you back?"

"Forty, fifty grand, for anything halfway decent."

"Fuck!"

"Right."

"Better hit up your cousin Charlie! Or have a dig around in one of those sofas; probably a few grand in change right there." She lowered her voice: "What's he make all his dosh from anyway?"

"Banking."

"Oh, right, Jana said."

"Plus he inherited a few million."

She snorted. "I inherited my mum's microwave."

"That's more than I got."

"Really? You sound posh."

"No more than you, I'll bet."

"Ooh! I'll have you know that behind this mockney is a genuine cockney. My Auntie Becca was known as the Pearly Queen of Bethnal Green."

Matthew laughed, warming to her despite her jagged manner. She slid off her stool, waving magenta-nailed fingers at him and swaying a little as she clopped away.

At dinner, after he'd served up the burgers, he found himself seated next to her at the stone table. She was vehemently disagreeing with Bill about an opinion he'd just offered concerning a well-known TV host.

"Rubbish! He's a prat, Bill. He's a talking colostomy bag, not a journalist. And definitely not 'evenhanded.'"

"Oh, I think he's pretty evenhanded," Bill retorted with a bland smile. He didn't seem terribly enamored of his houseguest.

"Crap! He's about as evenhanded as a fucking...lobster."

"A lobster. That's good, George."

After they'd finished eating, Matthew slipped away and did some cleaning up in the kitchen. When he went back outside the atmosphere had changed. George was talking loudly while the others sat listening in various attitudes of discomfort. She'd flagged a little during dinner, but now she was blazing away again. Apparently she'd just remembered, again, that Charlie was a banker, and found that she was compelled by her conscience to go on the attack.

"I'm having a go at you, Charlie," she was saying with a grin. "But face it, you're no different, *really*, from some Mafia boss or Mexican drug lord up here on your mountaintop, are you? Actually, you're worse—"

Bill cleared his throat.

"It's okay, Bill" she said, "I'm just having a go at our host. It's very English of me, I know, but Charlie doesn't mind, do you, Charlie?"

"Be my guest."

"Ha. No, but seriously, you actually *are* worse than a Mafia boss

or a Mexican drug lord, Charlie, because they at least risk getting killed or locked up for robbing defenseless people of their life's savings and stealing their houses, whereas you're not only *allowed* to rob people of their life's savings and steal their houses, you are positively *encouraged* to rob people of their life's savings and steal their houses. In fact, the more you rob people of their life's savings and steal their houses, the bigger your year-end bonus, right? And of course if it all goes *pear*-shaped, you and your chums in your six-thousand-dollar power suits can just get together with your other chums at the Treasury Department in *their* six-thousand-dollar power suits and arrange for an eighty-billion-dollar bailout, paid for of course by the very people you've spent the last decade robbing and stealing from. Right, Charlie?"

Charlie took a deep breath and exhaled slowly. Chloe was looking at him, as if waiting for him to defend himself. But he said nothing.

Jana, who'd been darting glances at her hosts, said, "That's kind of a not very nuanced way of looking at the situation, don't you think, George?"

"We've been watching a lot of Occupy footage," Bill put in, more dryly.

"Charlie's totally a supporter of Occupy," Chloe said. "Tell them, Charlie..."

Charlie frowned. Catching the look, Bill continued:

"Well, no, that wasn't my point. I mean, I give credit to Occupy for bringing their issues into the mainstream, but at this juncture I also think they need to leave off what basically amounts to little more than tomfoolery and let the grown-ups deal with what happens to be—"

"The *grown-ups*?" George interrupted. "The *grown-ups*?"

"—with what happens to be a highly complex situation—"

"Daylight robbery is *not* complex, and who the fuck are the *grown-ups*?"

"What I'm trying to say is blaming the bankers for the inevitable problems that occur from time to time in a free market is like blaming your stomach when you overeat. It's just facile. It's singling out a small group of mostly honest and decent people, and turning them into scapegoats for the consequences of wanting to have cars and houses and easy credit for everyone instead of just, you know, the lucky few. What I'm saying is we're all implicated."

"Bollocks. How am I *implicated* when Charlie here sweet-talks some little old lady into signing up for a mortgage she can't afford and then runs off and sells that mortgage on to some thicko pension fund manager, knowing that the little old lady and all the other little old ladies he's sweet-talked in similar honey-tongued fashion are going to default, and the pension fund is going to go *pear*-shaped, and all the pensioners are going to be living off thin *gruel* for the rest of their days? How am I *implicated* in that, pray tell? What do *you* think, Charlie?"

Again Charlie abstained from comment. His back was straight, his mouth slightly open. Looking at him, Matthew realized it was his meditating posture. Not the full lotus, of course, but the erect spine, the centering of the body mass on the abdominal triangle— the *tanden*, as Matthew had seen it called in the Zen books lying around the house—the belly breathing, regulated so as to achieve *mushin*, no mind. It was a technique, as far as Matthew understood, for reducing other people to mere disturbances in the visual field.

Charlie did break his silence, however, a little later. George had

moved on to the subject of the banks short-selling mortgage-backed securities even as they were aggressively marketing those same securities to their clients, a practice she seemed to consider worthy of a whole new palette of disgust-effects. While she was in full cry, Charlie muttered something that, perhaps because he'd been so quiet until then, caused her to stop midsentence.

"Pardon?"

"You're talking about Goldman Sachs," Charlie said. "I worked for Morgan Stanley. They didn't do that. "

"Oh!" George said brightly. "In that case I owe you a massive fucking apology, don't I? Here, darling..." Leaning across the table, she planted a big kiss on Charlie's lips and sat back, laughing.

The gesture briefly dissolved the tension at the table.

But then Hugh spoke. He'd been drinking steadily all through dinner, and Matthew had assumed he was more or less in a stupor. But that didn't appear to be the case. Quite the reverse, if anything.

"Not that Morgan Stanley was a model of rectitude, exactly..." he said.

"I wasn't—" Charlie began. Chloe looked at him expectantly but he broke off, seeming to decide in favor of stoical endurance over further argument.

"I've read quite a bit about them," Hugh said. "It's a subject that interests me."

"Uh-oh, Charlie," George said. "Now Hughie's having a go at you. This time you're really in trouble!"

Chloe poured herself a glass of wine and looked out across the dark valley, seeming to absent herself. Political debate, with its tedious moral one-upmanship, had never seemed to interest her much, and this too was something Matthew admired in her. It

was a kind of cleanness, he'd always thought; a refusal to join in the demeaning parlor game of judging and being judged. No doubt this English couple would dismiss it as the complacency of the overprivileged, but he knew her better than that: she'd have been the same Chloe rich or poor; taking whatever life offered, without guilt, and without envy. He was very certain of that.

"No, but I find it all very intriguing," Hugh said. "We tend to see subcultures like Wall Street or Silicon Valley as monolithic entities but in fact they're fascinatingly diverse. Goldman Sachs, as far as I understand it, got its sort of über-predator edge by recruiting purely on the basis of how clever and hungry applicants were. They filled their ranks with all these high-IQ but completely ruthless young blokes out of projects in the Bronx who'd never had any inhibitions about grabbing whatever they could. Morgan Stanley was more old school, wasn't it? You had to have connections to get a decent job there, which made the whole operation a bit, well, no offense, Charlie, but a bit less sharp. The only reason they weren't short-selling those securities was that no one there saw the crash coming. Isn't that right? Not that being slower off the mark made them any more ethical— then or now, by all accounts. Didn't they just handle the Facebook IPO?"

"I wasn't there," Charlie said. "I left in 2005."

"Ah. But now when was Eliot Spitzer's thing, the Global Settlement? 2003, wasn't it?"

A guarded look appeared on Charlie's face.

"Around then."

"Eliot Spitzer!" Bill said, rolling his eyes.

Hugh ignored him:

"And didn't Morgan Stanley get the biggest fine of any of them?"

"It's possible," Charlie muttered.

"I'm fairly certain they did. That's been their racket for quite a while, hasn't it? Getting their analysts to sex up the profile of companies on the verge of going public?"

George broke in: "Is that what you did, Charlie? Were you an analyst?"

In a breathy voice, Jana said, "I think we should give Charlie a break, already!"

"Me too," said Bill.

"I'm curious, though," George pressed. "*Were* you?"

Matthew happened to turn toward Charlie just then. He was thinking it was high time someone mentioned Charlie's long-established interest in ethical investment, and was intending to mention it himself. But as he caught Charlie's eye, a look of anger, hatred almost, flashed across Charlie's features. It was gone before anyone but Matthew could notice it, but it shocked him. He dropped his glance immediately.

"Yes, I was a telecom analyst," Charlie said quietly to George.

"*Really?*"

"Come on, guys," Jana said. "Let it go."

There was a silence, long and uncomfortable. In it, the distant sound of drumming wafted in on a breeze.

"What's that?" Jana asked.

Matthew answered:

"The Rainbow people."

"Who are they?"

"Bums in war paint," Bill declared.

"Actually, they're interesting," Matthew said. Seeing an opportunity to atone for whatever he'd done to upset his cousin, he began talking about his encounters with the Rainbow people at the creek. He'd already told Charlie and Chloe the story of his meeting with Pike and the two girls, but Chloe pressed him to repeat it, laughing again as he described the wizened old guy with his embroidered bag. She, at least, seemed grateful to him for steering the conversation away from banking.

"Tell them about those words they use," she said, smiling at him. "They have their own vocabulary for everything."

He rattled off as many of the words as he could remember. Hugh took out a notebook and asked him to repeat them.

"That's priceless," he said, writing them down. "Absolutely priceless."

"Now Hughie's going to write an article about them," George said, "and everyone's going to think we spent our time in America living in a fucking teepee!"

A more relaxed conversation developed. Charlie brought out liqueurs and Bill produced some medical-grade pot. The moon rose from behind the mountain, newish, and bright enough that even its dark part had discernible substance and shape. By the time the party broke up everyone was behaving as if nothing untoward had happened.

· · ·

Later that night, Matthew heard a sound from the pool. He got up and looked out of the guesthouse window. Charlie was in the water, swimming the steady, head-down crawl he used for doing laps. Reaching the end he turned, plunging back the other way, his

long, straight body cutting the same undeviating line through the water.

After a while he climbed out and dried off. But instead of going back to the house, he wrapped himself in a towel and sat in a deck chair, motionless. He didn't seem to be meditating. His slumped body suggested something more along the lines of brooding.

The English couple must have left him feeling bruised, Matthew supposed. He thought perhaps he should go down and commiserate. But he wasn't sure how welcome he would be. Charlie had been rather distant with him lately. Borderline unfriendly, in fact. The other day he'd come back from New York in an upbeat mood after a meeting with a former executive from Grameen America, the U.S. branch of the Bangladeshi bank that had pioneered microloans, and announced that he was going to adapt their approach for his own investment group. (He was no longer referring to this as a "consultancy" group, a fact Matthew had noted with the faint amusement his cousin so often provoked in him.) "It's exactly what I've been looking for," he'd told Chloe excitedly. "It puts money into exactly the kind of small-scale entrepreneurship I've always believed in, and it turns out to be a damn safe bet for investors." But as soon as Matthew had started asking him questions about it, expecting to join in the conversation, he'd clammed up. And then there'd been that strange look of outright hostility at the table tonight. What had that been about? Matthew wondered. He tried to think what he could have said to provoke it. But he'd hardly spoken at all by that point in the dinner.

On the other hand, it was possible he was just imagining all of it. Maybe the look was just a general expression of irritation that happened to have caught him in its beam. And maybe, by the same

token, the other episodes had equally innocent explanations. He did suffer from a certain social hypersensitivity. He'd read somewhere that it was called the "spotlight effect": a tendency to imagine other people were paying more attention to you than they really were. It made you self-conscious; inclined to attribute critical judgments about yourself to people who in fact weren't thinking about you at all.

Well, if that was all it was, then perhaps he should go down and talk to Charlie after all. Let him know he was on his side, whatever that English couple thought of him.

He put on some clothes and went down the path to the pool. The stars were bright, the midnight air throbbing with drums and katydids.

Charlie looked over as he opened the gate, his face lit by the pool lights.

"What's up?"

"I was wondering if you could use some company."

"Oh." Charlie glanced up at the guesthouse window.

"I thought you might want to talk."

"About what?"

The defensive tone stalled Matthew.

"I don't know . . . I thought they might have upset you at dinner—the Brits."

Charlie shrugged.

"It's not exactly news to me, what they were saying."

"I guess not."

Matthew was standing by the pool, uncertain whether to sit down. After a moment Charlie said, very coolly:

"Are you sure that's what you wanted to talk about?"

"What do you mean?"

Charlie stared at him, his smooth features unsmiling. Then he shrugged and stood up, giving a yawn.

"Just wondering."

"What else did you think I—"

"No, nothing." Charlie yawned again. "Sorry. I'm tired."

"I mean, Charlie," Matthew persevered, somewhat against his better judgment, "I'm always happy to talk about anything. You know that. Anything at all . . ."

Charlie smiled.

"I didn't mean that. But thanks anyway." He turned to go.

"Charlie—" Matthew heard himself blurt. At that moment he was as close as he ever came to telling Charlie about Chloe's lover. He often wondered, later, how things would have turned out if he had.

Instead he broke off. In the silence that followed, Charlie turned to face him again, giving a strange look of skeptical expectation, as if Matthew were in the process of fulfilling some damning prophecy someone had made about him. It wasn't the actively hostile look of earlier, but there was a total absence of warmth in it. Utterly bewildered, Matthew tried to think of some word or phrase to break the tension, but before he could, Charlie turned the exchange in an altogether unexpected direction.

"By the way, Matt, this is kind of awkward, but we have some friends coming and we're going to need the guesthouse, just for a few days."

"Oh . . . no problem. I'll move my stuff into the spare room."

"No, I mean we need that too. Also Lily's going to be back from camp, so she'll need her room."

"Oh. Okay."

"I was thinking maybe if you had things you needed to do in the city, you might want to go down for a few days."

Matthew didn't know what to say.

"I mean . . . as I think I mentioned, I've sublet my place . . ."

"That's fine. You can stay at the house. No one'll be there. I think it'll just be for three nights, and not for another week or so."

"Well . . . okay . . . thanks," Matthew said, trying not to feel aggrieved.

"Night, then," Charlie said.

"Good night."

Back in bed, Matthew lay awake for some time. Charlie's willingness to send him away in order to make room for other friends surprised him, but he didn't want to have to feel upset with his cousin. In fact, he wanted very much not to have to feel upset with him, and after a while he was able to persuade himself that from Charlie's point of view there really wasn't any callousness in it at all. He was just trying to solve a logistical problem.

He closed his eyes and curled up in a determined simulacrum of sleep, furiously barring his consciousness against the mass of thoughts clamoring for entry, until finally real oblivion descended.

eight

In the morning he found Charlie drinking coffee alone on the terrace. It was early, not yet seven.

"Good sleep?" Charlie asked. Tanned and relaxed in his gray T-shirt and drawstringed shorts, he seemed fully recovered from his brooding hostility of the night before. His lean legs sprawled forward, feet comfortably crossed at the ankles, tapping each other as if in mutual affection.

"Not bad."

"Have some coffee." Charlie nodded at the pot and looked back down at his iPad. He held the device in his left hand and scrolled with his right, dismissing current events that didn't interest him with a flick of his forefinger, and detaining others with a lightly proprietorial jab as if to say, "Just one moment, you."

"Chloe still asleep?" Matthew asked.

"No. She went out. She'll be back with pastries after Early to Bread opens."

"Where'd she go? I mean . . . I mean . . . it's kind of early for yoga, isn't it?"

Charlie looked up.

"She went to take pictures."

"Ah. More mailboxes."

"Right. She figured she ought to get out there while she still can. Lily'll be home tomorrow."

"Right. Of course. Make hay while the sun shines. So to speak."

Charlie gave him another glance, and turned back down to his screen.

"I think I'll get an early start too," Matthew said.

"Uh-huh."

"There's a farmers' market in East Deerfield . . . Always good to beat the crowds."

"Well, don't get anything for me. I'll be in the city."

"You won't be coming home?"

"Yeah, but late, and I won't be eating. There's a dinner."

"Anything interesting?" Matthew asked, eager to leave but at the same time anxious to ascertain where he stood with Charlie; still clinging to the hope that his cousin's hostility might have been purely imaginary.

"What?" Charlie was looking his screen.

"Anything interesting—the dinner?"

"Oh, those Grameen people. Ex-Grameen."

"That sounds encouraging . . ."

"We're getting there."

"Microloans, right?"

"Right."

"What exactly is a microloan? I mean, what sort of sum?"

Charlie looked up at him.

· "It varies." He seemed on the point of getting annoyed. Bewildered, Matthew dropped it.

"Well . . . see you later, then."

"See you later."

He drove fast, making the turns without thinking. The LeBaron was in the A-frame's short driveway, and this time so was the Lexus, squeezed in right next to it, both fenders gleaming in the morning light. The sight was strangely shocking; shattering almost. It was as if, until now, some part of him really had been clinging to a shred of hope that he'd been imagining things. He plunged on past, his head reeling.

So what? he told himself. *Her business, not mine.* At the same time, from some ungovernably autonomous region of his mind, other thoughts arose; crushing, and still more crushing. She didn't care anymore if she was found out . . . She *wanted* to be found out; wanted to precipitate a crisis, upend her marriage . . . Or no, she wasn't even thinking about her marriage: she'd just been in too much of a hurry to see her lover, get into his bed for an early morning fuck on this last day of easy mobility, before her daughter came back from camp. *So what? So what?*

He pulled out onto the county road and a garbage truck he hadn't seen blasted its horn as it bore down, snorting into his mirror. Shaken, he made an effort to get a grip on himself. After a moment a slightly more rational explanation for the car's pres-

ence right there in the driveway came to him: she must have simply thought she was safe from discovery at that early hour. It wasn't much of a comfort, but it countered the suggestion of uncontrollable desire, which made its effect on him less incendiary. The pitch of his own feelings appeared to be connected with Chloe's. If he could tell himself this was just an ordinary affair pursued out of ordinary boredom, and regulated by sensible caution, he felt he could manage this absurdly inappropriate anguish.

He was driving toward East Deerfield because he had told Charlie he was going to the farmers' market. But he didn't feel like going to the farmers' market and it wasn't as if Charlie would give a damn whether he went to the farmers' market or not. What he felt like doing, he realized, was going back to Aurelia, back to the A-frame. The farther away he got, the more strongly he felt drawn back to it, as if distance brought out some mysterious soothing essence lodged in that triangular building that wasn't discernible in the tumult of things he felt in its proximity. At the same time the very urgency of the desire to go back seemed reason enough to resist it. It was abundantly clear to him that he was becoming unhealthily fixated on that little house.

He turned off the county road and drove aimlessly along the winding lanes that spread through an area of old dairy farms. Some of these looked abandoned; broken barns standing open to the sky, machines rusting in tall weeds.

I should leave right away, he thought, not wait till Charlie's guests arrive. Just make my excuses and go.

But where? His own apartment was sublet. His few friends aside from Chloe and Charlie were all dispersed for the summer.

In the past he would have gravitated toward the house in Spain, near Cádiz, where his mother and her third husband spent their summers, but his mother had died two years ago, and the husband, who owned the house, hadn't seemed interested in continuing his relationship with Matthew. He could visit his sister, he supposed. She and her partner, both social workers, lived in Bristol, a city he liked. But they were religious and the last time he'd visited, almost ten years ago, their determination to drag him off to church had got on his nerves. He could go somewhere on his own, of course, but that would mean motels and restaurants, which would eat up the meager profit he was making on his sublet; money he was counting on to help get him through the rest of the year.

The rest of the year . . . It was only the second week of August, but suddenly he was aware of autumn. The leaves overhanging the narrow roads were dusty and frayed. The grasses already looked dry. And still he had made no progress in the task he'd set himself, of getting to grips with the curious stalling paralysis that had taken him over.

Part of the problem was that he'd counted on being able to talk to Charlie and Chloe about it, but in their different ways they'd both made themselves inaccessible. Not that he blamed them, he assured himself, fighting off an urge to do just that. Why should they concern themselves with his private problems?

I should leave, he told himself again. Find a cheap motel on the Jersey shore and hole up for the rest of the summer.

He'd come to an area of cultivated fields, with split-rail fences dividing them. A red Dutch barn came into view as he

drew level with a well-tended cornfield. It looked oddly famil-iar, and he realized it was the one Chloe had photographed the other day. He slowed down. There was the mailbox with the enamel-painted wild turkeys and the petunia in its clay pot. The thought that Chloe had been here with her cameras gave the little scene a poignancy that clutched at him. He stopped and got out of the truck, breathing in the warm, sweetish air. The sense of her was strong suddenly, saturating, as if he had come upon yet one more of those secret pockets of hers. He felt close to her, standing where she had stood; linked across the intervening days as if by hidden threads, like the threads at the back of a tapestry. The cornstalks were taller than he was, armed in their heavy cobs, with the yellow silks blackening where they spilled from the split sheaves. At the edge of the field, blue starry flowers—cornflowers, he supposed—stood out against the steel-green darkness of the corn. Their blue looked warm at first, but the longer he looked, the colder it seemed to grow, as if it too were an incursion from the future; a backward glance of arctic blueness from the winter ahead. He climbed into the truck and headed back toward Aurelia. It was past eight by the time he got there: Early to Bread would have opened. It occurred to him that, assuming Chloe had left, he could go and knock at the door of the A-frame; pretend he'd been sent by the owner of the house to check the furnace or look at a crack in the ceiling. The guy would have no reason not to let him inside.

But then what? he wondered, frowning in bewilderment at the scenario he'd created. Why would I want to get inside?

The Lexus was gone from the driveway when he reached the

A-frame. He slowed, looking in through the blur of a screened window. A light was on. A large head moved against it.

Matthew sped away, his heart racing.

. . .

Charlie had left for New York when he got back to the house, and Chloe was out by the pool. The breakfast things were still on the stone table, and Matthew cleared them away. A half-scooped-out cheese sat on the kitchen counter, oozing from its cavity. Matthew threw it out and put the dirty plate and spoon in the dishwasher. He couldn't help disapproving of the wastefulness of his cousin's habits. He would pick up novelty loaves from Early to Bread on his way home from tennis, bite off a chunk, and let the rest go stale in the back of his car. Or he'd buy plastic-encased raspberries and leave them around unopened till they grew a fur of mold.

The landline rang. Matthew picked up: it was Jana, wanting to speak to Chloe. He called out to the pool and Chloe came in, putting on a pale blue shirt over her swimsuit. Matthew stood out on the terrace while she talked.

After she'd finished she came outside.

"Matt, I'm going out for the evening. Jana invited me over for a girls' night. Bill's away."

"Ah. Okay."

She stepped close to him under the grape arbor. "Sorry to be deserting you."

"Don't be silly."

"I hope you weren't planning something special, for our dinner?"

"No, no."

The truth was he'd barely taken in the fact that they'd been supposed to have dinner alone that night, so estranged had he been feeling from her.

"I'd much rather stay here with you," she said, "but I think Jana's having marital troubles."

"No problem."

She put her hand on his arm.

"You should go out somewhere too, Matthew. Have a change of scene."

He looked at her, surprised at the sudden solicitousness.

"The bar at the Millstream's supposed to be fun," she said, grinning. "You should check it out. You might meet someone."

"Hey! Who says I want to?"

Chloe laughed, her small teeth flashing white. She opened the kitchen door. "Shall we have some iced tea?"

"Sure."

"Seriously, Matt. It would do you good," she said, coming back with the glasses of tea on a tray.

"To pick someone up at a bar? That's never really been my thing."

She looked at him across the stone table, the uncluttered beauty of her face with its expression of tender attentiveness pure pleasure to behold.

"I don't know—I remember a time when you had a new girl-friend every time we met . . ."

"Well, I didn't pick them up at bars!"

"What about that blonde you met at Rucola?"

"Alison? She was eating there, at the table next to me. Not the same as a bar pickup."

Chloe's cell phone made a sound. She ignored it.

"Okay, but wait, there was one actual bartender, wasn't there?"

"Yes. I met her at the Nitehawk Cinema."

"Right. I liked her. But I preferred the blonde. I'll tell you a secret: Charlie and I were actually hoping you might settle down with her. She seemed just right for you."

"How so?" Matthew asked, pleased by this evidence of interest in his emotional well-being, even though it was from several years in the past.

"Well, she was cheerful and, I don't know . . . easy-going. Wasn't she from the West Coast? Charlie said he could see the two of you running some nice little café together, in Portland or somewhere. Her at the front, and—"

"Me skulking at the back?"

"No! You doing the cooking. I thought she was perfect for you."

"I'm not sure I'd have been perfect for her, though . . ."

"Oh, who cares? You should only ever consider yourself when it comes to love. You think I ever cared if I was right for Charlie? No! I saw he was right for me and I pointed myself straight at him! And I've never regretted it."

Matthew laughed, ignoring the urge to ask why she was cheating on him in that case, so happy was he to be talking the way they always used to; light and bantering, and coolly frank. Already he could feel her familiar, clarifying effect on him. She had a way of restoring him to himself; an intuitive understanding of his deepest nature that he'd never encountered in anyone else.

"Anyway," she said, "I don't necessarily mean getting a date. I just mean you should go out, talk to people, see some new faces, cheer yourself up. That's all."

"Why? Do I seem unhappy?"

"No. Just a bit ... locked up in yourself."

"Hmm."

"Hmm, what?"

"Well, I have been feeling a little bit ... locked up. It's been bothering me, actually."

"Really? You should have told me."

"Oh ... I don't want to burden you with my woes."

"Come on! What are friends for? Tell me about it."

"Well ... it's nothing very specific, just a sort of ... stalled feeling ... if that makes sense ..."

"When did it start?"

"I think around the time I sold my share in that restaurant. You remember ..."

"I do. You were going to invest in some other project. What happened to that?"

"I'm not sure ... I think I just ..." He groped for words to express the strange loss of will that had begun afflicting him. It was an elusive subject, however, a process spread over time that had never quite crossed the boundary from the possibly imaginary to the definitely real, and anyway seemed not to want words to express it so much as a kind of childish sob of anguish, which he now found himself, to his embarrassment, suddenly struggling to contain.

Chloe's cell phone made another sound and this time she glanced at it. Picking it up from the table, she walked away, sig-

naling she'd just be a minute. She stopped a few yards off and listened, saying nothing. Then she walked briskly farther off, passing through the apple trees to the pool, and shutting the gate behind her.

Matthew took the opportunity to pull himself together. Much as he'd been longing for the opportunity to talk like this, he didn't want to make a fool of himself. The last thing he needed was for Chloe and Charlie to start thinking of him as an actual basket case, which would be the inevitable consequence if he gave in to this sudden mortifying impulse to weep. A dryly ironic attitude to one's own pain was, he knew, the only safe way of discussing it.

The emotions that had ambushed him had their origins in events from long ago; he was well aware of that. They had lived inside him for almost three decades, with an undiminished power. For periods they were dormant, but when they surged up like this, they could be overwhelming, and it was only with a determined effort that he was able to subdue them, fighting them back until he had achieved the requisite counterbalancing state: an arid indifference to everything.

Several minutes had passed, and Chloe was still on the phone. He could see her in glimpses between the apple trees, pacing around the pool, and he could hear her voice, rising intermittently between long silences.

It came to him that his reaction to her infidelity had something to do with these unmastered childhood feelings. Pursuing the intuition in Dr. McCubbin's precribed manner, he found himself forming the surprising thought that he was indeed experiencing jealousy: not from the point of view of his actual self,

but the self he would become if he were ever to be freed from the grip of those ancient emotions. Because that other, freer self regarded Chloe as nothing less (a look of amusement spread on his face as he articulated this thought) than his own true wife. Charlie, at that imaginary juncture, would be nothing more than a minor inconvenience. All this belonged, of course, to a purely latent version of reality.

When Chloe finally reappeared, she had put on sunglasses. She smiled as she approached the terrace, but she'd tightened into herself, gripping an elbow with one hand.

"I'm sorry that took so long."

"Everything okay?"

"Yes." She looked away, and then turned back to him.

"Actually, Matt, I have to go out for a bit. Do you mind?"

"Of course not."

She moved off quickly, as if afraid he might question her, grabbing her car keys from the kitchen table.

"We'll finish our talk another time, right?" She was still in just her shirt and swimsuit.

"Absolutely."

A moment later, he heard the Lexus start up and accelerate off down the driveway.

• • •

The silence of their aborted conversation reverberated in her wake. It seemed to press against him, pushing him into the house, and then out again. He went to the pool and lay on the wooden sunbed Chloe had vacated earlier. Its warm laths smelled of her suntan oil. Butterflies hovered on the zinnias

and cleomes. It came to him once again that he should pack his things and leave. Chloe could drop him at the green on her way to Jana's this evening, and he'd wait for the bus . . . He got up from the sunbed and climbed the rocky path to the guesthouse, trying to think of a plausible excuse for his departure.

But as soon as he entered the pleasant room with its rough plank walls and pine-scented air he changed his mind. What is happening? he thought. What am I doing? He went back to the house. In the cool of the sunken living room he picked up a gigantic volume of Helmut Newton nudes. As he leafed through the long-boned, silvered figures his thoughts moved forward to the moment of Chloe's arrival back from her lover (there was no doubt in his mind that that was where she'd gone), and he felt the impossibility of being able to step back into their briefly revived intimacy. Better not to be here at all when she returned than risk alienating her with the sullenness he was inevitably going to be radiating. He shut the book and went out to the pickup truck in the driveway, dimly aware, as he turned the key in the ignition, of having rationalized a desire he knew to be irrational.

Town was unusually busy, with traffic backed up a quarter mile from the green. Something was going on in the athletic fields that ran down one side of the road. A stage had been erected, and there was a woman on it speaking into a microphone. As Matthew drew level, her words became briefly audible: ". . . so for those of you who have ever needed the fire company, or enjoyed the flowers on the village green, or had a relative taken care of in the Aurelia hospice . . ." Farther along, hanging over the entrance to the field, was a sign reading VOLUNTEERS DAY PICNIC AND FIREWORKS.

James Lasdun

The traffic eased up after the green, and he was soon crossing the bridge over the creek and turning onto the leaf-dappled
twists and turns of Veery Road. The LeBaron was in the driveway. Right next to it, gleaming remorselessly in the hard sunlight, was the Lexus.

He drove on. What now? It was three in the afternoon. He
appeared to have exhausted his options. Waiting at the house for
Chloe, circling back to the A-frame, packing his things and leaving: every possibility seemed to bring him up against the same
intolerable reality.

A band of schoolchildren was on the stage playing "Crazy
Train" as he drove back past the athletic field. Troops of families
were gathered before them, cheering them on. Apparently the
town had an existence beyond supplying Charlie and Chloe with
convenient places to play tennis and conduct assignations.

Back up the mountain, he went straight to the guesthouse. At
least here he felt a degree of calm. He lay on the bed, reaching for
his father's old Penguin edition of Pascal's *Pensées*; this also more
for purposes of talismanic comfort than any more practical aim.

The book was part of a boxload his mother had sent him when
she'd remarried and decided to get rid of his father's things. For
a long time Matthew hadn't been able to face unpacking them,
but lately he'd begun thinking about his father from the point
of view not just of an abandoned child wanting to be magically
reunited with him, but of an adult curious to understand him.
A year ago he'd started reading through the books, hoping they
might have something to offer in this regard. It turned out his
father had had a habit of noting the date he'd read each volume,
enabling Matthew to follow him in chronological sequence, and

giving him the somewhat eerie impression of tracking down his absconded parent along a kind of trail or spoor of print.

As a young man Gerald Dannecker's tastes seemed to have run mostly to English comic novels, full of farcical plot twists and larky repartee. Later, after marrying and settling into his career, he'd begun to read more widely: political biography, travel, popular science. It was in the period following the Lloyd's crash that the books by Pascal and other philosophers had begun appearing. Having never before been a marker of passages, he had begun carefully underlining pithy phrases during this period, and this gave the books a peculiarly personal aura. Alighting on the markings, which were in pencil and always very neat, Matthew would feel a tantalizing proximity to his father's thought processes. The sense of an agitation crystallizing, dissolving, reformulating itself, was palpable. From the beginning, the question of suicide had been ominously present. In a book of Schopenhauer's writings Matthew had found underlined: *Neither in the Old nor in the New Testament is there to be found any prohibition or even definite disapproval of it.* Several months further along, in a collection of aphorisms by E. M. Cioran, the thought was still clearly on his father's mind, and its coloration had become even more positive: *Suicide is one of man's distinctive characteristics, one of his discoveries; no animal is capable of it, and the angels have scarcely guessed its existence.* In the same book, however, the underlinings had directed Matthew to stirrings of what appeared to be an entirely different impulse: *There has never been a human being who has not—at least unconsciously—desired the death of another human being.* Disturbed, Matthew had wondered whose death besides his own his father might have been desiring.

The directors of Lloyd's? Charlie's father—Uncle Graham—who had talked him into becoming a "member" of that accursed organization in the first place? But before he could answer the question, it too had undergone radical twists and refinements, culminating in a passage at once so opaque and so communicative, Matthew had committed it to memory: *Who has not experienced the desire to commit an incomparable crime which would exclude him from the human race? Who has not coveted ignominy in order to sever for good the links which attach him to others, to suffer a condemnation without appeal and thereby to reach the peace of the abyss?*

For at least a year after his father had disappeared, Matthew had been certain he was going to contact him, probably with some cryptic message that only Matthew would recognize as coming from him, and that only Matthew would understand. No such message had ever come, and yet as he'd read through this last sequence of books, it had begun to seem to him as if it was after all written right there in those neat pencil lines: just as cryptic as he had always imagined it would be, and at the same time just as powerfully eloquent. By the time of Pascal's *Pensées*, the last in this concluding sequence, the quandary over what course of action to take seemed to have given way to a more generalized mood of reflection and speculation. Perhaps a decision had been taken and his father was merely waiting for the courage, or the right moment, to act.

A coroner's verdict had declared him legally dead after the obligatory seven-year period, but the declaration had been a purely administrative event in Matthew's mind. Unlike his mother and sister, who had eagerly accepted the verdict, relieved

by this final official purging of the taint of disgrace, Matthew had never been able to assign his father conclusively to the category of either the living or the dead. He thought of him as a kind of vacillating spirit moving between both worlds, and these books had done nothing to settle this uncertainty. It had always been hard for him to accept the banal criminality of his father's deed. Emptying out his clients' accounts! The very fact that he'd had signatory power over these accounts in the first place was proof, surely, of his absolute probity; a measure of how thoroughly out of character the deed had been. And yet the books, with their cunning and convoluted moral arguments, only made it harder to reach any kind of stable verdict. He didn't know what to believe; wasn't even sure what he *wanted* to believe. In one fantasy his father had killed himself but stolen his clients' money first so as to make it look as if he'd just run off somewhere, and thereby spare his family the trauma of his suicide. In another, his father had reached some obscure philosophical justification for the theft and was still alive, living anonymously in some secluded place on the proceeds. Matthew even half fancied he knew where that place was. There was a turquoise house on the hillside high above the little secluded cove known as Tranqué Bay on the Caribbean island where the family had gone on holiday three winters in a row. Lying in his deck chair, his father used to gaze up and fantasize out loud about living there. "If we ever come into any serious money," Matthew remembered him saying, "that's the house I shall buy." Matthew had reminded his mother of this at the time of the investigation, and she had passed it on to the detectives from Scotland Yard. Nothing had come of it, and yet whenever he thought of his father as still living, his imagination persisted in

placing him there above Tranqué Bay, enjoying the sea breeze on the carved wooden veranda that was just visible from the white sands below.

Leafing back and forth through the pages as he lay on his bed in the guesthouse, Matthew read and reread the underlined passages, stalking his father's shade through the thoughts and aphorisms, some of them familiar to him, some forgotten, others encountered now for the first time. He found: *Incomprehensible that God should exist and incomprehensible that he should not*, and: *All men naturally hate each other.* He found: *Justice is as much a matter of fashion as charm is*, and: *It affects our whole life to know whether the soul is mortal or immortal.* And with each underlined phrase he felt at once closer to his father and more baffled by him than ever.

• • •

It was six-thirty. He had fallen asleep. The sky over the valley was lilac, with just a few dry-looking clouds. He had dreamed of the cornfield, only he was there with Chloe, and had asked her point-blank: Who is your lover? Leaning in so that her hair brushed against his face, she had said softly in his ear, I love you, and he had woken in a burst of happiness.

Through the guesthouse window he saw her floating on her back in the pool. He put on some clothes and went down.

"Hi, there," she called. "I looked for you."

"I fell asleep."

"I figured. I was hoping you'd take a walk with me and Fu. Thought we might talk some more. But I didn't want to wake you."

"I had a dream about you," he said impulsively.

She hung motionless on the water, her face impassive, and for a moment he wondered if he had transgressed the tacitly agreed-on limit of what could be spoken of out loud between them. But then she smiled.

"Did you? I hope it was nice."

"It was very nice."

"That's good."

He felt suddenly very close to her. God, it was good to have someone in his life he could speak to without inhibition! She didn't ask what had happened in the dream, but her very silence seemed proof that she didn't need to be told, and this surely confirmed that the closeness he felt was real.

That there was something abject, pitiable, in the nourishment he took from such barely discernible signs and tokens of affection, he was well aware. It didn't trouble him, though. He'd learned long ago not to torment himself about things over which he had no control. One went through phases of strength and weakness in one's relation to the world, and when one was in a phase of weakness, as he appeared to be now, there was no sense in pretending otherwise. That was a recipe for humiliation. With luck he would rally himself before long, and then who knew what might happen? In the part of his mind not subject to regular intrusions of rationality there was no doubt at all that his and Chloe's destinies were inextricably linked; even that at some point—in another life, if not this one (such concepts were perfectly admissible in this part of his mind)—it had been arranged for them to be together. But in the meantime it seemed important to content himself with whatever crumbs of affection he could glean.

"Want a drink?" he asked.

"No, I should wait till I get to Jana's. Actually, I ought to get going."

He nodded.

"Everything go okay earlier—in town?" he asked.

"Oh . . . yes." Chloe plunged forward in the water, submerging her head. Coming up, she said, "Yes, sorry I had to leave so suddenly. It was just this woman I do yoga with. She was in kind of a . . . crisis."

Matthew looked at her as she shook the water out of her hair.

"Well, I hope you got her sorted, as we say in Blighty."

"Yes, I did." A quick smile crossed Chloe's lips. "I got her sorted."

"Good."

"What about you, Matt? Are you going to go out somewhere?"

"I don't know."

"You should. You should go to the Millstream. It'll do you good."

"I'll think about it."

"If you think about it, you won't do it."

She swam over to the chrome steps and climbed out, squeezing the water from her hair.

"Go on," she said, turning back to him. "Live a little!"

He'd half decided to go anyway, and had really only been resisting for the pleasure of Chloe's continued attempt to change his mind.

"All right. I'll go."

She was upstairs getting ready to go out when he left.

"Let's have a nightcap later on, shall we?" she called down. "I don't plan on staying late at Jana's."

"Okay."

"We can swap notes."

He laughed.

"Yeah. I'm sure I'll have plenty to report!"

•   •   •

The Millstream Inn was at the low end of town on Tailor Street, just beyond the junction with the county road. The restaurant was surprisingly crowded considering how early it was, but the bar itself had few customers. It didn't look like much of a pickup scene, Matthew thought, sitting on a stool with a cushioned back. Too early, he supposed. He ordered a gin and tonic and gazed into space, thinking of Chloe's remark that afternoon, about his girlfriends.

It was true that during the years when he'd been part owner of the farm-to-table restaurant, he'd had a period of relative promiscuity. It was something that happened from time to time, without any particular effort or decision on his part; just coming in like the weather. To the extent that he'd analyzed it, it was that these were phases when the outward appearance of his day-to-day existence approximated most closely to the generally held idea of what constituted a "life": regular employment, sustained contact with numerous other people, an overall semblance of purpose. Not that this made him more attractive to women than he normally was: there was the same modest frequency of signals as there'd always been, from the same middlingly attractive women who seemed to consider him an

appropriate target for their attentions. It was just that during those periods pure sexual need seemed to overcome a certain aesthetic fastidiousness, and he took whatever came his way. Alison, the blonde girl Chloe had liked so much, was plump and highly strung, with a nervous, grating laugh. Chloe's report of Charlie picturing the two of them running some cozy café in Portland had vaguely offended him, though he sensed now that it was the West Coast part of Charlie's fantasy, more than the choice of girl, that had hurt. The suggestion of Charlie wanting to put a few thousand miles between himself and Matthew was upsetting; particularly in the light of Charlie's recent unfriendliness.

He finished his drink and ordered another one. A woman in her forties was looking at him.

"British, right?"

"That's right."

"I thought I detected an accent. Whereabouts?"

"London."

"I believe I've heard of it."

Matthew laughed politely.

"Going to the fireworks?" the woman asked.

It took him a moment to remember the sign he'd seen at the entrance to the town athletic fields.

"Oh . . . I wasn't planning to."

"Supposed to be a helluva show."

"Uh-huh?"

"That's what I heard."

She faced him squarely from her side of the bar, apparently confident in her ability to secure his attention. She wore a pale

silk blouse, open to show some cleavage. Her face had a sheen of makeup. Her glistening hair was teased into angled spears like a pineapple top.

She took a sip of her cocktail, setting the near-empty glass down before her with a deliberate air, looking at Matthew. He gave a slight smile and turned away. He was about to knock back the rest of his drink and leave when the door opened and Chloe's lover came in.

Matthew had to remind himself, as the shock jolted through him, that the guy had no reason to know who he was. Trying to appear unflustered, he took a sip from his drink, and laid the glass back down on the bar.

Passing to the other side of the bar, the lover parked himself on a stool, greeting the bartender and extending a general smile all around. He was wearing a loose shirt of white cotton. His beard looked freshly trimmed.

Ordering a drink, he proceeded to offer himself up for conversation with a series of remarks directed at no one in particular. The remarks were cheerfully banal, but soon two guys who'd been talking quietly over beers were laughing with him, and after a while the woman in the pale blouse joined in.

"You going to the fireworks?" she asked.

"Sure am. I have my picnic blanket, my thermos . . . I'm told it's quite the show."

"Oh, it's fabulous. I go every year."

The lover looked around.

"Anyone else going? We oughta form a posse."

"We're going," one of the two guys said.

"Game on, then! I have time to grab a little something to eat first, right?"

"Definitely."

The man asked for a menu. Perusing it with a wistful air, he informed the bartender he would just have an appetizer, and ordered a lobster quesadilla.

"But give me a side of the shoestring fries too, would you?"

He added in a stage whisper to the woman, "My doctor told me I need to gain weight," prompting a loud, full-throated laugh.

"You here on vacation?" the woman asked.

He nodded.

"Got me a little rental right by the creek there. Veery Road."

"Nice!"

"The A-frame?" one of the guys asked.

"How'd you guess?"

"The owner's a friend of ours. She has a couple other rentals in town but that's always been the popular one."

"Easy to see why."

There was a younger woman, seated to the man's left, whom he hadn't appeared to notice, but now he turned to her, peering closely at the book in her hand. She looked up.

"Oh, I'm sorry, miss. I was just trying to see what you were reading there. I always like to know what books people around me are reading. It's a weakness of mine. Actually more of a pathological compulsion."

She held up the book for him to see.

"*Chronicle of a Death Foretold*," he read. "Now, didn't they make a movie out of that?"

"I don't know."

"I believe they did. Ornella Muti played the girl, I recollect. I forget the director, but who cares about the director anyhow?" He chuckled, and the girl smiled vaguely back.

Matthew signaled the bartender for his check. A feeling of restlessness had gripped him: an urge to move. He paid quickly, with cash. Outside, the air was rich with the day's warmth. He saw the LeBaron in the parking lot and glanced in as he walked by; there was a folded tartan picnic blanket on the backseat and a canvas bag with a thermos in it. Climbing into the truck, he pulled out onto Tailor Street. The sidewalk was thronged with groups of people, presumably on their way to the fireworks. Traffic heading in that direction was almost at a standstill. He decided to take the back route toward the green, along the other side of the creek. Purely a practical decision, he told himself as he turned onto the county road and then again onto Veery Road. At the A-frame he slowed down. The driveway was empty and the house was dark—naturally enough, since its occupant was at the bar and Chloe on her way to Jana's. But the urge to stop, to plant himself there, was as strong as it was when he had reason to believe someone was inside. If anything, it seemed to be even stronger. He drove on, considering this as one considers a new symptom that has just appeared, of some persistent illness.

Instead of crossing the bridge, he pulled into the stony area just beyond, where people left their cars when they swam. He was in an odd state of mind; at once very conscious of his actions, and extraordinarily detached from them, as though they were being performed by someone else. Parking the truck, he began walking back along Veery Road. Evening sunlight

flowed in level rays between the hedges. It was magic hour, he realized, and the thought seemed to plunge him back again into Chloe's aura. He felt as if he were approaching her along some ceremonial, processional route. Pink lilies with long, frilled petals burned like traffic-accident flares above the ditches. The empty-looking houses had molten red suns in their black windows. Ahead of him was the A-frame's sharp tip, pointing up over a tall hedge. He slowed his pace. I am just walking by, he told himself. To do anything different would have required an act of will that he felt safely incapable of mustering. A feeling of extreme passivity had come over him, as though some powerful external process had gathered him into its motions. As he turned left into the short driveway, it was fully in the belief that he was just curious to observe his own feelings at a closer proximity to the place. Even as he lifted the lid from the Weber grill by the screen porch, it was still in a speculative sense; a harmless glancing out across the divide between the actual and the purely conjectural. The door key was under the lid of the grill. As he picked it up, holding it between his finger and thumb, the situation abruptly reversed itself: the same passivity that a moment before had seemed to be keeping him safely from entering the house was now drawing him inside. No strenuous act of will appeared to be required any longer, or only if he should decide to walk away. It was as if the dense materiality of the little key had sunk the object into him like a fishhook, and he was being reeled in. Already, as he approached the front door, it was the other life, in which he remained outside the house, that was becoming conjectural. This, now, was the actual.

At the same time, he was aware that ever since he had asked the bartender for the check, it had been his intention to do precisely what he was doing.

• • •

The door opened into a living area defined by a gray love seat and armchair with a low glass table in between. Beyond the armchair was a fixed wooden ladder leading to a partially enclosed loft under the narrow apex of the roof.

He shut the door behind him, putting the key on a ledge by the doorway, and stepped forward. An air conditioner clicked on.

Passing to the side of the ladder, he saw a door to a room under the loft. He pushed it open. An unmade double bed faced a wall with a narrow window. On the bed was a half-packed suitcase surrounded by piles of folded shirts and pants. Next to it was a desk with a laptop on it. Past the bedroom was a bathroom with shaving things on a shelf over the sink. Beyond, at the rear entrance to the house, was a small kitchen crowded with stainless steel pans, racks of matching utensils, a wooden knife block and some new-looking appliances.

The glass-paned back door, bolted on the inside, gave onto a stone path across a lawn that dropped off abruptly at what must have been the bank of the creek.

He didn't appear to be afraid. Tense, but not afraid. Even if the man changed his mind about going to the fireworks or decided to come home before, he had his meal to get through first. That ought to keep him at the bar for a good twenty minutes at least, which was plenty of time.

But plenty of time for what? A vague idea of finding out who the man was had certainly been a part of what had drawn Matthew inside the house, and he looked around for some document, a rental contract perhaps, or some other official piece of paper, that might have the man's name on it. But there was no contract or any other document visible anywhere, and he didn't particulary want to start rummaging in the man's things. Anyway, now that he was here, the question of who the man was didn't seem as pressing as it had. What difference would it make, to know the man's name, or his profession, or anything else about him? Whoever he was, he was the man Chloe loved, apparently more than her husband, and certainly more than Matthew. What could possibly make that fact any more tolerable?

Then why was he here? He wandered back into the living room and sat down in the chair, making a deliberate effort to take stock of things. In the manner Dr. McCubbin had taught him, he made himself as fully conscious of the situation he had created as he could.

What exactly am I experiencing? What do I want?

People who broke into houses usually wanted to take something, didn't they? Or destroy something. Or leave some nasty souvenir of themselves. He didn't seem to have any interest in any of that. What, then? Was it just the forbiddenness of being here? The feeling of having attained some secret intimacy with Chloe? Possibly. Certainly he did feel a kind of illicit closeness to her. And yet even as he acknowledged this, he became aware of a lack, an incompleteness in the feeling, and realized that even though he was here, he was still in some mysterious way longing to *be* here; as if inside

the A-frame there should have been another A-frame, with another doorway and another key.

He stood up and went back into the bedroom. Something had been nagging at him and he had realized what it was. Half hidden under the clothes in the suitcase was a magazine that had caught his eye, though he'd barely been conscious of it. He took it out of the suitcase. It was the entertainment magazine that Chloe had asked him to pick up for her in East Deerfield earlier in the summer.

He brought it back into the living room, where the light was better, and began leafing through the glossy pages. Near the end, he came to a section headed "Bioflash." There, occupying half the page, was Chloe's lover, filling a doorway with his broad frame, gazing cheerfully at the camera.

Holding the page up to the waning light, Matthew began reading the article. It was one of those shamelessly flattering profiles such magazines went in for: calculated to induce envious loathing in even the most well-disposed readers. The man's name was Wade D. Grollier. He was a filmmaker. He had been born in rural Georgia in 1978. He lived in Brooklyn with his long-term girlfriend, actress Rachel Turpin (another cheat, then!). He'd had a hit movie that Matthew had heard of, though not seen, about a scientist who creates a robot lover for his daughter. He'd won a Spirit Award, whatever that was, for Best Director. One of his close friends, a Hollywood celebrity, was quoted describing him as "an authentic American rebel." He had spent seven weeks in Haiti after the earthquake, building shelters with his own hands. Before making movies he'd been a rock drummer and he still hung out with rock musicians. Names were

given, listed with the deadpan lubriciousness that seemed to be de rigueur in these kinds of pieces.

The ignominy of having been asked to fetch this magazine for Chloe struck Matthew with a belated pang. For a moment he wondered if Chloe had been deliberately amusing herself at his expense; sending the rejected suitor (for they both knew he was that) on an errand to procure this tribute to his triumphant rival. But he quickly dismissed the thought, unwilling to believe she could have been capable of anything so petty, or so deliberately cruel.

The piece continued in the same unctuous style. Wade D. Grollier appeared to be successful modern urbanity incarnate, though at heart he was still a country boy (the piece was slavishly attentive to the formula) and admitted that despite the jet-setting life success had foisted upon him, he loved nothing better than fishing in the headwaters of the Chattahoochee River with his childhood pals. His current project was a cross-species murder mystery set in the jungles of Borneo and featuring an orangutan detective.

Finishing the article, Matthew went back into the bedroom and returned the magazine to the suitcase. As he'd predicted, knowing who the man was made no difference at all to his feelings about the situation. Nor did the discovery give him any satisfying sense of having accomplished some mission at the house.

He wandered back into the living room. Books, phone chargers, bits and pieces of clothing he hadn't noticed before, lay here and there. None of it looked particularly interesting. On the walls were framed hiking maps of the area, showing

streams and trails and tiny black individual houses among the contour lines of the green-shaded mountains. One of them had the little town of Aurelia itself in an upper corner: a dense sprinkling of black dots spread either side of what must have been Tailor Street, and he was able to trace his way across the creek and down along Veery Road to the bend that came before the A-frame, and then the A-frame itself, where he was standing. It was as though his coming here had fulfilled some already latent itinerary. The downstairs windows were darkening now, but the little loft had a skylight that was still bright. He climbed up the ladder to take a look. Behind the balustrade of carved wooden slats was a plywood floor with a rag rug on it and a rolled-up, single-width futon. The space was probably meant for a child. It clearly wasn't being used.

He sat down on the futon. A flock of birds crossed the skylight, catching the sun on their undersides as they banked upward. Distant sounds floated over the trees: traffic, a blurred screech of feedback from a PA system. But it was peaceful all the same, up here in the apex of the A, and he felt no urgency to leave. It didn't really seem likely that the man—Grollier, wasn't that his name?—would come home before going to the fireworks, but even the small possibility that he might was of oddly little concern to Matthew. If anything, he noticed, it seemed to excite him fractionally. He found himself toying with the idea of unrolling the futon and staying there all night; not as a serious plan, but with the bemused interest one experiences when an unexpected fantasy lays open some wholly new realm of speculative pleasure.

He was turning over the components of this peculiar fan-

tasy, trying to understand why it should cause this faintly pleasurable apprehensiveness, when he became aware of lights probing down the gravel of the driveway. He knelt up, peering over the balustrade through the front window. He had been in the house barely fifteen minutes! And anyway, hadn't he heard the man say he was going straight on to the fireworks? Hadn't he seen for himself the picnic blanket and thermos in the car? The lights approached, separating into two beams as they came around the slight curve in the short driveway. Alarm spread through him, and yet for a long moment he did nothing; merely stared into the approaching glare, surrendering to the situation with an almost luxurious helplessness, as if the inertia building inside him all these months had finally rendered him completely incapable of movement. Only by an extreme effort of will was he able to rouse himself. Grabbing the balustrade, he hauled himself to his feet and took a few steps down the ladder, trying to calculate whether Grollier would see him if he made a dash for the back door, and whether it would matter even if he did, since he didn't know who Matthew was.

But as the lights went out, he saw that the car itself was not in fact the LeBaron, but the Lexus.

For a moment he thought he must simply be seeing things. In his mind Chloe was so firmly on her way to her cousin Jana in Lake Classon, it was impossible to accept she was here, and he stared, waiting for the hallucination to dissolve. But it was Chloe. He watched her climb out of the car and walk over to the Weber grill, lifting the lid. A puzzled look crossed her face and briefly the hope rose in him that she would leave now. But she put back the lid and, undeterred by the absence of the

key, proceeded toward the front door. He stood on the ladder, unsure what to do. If he went any farther down, she would see movement through the window. Already she was almost at the door. Only as he heard the handle turn did some dim instinct of self-preservation galvanize him, drawing him back up the ladder and behind the balustrade in time to conceal himself before the door opened.

She had her phone to her ear as she came in. With her free hand she switched on the light. Afraid she might look up and see him between the wooden slats, which were carved at their edges in the shape of ornate brackets, Matthew sat clenched and unblinking.

"Wade," she said into the phone.

He saw her pick the key from the ledge where he had left it, examine it a moment and set it down again.

"No, I'm at the house . . . Your house, Wade . . . I thought you might want to come say goodbye one more time."

She was wearing one of her thin, patterned skirts with a short-sleeved top, tailored at the waist.

"I know. I'll call her."

She moved in quick steps through the room with the phone to her ear, placing her hand lightly on the love seat, the arm-chair, the side of the ladder. As she moved toward the back of the house, disappearing out of sight, Matthew let himself breathe again. Very carefully, he backed into the corner of the little space, as far as possible from view.

He heard her laugh.

"You know you want to, Wade . . . You know you do . . . Yes, but they never start before ten . . . I know, but this is Aurelia. All

the bands in town have to do their Jimi Hendrix impressions first . . ."

Then she was directly below him, in the bedroom.

"Oh, Wade," he heard. "You really are leaving, aren't you? I'm looking at your suitcase . . . Yes, there's an early bus, around six; easier than driving . . . I know . . . I know, Wade, I do too, but Lily's coming, and anyway, I just can't."

She came back out of the room, closing the door.

"Be quick, then . . . Okay, but don't feel you have to charm the entire restaurant on your way out. Anyway, did you see Matthew?"

The sound of his own name hit Matthew like an electric shock.

"Yeah, that was him . . . He did? Probably went to the fireworks . . . Well, thanks for going anyway . . . Okay, I'll wait till you get here."

Something her lover said made her laugh.

"I know. But he can't help that, can he?"

She laughed again, more tenderly. "Yes, but you're good at sizing people up. Anyway, I thought it might interest you to take a look at him . . . Okay, see you in a bit."

Back in the living room, she turned off the overhead light and switched on a small table lamp.

Matthew watched her, trying to fathom the implications of what he'd just heard. Now she was on the love seat, facing in his direction, making another phone call.

"Jana? Hi. Listen, I'm so sorry, but I'm going to have to be a little late. Some things have come up . . ."

The polite hostess smile Matthew had seen when Jana came

to visit reappeared on Chloe's face. Her small teeth showed like
a row of pearls.

"Oh, that's sweet of you . . . No, no, I definitely want to
come. I've hardly seen you all summer . . . Thanks, Jana. I
shouldn't be too long."

She stood up and drew the shades down over the living
room windows. Sitting again, she held the phone in front of
her face, adjusting her hair and rearranging the rounded collar
of her blouse, opening a button to reveal a lacy edge of bra. It
took Matthew a moment to realize she was using the phone as a
camera to see herself. She put it away in her canvas bag, crossed
her legs and waited. After a few seconds she stood up again and
went toward the back of the house, returning with a lit candle
in one hand and a small plate in the other, with kumquats on it,
and chocolate. She placed them on the glass table, and switched
off the lamp. In the candlelight the gray furnishings took on a
warmer tone. She stretched, popped a kumquat into her mouth,
and lay down on the love seat, closing her eyes. But she was still
restless. Standing up again, she slipped her underwear off from
under her skirt in a swift, practical motion. Coming around the
coffee table, she sat back down—this time on the armchair—
and tossed the pale garment onto the floor beside her.

Matthew looked down through the thin gaps, feeling like
an animal in a cage. His mouth had gone dry. In the distance he
could hear an electric guitar. Closer, katydids had begun their
nighttime chorus. She had sent her lover to the bar to check
him out. Why? he wondered. Am I such a mystery, even to her?
Is there something in me I don't see? The question, unanswer-
able as it was, sent a ripple of anxiety through him.

Headlights pierced through the shades, blading in vertically through the gaps between the balustrade, moving across Matthew's face like a pair of scanners. A moment later the door opened and Grollier stepped inside.

He paused in the entrance, taking in the little tableau Chloe had prepared for him. In silence, he smiled at Chloe across the small room with its flickering gold light. Closing the door behind him, he moved toward her, stooping midway to pick up her discarded panties and fill his lungs with their scent.

Above them Matthew stared down through the slats in the balustrade, scarcely breathing; wanting and not wanting to see.

nine

An hour later he was still there, his limbs stiffened into position as if he'd been turned to stone, his mind a near-blank. Chloe had left, driven off to her cousin, but Grollier was still down there, sprawled naked on the love seat.

Matthew stared down at him. If what he had seen had extinguished any lingering hopes concerning the extent of Chloe's involvement with this man, what he'd heard had spread a deeper, more insidious ruin. It was so disturbing, in fact, that for some time he couldn't bring himself to summon any of it back. He was in a state of benumbed shock. Only some minor functionary of consciousness continued about its business, assessing the practicalities of the situation in a businesslike way: catching the far-off strains of someone's imitation of a Hendrix guitar solo, observing that Grollier would

have to leave soon if he was going to make it to the fireworks, noting unexcitedly that this would make his own exit from the house possible.

Grollier stretched and yawned. A smile appeared on his face and he rotated his shaggy head slowly from side to side as if in disbelief at something. Pushing down onto the love seat, he hauled himself up and padded off. Light appeared from the bedroom and Matthew heard drawers being opened and closed. He was getting dressed to go out, surmised the same detached mental functionary. Dully, Matthew projected forward; saw himself finally able to move again, slipping out of the house, driving back up the mountain, continuing with his life. The evening would take its place in the chain of significant episodes that had given his existence its singular character, and there would be no more possibility of forgetting it than there had been any of the others. At the same time it would make no practical difference to anything.

But he was mistaken about Wade getting dressed. The man was still naked when he returned to the living room, and now he began ferrying odds and ends back to the bedroom. It became apparent that he was simply continuing with his packing.

He was flying out to Indonesia tomorrow—Matthew had gleaned this from the post-coital talk—interrupting his stay at the house in order to salvage an agreement with an orangutan wrangler. Or no, not the post-coital talk: this part had actually come mid-coitus. They'd had a lull during which Wade had reiterated what appeared to have been an earlier attempt to persuade Chloe to go to Indonesia with him. She'd told him,

with all too evident reluctance, that it was impossible, and the renewed sense of imminent separation had started them up again. "Don't come," she'd said as Wade's groans began to indicate critical levels of excitement.

"Say something unsexy, then," he'd muttered.

"Okay. Tell me what you thought about Charlie's cousin."

So that Matthew had been compelled to hear himself discussed, this time without the refuge of gaps in the conversation by way of intermittent relief. He could feel the exchange in its entirety now, pressing at him, urging him to replay it like some elaborate injury one has to relive over and over until its power to hurt runs out.

"Well, he's a short guy," had been Wade's first observation.

"You said. You're a fat guy. He can't help it, you can, so what's your point?"

"That's my point, sugar. I could lose weight if I wanted to, but he'll never gain height. That is a big old difference, not of degree, but of ontology—"

"Oh, stop it. Anyway, he isn't that short."

"No, but—"

"You didn't think there was something strange about him?"

"Not that I could tell just from looking at him."

"I think there's something deeply strange about him."

"You mean he has the hots for you? I wouldn't call that strange, sugar."

Wade had re-enveloped her in his arms at that point, face against the back of her neck, his large hand reaching around to her breasts. She'd snuggled back against him.

"No, that doesn't bother me. Or it never used to. Now I'm not sure . . ."

"He's getting more serious?"

"It's almost as if he's becoming possessive. As if he thinks we're in an actual relationship. He's started questioning me—asking where I've been, where I'm going. Also . . . Mmm."

His other hand was moving between her legs and she broke off, given over to some large wave of pleasure.

"Also?"

She'd had to bite her lower lip, hard, before she could control her voice enough to answer.

"He's been acting weird with Charlie," she said as the sensation ebbed sufficiently for her to speak. "Needling him . . ."

"Oh, yeah?"

"I mean, I haven't seen it myself, but I doubt Charlie's imagining it. Charlie doesn't tend to imagine things."

"Needling him how?"

"He keeps making these insinuations . . ."

"About?"

"Me."

"What about you?"

"That I'm being unfaithful."

"Well you are, sugar. You are being unfaithful."

"But he doesn't know."

"You're sure about that?"

"I'm careful, Wade."

"So why's he doing it?"

"I think he's deliberately trying to make Charlie suffer. He knows Charlie has a tendency to get jealous."

"But why would he want to make him suffer?"

"I don't know."

"Well, I wouldn't worry about it. Not like there's anything you can do about it. Right?"

"But it's so cruel. I mean toward Charlie."

"You're awfully considerate of your husband."

"I love him."

The words, so unexpected in the circumstances, had shocked Matthew. Her ability to confound him never seemed to exhaust itself. Wade too had seemed surprised.

"You love him?" he'd said, heaving his bulk above Chloe and moving more concertedly. Her phrase had seemed to drive the two of them into suddenly more intense realms of mutual desire.

"You know I love him."

"You love his dough, I know that."

"Maybe, but I love him too."

"More'n you'd love me? If I was that rich? *When* I'm that rich?"

"More than I'll ever love you, Wade."

"Jesus, you are the most . . . unfathomable . . . human being . . . I have ever . . ."

"Don't come."

"Met. And I grew up around Catholics."

"That has nothing to do with it. Anyway, there's something else."

"About you and Charlie?"

"No, about him. Matthew."

And Matthew had braced himself for another blow, but

James Lasdun

as it turned out neither Chloe nor Wade were able to distract themselves from the business at hand any longer, and for the next several minutes the only sounds inside the little A-frame were moans of pleasure and the occasional protest from a piece of furniture subjected to forces it hadn't been designed to withstand. Time had seemed to thicken then, the seconds growing sticky as clay. He'd forced himself to think of dates of battles, variant recipes for choux pastry, passages from Pascal. *Two errors*, he'd remembered: *1. To take everything literally, 2. To take everything spiritually*. Which of the two am I falling into? he'd wondered, contemplating the scene below, where Wade had just enthroned himself in the armchair and Chloe was kneeling down between his sprawled legs, positioning herself with a votive grace that reminded him of one of her butterflies as it settled on the stamen of some garish flower, slowly folding its wings; or again, as they'd moved and her face had reappeared through the next gap in the palings, cushioned sideways on the love seat with a look of rapture as she lay over its arm. Was there an erroneous sense in which this was literal? A true sense in which it was purely spiritual? Turning, she had reached up and drawn Wade down onto the floor below her, in turn lowering herself onto him with a cry of joy. *There are perfections in nature to show that she is the image of God and imperfections to show that she is no more than his image*. That was one his father had marked and that he, with childishly pleasurable irrationality, had written, *No!* next to, happily aware that nobody except his ghostly co-custodian of this mystic text could possibly have any idea what he meant.

They'd lain in silence for several minutes afterward,

144

Chloe's head on Wade's chest as she idly fondled his detumescing member and ate a piece of chocolate, Wade's eyes gazing upward, scanning the ceiling, the skylight, the carved wooden slats on the balustrade. For a terrifying moment it had seemed to Matthew the man had caught the glint of his eye in the candlelit darkness and was staring straight at him, trying to make sense of what he was seeing. The prospect of what would happen if he did had been so far beyond intolerable that Matthew could only think of it in terms of annihilation. Possibly in some court of ultimate, celestial arbitration his presence here would be found at least partly understandable, even partly creditable. (Was he not in some sense acting on Charlie's behalf?) Certainly mitigating factors would be given their due. But no earthly judgment would get beyond the point of pure outraged horror. And there would be no mercy. He was well aware of that. No mercy at all.

Wade's glance traveled on. But as if some unconscious agency had registered what his eye had failed to discern, he said:

"You were saying, sugar, about your friend."

"I'm afraid of him," Chloe had murmured. "That's why I wanted you to see him. He scares me."

"Ah, c'mon, sugar. Why?"

"I don't know."

"I'll tell you what I think, sugar, I think you're mixing up your own guilt about Charlie with the little dude's fixation on you, that's what I think."

"I don't feel any guilt."

"My point precisely," Wade had answered with a chuckle.

Chloe had stood up then, and begun getting dressed.

"He's blackmailing Charlie," she'd said matter-of-factly.

"*What*?"

Wade's astonishment was almost as great as Matthew's own. At first Matthew thought she was joking or exaggerating for effect, but as she spoke on, it became apparent that she really did think he'd been blackmailing Charlie! He didn't know whether to weep or laugh at the absurdity of it. As he'd listened to the strange warpings and distortions of reality that made up her tale, the urge to interrupt and proclaim his innocence, to stand up on the gallery and shout out the truth, had been almost overwhelming.

Yes, it was true that Charlie had lent him money on and off over the years since his arrival in the States. Yes, it was thanks to Charlie's generosity that he had been able to come up with his stake in the farm-to-table restaurant. Yes, it was also true (though he hadn't realized it was quite so obvious) that he'd hoped at some point to interest Charlie in his food truck idea. But he had always made it very clear that he intended to pay Charlie back as soon as he was in a position to, and in any case none of it was a secret, and it certainly wasn't blackmail!

Wade himself had made the obvious objection:

"I mean, how's that blackmail, sugar? There has to be compulsion of some kind to call it blackmail. He'd have to have some kind of *hold* over Charlie ..."

"He does."

"What?"

"Charlie's guilt."

"For what?"

"For having money. For being luckier than him. For his father giving Matthew's father some bad investment advice a million years ago. For being, you know, a banker. For everything!"

"Yeah, but that's not—I mean, at a stretch you could call that moral blackmail, but for actual legal blackmail there'd have to be specific information he was threatening to reveal."

"All right, so call it moral blackmail. To me there's no difference. He's using Charlie's guilt to extort money out of him. He has been for years. Basically Charlie's been paying his rent since Matthew followed him here to the States, which I imagine he did with precisely that in mind."

"Seriously? Paying his rent?"

"I've seen the checks."

Untrue! Matthew had wanted to shout out. Unfair! There were just three or four months when Charlie covered my rent! And it was all on the record, written down on the ledger along with the other odd sums. And what the hell, he wondered as the scene replayed itself now, had she meant about me following Charlie to the States? Over the trees, as he considered this, came the unmistakable introduction to Jimi Hendrix's "Hey Joe." It was a song Matthew happened to know well. There was a couple he used to supply in the early nineties; middle-aged hippies who'd had the track on a mix they played all the time in their Ladbroke Grove bedsit, where they'd insist he share a smoke with them whenever he visited. Nothing in the mix was really his kind of music, but he'd responded to the emotional build of "Hey Joe" and the stark economy of its tale of jealous passion. The words weren't audible as he listened now, but he

knew the simple call-and-response lyrics well enough. The gun, the shooting, then that frenzied dream of escape. *Hey Joe*, he heard as if from deep in his own past, *where you gonna run to now*? and from even deeper, saturated in some ancient sense of yearning and sun-dazzled release: *I'm going way down south, way down to Mexico . . .*

Another wobbly guitar solo stretched over the town and then "Hey Joe" gave way to the screeching bombardment of "Star-Spangled Banner." There was a dim roar from the crowd and suddenly the blackness framed by the skylight above Matthew's head exploded in gold and emerald starbursts with a blast that made the windows rattle.

Grollier was still in the house.

He was in a bathrobe now, sitting on the love seat again, with a beer and a lump of cold beef on a cutting board. Apparently he'd decided not to go to the fireworks after all.

Matthew gazed down on him with a sort of despairing indignation. Absurd as he knew it to be, he felt personally cheated by this change of heart; as if he'd been deliberately double-crossed. The man had as good as given his word that he was going to the display, hadn't he? But instead here he was carving himself slices of cold beef, thick as carpet samples, and gobbling them down on crackers in between chugging at a beer!

Whatever perverse appeal it had possessed earlier, the idea of being trapped here all night had lost every trace of it, now that it appeared to have become a real possibility. It was so appalling, in fact, that it was almost a relief to have Chloe's bizarre allegations to think about instead.

"Anyway there *is* something specific," she'd said, buttoning her blouse.

"Oh, yeah?"

"Charlie had some things happen at Morgan Stanley, which he naively told Matthew about, back in the days when he still thought of him as someone he could confide in."

"What things?"

"Oh, nothing he could get in trouble for at this point, but not the kind of thing you'd want spread around, and Matthew's apparently aware of that. When we had those English people over the other night they were talking about the financial meltdown and making insinuations about Charlie's career, and Matthew started leaning toward Charlie in this very overt way as if he was trying to remind him he had it in his power to make him extremely uncomfortable at that moment if he wanted to. I didn't take it in at the time, but when Charlie told me about it later I realized I'd seen exactly what he was describing. It was very deliberate, and it was menacing. He was threatening Charlie."

"Hm."

"What do you mean, 'Hm'?"

"That's still not a real *hold*. I mean, if Charlie can't get in actual trouble for whatever he did."

"So what are you saying?"

"I'm saying, sugar, that for Charlie to be guilty enough to pay the guy's rent for him, he'd a had to have something besides routine rich-boy guilt on his conscience. Else it just doesn't add up. There'd have to be some kind of genuine act of darkness on Charlie's part."

"No. Not possible."

"Well, then I'm flummoxed."

"Charlie's too decent for his own good. That's actually the problem. He has an overdeveloped conscience."

A smile flared on Matthew's face as he recalled these words. Certain secrets, he had learned, came into the world with a curious immunity to being divulged. Like well-armed viruses, they gave off invincible reasons for being preserved intact at every moment of possible violation. The irony, that if he could somehow convey the truth to Chloe, all it would do would be to confirm her view of him as a blackmailer, was merely a further manifestation of this quality. All kinds of bitter ironies, as a matter of fact, seemed to have begun proliferating around him. That her apparent fear of him, unfounded as it was, would have seemed fully justified, indeed insufficiently urgent, if she'd had any idea where he was at the very moment she was describing it—was one. That the accusation of obsessive behavior she had gone on to make ("forever loitering around our house in Cobble Hill," was how she'd put it) had come to acquire an accidental semblance of validity in recent days—was another . . . The litany of accusations unfurled again in his mind. "Needling" Charlie. (How could Charlie have possibly misunderstood him so badly?) Blackmailing him, for Christ's sake! Mooching, stalking, other assertions even more bizarre . . . "I think he wants to move into our home up here," she'd said at one point, "take over the guesthouse or something." It was as if she'd somehow tuned in to his innocent appreciation of the little cabin, and out of some incomprehensible hostility inflated it into a charge of sinister covetousness . . .

The existence of this hostility, so out of character in the Chloe he thought he knew, was as startling to discover as it was painful. What had caused it? How had she managed to conceal it from him so perfectly, and for so long? Why bother with all the smiles and gentleness; all those tender conversations they used to have, those protestations of interest, affection, concern? Why, if she hated him?

And yet that hadn't been the end of it either. If it had, it might have been easier for him to manage. He could have told himself she was simply two-faced; a hypocrite in whom a dissembling graciousness had become habit, no doubt from having spent too many years looking out at the world from the plinth of Charlie's riches . . . But there had been more to it, and of a nature so unexpected it had left him more bewildered than ever; more pierced and shattered, and—strangest of all—more in love.

"You really do not like this character, do you?" Wade had said.

Chloe had paused then, her face stilling as if the question had sent her unexpectedly inward. After a moment she'd replied quietly:

"I do like him, actually. In some ways I feel very close to him. That's partly why I'm so confused. There's some kind of strange connection between us. I've always felt that. I often have dreams about him, not sexual but intimate. As if we'd known each other in another life. It makes me want to help him."

"Really? Because he sounds kind of irredeemable the way you describe him."

Chloe grinned.

"Nobody's irredeemable, Wade, not even you."

Grollier had laughed.

"You're a piece of work, sugar. You really are."

"I'll see you in a week," she'd said, leaning down to kiss him goodbye.

At the door she'd turned back.

"By the way, you forgot to lock up before."

"I did?"

"You should be careful. There are some sketchy characters in town. Every summer there's a break-in somewhere. 'Bye, Wade."

"Bye, sugar. I'll miss you."

"I'll miss you too."

. . .

Meatspace, he thought now. It had been like a forcible induction into the meatspace of the real.

Wade blew out the candles and carried his dishes into the kitchen, dumping them with a clatter in the sink and then noisily urinating in the bathroom. After that he slid the bolt on the back door open and shut again, returned to the darkened living room to lock the front door and finally retired into the bedroom. The bedroom light snapped off and after a creak or two of bedsprings there were no further indications of movement.

Meatspace . . . Or not an induction, exactly, since it had left Matthew more confirmed than ever in his wariness of that particular realm. But a vision of it at its most vividly car-

nal, glistening with the redness of betrayed intimacy, of deep bonds being torn asunder, every fiber bleeding.

Outside, the fireworks were going off in steady succession. He could see them through the skylight: white chrysanthemums flaring blue at their tips, sequined purses spilling golden coins, the slam of each explosion reverberating off the mountains.

Meatspace . . . And yet even in the midst of it, to have heard her affirm precisely the most hoped-for, uncertain, purely speculative of those bonds; the ones linking her not to Charlie but to himself! *As if we'd known each other in another life* . . . The words rose in his agitated spirit once again like some immensely soothing substance. He was right. He hadn't been imagining things. There was something real, objective, fueling the compulsions that had drawn him into this strange situation.

The thought, however, intoxicating as it was, brought him back to the more prosaic question of how he was going to get himself *out* of this strange situation. He'd realized at this point that whatever difficulties might be entailed in leaving while Wade was still in the house, it was not going to be possible to spend the whole night crouched up here in the loft. For one thing, his bladder was already uncomfortably full and it was inconceivable that he was going to be able to delay emptying it until the morning. For another, the boards creaked, and sooner or later Wade was going to hear something.

His first thought was to wait till the small hours, when Wade could be presumed fast asleep, then scramble down the ladder, unlock the front door and run. Even with the noisy boards, it seemed a reasonably safe plan. It was no distance

from the ladder to the door, which would take only a second or two to unlock. Even if Wade did wake up, there'd be time to disappear into the shadows of Veery Road before he got to the door.

But as Matthew started focusing on the details, dangers he hadn't considered began to present themselves. What if Wade called the cops, or tried to rouse the neighborhood? The fireworks would be long over by then, and there'd be no crowds in which to lose himself. By the same token, he wouldn't be able to drive off unnoticed even if he made it to the truck. No: better to get out while people were still around.

The explosions of the fireworks, which were coming thick and fast now, merged with their own echoes to form a continuous roaring. The display must have been approaching its climax. This was the moment to do it. Immediately, without giving himself a chance to reconsider, he unfolded his stiffened limbs and let himself down the ladder. The living room was almost pitch-dark, but he'd seen the ledge where he'd placed the key. He found the ledge without difficulty, and ran his hand along it. But there was no key there. He checked the floor below—maybe it had fallen after Chloe picked it up— but it wasn't there either. Wade must have put it somewhere else when he locked up, or else taken it with him into the bedroom. He'd have to leave through the back door instead. Restraining an impulse to run, he crept quietly toward the rear of the house. Bursts of blue light in the sky gave a flickering glimpse of the back door and he was able to position his hand directly on the bolt without fumbling for it. He slid it back and grabbed the door handle. But the handle wouldn't

turn. He tried again, twisting as hard as he could: to no avail. In the next flash of blue he saw that the round black knob had its own small keyhole at the center. For a few seconds of panicked alertness he searched frantically for a key—over the doorframe, under the doormat, behind the sink. He was groping along the counter when he heard a voice directly behind him:

"Mister, I have a gun pointed at you. Don't move."

He closed his eyes.

"Don't move, okay? I see you move, I'm going to have to shoot you. You got that? You can nod your head."

Matthew nodded. He felt oddly unafraid, calm almost, as though experiencing some peculiar natural law whereby fear diminished in proportion to the closeness of its object, vanishing entirely at the point of convergence.

"Now. You're going to hear me look for my phone, which should take all of about four seconds, and then call the police, but I'll be pointing my weapon at you while I do that and I will shoot you if you move a muscle. It's a semiautomatic Ruger, just so you know, single-action, so really, don't make any kind of a move. Okay?"

Matthew nodded again, but less in acknowledgment of Grollier's question this time, than of his own sense of what was going to happen. It didn't frighten him at all. In a way, it was a relief. He thought—such was the strange lucidity inside him—of the words from his father's Pascal: *All men seek happiness. This is the motive of every act of every man, including those who go and hang themselves.* He'd often dreamed of being placed in a situation where survival was simply not an

option; where the small part of him still obstinately clinging to the little knot of pain and unhappiness that made up most of his existence would finally have no choice but to defer to the other, larger part, that craved only oblivion. It seemed very clear that he was there at last. Only a little courage was required.

Slowly, conscious of having long ago brought to mind every argument in favor and every objection against, he began turning toward his executioner. "Mister, I told you," he heard, "do not fucking move!"

There was something unexpected in the tone; an aggrieved, almost querulous note. On completing the turn, Matthew saw why. Wade, who was naked again, had been bluffing. His hand was empty.

The two of them peered at each other in the flickering blackness for several seconds.

"You!" Wade cried out in startled recognition. His large head turned back to glance into the living room and up toward the loft. Facing Matthew again, he hurled himself forward, his bulky figure moving with stunning agility, hands outspread, his fingers braced as if to grab Matthew's throat and throttle him.

ten

Cooler weather blew in that night. For the first time all summer, Matthew needed extra blankets from the cedar chest. Under their comforting weight he fell quickly asleep. In the morning the day was blue and clear, and the trees were sparkling. Locking the guesthouse door, he went down for breakfast.

Chloe and Charlie were at the stone table. They looked scrubbed and cheerful, both of them taking advantage of the lower temperature to sport new outfits. Charlie had on a seersucker suit with rolled-up sleeves. Chloe wore a leaf-patterned dress under a thin silky cardigan.

She took off her sunglasses and grinned at Matthew.

"You didn't wait up for me!"

"Ah, no, sorry. I was tired."

"How was your night?"

He reached for the coffeepot.

"Uneventful."

Charlie glanced up from his iPad:

"No luck at the Millstream?"

"I told Charlie I'd sent you on a mission," Chloe said.

"No."

"That's too bad," Charlie said. "The bar there's supposed to be pickup central."

"Well, I didn't see any action," Matthew answered, pouring coffee into his cup. His hand was remarkably steady. "How were your evenings?"

"Mine was nice," Chloe said. "I like seeing Jana on her own. I'm not crazy about Bill."

"The guy's an asshole," Charlie said, tapping on his screen. "He's a reactionary who thinks he's a progressive, which is the worst kind of reactionary."

There was a box of pastries from Early to Bread on the table. Someone must have driven into town.

"What about your evening, Charlie?" Matthew said.

"Exhausting. I didn't get in till almost two."

"He fell asleep on the Thruway!" Chloe said, putting her hand on Charlie's arm.

"I didn't fall asleep. I very responsibly pulled over and took a nap."

Charlie yawned, looking at his watch.

"And now we have to hit the road again, right, Chlo?"

"Soon. By the way, Matt, we'll be out for dinner tonight. Lily's in a performance and it'll probably run late."

"Okay."

He'd forgotten they were picking up their daughter from camp today.

He reached for a muffin from the cake box.

"How was town?" he asked casually.

Chloe shrugged.

"The usual."

They left after breakfast. As soon as they were gone, he got into the truck and drove into Aurelia, crossing the Millstream bridge and crawling slowly past the Veery Road intersection without making the turn. A man was trimming his hedge on a ladder and a couple of kids were biking around a front yard. Otherwise nothing was going on at that end. He circled back and checked from the county road end: also quiet. This time he made the turn and drove past the house itself. Nothing: just the LeBaron waiting in the driveway and the silent house jutting above the hedges.

Back at the bridge he parked and climbed down to the creek. Despite the drop in temperature, people were out on the rocks. He made his way downstream until he came level with the back of the A-frame. Summoning the air of a harmlessly inquisitive wanderer, he scrambled up the bank opposite, which sloped up to the fence of a building supply yard. Walking alongside it, he allowed himself a few quick glances across to the other side. Nothing. The back door was closed, the glass squares in its top half reflecting blackly. The small trees flanking the path, sentinel-like presences in last night's darkness, turned out to be dwarf pear trees, laden with small green fruit. A faux-bronze Buddha, Aurelia's ubiquitous totem, sat in the shade of a maple, smiling. The peacefulness of the place was a little uncanny. There ought to have been some outward sign of disturbance, he felt, if only visible to himself; a crack in that trim clap-

board exterior, a crooked glint in a window. But the house seemed entirely calm.

He moved on, climbing back down to the water a hundred yards farther along, where, for the benefit of anyone watching, he dabbled his feet in a pool, before turning back.

A group of Rainbows had taken possession of a rock near the bridge. One was strumming a small guitar; others had drums and tambourines. A guy with a coiled topknot was sharing a sandwich with a lean gray dog. Torssen was there, Mr. 99%, sitting off to one side with the two girls Matthew had met with Pike. He was talking, while the girls listened in silence. One of them lay with her head resting on his thigh. The other, the kittenish-faced one, was on her stomach with her head propped on her hands. Her green hair, to which she had added tints of violet and orange, stuck up in a soft thick tangle, and Torssen was absently plying his fingers through it as he spoke.

Matthew stared, wondering again what it was about the guy that provoked such hostility in him. Was it just his own jaundiced distrust of any attitude that divided the world into oppressors and the oppressed, when the only valid distinction as far as he was concerned was between oppressors and, as he put it to himself, "oppressors-in-waiting"? Or was there something more primitive and personal going on? It occurred to him, as he probed the feeling, that there was probably an element of envy in it; that this figure holding court from the throne-room of his own body, with his jesters and musicians and nubile consorts arrayed about him, might, in some sense, have been himself, had circumstances beyond his control not intervened. Not that this particular image of fulfillment had a monopoly on his capacity for envy; far from it.

Depending on his mood, almost any image of success or even just average functionality had the potential to initiate a kind of looping self-interrogation; the abject sense of being confronted by some viable version of himself provoking the question of why he couldn't become that version, which in turn would arouse the fleetingly hopeful sense that all it would take would be a determined act of self-adjustment, followed, however, almost immediately, by the recollection that this adjustment would have to take place in that tantalizing stretch of time we wander in so freely and yet can no longer alter in even the minutest degree, namely the past. Which brought him back, like some infernal Möbius strip of thought, to that condition of abject susceptibility to the lives of others...

Still, it was true that some of those lives had more obvious resonance with his own, which no doubt boosted their power over him, and this man Torssen's was certainly one of those.

One of the girls passed Torssen a small bag and he rolled a joint, executing the ritual with the solemnity of a priest preparing a sacrament. The group smoked it openly, and the smell drifted down to Matthew on the breeze. Good stuff, he noted, remembering the spalls of dusty foliage, half oregano, he used to sell in London. Rudy, his old supplier, impinged on his thoughts, and Rudy's wife Joan. He frowned, shutting them out, and moved on.

Back at the house, he went straight to his room and slid his suitcase out from under the bed, unzipping the lid. Inside, exactly as he had left it last night, was the plastic shopping bag he'd taken from the A-frame's kitchen, bulging with its clutter. He peered in. There was the TAG Heuer wristwatch, the iPhone, the little cheap Tracfone, the laptop, the bulging wallet, the Sabatier knife. All present and correct. No reason why it shouldn't have been, of course, but

the need to check had been sharply urgent. He closed the lid again, slid the suitcase back under the bed and left.

In the kitchen he cooked himself an omelette of duck eggs and aged Gruyère with some leftover romesco sauce that needed eating. He was famished, but after a couple of bites he felt abruptly nauseous and tipped the rest into Fu's bowl. Fu, who had a sixth sense for any action involving his bowl, came waddling in immediately, and guzzled the whole mess down.

What now? Swim? Walk? Read? Think more about this hamstrung existence of his? The latter activity had become a little beside the point, he realized. He supposed he should try to take stock of the immediate situation; start processing what had happened and preparing himself for what was to come. But it was hard to get any lasting purchase on it. Thinking about it was like trying to handle a blob of mercury that broke into slithering beads as you touched it. It was like trying to take stock of a dream, or some strange hallucination.

He'd drifted into the living room, and was sitting on one of the rawhide sofas. George's words came back to him from the time they'd talked in the kitchen. Absently, he dug a hand down behind the rawhide seat. Almost immediately he found an iPod Mini. For the next several minutes he distracted himself with a methodical search of the deep, faintly oily crevices of the two sofas. By the time he was finished he'd found several Scrabble letters, close to forty dollars in change and bills and a gold-and-quartz Montblanc fountain pen. He considered leaving it all on the kitchen table for Charlie and Chloe to find when they got back with their daughter, with a note explaining where he'd discovered it, but realized this would raise the question of why he'd been poking around in their sofa in

the first place. Mildly amused by the predicament, he stuffed the whole lot back down into the crack. For a moment he felt rather noble and honorable doing this. But then he felt hypocritical, as though it had just been an act for the benefit of some invisible observer, and he dug it out again, all but the Scrabble pieces. Why pretend he was anything other than he was? he thought. A teenage delinquent turned fully fledged adult criminal. In which case he might as well start acting like one.

The atmosphere of those grubby, forlorn years came back to him; ages fourteen to seventeen, running his little business with his scales and baggies out of the tiny bedroom in the West Kensington flat he'd moved into with his mother and sister. One incident in particular asserted itself through the drift of memory. It wasn't an incident he thought about often: it was so bizarre it had a quality of having happened to a third party, and when he did think of it, he could hardly connect it to himself. Dr. McCubbin would no doubt have been highly interested in it, but he hadn't discussed it with McCubbin; not because he was embarrassed, but because even by then it had already sealed itself off from him, existing more as an article of faith than a living memory.

He'd gone to the flat of his supplier, Rudy, in Hounslow. Rudy had apparently forgotten he was coming and didn't have the goods, which he kept in a garage in Hatton Cross. He'd told Matthew to wait while he fetched them, saying he'd be back in an hour. Joan, his wife, offered Matthew a cup of tea. She was a gaunt woman with long, platinum-white hair and white-polished fingernails. The two of them sat together at the kitchen table with its porcelain donkey centerpiece, in the paniers of which sat little glass cruets of condiments.

They hadn't been alone before and didn't have much to say to each other. Joan asked about his school and he told her about his crammer in Holborn. They discussed the unusually sunny weather. A silence descended on them. Then Joan looked at him— he never forgot the placid calm in her pale blue, crow's-footed eyes—and said, "Would you like to fuck me, Matthew?" He was startled, and yet the words immediately acquired a kind of fateful- ness, as if in some part of himself he had long been expecting them. He remembered walking down a corridor behind her, his forefin- ger linked with hers, thinking: So this is how it's going to happen. In the bedroom she took off her top and went to the far side of the bed, kneeling on the gold-brown carpet in her bra and skirt. She lit a menthol cigarette. He hesitated in the doorway, unsure what he was supposed to do. There was a mirror etched with Betty Boop on one wall, and paintings of a woodland scene in each of the four seasons on another. In the corner was a built-in white closet. "Come here," she said. He went over and she unzipped his fly, tak- ing him in her mouth and putting his hands on her breasts, holding her cigarette off to the side. When he was hard she took off her skirt and bra and lay on the bed. "Is this your first time?" she asked. He nodded. She stubbed out her cigarette and raised her knees. "Take off my panties." He remembered the thinness of her thighs as he slid her underwear down; the scant black wisps of her pubic hair. He remembered trying to kiss her as he lowered himself onto her, and the abruptness with which she turned her head away, mut- tering, "None of that." She brought him into her and they went at it missionary-style for a bit. "Very nice," she said, and then turned over, lighting another cigarette and thrusting her thin behind at him. "Now hit me. Smack me." Bewildered—at fifteen he was very

innocent in these matters— he gave her a tentative smack. "Go on, I like it," she told him. "Harder. Harder." After a while she said, "Now do me again. Put it in."

Rudy was in the kitchen when they went back, sitting at the table with another man, a soft-looking guy in his forties, with an unshaven double chin. It was this part of the experience that was so strange: so charged and yet so blank. Everyone acted as if nothing out of the ordinary had occurred. Nobody asked where he and Joan had been or what they'd been doing. Rudy introduced the other man to Matthew as his new business partner, Don, who'd given him a lift back from Hatton Cross. Joan put the kettle on and made another cup of tea while Rudy weighed out the grass and hash and counted off the acid tabs, and Matthew paid him.

That was all, and nothing ever happened with Joan again. But a peculiar feeling had lingered with Matthew as he left, a sort of confused dread, and for a long time his mind had gone compulsively back over the experience, itemizing every detail, and often recapturing small objects or words he'd overlooked before, but always sensing there was still some large thing that he'd missed.

Later, in his twenties, he'd surmised that Rudy and possibly the other man had been watching through the closet keyhole or some hidden hole in the wall, or maybe through the Betty Boop mirror. Still later, he'd recalled an earlier visit where he'd gone into the room they called the lounge, and had seen, without taking any particular notice of it, a home movie projector on the cocktail cabinet, and it occurred to him that he'd possibly been filmed. But oddly enough even when he interpolated these conjectures back into the memory, they did nothing to diminish its aura of mystery, or reduce the sense of vague dread it still aroused in him.

It was only recently, a year or so ago, that he'd remembered the last part of it, or what he hoped was the last part of it. Without any obvious trigger it had come to him one morning in New York, that Joan had also told him to burn her with the lighted cigarette, and that he had done it: stabbed the red ember, in response to her gasped commands, against her scarred white buttocks. It had seemed a momentous new fact to have discovered, or rediscovered, about himself, full of potential illumination. And yet it too had proved oddly enigmatic, yielding little usable self-knowledge, and adding to his confusion.

Only now, for the first time, did it occur to him that its real meaning might be less in the nature of illumination than of prophecy. For was it not, in its masque-like way, a foretelling of last night's culminating gesture: the same hand, a quarter century older, thrust out in an almost identical motion, the same bewildered shock at the unexpected weapon in its grasp, as though Joan had reached down through time and placed it there; the same sense of irresistible necessity drawing from him an act of violence as savage and surprising to him as if he had been given a lightning bolt to wield?

· · ·

He took the spoils from the sofa back up to the guesthouse and put them in the suitcase with Grollier's things. The suitcase had seemed the safest hiding place for the moment. Nobody was going to stumble on its contents by accident. He'd be in New York in a few days, assuming his luck held (though "luck" didn't seem quite the word), and there'd be plenty of places to get rid of everything. The Montblanc pen he could sell when the time was right, along with

Grollier's watch. The rest could be bagged and dumped in trash cans across the city, or thrown in the river.

He swam laps for an hour before going to bed that night, forcing himself up and down the length of the pool. Shivering, he ran up to the guesthouse and took a long, hot shower. There was a moment, as he lay in darkness, in which he could feel the proximity of tumultuous thoughts that, if engaged, would almost certainly rule out any possibility of sleep. But he'd managed to exhaust himself sufficiently that fatigue soon got the better of him, and he was asleep by the time Charlie and Chloe got back from Connecticut with their daughter.

• • •

A child's voice singing a Lady Gaga song rang out from the kitchen as he went down for breakfast the next morning.

Lily had been at music camp. She played the violin and clarinet, and mimicked a range of English and American pop divas uncannily well, complete with cheeky glottal stops and tremulous melisma. When she wasn't making music, however, she was a quiet, watchful girl, with something of Charlie's distrustful air, as if she thought you might be trying to get something out of her.

She broke off the song as Matthew came in, and gave him a friendly, if somewhat impersonal, greeting. He kissed her on the forehead and realized he should have brought a present for her. At one time she'd treated him as a family member, unselfconsciously jumping onto his lap with a book for him to read to her, but in the past couple of years she'd become more reserved.

"How was camp?" he asked.

"It was good."

"That camp is something else," Chloe said. "The show they put on was like Broadway and the Lincoln Center combined. They even served little tubs of ice cream in the intermission."

Matthew smiled. "I've always wondered what I missed out on, not going to camp."

"You never went to camp?" the girl asked.

"We didn't have camp in England."

"But it's so much fun!"

"That's probably the reason."

Chloe laughed and Lily, taking the cue, gave a polite chuckle. That was another thing about her; a habit of doing whatever her mother did: echoing her gestures, acquiescing in her moods and wishes; sometimes with a strange sort of cringing eagerness, as if she weren't quite certain about her mother's approval. There was no obvious reason for this: Chloe treated her with impeccable kindness and patience, and yet the effect of her daughter's behavior was to suggest something faintly strained in her own. It was the only aspect of Chloe that Matthew had ever found remotely troubling, and he preferred not to think about it.

The morning passed unremarkably. After breakfast Chloe and Lily went off to a Zumba class. Charlie worked upstairs in his office. Matthew sat on the terrace with his father's Pascal. From time to time he checked for news on his computer, an old Toshiba netbook with a cracked screen. He'd brought it down because the Wi-Fi only reached the guesthouse erratically. There was still nothing.

After lunch he joined the family by the pool, lying in the shade while Chloe and Lily splashed in the water and Charlie floated around in his inflatable armchair. The citrusy scent of some shrubs that had started flowering for the second time that summer drifted

on the breeze. Heat rose from the flagstones edging the pool. He gazed out at the three figures, noting his own calmness, again with that odd, though not disagreeable, feeling of detachment from himself. A fantasy took shape in his mind, in which time stalled in a kind of endlessly looping eddy and all the pleasant sensations of this moment, the warmth and soft sounds and gentle motions, simply burbled on forever like some changeless screen saver.

But by the late afternoon he was beginning to feel restless again. A part of him wanted this lull to last forever, but another part of him, he realized, was impatient for it to break. He stood up.

"I should get some things for dinner."

Chloe looked at him, shading her eyes.

"Can't we make do with what we have in the refrigerator?"

"I need nectarines. I want to make a cobbler."

"Yummie!" Lily called out. "I love cobbler!"

"Me too," Charlie said.

"Yes, but . . . it's late, and Matthew shouldn't—"

"It's no problem," Matthew interrupted her, opening the gate. "I like going into town."

He left before Chloe could make any more objections. His desire to drive by the A-frame was as sharp, suddenly, as it had ever been.

This time a Chevy pickup was parked in the driveway, with a metal trailer attached to it.

Forcing himself to keep driving, Matthew glimpsed a man on a riding lawn mower in the backyard, sending out plumes of grass.

He parked by the bridge and climbed straight down to the creek. The daylight seemed to be throbbing around him. At the top of the bank opposite the A-frame he found himself staring

straight into the eyes of the man on the lawn mower. He raised a hand as if in casual greeting, and the man waved back as he rotated his machine back toward the house. A second man, wearing goggles, was weed-whacking around some shrubs at the corner of the kitchen. He was stepping slowly backward, moving in the direction of the kitchen door. With an effort, Matthew made himself leave. It was possible that you couldn't actually see into the kitchen through the door unless you stuck your face right up to the glass, but he didn't want to be around to find out.

It was coming, he thought. If not now, then soon. Fear was pushing up through the numbed feeling he'd had for the past two days. It was as though what had occurred was only beginning to become real in his own mind, now that the prospect of other people discovering it was looming closer.

He drank copiously at dinner that night, sensing he was going to have trouble sleeping. By the time he'd finished the dishes he could barely keep his eyes open. In bed, he fell asleep instantly. But an hour later he came lurching awake, his heart pounding. Had it happened yet? An awful certainty that it had, gripped him. He got up and took his netbook down to the pool, to search online for news. Still nothing. He stood up, intending to go back to bed, but instead found himself sidling around the house and into the truck. If anyone heard him, he thought, he could say he'd been unable to sleep and had gone to listen to the drumming. Town was deserted. From the county road he turned onto Veery Road. The thin dark triangle of the A-frame reached up like a finger saying, *Sshhh*. The gardeners' truck and trailer were gone. Only the LeBaron stood in the driveway, its lonely persistence charged with odd pathos now, like that of some helplessly loyal pet. I ought to be relieved, Mat-

thew thought. But if anything the stillness of the place—as though he'd somehow sealed it in time—made him more restless than ever. Parking in the pull-off beyond the bridge, he felt as if there were two of him; a self and a second self, ghostlier and yet seemingly more in control of him than the first, as it replicated every movement he made: two of him climbing down to the stream, picking their way with identical motions from rock to rock among the white combs of falling water and the black pools; two of him climbing the wooden steps up the bank below the A-frame, and stepping silently across the lawn to the windowed back door, aware of the dark forms of the pear trees on either side of him, the little Buddha cross-legged under the maple.

Covering the door handle with his shirtsleeve, he turned it and stepped inside, closing the door behind him.

The AC had been on, but there was a bad smell already: human waste and the odor of spoiling meat. In the darkness he made out Grollier's naked body, slumped against the wall like a heap of pillows with dark stains. As he stepped forward, moonlight coming in from the skylight caught the slits of white in the half-open eyes and he flinched back. All right, he thought, steadying himself. Alright. This was why he'd come, wasn't it? To see what he'd done; confirm that he hadn't in fact been dreaming or imagining his long evening at the A-frame. Well, here was his proof: the bearded head slumped on the enormous torso, one arm on the floor, the other bent at the elbow with the hand turned back awkwardly as if caught in the act of batting off a fly, legs kicked out across the passage; the whole body, blood-splotched from the neck down, emanating a sort of confused reproach, like some felled colossus who believed he'd been promised immortality.

He stared on. *You!* the man had shouted, incredulous as he rec-ognized Matthew in the flickering darkness. *You!*—glancing back into the living room and up toward the loft as if suddenly under-standing everything, and then lunging forward with his empty hands outspread in front of him. That much Matthew remembered vividly. What happened next was less clear in his mind, and in fact never acquired a stable outline. The fireworks lights strafing the kitchen in bright flashes that made the intermittent darkness all the more impenetrable no doubt added to the uncertain nature of the episode. Sometimes he saw himself blindly grabbing the kitchen knife only as Wade came charging toward him. Sometimes he'd taken it deliberately out of the knife block the moment he'd reached the back door, and had been highly conscious of having it in his pos-session all along. Sometimes it really did seem to have materialized in his grip by magic. As for the stabbing itself, it appeared to have occurred in some purely interstitial realm, outside consciousness and intractable to memory. One moment Wade was charging at him like an enraged ape; the next he was thrashing on the floor with a five-inch Sabatier blade in his throat, blood fountaining out from the severed artery in a copious gush while Matthew staggered back to the wall and stood flattened against it, aware only of a roar-ing in his ears and the fact that his body was vibrating uncontrolla-bly, as if he were in the process of being sucked into a tornado.

eleven

At around five the following afternoon, he went out from the kitchen, where he'd been making focaccia dough, and walked over to the pool. Chloe was lying on a sunbed, wearing earbuds and laughing at something on her phone. She liked listening to comedy podcasts and on those occasions there would be the minor delight of seeing her break into helpless laughter without visible cause.

It was a beautiful afternoon, the light so clear he could see small insects at the far end of the pool, glinting in the air above the water.

"Coming for a swim?" Chloe asked, tapping her phone. She was wearing one of her thin cotton shirts over her swimsuit. Her hair was loosely gathered in a leather clasp, falling in dark strands.

"Thinking of it," Matthew said. "I was actually wondering if it was warm enough."

"I know. It's getting cooler. I think the monarchs may have started leaving." She gestured over to the butterfly garden, where a few desultory specimens were still wandering through the air.

"Where do they go?"

"Mexico."

"Lucky them!"

She smiled.

"Want to hear something hilarious?"

She held out one of her earbuds, leaving the other in her ear.

"Sure."

He went over and perched on the end of her sunbed.

"Come closer," she said. "It won't reach."

He slid closer to her and put in the earbud. Chloe said a name that didn't mean anything to him.

"He's an actor but he also does stand-up. This . . . this person I know who goes to a lot of comedy clubs put me on to him."

She tapped the phone and the comedian's voice came into Matthew's ear. He laughed along with Chloe, but he wasn't listening. To be sitting there, joined to her through the looping white scribble of the earbuds, close enough to feel the warmth of her body, was a novel experience, strangely intimate, and he found himself wanting to take note of every detail of it: her arm in its weightless shirt brushing against him as she laughed; the sunlight on her fine small teeth; her perfume, which was like the scent of something grown in paradise; above all the private atmosphere of happiness she dwelled in, that at this proximity was something you could almost touch and taste and see. The intense love he felt

for her seemed to dilate and sparkle inside him. He sat motionless, drinking in the unexpected blissfulness of the moment.

It was Charlie who brought it to an end, appearing at the gate in his swimming trunks. He was looking at his iPad.

"Hey, Chlo, didn't we meet Wade Grollier? The director?"

Chloe took out her earbud.

"What?"

Charlie walked in through the gate, still looking at his screen.

"Didn't we meet Wade Grollier?"

Very coolly Chloe said:

"Who?"

"Wade D. Grollier. Movie guy."

"I don't know."

"I think we met him at some fund-raiser. Big guy with a beard."

She shrugged.

"Maybe. Why?"

"He was renting a house up here this summer."

Matthew braced himself.

"Oh," Chloe said with perfect nonchalance.

"Yeah. He was just killed."

No sound came from Chloe for a second or two.

"What do you mean?" she said.

"He was found dead in his rental house."

"What?"

"Stabbed. They found him today."

"What . . . where?"

Charlie looked down at his screen. "Veery Road—that's the one that goes by the creek, isn't it?"

Chloe didn't answer. She had stood up, putting on her sunglasses, and was walking over to Charlie.

"I'm pretty sure we did meet him," Charlie said as she looked at the screen over his shoulder. "At that thing in Aspen, where they had the hot-air balloons . . ."

Chloe had turned pale and Matthew could see that her hands were clenched tight.

"Don't you remember? Must have been two, three years ago."

"Maybe. What else does it say?"

Charlie flicked the screen.

"That's all. It's just a statement from the sheriff's department. Found stabbed earlier today . . . Treating it as murder . . . That's his picture."

"Oh, god."

"Unbelievable, right?"

Chloe moistened her lips, but said nothing.

She detached herself from Charlie and walked to the gate, cradling her elbows. Matthew could feel, almost on his own nerves, the horror surging through her.

"Where are you off to?" Charlie called after her.

"Lily."

She moved quickly toward the house. After she'd gone, Charlie gave a quiet laugh:

"Psycho on the loose, she's thinking."

Matthew gave a vague nod. He'd known his reactions were going to have to be very carefully calibrated once the discovery was made, but he could tell already that this was going to be more complicated than he'd imagined. Aside from the need to hide any awareness of how Chloe would surely be feeling under

her own, equally necessary, masquerade, it was also going to be crucial not to seem out of step with the casual attitude that Charlie, who had no reason to feel personally affected, would naturally assume.

Charlie continued:

"I doubt that's what it is, though. Probably just some methhead burglar who wasn't expecting to find anyone home."

"You think?"

"Yeah, or one of those Rainbow people."

He plunged into the pool and began swimming laps. Matthew went inside. The TV was on in the upstairs bedroom. He could hear its muffled noise through the kitchen ceiling, under the squeak of Lily's clarinet from along the corridor. There was a radio in the kitchen, but he couldn't find any news on it. He fetched his netbook from the living room and found a couple of breaking news stories that had the same information Charlie had read from his iPad.

Charlie came in from his swim and joined Chloe upstairs. An hour later the two of them came down for dinner.

"Like I told you, Matt," Charlie said, "burglary gone wrong. They had the sheriff on the local news. So we're off the hook for anything creepier. Right, Chlo?"

"Right." Chloe poured herself a drink.

"What did they say?" Matthew asked, trying to strike a tone of neutral interest.

"Basically just that. Someone broke in thinking he was out, got surprised and stuck a knife in him. The owner of the house found the body this morning but it happened a while ago."

"They can't tell exactly?"

"I guess that takes some time to determine. Anyhow, according to the owner he was due to fly out to Malaysia the day before yesterday, so—"

"Indonesia," Chloe corrected him.

"No, I think she said Malaysia."

She seemed about to insist, but swallowed down her drink instead.

"I'm guessing it happened the night of the fireworks," Charlie said. "Everyone in town goes, so it's an obvious time for a break-in."

"Right."

"It'll put a damper on the summer rental market, that's for sure."

Chloe went over to the drinks cabinet. Matthew heard the bottle clinking against her glass but managed to stop himself from looking.

"Sorry, that was a callous thing to say," Charlie said. "I guess I'm spooked by the fact that we met the guy. Chloe does remember, by the way, Matt."

"Oh, yes?"

Matthew looked at Chloe. She nodded.

"What was he like?"

Her eyes met his, and he made himself hold their glance. Her poise impressed him. Aside from the shaky hands and the fact that she was drinking at three times her usual rate there was little outward indication of what she must have been feeling. Certainly Charlie didn't seem to have any inkling of it.

"Oh, you know . . . It was at one of those events where you chat to hundreds of people. He seemed nice enough . . ."

"Was he . . . did he have a family?"

"I have no idea."

"He lived with some actress in SoHo," Charlie said. "She's off filming in the desert. Apparently he was up here to rewrite the script of his new movie."

"What actress?" Matthew asked, trying to second-guess what a guiltless version of himself would be saying.

"I forget. Who was it, Chloe?"

"I have no idea," Chloe said with a brusqueness that made Matthew nervous. He was well aware that his safety depended as much on Chloe's ability to put on a convincing performance as it did on his own.

"But listen," she said. "Let's not talk about this right now, shall we? Lily doesn't know and I don't want to scare her."

"Agreed," Charlie answered.

The topic wasn't mentioned at dinner, and Chloe went off upstairs immediately after. Matthew cleared up while Charlie and Lily embarked on a game of Scrabble in the living room. When he was finished he looked online for more news. There were tributes from fans and colleagues, but nothing new about the investigation. He went to bed without any serious expectation of being able to sleep, which turned out to be the case, though he drifted off for a couple of hours just as day was breaking and the birds were beginning to sing.

Breakfasting alone, he found a report on the murder in the *New York Times* online, along with a short obituary. Neither contained anything he didn't already know. Later that morning Charlie came home from tennis with the *Aurelia Gazette* and the *East Deerfield Citizen*.

"He's all over the *Citizen*," he said, sprawling down on the sofa.

"Who is?" Chloe asked. She'd been upstairs most of the morning, but had gone outside a little while ago, and had just come back in with some wildflowers, which she was arranging in a vase. She was wearing more eye makeup than usual, Matthew noticed. Other than that, it was hard to tell whether there was any objective basis for the aura of precarious frailty he detected around her, or if he was only noticing it because of what he knew. Lily was up in her room, her voice rising uninhibitedly over the tinny accompaniment of a karaoke machine.

"Wade D. Grollier," Charlie answered his wife. "Want to hear what they say?"

Chloe cleared her throat before answering.

"Sure."

"Not interrupting you, Matt?"

Matthew had found a Sudoku book in the bathroom and spent the last couple of hours doing puzzles. Plunging his mind into the realm of pure numbers seemed to give him some relief from his own thoughts, which had begun circling around the variables of what might or might not happen now that the body had been found, and how best to react to each eventuality. This ceaseless but largely pointless activity was what had kept him awake for most of the previous night.

"Of course not," he said.

"I'll give you the highlights. Let's see. Police unable to pinpoint exact time of death but believe it occurred sometime during the Aurelia Volunteers Day fireworks. So I was right about that . . . Director survived by a sister, who issued a statement calling him one of the kindest, funniest, most creative blah blah blah . . . Staying in Aurelia to work on a screenplay . . . Not married but living in

New York with girlfriend, actress Rachel Turpin. Right, of course. Spokesperson for Turpin said the actress, who is currently on location in Arizona, was devastated and blah blah . . . Officers from the sheriff's department canvassing neighbors on Veery Road and throughout Aurelia for possible leads . . . Case being handled by detectives from Homicide and Burglary Divisions . . . Murder weapon believed to be a kitchen knife missing from the house . . . Any information from members of the public blah blah blah . . ."

He tossed the paper aside.

"East Deerfield Burglary Division. Now, there's a phrase to strike fear into the most hardened criminal's heart! Maybe the guy'll just turn himself in out of sheer terror." He laughed. It was a quirk of Charlie's to be contemptuous, on principle, toward the police and uniformed officials in general.

"Why are they so sure it was a burglary?" Chloe asked.

"As opposed to what? An assassination? Some rival director jealous of his awards?"

Chloe shrugged.

"I mean, was anything actually stolen?"

"Well . . . presumably."

After a moment, Chloe said:

"Does it say what?"

Charlie picked up the paper and scanned the piece again.

"No. But—would it, necessarily?"

"I guess not."

She adjusted some flowers in her vase, and picked up a photography book. Matthew glanced over, trying to guess what was going through her head. It occurred to him that she might have

been thinking about Grollier's disposable Tracfone; hoping it had been stolen, perhaps, so that the police wouldn't find her number on it. It was too bad he couldn't tell her he had it safely in his own possession.

Charlie looked at his watch.

"I should get going. Big meeting this afternoon."

He went up to take a shower. Before long Chloe put aside her book and casually reached for the newspaper. Grollier's face filled most of the front page, broad and smiling. Matthew watched out of the corner of his eye as she looked at the picture, her own face expressionless. After a while she stood up and, without a word, went out through the glass doors. Halfway across the lawn she stumbled on something, almost tripping over, though she moved on as though she hadn't noticed. Passing Charlie's meditation garden, she wandered into the woods at the edge of the property, disappearing behind the gray trunks. She was gone for the rest of the morning.

• • •

Lily had been invited to a birthday party that afternoon, for a girl she'd met at camp. To Matthew's surprise, Chloe invited him along for the ride.

"They sound interesting, the parents. You should come."

"Are you sure? I wouldn't want to gate-crash . . ."

"No. It's just one of those things where they invite the adults to stick around if they want to. I'd drop Lily off but it's all the way over in Klostville. Come, Matt!"

They set off in the Lexus. Chloe hummed quietly as she drove. She seemed dazed, absent, and Matthew wondered if

she'd taken a tranquilizer. Lily sat in the back, listening to music on her headphones. Veery Road was cordoned off, the words SHERIFF'S LINE DO NOT CROSS running in black letters along the yellow tape. News vans and police vehicles were parked on the county road verge. Chloe glanced down toward the A-frame as they passed. She didn't say anything but it wasn't hard to imagine what she was feeling. An urge to make some comforting gesture gripped Matthew. He almost felt he could touch her shoulder in silent sympathy without danger, as if there were some point of contact between them that existed outside the practical exigencies of the situation. He restrained himself, however, aware of the danger of giving even the remotest hint of what he knew.

Glancing in the mirror, Chloe said quietly:

"Did you ever see any of his movies?"

For form's sake Matthew thought he should ask whose.

"Wade Grollier's. That was Veery Road back there. Where he was killed."

"Ah, right. No, I don't think I have. Have you?"

"I've seen every one of them."

He looked for a tone of ordinary surprise.

"What are they like?"

"I think you'd enjoy them. They're very funny and warm and . . . human. Even though they're full of robots and talking animals!"

He gave a polite laugh. Was this why she'd invited him along? To talk about Grollier? If so, he felt he should do what he could to rise to the occasion.

"You said he was nice, that one time you met him . . ."

She was silent a long moment, and it seemed to him he could

James Lasdun

feel her struggling with an intense desire to talk, perhaps even to blab out the whole story of her affair.

"We barely spoke," she said, clearing her throat. "But he must have made an impression on me. I went out and got hold of all his films."

"I'd like to see them. Maybe we could watch one tonight..."

"Maybe."

She rummaged in her purse, bringing out a pair of sunglasses that hid half her face. Matthew turned away, doing his best to conceal any awareness of her emotion. In the mirror, he saw Lily take a pair of checker-framed shades from her backpack and put them on, gazing up at her mother's reflection. Chloe stared at her a moment before smiling. Again there was that slight impression of strain in her relationship with the girl. She started humming again; a light, tuneless sound that seemed designed to keep the world at arm's length. By uncertain processes of thought Matthew found himself remembering Charlie's comment about his first wife's reluctance to have a child—how he'd been afraid it meant she wanted to go on "fooling around with other guys"— and with a little jolt he realized he might have just stumbled on something interesting. Chloe had become pregnant with Lily almost immediately after she and Charlie were married. Charlie had told Matthew the news over the phone, and Matthew had congratulated Chloe the next time he saw her in Cobble Hill. She'd thanked him, but he'd been struck by a distinct lack of enthusiasm for the prospect of impending motherhood. "It's not exactly what I had planned for this moment in my life," she'd said. "But I guess that's the way it goes." He'd assumed the pregnancy must have been an accident, and that she'd simply

decided to make the best of it. (His later discovery that she was a practicing Catholic had seemed to confirm this.) But now, as he considered it in the light of Charlie's comment about Nikki, it seemed to him things might have been more complicated. Had Charlie somehow pressured his new wife into having a child before she was ready? Got her pregnant so as to lock her into the marriage tightly enough to ward off his own jealousies? Not that he'd have forced anything: his benign image of himself wouldn't have allowed that. But he was a good manipulator, Charlie; very proficient at getting what he wanted without seeming to twist your arm. You could say it was a specialty of his, in fact, Matthew thought. If nothing else, he was quite capable of being deliberately careless in bed. And of course he'd have been able to pretend to argue for terminating the pregnancy (Matthew could hear him doing it; all scrupulous devil's advocacy against himself), knowing full well that Chloe wouldn't consider it . . .

Was that it? he wondered, turning back to her. Was that what had pushed her into Grollier's arms, or at least enabled her to act on her attraction to him? There was nothing vengeful or calculating about her—he was certain of that—but the delicate mechanism of her psyche was such that even if she'd had no idea of having been manipulated, let alone of punishing Charlie for it, the sheer drastic fact of it, lodged in the living tissue of her marriage, was bound to have summoned into existence some equally drastic countermeasure somewhere along the line. In which case poor old Charlie had had it coming . . .

A few miles beyond Klostville, the GPS took them up a steep mountain road and onto a driveway that skirted a grassy meadow. At the end was a wooden house with a stone terrace

where several adults and young girls were gathered. Solar panels gleamed on the roof, and an open-sided shed of rough timbers filled with neatly stacked logs stood to one side. There was a fenced chicken coop, and a paddock with a donkey in it and some small goats. A pleasant farmyard smell scented the air, sweetish and mealy.

A tall man in his thirties greeted them on the terrace, introducing himself as Philippe. He spoke with a French accent but his wife, Caitlin, who came over a moment later, seemed thoroughly American: gangly and blonde, with a generous laugh.

"So great to meet you," she said, shaking their hands and looking from one to the other. "Natalie is very smitten with your daughter."

She seemed to assume that Matthew was Lily's father, and Chloe made no attempt to correct her. They were introduced to the other adults.

"Do you guys live around here?" a bearded man in a T-shirt asked.

"Aurelia," Chloe answered. She'd taken off her sunglasses and seemed to be making a determined effort to appear relaxed and cheerful.

"Aurelia!" another guest exclaimed. "Isn't that where that movie director was just killed?"

"That's right," Matthew said, answering for Chloe.

The guest, a woman with long silver hair, shook her head: "Awful! Do the police have any idea who it was?"

"Not as far as we know."

"Truly awful," the woman repeated.

Caitlin brought out dips and carrot sticks from the kitchen,

while Philippe led the girls off on a treasure hunt, piling them into a wagon attached to a small tractor. The dozen-odd adults chatted on the terrace, sampling the dips and drinking craft beers from the cooler. They were a mixture of locals and weekenders. The silver-haired woman was a sculptor. The bearded man worked as a fishing and wilderness guide. There was a chiropractor and a couple who ran a shoe store. It seemed to Matthew that they were all under the impression he was Chloe's partner, and he found himself slipping mentally into the role; sitting close to her, opening her beer, letting his arm brush carelessly against hers. He was oddly relaxed. The individual who had spent the last few weeks in a state of neurotic, spiraling obsession seemed utterly unconnected to him. He felt affable, even charming. It was as if, playing the part of Chloe's lover, he was able to draw on qualities he couldn't access as himself, most notably the sort of easy-going, half-serious curiosity that had always seemed to him the elusive key to getting along with strangers. He found himself in conversation with Caitlin about the enormous flagstones on her terrace. She described how she and Philippe had transported them from a disused quarry on the ridge above their house, using the old quarrymen's technique of building an ice road in winter and sliding the pieces down. Genuinely interested, he questioned her about the house, the animals, their lives here in general. They'd moved from the city three years ago, she told him, where they'd bought and sold houses that had gone into foreclosure. Philippe, a graduate of Wharton as well as some eminent-sounding French institute, still did some real estate, but their aim was to live entirely off the land. "Homesteading," Caitlin called it, though from the plans

she described—building cellars into the hillside for goat cheese, and raising pigs for charcuterie in mobile foraging pens through the woods behind the house—it sounded more ambitious than that. She herself had grown up in Manhattan, but her grandparents on both sides were Wisconsin farmers, and as she described her and Philippe's new life, she seemed to radiate a more than purely personal happiness, as though some large and significant destiny were being fulfilled.

After a while she excused herself and went back inside the house. The silver-haired woman and some of the other guests were still talking about Grollier's murder, trading theories about what had happened. Matthew turned toward them, listening in. One of the shoe store couple had heard that Grollier's body was found naked, and was surmising some kind of sexual assignation gone wrong. The chiropractor seemed to know for a fact that the police were planning a raid on the Rainbow encampment to search for the stolen property. The wilderness guide echoed what Charlie had said: "I'll bet it was just some drug-addled drifter who's probably halfway across the country by now..."

He tuned out. The air was cool, but the sun itself was pleasantly warm. He tipped his face to it, closing his eyes and basking in its intimate heat. A fantasy formed in his mind: living up here in the mountains with Chloe, opening a little restaurant with food from local farmers and "homesteaders," cultivating a group of friends like these. His visits to the A-frame felt very distant from him. The stabbing itself seemed to have receded to a point of almost imperceptible remoteness.

The little rural fantasy played on in his mind. A funny name for the restaurant occurred to him—*Discomfort Food*—and he

chuckled softly, knowing it would amuse Chloe too. The talk around him had moved on from Grollier and he listened in again as it turned to the price of firewood, the surge in the local bear population, intrigues at the Klostville Town Board ... There was something appealing about it all; an easy, expansive ordinariness he hadn't encountered for a long time; not in the pinched conditions of his own life and not in the more luxurious spaces of Charlie's either. Charlie's wealth made him guarded, wary of people's motives for befriending him, and he lived a rather solitary life as a consequence. He and Chloe had done almost no entertaining this entire summer. Even the people who were going to be ousting Matthew in a couple of days were, as it turned out, just a potential business partner and his family.

Caitlin came out of the kitchen carrying a tray of plates and glasses.

"They just had a guy from the sheriff's department on the radio. The barman at the Millstream Inn remembers seeing Grollier in there the night he was killed. Apparently he got a call from someone and left in a hurry right after. They're putting out an appeal for the caller to come forward."

Matthew forced himself not to look at Chloe, but he could feel her tighten beside him. The other guests began talking.

"Can't they just track the person down from the guy's call records?"

"Maybe his phone was stolen."

"They'd still be able to get the records, though, wouldn't they, from the carrier?"

"Depends what kind of phone it was."

Half-listening, he tried to gauge the seriousness of the devel-

opment. Assuming Chloe had called Grollier on his Tracfone, and that Grollier had paid for that phone with cash, there was no reason to think the police would trace the call to Chloe. But what if she'd called him on his iPhone? Or what if the disposable phone had been paid for with a credit card and was therefore traceable? Or suppose Chloe decided, regardless, to come forward as the caller? Her good Catholic girl's conscience was apparently flexible enough to permit an affair, but he wasn't so sure it would allow her to obstruct the investigation of a murder.

He turned to her. She was following the conversation with a plausible air of detached curiosity, even putting in the odd comment of her own. But there was a fragility in her bearing, a constriction in her smile, and even if no one else noticed it, he could feel the immense effort of self-control she was making.

She smiled at him—he'd been staring, he realized—and he smiled back, wishing he could beam some strength at her, or at least a sense of how dangerous it would be, for both of them, if she lost her nerve.

twelve

"There are forty-five million people living in poverty in this country," Charlie said, reaching for some smoked sturgeon he'd brought back from the city. "They can't put up collateral for a big loan, but relatively tiny amounts of money can make a huge difference, and the thing is they pay it back! Or at least the *women* do. The women actually have a near-one-hundred-percent repayment rate."

It had rained in the night; a soft drumming like fingers on a desk, and it was still coming down steadily. Charlie was in a good mood. His deal was coming together, and in his exuberance he seemed to have forgotten his earlier reluctance to discuss it in front of Matthew.

"Interesting," Chloe said. She seemed composed, if not exactly relaxed.

"Yeah, I think we're going to make microloan-lending to impoverished women a centerpiece of our strategy."

"That's excellent, Charlie."

"It'll take some packaging, to get it across to investors, but it stacks up. It's kind of exciting. We're actually feeling rather proud of ourselves!"

"You should be. Isn't that great, Lily? Did you hear what Daddy said?"

"That's great, Daddy."

Matthew listened absently, smiling and nodding in the right places, though his mind was on other things. As of tomorrow he'd be gone for four days, which seemed a long time not to be able to follow developments firsthand, and this was nagging at him. Chloe's state of mind, in particular, was something he felt he needed to monitor closely and he wasn't going to be able to do that from the city. So far she seemed to have decided it was more important to protect her marriage than help the cops. But that could easily change, and he'd have preferred to be able to see it coming.

Lily wanted to play Scrabble after breakfast. Matthew began to clear the dishes, but Chloe insisted he come and play with them.

"We'll clean up later."

They went into the living room and set up the board on the coffee table. For a while they played without speaking, lulled by the steady rain into a peaceful silence. Even Matthew was able to relax a little. His mind drifted back to that first game of the summer, when Charlie had been so unamused by his joke word "siouxp." He found himself thinking of family Scrabble games when Charlie had come to live with them in London: the way he'd been torn between wanting to be a part of the household

and wanting it known that he considered the whole rigmarole to be, in some crucial way, not "cool."

"Coolness" had been extremely important to Charlie at fourteen, Matthew remembered. He'd arrived a year late at their school, which made it difficult for him to make his mark, or at least to get the kind of immediate high-status social ranking to which he seemed to feel entitled. Being cool had evidently been something he believed he could turn into a ticket to popularity. He was already somewhat cool, intrinsically, from the other boys' point of view, just by being American, but he took a lot of trouble to finesse it. Matthew had shared a bedroom with him for over a year, so he'd been able to observe the process close up, and it had been a revelation. The Dannecker family had never been remotely interested in fashion or pop culture, but suddenly here was this boy in their home who, to Matthew's admiring astonishment, would spend hours in front of the mirror, gelling his hair, trying on different outfits, with and without Ray-Bans, Discman, Yankees hat, Converse sneakers. Even on schooldays he'd do things with the school suit to sharpen it up. Fancy belts, a pair of cowboy boots he ordered from Arizona ... But it had been about attitude also, Matthew thought, remembering the subtle sneer fixed permanently on his cousin's handsome face at that time, and the way he had of rolling his eyes that made you feel ashamed of whatever crime against coolness you'd just committed. He'd do it when anyone in Matthew's family used one of the pet words they'd held on to from when Matthew and his sister were little—"polly" for porridge, "mimi" for milk ... It was just their way of amusing each other, but Charlie had made the whole family self-conscious about it.

All of which had impressed Matthew deeply. He'd been Charlie's fan from the start. He'd begun imitating him slavishly, which turned out to be a highly effective way of gaining his friendship. Charlie had seemed to enjoy having his younger, smaller acolyte at his side, piloting him across the schoolyard when he first arrived, or showing him how to get around London on the bus and Tube. Matthew had accepted his role as the junior partner unprotestingly, but he'd also felt proprietorial about Charlie. He'd liked showing him off, basking in the reflected glory, though he was also just plain proud of him in himself. He'd heard his sister describe him to a friend on the phone as "princely," and the word had seemed to sum him up precisely.

"Matt, weren't you at the Millstream bar the night of the fireworks?" Charlie said, jolting Matthew back into the present. He'd been reading on his iPad in between turns.

Matthew answered carefully.

"Yes . . ."

"Like at around seven, seven-thirty?"

"Probably."

"That guy Grollier was there. The barman remembers seeing him."

Matthew paused, waiting for Chloe to remind Charlie not to talk about this in front of Lily, but she seemed to have forgotten that useful restraint on Charlie's stubborn interest in the story.

"That's right," Matthew answered. "It was on the news yesterday. They were talking about it at Lily's party."

"You must have seen him there yourself."

"Huh. I hadn't thought of that."

"Apparently he got a call at the bar around seven-thirty and left in a hurry right after."

"Right. That's what they said."

"So you might have seen him talking on his phone."

Matthew was about to say he'd already left by seven-thirty, but decided to remain vague about the timing of his departure.

"I guess it's possible."

"Was the bar crowded?"

"Not especially."

"But you don't remember seeing him?"

"I mean, I don't really know what he looks like."

"Oh, he's unmistakable. He's a big guy, built like a tank. Kind of a loudmouth too, right, Chlo? You'd definitely know if you saw him. What I'm saying, Matt, is if you remember anything about him, it might be worth letting those people at the sheriff's department know. They obviously need all the help they can get."

Chloe had stood up. For a moment she remained motionless. Then, as if to explain the action, she went into the kitchen, murmuring that she'd be right back.

"You're right," Matthew said. His mouth had gone very dry.

"Even if it was just whether he was looking happy or upset while he talked."

"Yes. I'm trying to remember if I saw him."

"Your turn, Daddy," Lily said.

Charlie looked at his letters. Chloe came back in from the kitchen with a saucer of kumquats and chocolate. She put her hand gently on Charlie's shoulder.

"Maybe you shouldn't be on your screen while we're playing."

"Right. Right. Sorry."

They played on.

A few minutes later the game was interrupted again, this time by the ringing of the front doorbell. It was such a rare occurrence that all four looked at each other, as if unsure what the sound actually was.

Charlie stood up.

"Better not be those *Watchtower* people."

"Don't be rude to them if it is," Chloe called after him.

They heard the door opening and muffled voices. Charlie called back from the kitchen:

"Uh . . . it's the police, Chloe. They want to talk to us about Wade Grollier."

Chloe was still for a moment; her slight figure seeming to brace itself.

"Go to your room and practice, sweetheart," she said to Lily.

The girl left obediently. Chloe stood up, her face glassily expressionless, and climbed the three steps to the kitchen level. Matthew, whose first instinct was to absent himself, decided on second thought to follow after her.

In the kitchen Charlie motioned at a man in a jacket and tie.

"This is Detective—"

"Fernandez," the man said. "And my colleague, Officer Lombardi." He nodded toward a woman in uniform, who was wiping the rain from her face with a handkerchief.

Charlie introduced Chloe and Matthew. The detective shook their hands, wafting a scent of cologne from his jacket.

He looked about forty, with a thick black mustache and tired, dark eyes. The uniformed woman was younger, wide-shouldered and pale, her face a studious blank.

job, but it might be worth asking the barman if he remembers the book this woman was reading, if you're trying to track her down. Barmen notice that kind of thing."

The detective gazed at him mildly for a moment.

"That's a good idea."

"Maybe she could shed some light on this call Grollier got at the bar," Charlied continued, "because that's the real question you want answered here, isn't it? And why he left in such a hurry right after?"

"We'd certainly be interested in knowing that."

"The obvious inference, to me," Charlie said, "assuming you haven't traced the call—"

The detective kept his face impassive.

"—is that he was using a cash-only phone, which suggests either he was involved in something criminal, which I highly doubt, or else he was having some kind of clandestine relationship, in which case presumably there'd be traces in the house."

"Wasn't he living with that actress?" Matthew put in.

"Rachel Turpin, yeah," Charlie said. "But people do have affairs, you know. Maybe he was seeing someone up here." He laughed, pleased at his powers of deduction, and turned to the detective. "Did you guys think about that? Maybe that's why he was in Aurelia in the first place!"

Chloe, who'd been silent until now, said in a calm voice:

"Then why would he be picking up random women at the Millstream?"

That seemed to flummox Charlie.

"Good point, Chlo. Unless he was just some kind of compulsive philanderer . . ." He turned back to the detective. "Anyway,

all I'm saying, for what it's worth, is I personally don't think this mysterious phone call could have had anything to do with him getting killed. Because what would the scenario be? Someone luring him back to the house in order to murder him, which they did by stabbing him in the throat? That just sounds ridiculous."

The detective turned to Chloe.

"You say you talked to Mr. Grollier at this fund-raising event, when was it, two years ago?"

"About that."

"How would you describe him?"

"Well... we didn't talk for long. I actually didn't even remember I'd met him at all till my husband reminded me."

"Do you remember what you talked about?"

"No. I'm sure it was just, you know, party conversation."

"And he didn't make any particular impression on you?"

Chloe frowned.

"I seem to remember he was funny."

"He made you laugh?"

"I guess he must have."

"Had you seen any of his movies?"

Chloe hesitated fractionally.

"No."

"But you've seen them since?"

She looked at the detective, seeming to wonder how she'd prompted that question.

Lie, Matthew told her silently.

"Not that I recall," she said. "We haven't, have we, Charlie?"

"Definitely not."

She turned back to the detective:

"I didn't think so."

"And he never contacted you again after that meeting?"

She looked at Fernandez with an expression of placid indifference, as if she had no idea what he was driving at, and no interest in trying to guess.

"No," she said.

Attagirl! Matthew wanted to tell her. She'd been nervous, but when it came to it, her performance had been flawless.

The detective finished his coffee and set his mug down on the table next to the Scrabble board. He looked back through the pages of his notebook.

"You know what?" He smiled at each of them. "I think we're done."

He put his notepad away.

"You've been extremely helpful. Thank you all."

He leaned forward to get out of his seat. As he was rising, though, something seemed to stall him. The uniformed officer, who'd been sitting silently in the window seat, had just taken out her handkerchief again and blown her nose. Whether or not that had anything to do with it wasn't clear to Matthew, but some new thought appeared to register on the detective's face as he came to a halt, his unfolding body suspended midway between sitting and standing, his balding head angling back down toward the coffee table, staring at it. Slowly, carefully, as though an abrupt move might cause whatever it was he'd thought or seen to vanish, he lowered himself back down into the sofa.

"Although now, since we're here, maybe I should ask you just a couple more questions. Save us having to come back further down the road. Would that be okay with you?"

"Of course," Charlie said. "We're all extremely eager to get this cleared up. It isn't too relaxing knowing there's a killer wandering around out there. I was actually wondering at what point do you call in the big guns—you know, the state police, the FBI, whatever..."

Matthew let his eyes drift casually toward the coffee table, wondering what had caught the detective's attention. Could it have been something on the Scrabble board? He scanned the crisscrossing words, but on reflection the idea of a detective picking up some cryptic clue from a Scrabble game seemed unlikely.

"What I'm thinking"—Fernandez was tapping his pen against his notepad—"is that it would be helpful to have a record of what you were doing yourselves the night Mr. Grollier was killed."

Charlie gave an incredulous snort. "You mean our alibis?"

"Like I say, it's just so we have it on record," Fernandez said affably. "Dotting our *i*'s and crossing our *t*'s, so to speak."

"Of course," Chloe said politely. She had turned ashen since the detective had sat back down. "Charlie was in New York having dinner. Matthew and I were here all afternoon. Matthew went out to the Millstream bar—I think around six-thirty, right, Matt?" Matthew nodded. "And I left about ten minutes later to spend the evening with my cousin Jana in Lake Classon. Our daughter was still away at camp—that's her upstairs practicing. I can give you my cousin's number if you like."

"Thank you. We'll get all your details before we go."

Might it have been something about the books, then? Matthew looked at the lavish monographs and *catalogues raisonnés* of

Chloe's favorite photographers as closely as he dared: Nan Goldin, Robert Frank, the Helmut Newton book ... Was it possible that one of these had some unsuspected suggestion of Grollier about it? But that too seemed unlikely. He thought perhaps he'd been imagining things after all, and Fernandez really was just trying to make sure he didn't have to come back unnecessarily.

The detective had turned back to Charlie:

"And just so I have it straight, you came home after your dinner in New York, or you spent the night somewhere in the city?"

"Well, we have a home in the city too, but I came back here."

"What time did you leave?"

"Around ten. Happy to give you contact details of the people I was with."

"Thanks. So you got back here, what, around midnight?"

"Yeah, twelve, twelve-thirty," Charlie said airily.

"Twelve, twelve-thirty," the detective said, writing in his notepad. "And went straight to bed?"

"Yes," Charlie answered.

"Actually, Charlie," Matthew heard himself say, "wasn't that the night you had to stop for a nap on the Thruway?"

Charlie looked at him. He'd obviously thought the nap wasn't worth mentioning.

"Oh, yeah, you're right. I'd forgotten that. So it was probably a bit later."

"So ... what time, then, approximately?" the detective asked.

"Yeah, probably closer to one-thirty, two."

The detective looked down at his notepad, stroking his mustache for a moment.

"Thanks," he said, and turned to Matthew.

"And just to go back to the Millstream Inn, sir. You left at what time, approximately?"

"I'd say around seven-fifteen, seven-thirty."

"But you didn't see Mr. Grollier take a call on his phone."

"No. I think I'd have remembered if I had."

"Did you go to the fireworks?"

Matthew had already decided there was nothing to gain by pretending he'd been at the fireworks.

"No, I came back here. Got an early night."

The detective nodded, writing in his pad.

"All right." He turned to face Chloe and Charlie. "Now, if I could just ask if either of you have plans to travel over the next few days? Just in case we have other questions for you."

"No," Charlie said dryly. "We have friends coming to visit. I doubt we'll be leaving the house. Feel free to drop in anytime."

"I'm actually going to New York tomorrow for a few days," Matthew volunteered. "I'll be back on Thursday."

"Okay," the detective said, without great interest.

He stood up, his glance lingering a moment on the coffee table.

"What's the word for those little orange guys?" he said, pointing at the plate Chloe had brought in earlier. "My mom used to call them *quinotos* . . ."

"Those? Kumquats," Charlie said. "My wife's addicted to them. Kumquats and chocolate together. Preferably in the same bite. Right, Chlo? Help yourself."

"Maybe I'll take one for the road, and a little piece of chocolate." The detective took a kumquat and a piece of the dark chocolate.

"Let me just get those contacts from you," he said. "Then we'll be out of your hair."

The uniformed officer took down the contact details. Matthew looked at her, wondering again if she'd seen something, but there was nothing to be gleaned from her blank expression.

It was still raining when they left. Their car, an unmarked black Ford Explorer, sizzled on the wet as it pulled out. A few yellow leaves, fallen from the trees along the driveway, gleamed behind them on the darkened gravel.

.   .   .

"Morons," Charlie said, closing the door.

Chloe looked at him.

"You weren't very polite."

"I don't grovel to flunkies. Not my style. Anyway, the guy was completely out of line."

"He was just doing his job."

"His job? His job is to be down at that Rainbow encampment or over in Crackville or Methville"—those were Charlie's names for the two little run-down communities west of Aurelia where the county's poorest residents lived—"finding out whose deadbeat neighbor just tricked out his Chevy or came home from Sears with a brand-new log-splitter. Not lounging around nice people's houses sipping coffee and pretending to be Hercule Poirot. 'Dotting our *i*'s and crossing our *t*'s' . . . For fuck's sake!"

"Calm down, Charlie." Chloe was clearing off the table now, moving slowly, as if through some thicker element than air. She had the look of an accident victim trying to assess the damage while still absorbing the blow.

"I mean, he seemed to think it was seriously possible we had something to do with this business!"

"I don't think so."

"Come on, Chlo, he practically accused you of having an affair with the guy."

Chloe looked at her husband, her face wrung tight. For a terrible instant Matthew thought she was going to crack; spill it all. But she said quietly:

"You're getting carried away, Charlie."

Charlie glanced at her, holding her gaze for a moment before turning aside with a subdued, sheepish look.

"Sorry."

"Why don't you take Fu for a walk? He needs exercise."

"Good idea," Charlie muttered. "I could use some air myself."

Fu came padding in at the sound of his own name, and Charlie clipped on his leash. He'd put on his Burberry rain jacket and was just leading Fu out through the sliding door when he turned back to Matthew.

"By the way, Matt. I thought you were leaving us for good tomorrow. I didn't realize you were coming back."

"Oh!" Matthew said. "Well, if you'd rather I didn't . . ."

"No. I'd just forgotten."

"Of course we want you to come back," Chloe said, looking sharply at Charlie.

"Of course," Charlie echoed. "I'm just saying, I'd forgotten. I'll see you later."

He went out with the dog.

He's upset about me contradicting him in front of Fernandez, Matthew thought, watching Charlie through the glass

doors. Well, he'd certainly made Charlie look like a liar. Had he intended to? He hoped not. It was a matter of principle with him not to indulge any feelings of ill will toward Charlie. Not for Charlie's sake, but his own. His sense of personal dignity was tightly bound up in the disavowal of anything that might have been termed resentment. The position he had taken, from the start, was that he was above such pettiness. He preferred to be thought pragmatic, even coldly detached, than vindictive.

He stared out at his cousin: the tall, straight figure walking away from him, as it always was in Matthew's imagination; the slight stiffness of his bearing conveying, as it always had, Charlie's obstinate sense of the world's being forever in his debt. For a brief moment Matthew allowed himself to recall how he had acquiesced in that sense; unprotestingly handing over his own existence when Charlie had required it of him. *After all, Matt, things are already screwed for you, so you might as well . . .* It was the first time since coming to America, he realized, that he'd permitted himself a direct glance at this incident through the intervening years, but the words came back as clearly as if Charlie had just spoken them.

Lily was still upstairs. Alone with Chloe, Matthew felt an unaccustomed awkwardness. She seemed to be waiting for him to say something about the interview, but it was hard to think of anything that wouldn't sound either too knowing or too bland. He wondered if he should make some comment on her lie about not seeing Grollier's movies. It occurred to him that if he didn't, she might think he was deliberately making things easier for her—effectively colluding in the deception—which in turn

might make her wonder why. Maybe that was what she was waiting for: some harmless explanation. He plunged in:

"I thought that was extremely cool of you, telling the detective you hadn't seen Grollier's movies."

She looked away, but he had a feeling he'd been right.

"Oh ... I just didn't feel like going into it."

"That's what I assumed," Matthew said quickly. "I'd have felt the same. The guy was obviously just stirring things up for the sake of it. Making insinuations, like Charlie said. Why should you play along with it? I was impressed. It showed real sangfroid, as my father would have said."

She opened her mouth, closed it again, and then said:

"What if I *had* been having an affair with Grollier?"

"Ha!" Matthew exclaimed, trying to sound lightheartedly amused.

"Seriously ..."

"Well ..."

"I'd be in trouble right now for not having told them, wouldn't I?"

"I guess so. If they found out."

"They'd find out, don't you think?"

"Why?"

"Like Charlie said, if he was having an affair up here, there'd be traces of it all over the house, wouldn't there? Hair, body fluids ..."

"I suppose. But they'd have to have some reason to try to match them to any particular individual, wouldn't they? I mean, they couldn't just demand DNA samples from every beautiful woman in Aurelia ..."

"I imagine they'd figure it out, sooner or later," Chloe said, ignoring the compliment. "They aren't actually idiots, whatever Charlie thinks."

"Well, even if they did, so what? It's not as if it would help solve the murder. Unless you did it yourself!" Matthew laughed.

"All the same, I should probably tell them, shouldn't I? I mean, if I *had* been having an affair?"

She was practically confessing. In fact he wondered if at this point it would even be plausible for him to go on pretending she wasn't. But if he let her talk, he knew he'd have to tell her to go to the cops, or else risk looking shifty himself. It struck him that she probably *wanted* him to tell her to go to the cops; that she was looking to him precisely for reassurance that it was the right thing, and that she shouldn't be afraid. Well, he was damned if he was going to do that.

"Depends if you wanted to get dragged into a murder investigation," he said. "Have the affair splashed all over the papers . . . I don't imagine the police would keep it secret for long."

"I thought they sometimes made deals about that kind of thing . . ."

"That seems highly unlikely. Anyway, since you presumably *weren't* having an affair with the guy and didn't kill him, there's no need to torment yourself, is there?"

Matthew smiled at her as encouragingly as he could, wishing he could just tell her she'd handled the detective impeccably, and that she had nothing to worry about.

She nodded vaguely.

"I should go and shop for dinner," he said, eager to change the subject. "Anything you need?"

"No, thanks.

"I'll make something nice."

She managed a frail smile.

"You always make something nice, Matt."

He drove off. At a deer farm by the Thruway that advertised all-season meat, he bought a short loin of venison. She'd told him once that venison was her favorite meat, and he wanted to cook something special for her. He'd begun to think he might not be coming back after all. Not that he felt in any immediate danger, but it seemed tempting fate to come back to Aurelia while the police were—effectively, though they didn't know it—looking for him. Also, Charlie obviously didn't want him around.

• • •

Both cars were gone from the driveway when he got back. He was putting his purchases in the fridge when he saw what had been somehow invisible to him earlier: the little dish of kumquats and chocolates that Chloe had brought out during the game of Scrabble. They'd been on the coffee table, staring him in the face all the time he'd been trying to figure out what the detective had seen. She'd left the same snack in the A-frame. He could see it in his mind's eye, down on the glass table beside the love seat. He'd even been dimly aware of it in the darkness and tumult of his departure, but far from thinking he should get rid of it, he'd thought it added a natural touch to the scenario he'd tried to create, of a random burglary gone wrong. *Quinotos*, he thought, remembering the detective's word ... Had the guy been deliberately signaling to Chloe that he was on to her? Giving her

a chance to tell him about her affair in private? Was that where she'd picked up the idea of some kind of confidentiality deal? In which case, he wondered uneasily, what was she doing right now?

He was still unpacking the food when he heard a car pull up outside. Chloe came into the house. She was wearing a white blouse, gray skirt and blue Mary Janes.

She regarded him a moment, the bones of her face outlined by a shaft of sunlight piercing the trees along the driveway. He smiled at her.

"You look like you've been to a job interview!"

"I went to church. I haven't been for a while."

"They have services in the afternoon?"

"Yes."

He turned away, not wanting to look too interested.

"Did you go to confession?" he asked, putting the meat in the fridge.

"Of course."

"I can't imagine," he said, "what someone as saintly as you could possibly find to say inside a confessional."

"Oh, there's always something."

He turned back to her.

"Charlie took Lily tubing," she said. "They'll be home by six-thirty. We should eat early if that's okay."

She went out of the kitchen. He heard her open the bar fridge by the drinks cabinet in the living room, before climbing the stairs up to her bedroom.

He wasn't sure what to think. It made a certain amount of sense, he supposed, that she'd go to church. She'd certainly have

been in need of relief from the unremitting tension of the last few days, and maybe she'd decided this was a safer bet than going to the police. Priests were sworn to secrecy, as far as he knew. Anyway she'd have been careful about that, knowing her; kept anything identifiable with Grollier out of whatever story she'd told. No doubt there were established formulas she could use without going into details. Father, I've strayed from my vows, or something. The priest would have given her some Hail Marys, and told her to end the affair. And, of course, she'd be able to assure him that she already had.

But he had a feeling that she'd been lying to him: that she had in fact just been confessing her affair to Detective Fernandez.

Well, suppose she had? That didn't automatically spell catastrophe. It was even possible, he thought, peering into the murky entanglements of the situation, that it might actually do some good. It would clarify Grollier's connection to the household, which in turn might put an end to further investigation. Even if it didn't, suspicion would naturally fall first on Charlie, as the deceived husband, especially after Charlie's lie about what time he got home the night of the murder, which at the very least would buy Matthew some time, for whatever that was worth. All the same, he realized, he'd feel better if he could convince himself that Chloe really had just gone to church.

He poured himself a stiff gin and tonic. Aside from everything else, he didn't think he could face Charlie, after that little clash earlier, without some alcohol inside him.

· · ·

There was a Sous Vide machine in the pantry, which Charlie had given Chloe a couple of years ago, after she'd raved about the food at some French place out in Sag Harbor. Neither of them had learned how to use it, so it had stood on the shelf in its manufacturer's box ever since Chloe had unwrapped it. Matthew, who found the whole Sous Vide system with its high-tech pretensions and nasty little cooking bags thoroughly unappealing, had avoided it all summer despite some strong hints from Charlie. But he'd decided to inaugurate it tonight. Along with the venison itself, it would make a nice parting gesture for Chloe. She'd have no idea that that was what it was until much later, of course, but that was fine. She would look back and remember he'd cooked venison for her, using a troublesome method that he'd never shown any personal interest in mastering, and it would cast him, retroactively, in just the right light of sentimental self-abnegation.

Topping up his drink, he salted the lean crimson meat, vacuum-sealed it in one of the plastic pouches, and set it to cook. He'd picked up boysenberries for a compote, a red cabbage to braise with a slab of pig cheek, and potatoes for a herbed spaetzle.

At six-thirty the convertible drew up outside, disgorging Charlie and Lily.

Charlie barely greeted him. He glanced at the Sous Vide machine as he walked past it, but didn't comment.

"I thought I'd set up the Sous Vide," Matthew said.

Charlie turned back briefly.

"Oh, that's what that is."

"I bought some venison."

"Uh-huh? Chlo likes venison. I'm not crazy about it myself. When are we eating?"

"Shouldn't be long."

Charlie moved on out through the kitchen and disappeared upstairs, Lily following briskly behind. Matthew didn't know whether to be amused or offended by Charlie's rudeness. It was weirdly crass, but then Charlie had never been one to disguise his feelings, and he was obviously still angry about being contradicted in front of the detective.

Chloe made a little more effort to seem interested in the Sous Vide, when she came down.

"That's exciting," she said, filling her wine glass.

"Well . . . I hope it lives up to expectations . . ."

She gave a distracted smile. She seemed to have retreated somewhere even deeper inside herself during the last hour. She'd clearly drunk quite a bit too. Not that Matthew was exactly sober himself.

The meat came out of its pouch the same raw burgundy color it had been when it went in. He'd forgotten that peculiarity of the Sous Vide. Along with the boysenberries and red cabbage, there was something unnervingly purplish about the whole dish.

"You don't have a blowtorch, do you?" he asked, catching a flicker of dismay on Chloe's face. "I could sear it . . ."

"I'm sure it'll taste fine."

"You know what?" Charlie said, looking at it. "I'm just going to grab some cheese and eat up in my office. I have a ton of work to do before these people come tomorrow. You don't mind, do you, Chlo?"

Chloe looked blankly at her husband, and then shrugged. Under normal circumstances, Matthew felt, she wouldn't have let him get away with that. But she clearly wasn't in a state to confront anyone just now.

She barely said a word throughout the meal, and barely touched her food. Lily gazed at her anxiously.

"Are you okay, Mommy?"

Chloe gave her daughter a helpless look, her eyes wide and searching, as if trying to locate her through some thick mist.

"I'm fine, sweetheart."

The girl drifted off upstairs.

Alone with Chloe, Matthew said, before he could stop himself:

"Charlie's angry with me, isn't he?"

He could tell at once that Charlie had already talked to her. They must have spoken before Charlie took Lily tubing.

"Is he?" she said. "About what?"

"I don't know. I should ask him, I suppose."

She looked away uncomfortably.

"Well, actually, I think I do know," he said.

"Why?"

"He thinks I was trying to make him look like a liar in front of that detective. Chipping in about his nap on the Thruway."

"Well . . ." She looked up at him, her eyes settling candidly on his. "Were you?"

Something in her expression, a look of deliberate challenge, made him think of the things he'd heard her tell Grollier; all that crap about blackmailing Charlie.

"No, I wasn't. It just happened to be the truth."

"You weren't trying to—" She broke off.

"What?"

"I don't know . . . damage his reputation or something?"

"Huh?"

"Right before his deal goes through?"

So that was what Charlie had thought! As usual his cousin was a degree or two more cunning than him in his thinking. Chloe faced him again.

"I mean, it wouldn't be good if his partners knew he'd been brought in for questioning in connection with a murder, would it?"

"Why would I want to spoil his deal?"

"I don't know. Maybe you have something against him?"

She was looking at him more coolly than he liked.

An urge to set her straight seized him. Why *not* tell her? he thought. It wasn't as if keeping the damn thing to himself all these years had done him any good. He'd told no one; not his mother or sister, not even Dr. McCubbin. It would have seemed a kind of special pleading, a bid for mercy or—worse—pity, and he'd had too much pride to allow himself that, even as a fourteen-year-old. Pride, courage, dignity . . . all those fine qualities were supposed to be their own reward. But really, what good had they done him? What difference had it made to be a proud wreck, a dignified fuckup?

"How could I possibly have anything against him?" he said, and then added, with careful nonchalance, "I mean, aside from that business when we were at school together. But that was a million years ago. Besides, I never held it against him."

"What business?"

"He hasn't told you about it?"

"No."

"You knew I was thrown out, though?"

"Yes ... but I didn't think it had anything to do with Charlie."

She looked a bit apprehensive suddenly, which was certainly better than that coldly appraising stare.

"Ha. That's funny, I thought he would have told you."

She caught his eye, and he could tell she knew he was being disingenuous. He didn't care, though.

"I mean, it was nothing, really, just schoolboy stuff. I wouldn't have mentioned it if I didn't think you already knew ..."

He paused, savoring the look of alarm on Chloe's face. Something actively malignant seemed to have awoken inside him.

"What are you trying to tell me, Matthew?"

"Nothing at all. I'll stop right now if you don't want to hear it."

"What did Charlie do?" she said quietly.

"Oh, you know, he'd been through a rough time. His mother had just died. He'd started a year late at this very English school, not knowing anyone, except me, of course, but obviously feeling he deserved a place somewhat higher up the social hierarchy. You know how Charlie is. He did rise pretty quickly, but there was a little cabal at the top of our year that he couldn't crack; kids friendly with the year above, which was where girls started—below that it was still all boys—which in turn meant parties and clubs and all that stuff. There was one kid, some sort of delinquent aristo with access to high-grade

drugs, who kept the group supplied till he was busted smoking a joint in St. James's Park and the headmaster expelled him. Charlie stepped into the breach."

"Dealing?"

"Yes. Right away, before he even knew where he could procure anything, he let it be known to this group that he was open for business. This all happened in the period right after my father's disappearance, by the way. Our household had been turned upside down. My mother could barely put a sandwich together for our meals. My sister, who was supposed to be going to university, went off to live with some Anglican nuns instead. I was just in a sort of zombie state most of the time, too confused to know what I was feeling. Helping Charlie find a supplier seemed a perfectly natural thing to do. I took him to the Kensington Market, which was this place full of goths and punks and old gray-haired hippies. We were offered grass right away and for a while Charlie just bought the stuff there and resold it at school for a small profit. But then he realized he could do better buying it wholesale. Also people were asking for other things—speed, acid, coke . . . Anyway, we persuaded the guy we were buying from to introduce us to his dealer—"

"We? You were partners in this?"

"No, not really. I was more like his assistant, his gofer. Or maybe 'apprentice' would be the word, given the illustrious career I went on to later. We'd fetch the stuff from our new friend Rudy out in Hounslow together and bag it up in my bedroom, and sometimes I'd be the one who actually handed it over to the kids buying it. But it was his operation. All the

money was his—incoming as well as outgoing. Anyway, there was this girl in the year above who bought a tab of acid from Charlie. Henrietta Vine. She dropped it at a birthday party in Manchester Square and ran out into Oxford Street on her way home while she was hallucinating. She thought the buses and taxis were weightless as balloons."

He paused again, aware of the tension in Chloe's body in her chair opposite him.

"What happened to her?"

"She was hit by a taxi. She had both legs broken and most of her ribs cracked. The school moved quickly to find out where she'd got hold of the stuff. It didn't take long for our names to come up."

"Yours and Charlie's?"

"Yes."

"But ... Charlie wasn't thrown out?"

"No."

"Why not?"

"Why do you think?"

She looked uncomprehendingly at him a moment, until it dawned on her.

"He got you to take the blame?"

Matthew shrugged.

"Well, as Charlie said when we were told to report to the headmaster's office, 'After all, Matt, things are already screwed for you, so you might as well.'"

She was staring at him, her eyes very wide, and he stared back, feeling the words go in hard and deep.

"And ... you agreed?"

"It seemed reasonable to me."

"Reasonable?"

"I mean, I'd have been kicked out anyway, so why not at least try to save Charlie's skin? There was no point both of us going down if we didn't have to, was there?"

"Why you, though? Why not him?"

"Oh, because he was right. Things *were* already screwed for me."

His voice had started thickening, he realized. Telling her the story was having an unexpected effect on him. It was as if he were hearing it himself for the first time, and only now grasping the full extent of its implications.

He looked away; unsure, suddenly, if he was speaking out of a wish to avenge himself on Charlie or just, somehow, to account for himself to Chloe. Maybe the two motives had become inseparable.

"That's what the whole incident made clear—really for the first time," he said, managing a dry smile. "I hadn't actually seen my father's disappearance as quite the unmitigated disaster it was until Charlie pointed it out, if you can believe it. But he was right. So, yes, I agreed to take the blame."

He cleared his throat.

"But, you know . . . it's all water under the bridge as far as I'm concerned. Extremely ancient water under an extremely far-off bridge."

Chloe looked acutely distressed.

"Oh, Matthew," she said. It wasn't much, but it seemed to him he'd never heard anything quite so sympathetically anguished in his life; not on his behalf. He'd never wanted

pity—hers or anyone else's—and he hoped that wasn't what she was feeling now. But whatever emotion was filling her eyes with that look of infinite tenderness, it seemed to be doing him good.

In the silence that followed, he became aware of a familiar ticking sound behind him, in the entranceway to the kitchen. He turned around. Charlie was standing there. Judging from his posture, fully immobile and utterly silent except for the ticking of his Patek Philippe, he'd been there for some time. Chloe must have seen him appear and decided to let him listen. He looked right through Matthew. Chloe spoke:

"You never told me any of that, Charlie."

A scoffing sound came from Charlie.

"You should have told me," Chloe said.

Abruptly, Charlie stepped forward into the room, grabbing his rain jacket.

"I'm going into town to get something decent to eat," he said. "I'll see you later."

He strode out through the front door, slamming it behind him.

"Charlie!" Chloe shouted. A moment later she ran out after him. Matthew could hear her calling Charlie's name in the rain, then the slam of a car door and Chloe yelling, her voice louder than he'd ever heard it: "Don't you dare! Don't you dare, Charlie!" followed by the pounding of a fist on the car roof: hard enough to dent the paneling, by the sound of it. Charlie must have got out of the car then: Matthew heard the car door close again, more quietly, and Charlie's voice, very controlled, saying: "I don't have to defend myself against that

little shit," followed by Chloe, her voice audibly constricted with rage, answering: "You'd better, Charlie, or you'll regret it." There was a long pause, then Charlie's voice hissed: "Not here." Matthew heard their brisk footsteps crunch on the gravel as they walked around the side of the house. A few minutes later they came in through the glass doors and went silently upstairs. For some time, as he cleared up the kitchen, Matthew heard voices through the ceiling. He'd never heard them fight before, and would have liked to hear what they said, but he couldn't make it out. Still, the anger in Chloe's muffled voice was unmistakable, and it seemed to him inconceivable that there weren't going to be some painful repercussions for Charlie, down the line. Chloe might be capable of loving a man she was betraying, but he seriously doubted she'd be able to go on living with a man she despised. And how, he wondered, allowing himself for the first time a steely satisfaction in what his words had surely wrought, how could she not despise Charlie after this? He felt as though he'd discharged himself of some indissolubly corrosive substance. Now let it spread its ruin somewhere else.

· · ·

It was still raining when he went to bed. The pines stood dripping behind the guesthouse, dark and immense. Glittering strings ran from the ungutttered octagonal eaves. He opened the door and slid the suitcase out from under the bed, half expecting, as he always did, the things inside to have rearranged themselves, so bristlingly volatile had they become in his imagination. They lay exactly as he had left them. Still,

that was something to look forward to: getting rid of this junk. It made him nervous having it there. Several times he'd been on the verge of taking it out; bringing it to the town landfill with the rest of the household garbage. But the thought of some dogged detective or beady-eyed municipal worker spotting something had held him back. Better to dump it all in the city.

It came to him as he lay in bed that he should put the knife in Charlie's safe.

The idea filled him with a strange delight. He pictured the knife lying there, where the Tiffany bracelet had lain at the beginning of the summer. There was something apt and satisfying about the image. It was where Charlie himself would have put it, he decided, if he really had killed Grollier: stashed it there till he came up with a foolproof spot to get rid of it once and for all. Or no, perhaps he'd want to keep it there: hold on to it as some sort of perverse souvenir; the next best thing to the actual scalp of his wife's lover . . .

He imagined Detective Fernandez turning up in Cobble Hill after an anonymous tipoff, armed with a warrant; Charlie's disdainful grin as he showed him the safe and keyed in the date of his mother's death; the look turning to bewilderment as the steel door opened . . . That would be a sight to behold! But of course I'd be long gone by then, Matthew remembered . . . That seemed to be an indispensable element in the idea taking shape in him; the sense of himself radically elsewhere, under a hot blue sky in some place well out of reach of Detective Fernandez and the East Deerfield Sheriff's Department. Because Charlie, knowing Charlie, would surely wriggle out

of it one way or another, and sooner or later the trail would resume its original course and destination.

Not that you could physically disappear anymore. That option, such a primordial human yearning, had gone the way of those off-the-grid backwaters that had once made it possible. But you could still vanish by becoming someone else. There'd been endless talk about that when his father ran off. People had suggested he might have found his way to Belize or somewhere in Southeast Asia; acquired a false passport through one of the document-forging operations in Port Loyola or Bangkok, and started life afresh in some tropical hideaway.

Why not follow in his father's footsteps? The idea had a certain inexorable logic about it, after all, or at least a certain fateful appeal. And it wasn't as if he hadn't thought about it before. It had been present in his mind intermittently throughout his adult life; a fantasy of familial reconvergence that had often comforted him in times of stress.

Of course, there was the little matter of money to consider. His father had had the equivalent of well over a million dollars with him when he disappeared, whereas Matthew, when he last checked, had a little under five grand. The disparity made him smile in the darkness of his room. What a failure he was, compared to his old man! How petty and unambitious the field of his own endeavors!

It was only at this juncture in these drifting nocturnal ruminations that what might have been obvious from the start, had he been more willing to accept the role of vengeful malcontent that life seemed so eager to confer upon him,

became apparent. Not that the timing of it altered its complexion in any fundamental way; he was aware of that. But it meant something to him that the idea hadn't been premeditated.

The money would come from Charlie's safe.

The knife would go in and the money would come out.

It was so simple, and so obvious, that the registering of it felt almost irrelevant; as if it had been arranged long ago by providence, and had always been going to happen, whether or not he knew it in advance.

He saw, in his mind's eye, the blocks of cash in the shadows behind the Cipro bottles, stacked in towers of different heights like their own little Financial District. A million and a half dollars: Wasn't that what Charlie had told him?

He remembered how disappointed Charlie had seemed by his reaction to the sight of all that "moolah." He'd seemed to want Matthew to be impressed, and so Matthew had obligingly pretended to be. But in the peculiar mood that had risen in him now—a sort of euphoric clairvoyance—it occurred to him that perhaps Charlie had wanted something else too: that he'd wanted him not just to be impressed by the money, but to *take* it.

Was that possible? Was that, at some half-conscious level, why Charlie forgot the bracelet in the first place and had Matthew go back and open the safe and see what it contained? Had he been *offering* me the money? Matthew wondered. Hoping I'd scoop it up and disappear out of his life once and for all? Was Matthew's failure to do so the real reason why Charlie was sending him back to the house now?

Absurd! And yet there was something persuasive about the

notion; an insidious plausibility that seemed to require him to weigh it seriously in his mind.

Because Charlie owed him; there was no doubt about that. And Charlie knew it too. He surely remembered as well as Matthew those words he'd spoken as they crossed the schoolyard to the headmaster's office a quarter century ago. Or even if he'd forgotten the words themselves, he couldn't have forgotten the intent behind them. Because he'd certainly given every indication of *regretting* that intent. Even of wanting forgiveness for it. God knows he'd been eager enough to fork over the little loans Matthew had been compelled to ask for at moments of desperation over the years; often throwing in a few hundred dollars extra as if to convey his awareness that it was he, Charlie, who was getting the real relief from these transactions, the real easing of burdens . . . And judging from his behavior these past few weeks, he'd have been happy, more than happy, to make one last act of contrition in order to secure the permanent disappearance of his problematic cousin.

A million and a half dollars. It wouldn't seriously harm Charlie, but it was a decent sum. Not excessive, considering the fact that, in addition to everything else, Matthew had also done Charlie the favor (he hadn't seen it in quite this way before, but it was indisputable now that he thought of it) of eliminating his wife's lover. But certainly an acceptable sum. A person could surely get whatever it took to start life afresh, with a million and a half bucks, and still have plenty left over. It wasn't as if he intended to be idle. He'd go somewhere quiet, low-key. Buy a place with a little land. Find some locals to go

into business with. Plant gardens and orchards with them; raise chickens and goats. He'd always liked the idea of a communal enterprise; the company of some like-minded people to nourish the spirit and soften the drudgery of work. He'd accepted too unprotestingly the isolating conditions of work in London and then New York; the ethos of every man for himself. His new life would be more openhearted, more spacious and purposeful, than the mere getting-by he'd settled for in the past. He'd always known there was something narrow and aimless, something wearyingly selfish, in the way he'd gone about things in the past. An absence of thought for anything beyond the limits of his own immediate wants and needs. It was never the life he would have chosen, but choice had never seemed a very serious component in his existence. You just grabbed what you could from the few things that presented themselves. Even when he'd gone in with those others—an entertainment lawyer, a couple who invested in artisanal food start-ups, a former City Hall official who knew how to oil the wheels of the city's permit bureacracy—on that farm-to-table project, they'd each been in it purely for their own private gain. It was just business; only ever just business, which was perhaps why it hadn't excited him in the end, even though he'd made a little money out of it.

Well, here was his opportunity to do things differently. To be a better person; live a more generous life! Wasn't that what he wanted, more than anything? Wasn't it what everybody wanted? He could work hard; physically as well as mentally: he knew that. Everyone could work hard under the right conditions, and it was possible to enjoy hard work, even the most numbing, backbreaking toil. But you had to have a sense of participating in some greater good than just the maintaining of your own small existence; some human quorum or congregation of a size sufficient to align you *with* the world instead of against it. The imagination had to be fired, and kept alight. The heart had to feel the presence of joy and warmth. He saw that very clearly now, and for a moment he seemed to see himself as if in a dreamlike film, surrounded by kindred spirits at the warm center of some bustling enterprise in which food, wine, starlight, warm breezes and the sounds of human conviviality combined like the elements of some ancient ceremony to plunge the parched spirit back into the flow of life's inexhaustible abundance.

It struck him that in a peculiar way the difficulties he'd hoped to resolve during his stay up here in Aurelia were being resolved, now, in spite of everything. Perhaps even *because* of everything! It was a strange thought: that in order to win this reprieve, he'd had to do precisely the things he had done. That killing Grollier was, in fact, the necessary condition for this second chance at life . . . A vertiginous thought. And yet it too seemed to have something dimly plausible about it. In the darkness of the little guesthouse with the dwindling rain pattering erratically on the shingle roof, it seemed to him he might have just stumbled, rather late in life (and very late, in comparison with his cousin Charlie), on some fundamental secret about happiness and fulfillment.

He knew where he was going to go, of course. He hadn't been there since he was a boy, but as he lay thinking of it now it was as vivid to him as though he'd been living there all his life. He saw the bustling port with its pink customs building and wooden houses drowning in hibiscus and frangipani. He remembered the narrow cement road that wound up through the old coconut plantations into hills where the air smelled of goats and nutmeg and woodsmoke. He thought of the little restaurant high above the yacht harbor where they'd sit on the balcony every afternoon, counting the different blues of the bay and watching the sinking sun throw javelins of shadow through the forest of masts. There was no airstrip on the island, and at that time there was no ferry either, and the journey itself was one of the highlights of the holiday, with its combination (irresistible to a schoolboy) of luxury and inconvenience. They'd fly to Barbados, then squeeze into a series of successively smaller planes and air taxis until they arrived on the neighboring island, where, as night fell, they'd board the "schooner" (an old wooden banana boat) to their own island, sharing the broad-planked deck with islanders carrying caged guinea fowl and sacks of mangoes and soursops. Once they'd reached the open sea, the crew would raise two rust-colored sails that bellied out enormously in the warm breeze, and the rest of the journey would pass without any engine racket, just the bubbling of their wake and the chatter of island voices with their beautiful, lilting English. The stars would come out and after an hour they'd start to see the glitter of the little port and catch that sweet fragrance from the hills, and the feeling of imminent adventure would be almost overwhelming.

Drifting to sleep, he saw the blue-shuttered Tranqué Bay Hotel where they'd wake to the brilliance of the Caribbean morning, and race each other past the old stone ruins to the beach. It was there, after they'd swum and breakfasted, and installed themselves on deck chairs in the shade of the stately palms, that his father would look up at the turquoise house on the hillside across the bay, half hidden in foaming blossoms, and announce that if the family ever came into any serious money, *that* was the house he would buy.

Well, the family was about to come into some serious money.

thirteen

He woke early. The air was moist, cluttered with scents from the wet trees and some late-blooming roses. He breathed in deeply as he walked down the little rocky path. It was his last day at the house: he was sure of that now, and he felt a sentimental wish to supply himself with good things to remember about it. The air, always so fresh and sweet compared to Bushwick, was one of those things.

Chloe was in the utility room off the kitchen, putting sheets in the dryer. She straightened up, hearing him come in.

"Hi, Matthew."

There were dark circles under her eyes. She and Charlie had still been quarreling when he went to bed last night. He was curious to hear what Charlie'd had to say for himself, though he didn't feel he should ask directly. Chloe was looking at him,

her expression a little uncomfortable, as if she had something difficult to report but wasn't sure how to broach it.

"Want some breakfast?" he asked airily. "I thought I'd make shirred eggs."

"Actually, I was wondering if I could ask you a favor?"

"Of course."

"Would you mind running into town and picking up some pastries? It's just that we have to get the place ready for these visitors, and Shelley's away, so I thought we'd keep the cooking to a minimum." Shelley was the cleaner.

"No problem."

"Thanks, Matt."

He drove into town, reluctant to believe this errand was really all she'd had on her mind. She'd wanted to talk about Charlie, he sensed, but had qualms about doing it. Which suggested she'd had something less than flattering to say about her husband. In other words, it was all exactly as he had predicted! The only surprise was how quickly the process had begun. It crossed his mind that Chloe had spent the night in the guest room, too appalled by what she'd learned about Charlie to sleep with him. He quelled an impulse to rejoice, but he couldn't pretend he wasn't gratified by the idea of Charlie's domestic contentment being shattered.

He pulled in behind the hardware store, parking by their fleet of hydraulic machines—diggers, augurs, log-splitters, leaf-mulchers—that stood along the rental section like strange, demonic beasts. Early to Bread was busy, and it was several minutes before his turn came at the register. He ordered the usual selection of muffins and scones and took them back to the truck.

There was no sign of life in the house when he got back. He arranged the pastries on a dish at the center of the kitchen table and went to the guesthouse. His bus didn't leave Aurelia till two in the afternoon but he thought he might as well get his packing done. It didn't take long. As he looked around the octagonal room one last time, it occurred to him he could replicate it where he was going. Not the view, of course; he'd be looking over the sapphire waters of Tranqué Bay or somewhere like it, assuming all went well, but the furnishings and the rough plank walls. And maybe there *would* be a view of a pool through one of the windows someday, with a butterfly garden next to it just like Chloe's. At this thought the image of Chloe herself, charged by the realization that he wouldn't be seeing her again, flooded him with an emotion so intense she seemed almost palpably present in the room, and for a moment he had the impression that he could smell her scent, and that if he were to reach out he could touch her living hand.

As he wheeled his suitcase through the pool gate, she came out of Charlie's meditation garden, carrying her phone.

"Oh, hi," she said, putting the phone away. "You're back."

He smiled, feeling the familiar jolt of reentry as he passed from that realm of secret communion with her to the plane of ordinary conversation.

"I put the pastries on the kitchen table," he said.

She thanked him vaguely, and offered to reimburse him.

"Don't be silly."

She was looking even more uncomfortable than she had before.

"Listen, Matthew..."

He tilted his head sympathetically, convinced he was finally about to hear that his story last night had forced some fundamental reappraisal of the man she was married to. But he was wrong again.

"I've just found out there's a direct bus from East Deerfield at nine-thirty," she said, speaking quickly. "I need to go in this morning anyway, so I thought maybe I should take you to that instead of the later one. How would that be? It'll save us having to go out again in the afternoon, and it'll also be a much quicker journey for you..."

She sounded nervous, he thought. She must have been afraid he'd be upset about being turfed out early. But he was actually relieved not to have to linger. Aside from giving him more time in New York to organize himself, it would get him out of having to confront Charlie before he left, which he'd been dreading.

"Whatever's easiest for you."

"We'd have to leave right away."

"No problem. I'm all packed. I just need the key."

She looked blank.

"To your house. I'm staying there."

"Oh. Right. I'll get it."

She went ahead of him, moving briskly while he wheeled his suitcase over the lawn, and met him in the kitchen with the Cobble Hill keys.

"Charlie's still in bed, but..."

"That's okay. I'll see him on Thursday." It seemed important to maintain the fiction that he was going to be returning later in the week. "Assuming I'm allowed back..." He smiled

ruefully, hoping the remark might finally get them onto the topic of last night's row. But she didn't respond, and as soon as they got into the Lexus she started her infuriating humming once again, the soft drone as effective a barrier to conversation as a diving bell would have been. She kept it up all the way through Aurelia and onto the county road beyond. He gazed out through the window, doing his best to ignore both the humming itself and the insensitivity it seemed to imply. Small houses straggled from the outskirts of town: dilapidated old clapboard cottages and the vinyl-sided bungalows referred to, in the optimistic American parlance, as "ranch" houses, as if they had a thousand head of cattle around the back. His mind went to his cramped apartment in Bushwick, with its living room window facing a wall, and a momentary gloom descended on him until he remembered he wasn't going to be living there anymore. The new life he'd charted out last night seemed to be only fitfully present in his mind. He concentrated, trying to make it more real for himself.

Still humming, Chloe turned onto Route 39, the busy highway into East Deerfield. He couldn't help feeling a little hurt by her uncommunicativeness. He'd bared his soul to her, after all, and she'd obviously been moved by what he'd told her. At the very least, he thought, she owed it to him to reveal what Charlie had had to say for himself. Had he professed any guilt about his actions? Matthew wondered. Any remorse? Not that it would make any material difference at this point, but he'd have liked to know. He stared out again, watching the familiar old landmarks reel past: gravel quarry, furniture liquidation store, Swedish Auto . . . As they loomed up and disappeared, he tried

to impress on himself that it was the last time he'd be seeing any of them; that this phase of his life, the American phase, was over. Here were the unfinished McMansions of a residential development abandoned after the financial meltdown, plywood walls blackening under peeling skins of Tyvek. Charlie liked to point these out as an example of why bankers needed to be regulated. "Repealing Glass-Steagall," he'd declare in that righteous way of his, "was the banking equivalent of legalizing assault weapons." It occurred to Matthew that Charlie too had disappeared out of his life for the last time; striding out through the kitchen last night and slamming the door behind him.

"So what did Charlie have to say about what I told you?" he blurted, unable to contain himself any longer.

Chloe stopped humming. They'd reached the traffic circle outside East Deerfield and she slowed down, taking the exit for the bus station. He saw the tip of her tongue dart out to moisten her lips.

"You mean about the . . . thing at your school?"

"Yes."

She paused for a long moment before answering, and kept her eyes steadily on the road as she finally spoke.

"He said you were lying."

Matthew was too stunned to speak for a moment. It was as though Charlie had just punched him in the face.

"What?" he said.

"He said you'd made the whole thing up."

"My god! Did you believe him?"

"No. I told him I thought that would be totally out of character for you."

"Thank you," he said, hugely relieved. "And what did he say to that?"

Chloe glanced in the mirror, but stared forward immediately, as if avoiding his eye. He understood: she'd been put in an extremely awkward position, effectively having to choose between himself and her husband. No wonder she'd been looking so uncomfortable earlier. Still, at least she'd had the decency to abide by her own instinct for the truth. It certainly would have been easier to go along with Charlie's monstrous little invention. She answered him, speaking with a kind of wavering but determined firmness:

"He said you were a crook. He . . . he said you always had been."

"Christ! That's a bit desperate, isn't it?"

"He said you'd been stealing things from him all summer . . ."

"You're kidding! What things?"

She swallowed. She was gripping the steering wheel tightly, he noticed; her knuckles bright as candle flames.

"Oh, little things . . . A pair of cuff links. Some money from his wallet. He said he'd seen you eyeing his father's watch by the pool one day, like you were planning to take that too."

"I don't believe it! Don't you think he'd have mentioned that earlier if it was true?"

"I told you, I didn't believe him. We had a big fight about it, in case you didn't notice."

Matthew nodded. They stopped at a red light. Chloe stared forward in silence. He could see the vein in her neck pulsating in sharp throbs. She'd closed her mouth and was breathing in

deeply through her nose as if to steady herself. The light went green and as they moved forward she spoke again:

"He said the reason he didn't mention it earlier was that he felt sorry for you."

"Christ almighty!"

"Personally, I think—"

She broke off. The bus station came into view ahead, the grimy white pillars of its open hangar gleaming in the sunlight.

"You think..." Matthew prompted her.

"I think it was because he felt guilty."

"For what he did at school?"

"Yes."

It took a moment for the implications of this to sink in.

"Wait, you're not saying you believe him, though, are you? You don't actually think I stole from him, do you?"

They'd reached the bus station. She pulled in and found a space at the back of the parking lot. She seemed extremely agitated, her small upper teeth biting down on one side of her lip as she maneuvered into the space.

"Your bus is here. You'd better hurry," she said. Her voice was breathy and he could hear a distinct tremor in it.

"I'm confused, though, Chloe ... You're not saying *you* think I lied or ... or stole from him, are you?"

"Go on. You'll miss your bus."

"But Chloe ..."

"Get out, Matthew!" she said, turning to him with sudden savagery.

He opened the door, his confusion seeming to migrate

to his legs as he climbed out and took his suitcase from the trunk. As he rolled it to the front of the car to say goodbye she pulled forward with an abrupt lurch.

"Chloe!" he called.

She stopped, just as abruptly, a few yards off from him. As he moved toward her he saw she was rummaging in her canvas bag. She thrust something toward him as he reached her window.

"You stole *this*," she said. "Didn't you?"

It was the gold and quartz Montblanc pen he'd found in their sofa.

"I looked in your suitcase," she said. "Just now when I sent you into town. I had to know if Charlie was lying to me."

"Oh." His voice came like a strange sigh.

"It wasn't all I found."

He seemed to feel all the strength sluice out of him.

"You were in the house that whole time, weren't you?" Her face had darkened in blotches, contorted. She seemed barely able to speak. The pen was shaking in her hand like the needle on some dangerously overburdened measuring instrument. "You'd gone there to watch us, hadn't you?"

"No! That isn't—"

"And then you killed him."

"That's not what happened. Wait, Chloe—" She'd started pulling away again. "I'll tell you what happened—"

"I was nice to you, is what happened," Chloe said.

He wanted to tell her everything suddenly. It seemed to him she'd understand. If anyone could understand, it was Chloe. But she'd pressed the window button and the glass was sliding up between them.

"Chloe—"

"I hope you rot in hell, Matthew."

She'd reached the parking lot exit.

"Chloe!" he called after her, his mind reeling. The window had closed. He watched her ease the car back into the traffic and drive off. For several seconds he was unable to move. Immense forces seemed to be pressing down, immobilizing him. It was as if the moment were too densely freighted with reality to pass through. He heard her words again: *I hope you rot in hell* . . . She knew what he had done, and her knowing it seemed to make it real for the first time. He had killed Grollier, taken his life. A feeling of horror surged inside him. The stark fact seemed to lie all around him suddenly, like some vast, untraversable desert. And yet, he thought, trying to steady himself, she'd brought him here, hadn't she? She'd brought him here to the bus station, and that surely meant something. She could have called the cops to the house, told them what she'd seen, but she'd brought him here instead. So maybe she *had* understood in some way; seen that he wasn't to blame for it; that Grollier, no less than himself, had been *Charlie*'s fall guy, one more surrogate for Charlie's pain. Or maybe it was just that she was so intent on keeping her affair a secret from Charlie she'd chosen to pretend not to have seen what she'd seen. Either way she'd let him go, hadn't she? Told him she knew what he'd done, told him to rot in hell, but let him go. Well, then, he thought, moving forward, he owed it to her to make it work.

Buses were lined up on either side of the outdoor shelter, engines throbbing, fumes spewing out into the morning

air. He'd be in New York in a few hours, he told himself; on a plane as soon as possible after that. Meanwhile he needed to get a ticket, a bottle of water, something to eat. He passed between the buses, focusing determinedly on his objective as he breathed their acrid stench: Tranqué Bay, the land he was going to buy with Charlie's "moolah," the turquoise house on the hill. Dimly, as he came out into the open forecourt, he became aware of something encroaching on him, some vague darkness that seemed more an emanation of the horror still present inside him than anything external. He ignored it, keeping his mind on the vision he'd had the night before, of a new existence, the new person he was going to become. He made himself think of the joy of those sparkling mornings, racing past the old stone ruins to the beach and plunging into the waves with the smell of salt air filling his lungs and the palms along the shoreline tossing in the breeze as if in their own raptures of delight. People were jostling around him: passengers going in and out of the ticket office, taxi drivers looking for fares, officials from the bus company. Again the sense of some encroaching darkness intruded; a shape that was somehow both a solid object entering his field of vision and at the same time a kind of blackly spectral embodiment of what he had done, looming back on a surge of renewed horror. He focused tenaciously on the bright image, as if the sheer glittering intensity of it, pictured with sufficient conviction, might be enough to draw him forward through the many obstacles and difficult passages that lay ahead.

He was still seeing it in his mind's eye when the black Ford Explorer that had emerged from behind the ticket office and

been slowly approaching him all this while came to a halt a few feet off. The doors opened, but even as Detective Fernandez climbed out and strolled calmly toward him, followed by Officer Lombardi, it was some time before he was able to adjust from the glare of that sunlit future, and understand what was happening.

Acknowledgments

Special thanks to my editors, Jill Bialosky and Robin Robertson, for their patience and astute advice.

A NOTE ABOUT THE AUTHOR

Fiona McFarlane was born in Sydney, Australia. She has degrees in English from Sydney University and Cambridge University, and was a Michener Fellow at the University of Texas at Austin. She lives in Sydney.

ACKNOWLEDGEMENTS

I would like to thank my family, Lyn, Ian, Katrina, Evan, and Bonita McFarlane; I think also of my grandmothers, Hilda May Davis and Winifred Elsie Mary McFarlane. I'd also like to thank my teachers, especially Elizabeth McCracken, Steve Harrigan, Alan Gurganus, and Margot Livesey. I'm grateful to Stephanie Cabot, Chris Parris-Lamb, Anna Worrall, Rebecca Gardner, Will Roberts, and everyone at the Gernert Company; also to my editors, Mitzi Angel, Ben Ball, Meredith Rose, and Carole Welch. This book was written with the generous assistance of the Australia Council for the Arts; the Fine Arts Work Center in Provincetown; St. John's College, Cambridge; Phillips Exeter Academy; and the Michener Center for Writers—in association with these wonderful places, I'd like to thank Salvatore Scibona, Roger Skillings, Charles Pratt, Marla Akin, Debbie Dewees, Michael Adams, and Jim Magnuson. Finally, I must thank my friends, especially Mimi Chubb, Kate Finlinson, Virginia Reeves, and, most of all, Emma Jones.